Séance in Sepia

SÉANCE IN SEPIA

MICHELLE BLACK

FIVE STAR
A part of Gale, Cengage Learning

GALE
CENGAGE Learning™

Detroit • New York • San Francisco • New Haven, Conn • Waterville, Maine • London

GALE
CENGAGE Learning™

LIBRARY OF CONGRESS CATALOGING-IN-PUBLICATION DATA

Black, Michelle.
    Séance in sepia / Michelle Black. — 1st ed.
        p. cm.
    ISBN-13: 978-1-4328-2548-5 (hardcover)
    ISBN-10: 1-4328-2548-8 (hardcover)
        1. Spiritualism—Fiction. 2. Photographs—Fiction. 3. Murder—Investigation—Fiction. I. Title.
    PS3552.L34124S38 2011
    813'.54—dc23   2011024999

First Edition. First Printing: October 2011.
Published in 2011 in conjunction with Tekno Books and Ed Gorman.

Printed in the United States of America
1 2 3 4 5 6 7 15 14 13 12 11

In Loving Memory
Ross Robert Reagan
1985–2006

CHAPTER ONE

"Another person's marriage is a foreign country to which visas are never granted. Don't ask me how I know, I just know."— Flynn Keirnan (2006)

"You live long enough and you know what you get?" Mrs. Belton said. "You end up dyin' alone." A cigarette dangled from her brightly painted lips as she oversaw the estate liquidation of her deceased tenant, Mrs. Pilcher.

Flynn Keirnan glanced up from the floor of the tiny apartment, amazed that the ash on Mrs. Belton's cigarette did not fall despite the bouncing ride it took through the old woman's monologue. She sat there sorting through the deceased Mrs. Pilcher's dusty collection of books and tried not to feel like a carrion crow picking the remaining flesh off a festering corpse, yet what was she but a scavenger, searching for pearls among the detritus of the recently departed?

"I guess there's no real victory in being the last man standing, after all," Flynn offered in an attempt to be polite. She was not anxious to make conversation.

"What? Yeah, well, whatever," said Mrs. Belton.

The morning sun filtered through the old chintz curtains to illuminate a hazy flotilla of irritating particles in the air. The dust, combined with the cigarette smoke, was starting to give Flynn the fine edge of a headache.

I'm doing this for Dad, was her silent mantra on these occasions. Performing a disagreeable task for the benefit of someone

7

else ennobled it somehow. At least, that's what she tried to convince herself.

"The poor old dear must have been ninety-five if she was a day. Outlived two husbands, all her friends, even her two kids. Nobody came to her funeral 'cept me and my pastor."

Mrs. Belton paused and removed the cigarette long enough to blow her nose on a tissue that she kept rolled into the sleeve of her pink cotton robe. Or was it called a housedress? Ladies of that vintage wore housedresses.

Flynn wondered how old Mrs. Belton was, given her disparaging remarks on the late Mrs. Pilcher. She didn't look that much younger herself.

"The sheriff gave me the right to sell her stuff to cover the back rent she owed me. I got the paperwork from the probate court."

"Any kind of a receipt would be fine. I just need it for the taxman."

"You're buying then?"

"Maybe. Probably." Flynn tried to keep her voice as neutral as possible. She didn't want the old woman thinking she was too excited. She might jack up the price. Flynn wasn't a pro at this by any means, but in the last four months, she'd picked up a few tricks.

"You sure you don't want to see the rest of the place? She had some real nice bedroom furniture."

"No, just the books. My dad owns a used bookstore up in Weston." She had learned early on not to call her father's shop an "antiquarian" bookstore. Otherwise, Mrs. Belton might think she was interested in antiques generally and would have tried to convince her that everything in the house was a priceless rarity. Better she assumed Flynn was looking for junk.

Every Thursday was estate sale day, so she went shopping armed with a cardboard box and a checkbook, plus a healthy amount of cash in case the sellers didn't take checks.

Brody, her fourteen-year-old son, derisively called these expeditions "dumpster diving" and some days he was not far off. The phrase "estate sale" was broad in its interpretation and they ran the gamut from elegant to ghastly. She had learned to wear her oldest jeans and least-loved tee-shirts on such forays.

This present *opportunity*—to put a fine spin on it—fell somewhere in between. The little ground-floor apartment sat in an early twentieth century house, a good old American Foursquare that towered over its Craftsmen bungalow neighbors. The home had been converted into four apartments sometime before Nixon resigned and the whole place smelled a little moldy. That wasn't so bad. The smells Flynn couldn't identify bothered her the most.

"Weston's a cute little town," said Mrs. Belton in a disinterested, conversational tone. She began to wander around the room, now accepting the fact that she was not going to sell anything other than books.

Flynn pulled one volume after another off the rickety wooden bookshelf built into a fireplace mantle. It was just a wooden mantel, no fireplace anywhere to be seen. Sadly, most of the books were worthless. The majority were *Reader's Digest* condensations from the 1960s that her dad would scorn. A couple of cookbooks from the forties or fifties caught her eye, but they were so soiled and dilapidated at the hinges that they could not be opened without falling into several pieces.

There was a nice-looking old dictionary though, a Webster's dating from before the First World War. Her dad might make something of that.

As she thumbed through it, trying not to breathe and thus sneeze, she caught on a hard page inserted in the middle. An old photograph. Really old. Pre-1900, certainly.

It seemed to be a portrait of some sort, but not the typical stiff Victorian pose usually found in studio shots from that era.

In the fading sepia tones a young woman sat before the lens with an unsmiling gaze. She had dark hair that cascaded down her shoulders. That alone drew Flynn's attention. A woman sitting for a portrait in those days would never have worn her hair down. The unorthodox coif gave her a bohemian air. Maybe the sitter was an artist or an actress, someone not afraid to look unconventional.

Her dark eyes were large and heavy lidded, but they squinted slightly, hinting at defiance. Or maybe she was just annoyed at the photographer for making her sit still so long.

The young woman was not alone in the picture. At least, not exactly. The semi-transparent faces of two men floated above her on either side. Only their disembodied heads were visible. Their images must have been added in by a double exposure or perhaps the printing of more than one negative at the same time. Each of their faces was surrounded by a wreath-like circle of clouds that seemed painted-in somehow.

The men appeared to be about the same age as the woman, mid-to-late twenties, perhaps. One had thick, dark hair and a full beard. The other was a curly blond with a pale mustache. Both were attractive though in different ways. The dark-haired man's expression bore an intensity the fair-haired gentleman lacked. She wondered if the young woman and the bearded man might be brother and sister, they seemed so alike.

"I found a photograph, Mrs. Belton. Do you think it could be of Mrs. Pilcher?"

The landlady politely blew her smoke away from Flynn, out of the corner of her prune-like mouth as she sidled in close for a look.

"Naw. She was old, but she wasn't *that* old."

Of course she was right. A silly question. Even if the dead woman were a hundred, she couldn't have been born when this photo was taken.

"Must be another one of her 'treasures,' " Mrs. Belton chuckled, somewhat unkindly.

"Treasures?"

"The poor thing had Alzheimer's. Started hiding things. They do that, you know. She was forever hiding her checkbook—afraid someone would steal it. Then she'd forget where she hid it, of course. She and I would have to tear this place apart looking for it about every month, so she could pay her rent."

Flynn noticed an empty picture frame on the faux mantel. It looked to be the right size to fit the photograph. It would have been much better protected in that frame than shoved into a book.

"I'd like to buy this dictionary and the photo, too."

The old woman scowled at such a small sale. "All the books, plus the photo, for twenty bucks."

"But I don't want them all. Just the dictionary and the picture."

"All or nothin.' That's the deal."

She just wants me to eliminate the mess she has on her hands, Flynn inwardly griped. "Okay."

She handed Mrs. Belton twenty dollars in cash and got a scribbled receipt of sorts. She piled the old books in her cardboard box, placing the dictionary on top since it held the photo, and she was on her way to the next sale.

"A fair day," said Daniel Keirnan to his daughter as he checked out Flynn's inventory purchases. He sat each book on his counter to examine it. Occasionally, he turned to his computer, which served triple duty as a cash register, inventory keeper, and—thanks to its Internet connection—price checker.

Flynn was impressed with her dad's computer skills. He had embraced the digital future before she was even born. Back then, computers filled whole rooms. He had been the first in his law firm to use them in his practice and he was still as up to date as his teenage grandson.

Dan was particularly delighted by the search engines. He had long ago taken to calling the Internet, in mock reverential tones, his "Oracle." Whenever he needed to look up some fact or bit of knowledge, he would announce that he was "consulting the Oracle."

"I'm turning into a pretty decent book scout, you've got to admit," she said.

"Yes, I'm so glad I spent all those thousands sending you to graduate school."

"You should talk."

"Hey, I get a pass. I'm officially retired. Remember?" He winked at her over his little half-frame reading specs.

His name was still at the top of his law firm's stationery, but he had not actively practiced since the death of Flynn's mother the year before.

"If you don't watch out, Dad, I'll demand a raise."

"Sweetie, you know I wish I could pay you—"

"Dad, I'm kidding. You know that."

The last thing she expected was a paycheck. Her dad had insisted on giving both her and her son room and board since she had offered to take a leave of absence from her college teaching career to move to Weston and help him set up his shop.

Dan had opened Weston Books in February and his receipts had yet to even make the modest rent on his space. Still, Weston was a summer town. June was only a couple of weeks away. Soon they would have the bookshelves fully stocked with a wide variety of out-of-print, rare, or otherwise collectible books that would presumably enchant the hordes of summer vacationers who would wander the quaint, antebellum streets of Weston, Missouri.

She pulled out the old dictionary from the Pilcher estate and drew from it her oddball treasure of the day.

"Look at this photograph, Dad. It must be really old. Do you think it might be worth anything?"

He examined the picture, tilting it to catch more light. The vintage overhead lights that resembled old gaslight fixtures had looked so stunning in the antique reproduction hardware catalog when Flynn had ordered them. Unfortunately, they gave off a disappointing amount of illumination, especially bad for a bookstore. Fashion had trumped function, as usual.

"I don't really know. Go ask that guy at the antique store on the corner. He might know something."

She left the shop and headed over to Heilbocker's Antiques, the largest of the town's four antique stores. She unconsciously smiled as she walked. The late May afternoon swelled ripe and lovely. A fresh, flower scented breeze wafted over from the yard of the large, yellow Victorian-era bed and breakfast called the Sunshine House. Flynn thought the house's Queen Anne detailing looked out of place in Weston since the little city had reached its peak as a Missouri riverboat town before the Civil War.

Most of the Main Street architecture dated from the 1830s and 40s. A simpler, Colonial revival style was in vogue then. The surviving houses from that period tended to be more Carpenter Gothic than Victorian. Some even had slave quarters in their backyards, a chilling reminder of Missouri's Border State past.

When the railroad came West in the 1860s and chose Kansas City—forty miles to the south—as its locus, the river traffic dried up and Weston slowly died. It didn't help that a devastating flood hit the town in the 1890s. When the waters receded the Missouri River had changed its course, ending up four miles from the city docks.

"It's an albumen print," said Mr. Heilbocker. He squinted through his bifocals at the picture, curling his upper lip in the effort. This displayed some unsightly brownish dentures, so Flynn glanced away. His shop was a mess. How did he ever find anything? Her dad's store was practically antiseptic compared to this place.

"You mean like egg whites?"

"Yes, they used it as a base to coat the glass negatives as well as the paper prints. It held the silver nitrate, you see."

"You seem to know a lot about old photographs, Mr. Heilbocker."

"Call me Don, young lady."

"I'm Flynn Keirnan." She smiled at being called "young lady." At thirty-six, she didn't hear that much anymore. But she was young enough to be his daughter, maybe even granddaughter, so she supposed that justified his use of the term.

"My dad just opened Weston—"

"—Weston Books." He grinned. "This is a small town, Missy. Not much escapes our notice."

He flipped the photograph over and looked at the markings on the back. No date, sadly, but a name in scratchy, faded ink: "Medora Lamb."

"The photographer?" she ventured.

"Or the subject."

"I wonder which?" Certainly the subject, given the era. Male photographers had to outnumber females by a thousand-to-one back then, she assumed.

"This size was called a 'cabinet card.' Definitely pre-1880." He studied the photograph further and scratched his chin.

"I think this might be one of those—oh, what were they

called?—ghost pictures, spirit pictures?"

"These two guys are supposed to be ghosts?" She grinned as she looked at the two floating young men once again. They seemed like such opposites. Did they represent an angel and a devil sitting on the girl's shoulders?

He shrugged. "Who knows? I just seem to remember a special on the History Channel about Victorian séances and the like. Spiritualism was very big back then. There were photographers who claimed they could take pictures of the departed."

"What a scam."

"I suppose. Folks believed in those séances, though. And photography was just in its infancy, remember. People weren't too sophisticated about it. I suppose a grieving relative was even more gullible than most."

"Easy marks." She smiled sadly and he nodded in agreement.

"I'm willing to offer you a hundred dollars—just on spec— that this might be one of those spirit photos."

She practically had to pick her jaw up off the worn wooden floor of his shop. So much for her poker face. She had hoped he might give her twenty bucks, maybe twenty-five, tops.

"Of course, I would offer more," he continued, "if you had a provenance on the thing."

"Excuse me, a providence?"

"Pro-ve-NANCE." The old man squelched a sigh, but it exited his hairy nostrils so she heard it anyway.

"The history of its ownership, dear. *Where* did it come from? *Who* are these individuals? Were they or the photographer someone famous?"

Flynn thanked him for his time. She told him she would consider his offer, but her plans were already speeding in a different direction. If this old guy was prepared to pay her a hundred bucks for the thing, she might make some real money auctioning it on the Internet.

She left the shop tingling with the sense that carrion might be a taste she could acquire after all.

CHAPTER TWO

The People of the State of Illinois
versus
Alec Ingersoll
Testimony before the Criminal Court of Cook County, in said
County and State, held at the Criminal Court House, in the
City of Chicago on Monday, being the 12ᵗʰ day of April in the
Year of Our Lord one thousand eight hundred and seventy-five
and of the Independence of the United States, the ninety-ninth.

Joseph Simon, a witness called and sworn on behalf of the People, who examined in chief by State's Attorney Mr. Lynch.

Mr. Lynch: Please state your name, age, and occupation.

Simon: My name is Joe—I mean Joseph—Simon. I'm twenty-three years old and I work for the Post Office. I deliver the mail.

Lynch: Tell us what brought you to the home of Alec Ingersoll on the afternoon of Tuesday, March the second.

Simon: Delivering the mail, of course.

[Laughter in courtroom. Judge calls for order.]

Lynch: Did you know Mr. Ingersoll by sight?

Simon: Oh, yeah. I knew 'em all. He and his wife and the other man living there, Mr. Langley. They all received lots of mail from back east.

Lynch: What time did you arrive at the house?

Simon: One or so. The usual for the P.M. delivery on that route.

Lynch: What caused you to enter the home?

Simon: I had a C.O.D. Three dollars due. So I rang the bell. Rang it a lot. Nobody answered so I was about to leave a note when Gracie—that's a girl who works for the Ingersolls part time—she saw me at the door and called hello. See, she also works for the folks across the street, housecleaning and odd jobs and such. She was on the neighbor's porch beating rugs when she saw me.

I said, "Hey, Gracie, where is everybody?"

She said the servants got every Tuesday off, but that she was sure Mr. Ingersoll was home. She saw him go in the house not half an hour before and she didn't think he'd come back out yet.

Lynch: Then what happened?

Simon: She came over and opened the door—it wasn't locked—and she stuck her head in and called for the Missus.

Lynch: Mrs. Ingersoll?

Simon: Yeah, though she don't go by Ingersoll, you know. She calls herself, I mean, *called* herself Miss Lamb. That was her maiden name. Gracie said she didn't use her husband's name because she was a famous painter, but I never heard of her. I guess she was famous back in New York.

Lynch: Did anyone answer when the girl called for her mistress?

Simon: No, not a sound. We thought the place had to be empty, so Gracie asked me if I wanted to come into the front parlor to see the bloody lions.

The Court: Young man, I do not allow profanity in my courtroom.

Simon: Oh, no, Your Honor, sir. I didn't mean any profanity. These lions on each side of the fireplace, they were carved out of some kind of rock that looked like bloody ice so Gracie called 'em the "bloody lions" as kind of a joke.

18

[The defendant is heard to say the words, "Rose quartz."]

The Court: Mr. Oberholtzer, instruct your client not to speak until he is placed on the witness stand.

Mr. Oberholtzer, on behalf of the defendant: Yes, your honor. He merely wished to clarify that the lions were carved from rose quartz, to clear up the confusion.

The Court: Proceed, Mr. Lynch.

Lynch: Why were you so interested in seeing these things?

Simon: Gracie talked a lot about 'em. Sounded curious, that's all. I didn't mean any harm by it.

Lynch: You didn't think of yourself as a trespasser?

Simon: [Hesitates]

The Court: Answer the question, son.

Simon: I always wanted to see inside that house. Curiosity, plain and simple. I admit it. Suppose it was wrong, but I was curious because of all the scandalous stuff that Gracie said went on in there.

Lynch: What did she tell you about the Ingersoll house?

Oberholtzer: Objection, Your Honor. Hearsay.

Lynch: I'm not offering it for the truth of the matter, your Honor, but just for what the witness had been told. To establish his motive for entering the house.

The Court: I'll allow it for that narrow purpose. Continue.

Simon: Gracie said that Mrs. Ingersoll took naked photographs of Mr. Langley. She walked into the studio one day and saw 'em. He was posing for a picture and wasn't wearing nothing but a smile. [Laughs]

[Laughter in the courtroom. Judge calls for order.]

Lynch: So you went in there hoping to see Mr. Langley naked?

[More laughter in the courtroom]

Simon: No, sir! I just thought, you know, there might be some pictures lying around. Of people, maybe even women. And anyway, Mr. Ingersoll was supposed to be home and I needed him to pay for the parcel. Well, we went in. Before we even got to the parlor, though, we both heard a sound from upstairs.

Lynch: What sort of sound?

Simon: Strange. Like a sob. Only it wasn't a woman's voice. Gracie thought we should go see what it was, but she was scared to go upstairs because the house had got broken into just the week before.

Lynch: So you took it upon yourself to investigate?

Simon: Guess so. I mean, if someone was home, they could pay the cash due on the parcel and I wouldn't have to haul it back again. It was kind of heavy—a box full of photographic chemicals that Miss Lamb ordered from a firm in Boston. I recognized the return address.

She got a package like that every couple of months. She told me what was in it. She wanted me to be careful with the packages as some of the chemicals were dangerous.

Lynch: Dangerous in what way?

Simon: I don't know. She didn't say. Anyway, Gracie and me went upstairs and we didn't see nobody in any of the rooms, but there had to be somebody home so we thought they must be up in the tower room where Mrs. Ingersoll had her studio. I told Gracie to stay put and I went up by myself.

Lynch: Describe what you saw when you entered the tower room.

Simon: Well, first I saw Mr. Ingersoll. He was sitting on a bench or something.

Lynch: What was he doing?

Simon: Nothing. Just sitting. He was kinda slumped forward with his elbows resting on his knees. He looked up at me, but he didn't say anything just then. He seemed strange, like he didn't even know me though he used to see me on my Saturday deliveries and called me by name sometimes.

I started to explain why I was looking for him—you know,

the C.O.D—but then I saw the others.

Lynch: What others?

Simon: Well, Miss Lamb—Mrs. Ingersoll—was sitting at a table or desk of some kind and she had her head down on the table like she was sleeping. I assumed she *was* sleeping until I saw Mr. Langley. He was sitting in a chaise lounge and staring out of the windows like he might be enjoying the view, but where his head rested back on the upholstery there was this big, dark stain, like spilled wine.

Then it hit me—he was dead. I turned to Mr. Ingersoll and I said something like, "What in hell is going on here?"—pardon my language, Your Honor, but that's what I said.

He opened his mouth like he wanted to say something but no words came out. He had such an empty look in his eyes that he made me think of those stories you read in the penny press about hoodoo zombies. And then I saw it.

Lynch: Saw what?

Simon: The gun. Mr. Ingersoll had a pistol in his hand.

Lynch: Did he point it at you?

Simon: No. He seemed to be just holding it. It was pointing at the floor, I guess. He said, "Something terrible has happened here." He said it in such a strange way, it chilled my blood. Like a little child might say it. And his voice had a catch in it like somebody does when they've been crying. And then I saw that his face was wet, with tears, I guess.

Lynch: Then what?

Simon: I took off running. I didn't care to talk to anybody holding a gun. I dashed down the stairs, grabbed Gracie's arm, and dragged her out with me. We didn't stop running 'til we found a policeman two blocks over.

CHAPTER THREE

A quick tour of three different Internet search engines failed to turn up any reference to a "Medora Lamb." So much for the all-knowing properties of the Oracle.

"Spirit photography," however, yielded enough returns to satisfy Flynn that she may indeed have a specimen of the genre. Practitioners like William Mumler and Bertrand Norris came up frequently, though both had been forced to defend themselves against fraud charges during their careers.

The antique dealer was right about séances and the occult being all the rage in nineteenth-century America. A pair of sisters named Fox got the ball rolling in 1848 when they claimed to have contacted the spirit of a man who told them he was buried in their basement. When a skeleton was indeed excavated, they became celebrities. Séances featuring floating tables and tapping ghosts became the parlor entertainment of choice.

The end of the Civil War brought spiritualism its greatest popularity, though with a more solemn turn. The unprecedented loss of life in that war created a boom for spiritualists promising grieving relatives contact with their lost sons, brothers, and husbands.

Spiritualists even had their own national trade societies, complete with annual conventions and such. Photographers who claimed to be in contact with the spirit world jumped on the bandwagon to offer visual glimpses into the great beyond.

Sherlock Holmes's creator, Arthur Conan Doyle, was a vocal

supporter of the movement, writing a book on spirit photography. By the early twentieth century, though, the world was becoming increasingly skeptical. In 1902 there was already an amateur guidebook to "trick photography" instructing the home hobbyist in how to create fake "ghosts" in pictures.

The photographs Flynn viewed online by Mumler, and particularly Norris, bore a striking similarity to her photograph. With this encouragement, she offered the photograph for auction on eBay and started the bidding at $99.00 to see what might happen. If she got no bids after ten days, she could at least go back to Heilbocker and ask if his hundred-dollar offer was still open.

She scanned the picture, sent it to the auction site, and wrote up a description of the thing as best she could, hoping no one would accuse her of too much exaggeration to compare the style of the photograph to that of Bertrand Norris. His pictures had a cloud-like quality encircling the spirits, just like hers.

She devised the moniker WESTONBOOKGRRL to cloak her true identity, as all the other auction mavens did. Then she giddily pressed the SUBMIT button.

Let the bidding begin.

She checked the auction listing the following morning: no bids. Fourteen people had looked at the page. She had auctioned a few items before under her son Brody's account, but not enough to remember if this was a high or low number. She tried not to get discouraged.

She checked it at noon: still no bids, yet one hundred and thirty-three lookers. What did this mean? Had she set the opening bid too high? Maybe she should have started at a dollar, but kept a reserve price of a hundred.

She checked the page one last time before bed. Nothing . . . but there was a question emailed to her about the auction. The message was from someone with a user name of "WOODHULL28."

Dear WESTONBOOKGRRL:

Where did you get this photograph? Is it authentic? Not a reproduction?

She wasn't sure how to respond. Where she got it was none of his (or her) business. Or was it? She frowned at the screen. That pesky *provenance* issue again.

She had nothing to lose by being truthful. She'd come by the photo honestly.

The image of the carrion crow loomed up out of nowhere once again. What she now did for a living made her feel faintly dirty, tainted. She never admitted this to her dad for fear of hurting his feelings. He believed antiquarian bookselling was a noble calling. He enjoyed the thrill of the hunt, the treasure trove adventure of it. She had even felt that herself momentarily yesterday when the old antique dealer offered her a hundred dollars for something she had bought for twenty.

Dan Keirnan undeniably loved his newly adopted profession. She had to respect that. He even had wild dreams of turning Weston into a "book town," like Hay-on-Wye in Wales. They had visited the U.K. together the summer before on a bittersweet dad-and-daughter vacation right after her mom died. When they arrived in Hay just a week after its famous book festival, something in Dan just clicked. The tiny town was home to over thirty antiquarian bookstores.

They were soon to learn that, unlike their counterparts who sold new books, used and antiquarian booksellers *benefited* from competition, rather than being diminished by it. A synergy developed. The more used bookstores in close proximity, the more customers they drew because they each offered unique merchandise. You seldom saw the same books twice as you ventured from store to store. Each shop reflected its owner's passions and idiosyncrasies in a way new bookstores—chained to the dictates of the bestseller list—never could.

As her dad poked around the many shops and bookstalls of Hay-of-Wye, his future was sealed. Throughout their visit, she noticed that he had begun to furiously scribble notes to himself in his travel diary. He announced on the plane trip home to Kansas City that he was retiring from his law firm and moving up to Weston to open his own shop.

The buyout from his practice more than set him up for his first couple of years in business. So there he now was spending sixty-plus hours a week remodeling and stocking "Weston Books": his new baby, his sunset career.

And she knew he wanted to share it with her. She had taken a year's leave of absence from the college where she taught to spend some time with him getting the shop off the ground, but she usually changed the subject when he suggested they make the arrangement permanent. She had moved to Weston more because she wanted a new environment for her son, Brody. She didn't like the friends he hung out with in California. She just didn't see a career for herself as a bookseller.

She returned to her auctioneering duties.

Dear WOODHULL28:

I bought the photograph at an estate sale. A local antique dealer told me it was an "albumen print." That is the extent of my knowledge, I'm afraid.

Thanks for your interest,

—WESTONBOOKGRRL

She hit the SEND button and was about to start paying her utility bills online when she heard the *ping-ding* of her email in-box announcing she had a new message.

WOODHULL28 had sent an immediate reply to her post.

Whose estate? the bidder demanded.

Okay, maybe she was reading in the "demanded" aspect, but

the abruptness of this post annoyed her. No salutation, no pleasantries like "Thanks for your prompt response." Maybe she was being too sensitive but she felt an unspoken, *"Whose estate was it, moron?" in his question. She replied in a businesslike fashion despite her annoyance:*

The estate of a Mrs. Loretta Pilcher in Kansas City, Missouri.

This brought another near–real time reply:

I have to know more about this thing if I'm going to offer over a hundred dollars for it.

She could not believe it. Someone was actually going to offer her more than a hundred dollars! Her heart took off like a jackrabbit. Before she had a chance to respond, she got her first bid on the auction.

Someone calling themselves *ORDLAW17* agreed to her opening bid of ninety-nine dollars.

WOODHULL28 didn't bother to wait for further answers and jumped in with a bid of $150.

CHAPTER FOUR

"Alec Ingersoll is dead and thus the true story of this man and his wife and their friend can now fully be told. They were certainly not the first three people to try and file the corners off a romantic triangle until it became a circle of love. Never an easy task but not one they imagined would end in tragedy. Of course, simple geometry would suggest that the corners of a triangle can often prove sharp enough to cut glass, much less fragile human flesh."

—Victoria C. Woodhull

Friday, April 23, 1875

Franklin Oberholtzer did not believe in the occult and felt slightly uncomfortable in his present endeavor, but as a courtesy to his client, Alec Ingersoll, he stood on the steps of the courthouse and waited in the unusually warm April sun of a Chicago afternoon for the arrival of Mrs. Victoria Woodhull. He pulled off his short-brimmed felt hat to fan himself. He was a portly man and did not care to perspire. He stepped back under one of the archways of the south doors to gain what shade he could.

The sun was not the only cause of his moist brow. He had to admit he shared some of his client's anxiety at meeting a nationally known personality. One so famous, in fact, the newspapers often referred to her simply as "The Woodhull." That she was also a woman and a bit notorious, thanks to her radical beliefs, heightened the suspense of his wait.

Though she began her public career as a spiritualist and was currently the president of the American Spiritualist Association, her greatest gift seemed to be making headlines. When she wasn't opening the first female-owned brokerage house on Wall Street, or addressing the U.S. Congress on the subject of woman's suffrage, or running her own radical newspaper, she was known to run for the presidency of the United States. *The presidency of the United States!* No endeavor on earth seemed to intimidate this woman.

Like every other member of the newspaper-reading public, Oberholtzer had followed her exploits for the last five years. He was not sure what she looked like, though. He had never seen a photograph of her. He had read she was attractive, dark haired, and in her middle thirties.

That she might be wearing her hair shorn in some masculine style was a possibility. He had read that she disliked the time and fuss long hair required and abandoned fashion for expedience. Oberholtzer did not wholly agree with such a drastic decision, but he bore a grudging admiration for a woman with the daring to make it.

It was said that her face glowed with an unnatural light whenever she entered the trance state to commune with the spirits. At least that was what Theodore Tilton alleged in his breathless, gushing biography of her. But the writer obviously had been smitten with his subject. Smitten, in fact, was too mild a word. Obsessed was probably closer to the mark.

A hack pulled up and a lady of medium height wearing a teal green veil alighted. Might that be her? He had specifically requested that she cloak her appearance when arriving at the courthouse. He knew that reporters followed her everywhere like hungry dogs, hoping she might toss them a tasty quotation, preferably something shocking or outrageous.

Additional publicity was the last thing his poor client needed right now. Ingersoll's case had gone to the jury only two hours previous. The unfortunate young man now began his painful wait for the decision that would determine whether the remainder of his life might be measured years or days.

The woman he watched wore a black suit of sturdy silk fabric with a conservative demitrain—a tasteful and unassuming traveling costume, to be sure. Two other persons also exited the carriage and followed her up the stone steps: a young woman with golden curls who smiled at all she passed and a handsome gentleman of perhaps forty years in age with a fashionable mustache and luxuriant side-whiskers in the Dundreary style. He wore a much less sanguine expression.

Oberholtzer tentatively approached the veiled woman and whispered, "Mrs. Woodhull?"

The woman lifted her veil just enough to reveal a comely and composed countenance. Could this dignified young woman really be the same person that the cartoonist Mr. Nast lampooned in *Harper's Weekly* as "Mrs. Satan"?

"Lawyer Oberholtzer, I presume?"

"At your service, Madam, and may I thank you for coming here today?"

"The pleasure is mine, sir. May I present my husband, Colonel James Blood, and my sister, Miss Tennie Claflin?"

The lawyer looked at the husband in confusion.

Blood was used to this reaction and immediately offered an explanation along with his hand. "My wife retains the name of her first husband, the late Dr. Woodhull. She is best known to the public as such."

"Of course, of course," stammered Oberholtzer with an apologetic smile, now understanding she had a "stage name," as it were. With a gesture, he hurried them into the newly built

Cook County Criminal Courthouse. The current building had only been open a few months. All court buildings and county offices had been destroyed in the Great Fire of '71. At least the criminal courts now had a permanent home. The county courts, probate and the like, were still moving about the city from one temporary location to another.

"I am sorry we have arrived so late in the afternoon," said Mrs. Woodhull. "Our train was delayed. A dead cow on the tracks, as fortune would have it."

"Poor cow," said the blond sister with a girlish pout.

"My client is so eager to make your acquaintance, he would be thrilled to receive you at any hour of the day, Madam."

"Will my wife be in any jeopardy?" said the concerned husband of Mrs. Woodhull.

"Absolutely not," said the lawyer. "My client is a most refined and educated gentleman. And thoroughly innocent of these charges, it goes without saying."

"Has a jury of his peers found him so? That's the more pertinent question, is it not?" pursued Colonel Blood.

"They debate the matter as we speak, sir, but there are no doubts in my own mind." They mounted the stairs to the second floor and headed down the corridor to the arranged meeting place.

Only twice did reporters approach and then only to beg the lawyer's opinion on how long the jury "would take to convict" his client. He brusquely told them to step aside, but inwardly sighed with relief that they did not recognize the famous woman at his elbow who staunchly matched his rapid-pace step for step even as her family members fell behind.

She had been the subject of two opposing editorials in the *Chicago Times* only just this morning. She was scheduled to give a lecture on controversial topics related to social reform, among them the relaxation of the current marriage laws, which she claimed amounted to legalized sexual slavery of women.

One editor wrote a scathing condemnation of the proposed speech and warned the good citizens of Chicago to give the radical woman wide berth lest they be corrupted, nay, *polluted* by her upsetting ideas. His associate on the editorial page took a broader view, stating that controversy was healthy in a free society. Mrs. Woodhull's oratory gifts were legendary, said the editor—she had well earned the title of "Queen of the American Lectern"—and all who heard her would be well entertained by her presentation, whether they chose to embrace her philosophy or not.

Oberholtzer ushered Mrs. Woodhull into a large meeting room often used for conferences between defense attorneys and their prosecutorial adversaries.

Only a single policeman stood guard at the door. Alec Ingersoll was, after all, a partner in one of the most respected architectural firms in the city. He had worked among the highest members of Chicago society. Though he had been denied bail because he was charged with capital crimes, no one, including the esteemed district attorney, considered him a threat to public safety.

Oberholtzer opened the door where his client waited and allowed only Mrs. Woodhull to enter. He used his significant girth to block the other two, smiling and winking to try and pacify them.

"Alec, may I present your highly anticipated guest?"

Ingersoll rose immediately and nervously whispered the words, "Oh, God."

The lawyer excused himself to join the others in the busy hallway.

"Why did you ask me to be your medium to the Spirit World, Mr. Ingersoll?" Victoria said without preamble as she raised her

31

veil with a motion both elegant and simple. This revealed a pair of penetrating blue eyes and a frank but courteous smile on her lips. "There are many able practitioners here in Chicago and I must tell you that I don't conduct séances professionally anymore."

"My wife idolized you, Mrs. Woodhull. She could quote from your published speeches, chapter and verse. She subscribed to *Woodhull & Claflin's Weekly* and even went to the expense of having it mailed to her when she moved here from New York. When she first heard you speak at Steinway Hall in '71, she was mesmerized. Of course, you made quite an impression on everybody that night. I'm sure you recall it."

"Indeed I do." One does not forget a night speaking to a cheering crowd of three thousand who came out into the wettest, coldest, most disagreeable November night the city of New York could offer. That night was a triumph and glowed in her memory still.

"She said hearing your speech altered her outlook on life. Looking back now, I suppose it did. You spoke on the subject of Free Love."

The words "Free Love" seemed to burn his tongue.

"Your wife was a follower of the doctrine, I take it?"

A bitter laugh was his reply, but then he added, "I should think that was obvious. If you read the papers, I mean."

She knew that the Chicago press had dubbed the double slaying of Medora Lamb Ingersoll and her reputed lover, Cameron Curtis Langley, the "Free Love Murders." The newspaper reporters had made such a meal of the story it came as no surprise that the lawyer had specifically requested she come to the meeting incognito so that they might not recognize her and feast upon his poor client further.

Such was the price of fame, or ill-fame. She'd acceded happily to his request, having no desire for interference with her own journalistic endeavors.

Woodhull & Claflin's Weekly, the newspaper that Victoria, her husband, and her sister struggled to keep going, had landed the story of a lifetime. Alec Ingersoll's tale of a deadly love triangle would surely staunch the current flow of blood-red ink on the *Weekly's* balance sheet.

Victoria had heard rumors that a major New York daily had offered Ingersoll twenty thousand dollars for his story. This was money he doubtlessly needed. No one knew better than she the ruinous cost of litigation. She had been forced to defend herself in court three times in as many years, and though she had prevailed in every case, it did not make the effort less dear.

The price Ingersoll now demanded for his story was not a monetary one. He simply asked that she perform a séance and summon the spirits of his departed wife and his friend, Mr. Langley, to find out the actual manner of their deaths.

"But you didn't share her feelings on Free Love?" she asked cautiously.

He sighed. "I don't know. Maybe I thought that I did for awhile. I certainly told her I did. But then, I would have said anything to keep her love. Anything." He raked his hand through his dark hair and continued.

"You and all those other reformers make your living peddling these ideas from the lectern. Well, it all sounds good in *theory,* doesn't it? Whereas, in practice . . ."

"One must be careful not to confuse freedom with anarchy," she said, her voice turning chilly.

"I'm sorry. I did not intend any disrespect. You are doing me a great favor by coming here and I am grateful for it. Believe me, I am." He rose and faced the window opposite the long, highly polished oak desk. Then he turned, silhouetted by the afternoon sun, and uttered a heartfelt explanation of sorts:

"We do not *choose* whom we love . . . or surely we would

make wiser choices."

"That is true," she said, relaxing for a moment to consider his remark. It touched her in a way that she could not immediately discern.

"It would be such a relief to actually converse with someone who might understand my unusual marriage, if not its unfortunate aftermath. I hoped that you, alone among everyone in the country, might be such a person. I mean I've read about how you once lived under the same roof with both your former husband, Dr. Woodhull, and your present husband—"

"I think we should focus on the matter at hand, Mr. Ingersoll. We meet today to discuss the details of *your* life, not mine."

"Yes, of course. You're right. I imagine my story will make a good article for your paper."

"I suppose that will depend on how it ends."

His sad, self-mocking smile was painful to view. "I think I know how it will end. I have no reason to be optimistic. 'Lynched' by Lynch. That's a popular saying among my jailers. Mr. Jeremiah Lynch is the state's chief prosecuting attorney, that is."

"You never confessed to the crimes, yet your lawyer said that you refused to testify in your own defense."

"I couldn't bear to speak of it. Even now, in some ways I still can't. But for what I ask of you, Mrs. Woodhull, I am willing to give up what little privacy remains to me. I *must* find out what really happened to my wife and my friend. I did not kill them, it goes without saying, but I cannot bear to die still wondering."

"Have you ever attended a séance before, Mr. Ingersoll?"

"Once," he said. "About five or six years ago. I walked into it assuming it would be nothing more than an amusing parlor game. But when the medium contacted the spirits of my dead parents—it could not have been a trick. She told me things only I and my parents could have known about the day they died. I was utterly amazed. I didn't get an ounce of sleep that night, I can tell you."

"I'm afraid my services as a spiritualist come with no guarantee. Some unscrupulous practitioners would tell you otherwise, but I will not give you false hope, even though I am most anxious to print your story in my paper."

"I appreciate your candor, truly, but I have thought this through and believe, if anyone, you might be able to help me. I was greatly relieved when you answered my letter, in fact. You probably receive so many letters, as famous as you are. I worried mine might get lost in the pile unread until . . . until it was too late."

"My daily mail is not the avalanche you imagine. And you are famous in your own right, don't forget."

"Infamous, you mean."

"You *are* a famous man, Mr. Ingersoll. Quite apart from your recent . . . uhm, difficulties. Your architecture will live long after you, now won't it?"

Once again, Ingersoll's cynical smile returned. "I expect they will try to separate my blighted name from association with those fine houses and buildings now."

As he spoke, Victoria's busy mind raced with ideas, questions, and logistical complexities. She wondered how best to approach this tantalizing new assignment.

She feared the story might now prove a case *against* the cause of Free Love if the gentleman were found guilty of the crimes. That would not please her husband, who served as editor in all but title to the *Weekly*. They might have to frame the story as a cautionary tale, indicating the husband's lack of faith in the Free Love doctrine proved his own downfall.

But what if he was telling the truth? If he did not kill his wife and her alleged lover, how did their deaths occur?

Victoria studied this strange and perhaps even pitiable man

in an attempt to feel some connection to him, some means of understanding him. He was a handsome man, though she had to look closely to appreciate this at the moment. His suit was rumpled and dirty. His hair and beard had grown unruly and unkempt during his incarceration. Shadows beneath his dark, penetrating eyes made him look a decade older than his twenty-nine years.

"And your wife is well known in her own right. This may surprise you, Mr. Ingersoll—I once sought to interview her."

His lips parted in amazement. "You did? My God, Dora would have been in ecstasy to meet you—her idol. How could this be? She never mentioned—"

"I doubt she was informed of the matter. My sister and I called on her at her home after her arrest, a few years ago. I assume you are aware that she and I have both been targets of Mr. Anthony Comstock. He marched her off to the Tombs just two months after he arrested me. When we tried to contact her, we were told by a servant of her grandmother that she would not speak to the press."

"Ah, yes, her grandmother—that explains everything. If only poor Dora had known, how happy she would have—" Emotion cut his sentence off. He clenched his fists before him on the table and drew a deep breath to recover his composure.

"Before we begin our formal interview, I must ask an indelicate question and I beg you not to take offense. Judging by recent court actions, if you had simply played the betrayed husband, a sympathetic jury might have acquitted you."

She knew that only a few short years ago, Daniel McFarland had shot and killed his divorced wife's paramour, the *Tribune* reporter, Albert Richardson. The jury acquitted him of the murder, even though it was the *second* time in two years the man had shot poor Mr. Richardson!

And even more recently, a California court had acquitted a

photographer, Eadweard Muybridge, of shooting his wife's lover on the grounds of justifiable homicide. Whether technically legal or not, it seemed a man killing his wife's lover was authorized to do so in modern America.

"But that is *not* what happened, Mrs. Woodhull. I did not kill my wife *or* Mr. Langley and *I did not care to lie in court,* even if it meant saving my own skin."

He suddenly glanced away and after a moment's reflection added, "But I also did not dare to tell the truth."

"What in heaven's name do you mean by that, sir? If I am to interview you, you must promise not to talk in riddles." She began to doubt his earnestness.

"Fair point. I fear I am so distracted at times that my mind wanders most dreadfully. You see, I could not bear to tell you my story now if I weren't certain I would not live to read it."

"Oh, Mr. Ingersoll, I am grieved to hear you speak thus—"

An urgent knock at the door interrupted their discussion. Victoria's sister, Tennessee, poked her pretty head in. "Not much longer, Vicky, dear, surely?"

"Let's begin fresh tomorrow, Mr. Ingersoll. I'm afraid I am much pressed for time."

He looked alarmed by this statement. "Does that mean you won't conduct the séance tonight?"

"Mr. Ingersoll, it's nearly four o'clock. I'm destined to speak to a crowd of nine hundred at seven this evening at the McCormick Music Hall."

"But can't you cancel it?"

"The tickets are already sold. And besides, you have your end of the bargain to uphold. You promised to tell me your entire story. Actually, I think that the more I know about your wife and your friend, the better chance we have of contacting—"

"But—"

"Sir, you will have to excuse me. I must now take my leave."

He rose from his seat, much agitated by her threatened departure. "Please, have pity on me—a condemned man."

"You're not condemned yet, Mr. Ingersoll. The jury is still out."

CHAPTER FIVE

Flynn must have finally fallen asleep sometime after three. She woke up at seven, stiff and groggy at her computer desk. She massaged her cheek, which now bore an indentation in the shape of her watch face, her left wrist having served as a pillow.

She decided to check the auction before stumbling off to the kitchen. What she found there woke her up more than any caffeine could hope to.

The current bid stood at a staggering $1,840.00.

She laughed out loud with delight. She finally felt like she was making a meaningful contribution to her dad's business. She couldn't wait to tell him.

She went upstairs and tapped on his door. A groan was the response.

"Hey Dad, sorry I woke you. Mind if I open the door?"

"Oh, sure. Is everything okay, honey?" He sat up in bed but did not look too sentient.

"Yeah, great."

"Brody is fine?"

"Yes, yes."

"Are you sure?"

She held back a sigh of irritation. The incident of last weekend was obviously still on his mind. She had taken the matter a lot less seriously than he had.

They had gotten a call from the police at just before midnight last Saturday to come pick Brody up from the station. Frantically pulling their clothes on and rushing down, fearing all the terrible outcomes that only parents of teenagers can imagine, they discovered that Brody had not really committed any crime at all.

"We were just playing a game of 'Riding Coach,' " he complained, still outraged that the officer had made him come to the station until he was picked up by a parent.

"What the hell is that?" said his grandfather.

"One guy gets into the trunk while the others drive around. When you stop at a light, the driver pops the trunk release and the guy gets out."

"I don't get it," Flynn said.

"We were just messing with people. Sometimes we get out of the trunk and run away screaming like we've just escaped from being kidnapped. Other times we get out of the trunk, close it, and calmly walk away, like nothing's happened. The people in the car behind don't know what to think. It's just for laughs. What the hell else are we gonna do on a Saturday night?"

Flynn thought it was brilliant street theater, and could barely avoid saying so. Dan Keirnan clearly was not amused.

"Dad, this is good news. Great news! We've made our first major score."

"I'm not tracking, honey. Score on what?" He stretched and looked like he was not ready to get up yet.

"I'm auctioning that old photograph on eBay and the bidding has gone wild." She took a deep breath to regain some level of composure. "We're going to make a lot of money, Dad."

"Oh, honey, that photo's *yours* to sell."

"The bidding is at almost two thousand dollars and the auction isn't near being over with."

"My god. What's so special about that photo?"

"Beats me. Something's going on here and I've got to find

out what it is."

"You may need to consider whether that eBay website is really the proper venue. I got the impression from talking to you and Brody that it was more like a glorified garage sale."

"You may be right."

"Well, try to find out all you can and good luck, honey. I'm going to hit the sheets for a little while longer. You know me, not a morning glory like you. And that picture's *yours*, by the way. No question about that."

"But Dad, I don't feel right about—"

"I'm serious."

"Why don't we split the take? There's going to be plenty here for both of us."

"Nope, it's yours. If nothing else, it's my way of saying thanks for all your unpaid help at the store these last few months."

She longed to tell him that he probably needed the money worse than she did, but that would require far more disclosure about her personal life than he—or anyone else—had a right to know.

She returned to her computer and saw the bidding edging ever closer to $2,000.

Still the same two bidders. Why on earth was this so important to them? Were all spirit photos this valuable or was there something special about this one?

An email arrived from **ORDLAW**:

Hello—

I have been bidding on your spirit photograph and—yikes— it's getting pricey. I am about tapped out. I don't want to ruin your auction or anything, but is there any way you could just let me look at the picture and maybe make a good, high-resolution scan of the thing? I need it for my research on a book I am writing.

41

You would be well compensated for this, I promise you. I am located in Chicago and the listing says you are near Kansas City. I could catch a commuter flight and be there long before the auction ends.

Can I talk to you further about this, at least?

Thanks for your time,

Sincerely,
Matt Holtser

Flynn twisted her mouth as she read the screen. She hated to see a good bidder drop out, but she was eager to learn more about her mystery photo. This guy obviously knew something, maybe a lot.

She would have to discuss this with her dad later this morning at the shop. She needed a second opinion before going forward.

"My guess is he's a lawyer from Chicago," said Dan Keirnan when Flynn pulled up the email on her father's computer at Weston Books.

They both sat behind the counter with propped elbows, staring at the screen as though it had magical, enthralling properties.

"Where do you get that from? He said he was a writer."

"—who calls himself 'ORDLAW.' O-R-D are the call letters of Chicago's O'Hare Airport. I'm betting money he's a Chicago lawyer."

"Should I talk to him?"

Dan frowned and removed his reading glasses. "I hate to see you getting involved with strangers. He might be a flake. Maybe even a dangerous flake."

Flynn nodded and thought about it further, playing the good daughter. But how could you fear a guy who uses the word "yikes"?

"What if I give him the bookshop address? That's public. And if he wants to meet, he can come here. That would be pretty safe, right?"

Her father chuckled and shook his head. "Curiosity killed the cat. Or so I've been told."

"Forewarned is forearmed, Cliché-boy."

CHAPTER SIX

Testimony of John Blevins, M.D.
Examined for the People by Mr. Lynch

Mr. Lynch: What is your name and occupation?

Dr. Blevins: Dr. John Blevins. I work at City Hospital. My primary duties are to perform post-mortem examinations at the request of the county coroner.

Lynch: By that, do you mean you perform autopsies?

Blevins: Yes.

Lynch: Dr. Blevins, I wish to show you these two reports and introduce them into evidence. Do you recognize them?

Blevins: Yes, these reports are based on my examinations of the bodies of Mrs. Medora Lamb Ingersoll and Mr. Cameron Curtis Langley. The bodies were identified to the officers at the scene of their discovery by Mr. Alec Ingersoll.

Lynch: When were these examinations performed?

Blevins: I performed both of them on the day subsequent to the discovery of the bodies.

Lynch: Were you able to deduce the time of death for the two individuals?

Blevins: From the description of the bodies—temperature, degree of rigor, and so forth—given to me by the investigating officers who first arrived on the scene, I would suggest that both deaths occurred more than one hour and less than six hours prior to the arrival of the officers.

Lynch: So we are to assume that both individuals perished

44

sometime during the morning of March the second.

Blevins: Yes, that would be my assumption based on the evidence.

Lynch: Can you say which death occurred first?

Blevins: I cannot say with confidence, no.

Lynch: Could you summarize your findings as to the cause of death for the court, beginning with Mrs. Ingersoll?

Blevins: It is my opinion that Mrs. Ingersoll died of cardiac arrest occasioned by the consumption of potassium cyanide.

Lynch: What first made you think that cyanide was the cause of death?

Blevins: The unusual pallor of the face and the strong smell of almonds. This scent is a telltale indicator of the presence of cyanide, though, curiously, not everyone has the ability to smell it. It's not known why that is.

Lynch: And in testimony previously offered by the investigating officers, a jar labeled "Cyanide of Potassium" was discovered in Mrs. Ingersoll's photographic studio?

Blevins: Yes, I asked the investigators to look for this chemical once I had determined that it played a central role in her demise. I knew that the deceased practiced the art of photography and this chemical is frequently employed in that process.

Lynch: And was the amount of the chemical found on the premises sufficient to cause death, if ingested?

Blevins: The half-filled jar they produced still contained enough poison to kill an entire neighborhood.

Lynch: So it is a highly toxic substance. And sufficient quantities of this chemical were found in the body of Mrs. Ingersoll?

Blevins: Her mouth, throat, and stomach contained a highly lethal dose, such as to produce an almost instant case of acute poisoning.

Lynch: Instant?

Blevins: Yes, in that concentration, the individual would likely lose consciousness almost immediately. Convulsions and heart arrhythmias would likely follow and death by cardiac arrest would be the final outcome.

Lynch: How long would this process take, from ingestion to death?

Blevins: Anywhere from a few minutes to an hour at most.

Lynch: And how was this poison administered?

Blevins: Through the oral cavity, that is to say, the mouth. Potassium cyanide is crystalline in character. Looks very much like sugar, in fact. And it dissolves in water just like sugar.

Lynch: Was the physical evidence entirely consistent with someone willingly drinking the substance?

Blevins: No, not entirely. There were stains on the woman's collar and neck that made it seem as though she—or someone—spilled the beverage containing the poison in an odd direction.

Lynch: Odd in what way?

Blevins: Well, if someone spilled a drink on themselves while sitting or standing upright, the stains would run down. [Witness indicates the shirtfront area.]

These stains on the woman's collar and neck went in a backward direction as though she were lying on her back when it happened.

Lynch: Are you suggesting that she might have been held down and someone poured the liquid into her mouth?

Blevins: That would be one possible scenario.

Lynch: Now, Doctor, may I direct your attention to the details of Mr. Langley's death.

Blevins: Mr. Langley died of a single gunshot wound to the head.

Lynch: Was it possible that Langley's wound was self-inflicted?

Blevins: It was possible, though the angle of the wound was unusual for a suicide.

Lynch: How so?

Blevins: The point of entry and the angle that the bullet traveled were not ones I've seen before in a suicide situation. Most persons taking their own life point the gun at the temple or into the mouth or under the chin.

Mr. Langley's wound began at the corner of the jaw and traveled up and back through the skull cavity, exiting the upper rear portion of the skull.

Additionally there was no contact powder burn at the entry of the wound, indicating the barrel of the revolver was not pressed directly against the skin.

Lynch: So the gun might have been fired in the midst of a struggle over the gun?

Mr. Oberholtzer: Objection, Your Honor. The prosecution is calling for the witness to *invent* circumstances to further his case.

Lynch: Your Honor, my witness is an established expert in this area and, as such, may offer his professional opinion.

The Court: Narrow the question, Mr. Lynch.

Lynch: Dr. Blevins, in your *professional* opinion, could the gunshot wound have been fired by another person?

Blevins: It is possible, yes.

Lynch: No further questions, Your Honor.

Cross-examination by Mr. Oberholtzer for the defense.

Oberholtzer: Dr. Blevins, when you examined the body of Mrs. Medora Ingersoll, did you find any evidence that she had been injured or mistreated in any way?

Blevins: I did not find any unusual bruising or cuts, if that is what you mean.

Oberholtzer: No sign of a struggle?

Blevins: No.

Oberholtzer: So we may infer that the unfortunate woman drank the poison willingly? In other words, she was not forced?

Blevins: That is possible, yes. Especially given the amount that was ingested.

Oberholtzer: What do you mean by that, Doctor?

Blevins: Well, if she were offered the poison by stealth—hiding it in a beverage or food, she might not have ingested the quantity of the poison as it is highly irritating to the mucus membranes of the mouth and throat.

Oberholtzer: So she might have immediately assumed that something was amiss with the beverage and stopped drinking it.

Blevins: I would assume so.

Oberholtzer: But she did not. She drank a large quantity. As if she wished to insure her own death.

Blevins: That is one possible explanation.

Oberholtzer: And if you were presented with a victim suffering this exact malady and the only thing you knew about them was that they had a history of at least one previous suicide attempt by poisoning, what would your ruling most likely be in that case?

Blevins: Absent any other information, I would likely rule it a death by suicide.

Oberholtzer: Thank you, Doctor. Now let us turn our attention back to the second victim, Mr. Langley. Was there evidence that he fired the pistol that caused his death?

Blevins: There was powder residue on his right hand, consistent with having fired the weapon for at least one of the two times it was fired.

Oberholtzer: No further questions.

CHAPTER SEVEN

Saturday, April 24, 1875

Was there any sound on earth sadder than a dove calling to his mate? Victoria Woodhull wondered. She awoke just before dawn and opened, with some difficulty, the window of her hotel room at the Palmer House for a breath of air. The rainstorm last night had settled the pervasive dust and the winds had carried the omnipresent stench of the town to some more rural location.

The sleeping city lay still in its unnatural quiet. In the dim, gray light she could see the cooing dove perched upon the ledge of the building across the alleyway. She felt a wistful comradeship with the mournful little creature. Her own mate, after all, had left on the midnight train.

"I'm not needed here, I can see," he had said while angrily re-packing the valise he had just emptied four hours earlier.

"Just because I'm canceling the remainder of my engagements for the week doesn't mean—"

"It means you're throwing away good, hard cash on the . . . the . . . mere *possibility* we might sell a few extra copies of the *Weekly*. And maybe, *maybe* not land in jail in the bargain."

"This situation is completely different from the Beecher matter," she said. "We have the participation of the subject this time. He initiated it. And we'll be careful in our choice of words to keep Comstock out of this."

Her usually cool-headed husband, Colonel James Blood, who had shared her bed and her extensive business ventures for the

49

last nine years, had every reason to worry about this latest gambit.

When Tennie and Victoria first broke the story of the Reverend Mr. Beecher's marital indiscretions with the wife of his friend Theodore Tilton, the world as they knew it turned on its ear. First and foremost, the edition could not have sold faster had they been delivered by the winds of a hurricane. Copies of the *Weekly* went for as much as $40 each on the streets of New York!

Such was the public's need to learn of Mr. Beecher's personal life. What a wicked thrill to find out that the minister the *New York Herald* had proclaimed "the most trusted man in America" was as human as the next. (Trusted, indeed! Victoria would not trust Henry Beecher with her hack fare, much less her immortal soul.)

Of all the flaws humans are heir to, she despised hypocrisy above all. And she thought Mr. Beecher the most deceitful and Janus-faced man on the planet. She did not begrudge him his little affair with Libbie Tilton. She, of all people, felt one should, one *must* follow the dictates of the heart. That was the essence of the Free Love philosophy: Let not Man, nor God, nor—most of all—the State stand between individuals and the truth of their own hearts.

But while Mr. Beecher practiced this philosophy in private, he damned it from his pulpit. The East River filled with "Beecher boats" every Sunday morning as hordes of the faithful left Manhattan to invade the borough of Brooklyn to receive the Word of God according to Henry Ward Beecher's eloquent, if curious, understanding of it.

Mr. Beecher's allies proved to be as relentless as they were ruthless in defending him. In the two years following the Beecher Scandal issue of the *Weekly,* Victoria and her family had lost nearly everything they valued—the beautiful mansion on Thirty-Second Street, their brokerage house, and frequently their liberty. The Beecher minions, at the direction of Anthony Comstock, had arrested them countless times, demanded thousands for bail—for an alleged misdemeanor, of all things!—leaving them broken financially but unbowed, unrepentant.

Thus she knew her husband was on some level correct to question her current course and yet, she would not allow the Beecher forces to change the direction of her life. She would interview Alec Ingersoll and publish his story and let the Devil take anyone who stood in her way!

She opened her beloved red Moroccan bag in which she kept her speeches. She pulled out the notes she had taken the previous afternoon at the courthouse.

"Vicky?" came the whispered voice of her sister over the glass transom.

Victoria opened the door a crack, not wanting to officially rise for the day quite yet, but Tennie seldom tolerated neglect and actively ignored attempts at subtlety.

Tennie stood on tiptoe to peer over her shoulder. "Where's the Colonel?"

"Left on the train last night." She admitted her sister to her chamber.

Tennie plopped herself on the bed with a childlike bounce. "Where's he going?"

"New York, or so he claims. I would more likely guess St. Louis, at least for a day or two."

"Don't worry, darling. He just wants to see his daughters. Not the wife. It's only natural."

"I know, I know. He was angry at me when he left, though."

"He has a point, Vicky."

"Don't tell me you're on *his* side. This Ingersoll matter is going to be a splendid story for the *Weekly*. It will get us out of debt, *finally*, and I can stop this positively ghastly lecture tour.

51

You know it's killing me. I think I shall strangle if I have to breathe one more day of cold air on a rail car or in a drafty lecture hall."

"But Spring is here. The weather is bound to improve. And soon little Zula can join us on the road again. I love it when she gives that reading from Mr. Shakespeare as an opening. She's so advanced for her years. Only thirteen and such poise on the stage. I hope I have a daughter someday."

Victoria pulled on the bell to summon the staff. She desperately needed some hot coffee to fortify her for the day ahead. After placing her order with the room service attendant at her door, she turned back to her sister, "What wakes you at this unholy hour, dear?"

Tennie pulled a yellow slip of paper—obviously a Western Union telegram—from the pocket of her dressing gown.

"The hotel got our rooms confused and sent this up to me instead of you. It's another one from Mr. Nostrils. He's caught up with us again."

"Mr. *Norris*," Victoria said, chuckling in spite of herself. The gentleman in question did have rather large nostrils though. She quickly perused the message:

Urgent [stop] Must call upon you when you reach Chicago [stop] Am desperate [stop] You are my only hope [stop]—B. Norris

"Why is Mr. *Nostrils* so 'desperate,' darling?" asked Tennie.

Victoria could only groan. "He's been charged with fraud. He's a spirit photographer and someone is suing him, claiming that his photographs are hoaxes. Then the district attorney's office here in Chicago began to investigate him. He now may even face criminal charges. The poor man is frantic. He wants me to testify on his behalf as an expert witness."

"Why are you an expert? You don't know anything about photography—except how to pose!" She gave a teasing wink.

"He wants me to testify in my position as the president of the

American Spiritualist Association, of course."

Had she only known what strange tasks would be asked of her in that role, she was not sure she would have consented to it. The lofty title had seemed like such an honor at the time.

"I think he asked you because you are famous and he will be guaranteed some free press coverage on the day you testify."

"My, my, aren't we cynical?" She would have teased more had not the room service waiter arrived with the coffee tray. Poor Mr. Norris had been following her from town to town for the last two weeks of her tour, begging to meet with her. Her husband had held him off so far, as she was usually so drained of energy by a vigorous speaking schedule she did not have time to pursue extraneous matters. With her protector now gone she would have no buffer between her and the public. She knew she would have to meet with the photographer.

The hotel restaurant had sent up some muffins and toast, though she had not ordered them. In any case, the toast was spongy and the muffins were cold. She did not really care as she planned to breakfast with Mr. Oberholtzer to talk about his client, Alec Ingersoll.

"Why don't you share my room, Tennie, dear? We could save money by doubling up. Mr. Ingersoll is only paying for *my* room, you know."

The suite was large and elegant to a fault. Fourteen-foot ceilings, a large mahogany writing desk with its plushly upholstered chair, a profusion of gold brocade and fringe on every fabric surface, from the richly hung bed curtains to the generously sized couches and chairs in the sitting area. She could have happily lived there forever had not the looming threat of eventually paying the bill confined her extravagance to merely the nights Mr. Ingersoll would underwrite.

"But Vicky, if I don't have a room of my own, how am I to entertain interesting callers?"

"Shame on you," said her older sister with a chastising laugh. "Just take care."

"My dear Mrs. Woodhull," said Franklin Oberholtzer in a booming voice, much-befitting a courtroom.

He pulled off his smart hat with a grand gesture. He wore a well-cut suit of iron gray wool that only partially concealed a wildly colorful vest of violet and yellow plaid. That a man in so cautious a profession as the law would choose such lively accents to his wardrobe surprised Victoria in a favorable way.

"Allow me to escort you to the Dearborn Cafe," he said. "Just a short walk. A fine breakfast can be had here. And certainly a bit more privacy."

Victoria left the entrance to the Palmer House restaurant with regret. It was universally acknowledged to be the most elegant in the city. Just to sit under its magnificent dome was an elevating delight.

Upon the street, Victoria's senses were assaulted once again by a pervasive, noxious odor. The dawn respite had now expired. She instinctively covered her nose with her handkerchief, an action noticed by her walking companion.

"The winds have changed direction," he said with a chuckle. "Now you are reminded how our fair city makes its fortune. You smell the Union stockyards, Mrs. Woodhull. If you owned livestock or a railroad, you'd call that the smell of *money.*"

"Perhaps there are worse things than being poor."

He threw his head back in a hearty laugh and swiftly guided her toward their destination.

"I take it you are not a frequent visitor to our city."

"On the contrary, sir. I used to live here, many years ago. The city has emerged from its own ashes remarkably."

"Indeed," said the lawyer with a note of pride. "Not even the Panic of '73 could slow us down. We will be stronger for having been tested, as they say."

Tested, to be sure. The fire of October 1871 had devastated the city and the recovery was still in progress. Ninety thousand people lost their homes to that unprecedented inferno. Hardly a single building of consequence was left in the busy commercial center of town.

Once seated at a semi-circular banquette in the far more humble eating establishment than the grand Palmer House offered, Victoria saw Oberholtzer tip the waiter more than one bill to keep the tables on either side of them empty. He had obviously thought of everything. She folded back her veil.

"You have already had a favorable effect upon my client, Madam. After you left him, he requested a clean set of clothes and the services of a barber. He said he was ashamed of his appearance and afraid he had offended you."

"Not at all. Knowing his ordeal and the length of his incarceration, I was most sympathetic."

"I just wish I could have gotten him more interested in his appearance before the jury. He did not seem to care a rap what they thought."

They placed their orders and began to sip their coffees as he commenced the little meeting she had requested the afternoon before.

"I must tell you straight out, Madam, I don't believe in spiritualism. I don't mean any offense by this—"

"None taken, Mr. Oberholtzer. I am frequently confronted with nonbelievers."

Victoria used to boast that she could smell a doubter at twenty paces. Picking up on the subtlest of nuances is all part of the medium's gift. Tennie said she was never offended as long as they were willing to pay. Victoria, on the other hand, retained a tad more scruples on this subject.

The temptations could be overwhelming, however. Such is

the spiritualist's power over her eager and often desperate clients. Victoria could say with unequivocal pride that she had never humbugged anyone.

"I've known Alec since he first came to Chicago," said the lawyer. "I believe I was his first client. He designed my house. Labored ceaselessly to please me and my wife. And when it was completed the *Times* wrote a story about it in their Sunday edition. After that, he could not handle all the commissions he received."

Oberholtzer paused a moment and added quietly. "He is the exact age my Frank, Jr., would have been."

"You lost a son?" Victoria inquired with delicacy.

He nodded. "The last year of the War. Barely nineteen, but so proud to wear the uniform of the Republic."

"I'm sorry."

He dismissed the matter with a slight wave and returned to his original topic. "Alec was a rising star here, to be sure. How his senior partners enticed him away from New York, I'll never know, but they were delighted to have him. Couldn't do enough for him.

"Until this, that is. It's such a tragedy. All his damned wife's fault, if you ask me. Excuse my language, but I'm far from neutral on the subject. My wife and I considered—still consider—Alec a good friend."

"Why did he make this request of me, do you suppose?"

Oberholtzer let out a long and pensive sigh. "He's desperate. Whatever demons are chasing him, they are definitely gaining ground. I have come to question his sanity as this matter has dragged on. He's been saying the oddest things of late."

"Such as . . . ?"

The lawyer thought for a moment, seeming to have many examples of Alec Ingersoll's mental instability to choose among.

"He said, out of the middle of nowhere last week: 'Once the

blood freezes in the veins, little shards of ice begin to prick and scratch the heart in a most painful way, but like anything else, one gets used to it.' Now what in the world are we supposed to make of that?"

"I think it's a rather poetical observation, Mr. Oberholtzer. Though I agree, I cannot discern its meaning."

The large man shrugged. "I think he was referring to his marriage."

"They were not happily wed?"

"Damned if I know. If you're able to contact his dead wife and friend, Godspeed. I will be curious to know if Alec tells you more than he was willing to tell me. He gave me blasted little to hang a defense on. The best I could do was force the State to prove its case and hope to raise a reasonable doubt.

"The coroner was never able to swear that Langley's wound was not self-inflicted. Langley had a suicide attempt in his recent past. And the wife drank poison. Cyanide of potassium, it seems—found among her own photographic chemicals. That, too, could have been a suicide. We were able to suggest that she had also attempted to take her own life on at least one occasion that we know of."

"A happy crew indeed," Victoria mused. This new information caused her to contemplate the situation in more depth. "Would there not be some physical evidence on the dead man's hand if he had fired the weapon to kill himself?"

"An excellent point, Mrs. Woodhull! Bravo. I am gratified by your astute observation." The lawyer said this with a broad and congratulatory smile that flattered her a good deal. "The late Mr. Langley's hand indeed bore the powder residue one would expect to find on a hand that had fired such a weapon."

"And the hands of Mr. Ingersoll?"

The man's good humor faded at this question. "Alas, my client had the misfortune to pick up the pistol at issue. His own hand was soiled in the process. And the weapon appeared to have been fired *twice*. Two bullets were missing from the revolver's chambers and one most definitely ended up in Mr. Langley's head. They found the other imbedded in one of the walls.

"When the officers arrived, Alec was holding the gun in his hand. He's lucky they did not shoot him for refusing to drop it. He didn't threaten them with it, mind you. Just sat there in some kind of daze.

"The prosecution advanced the theory, somewhat successfully I must admit, that the two men might have struggled over the gun in some fashion. They hinted that Langley may have been trying to defend himself against Ingersoll and fired the weapon once in that endeavor. Then they asserted that my client overtook the pistol and fired it at point-blank range into his friend's jaw.

"I was able to introduce that business about Langley's former roommate, Jackson Hurley, showing up unexpectedly in late February. I still consider him to be a suspect. He had a warrant outstanding on him from New York. Just fraud of some sort, but an active warrant, nonetheless. Unfortunately, the police could never locate him for questioning after the murders. I hope it all mixed the stew a bit in the jurors' minds."

"What did you know for certain about that day?"

"Alec told the police that he was summoned home by a message purportedly sent by his wife. A young boy stopped in at his office and delivered the message verbally, then left. Alec thought it odd that Medora didn't send a written message, as she usually did. He sensed immediately that something must be wrong."

"He didn't know the boy, I take it?"

"Never seen him before. The police got a description of him from both Alec and his draftsman. There's no question he existed. The officers *said* they looked for him."

"You sound like you don't think they did look."

The lawyer frowned to affirm this suggestion. "They've been overconfident from the start. The police and the prosecuting attorney, that is. They felt certain they had the guilty man and didn't go looking for anyone else. I guess I can't blame them. Lovers' triangle, husband found with the bodies and holding the gun that killed his friend. What more did they need, after all? Signed confession would have made it tidier, I suppose. At least Alec denied them that."

"You said yesterday you had photographs . . . ?"

"Are you sure you want to see them while we eat?"

"I've plunged myself into this, Mr. Oberholtzer. I can't afford to be squeamish."

"All right, then, but don't say I didn't warn you."

He pulled his briefcase from beneath the table and opened it on his lap. "Before I forget it, here are the copies of the newspapers you requested from the trial days. You will find extensive coverage of each witness's testimony."

"Bedtime reading?" she said with a chuckle.

"Might give you nightmares." Some moments of leafing through the remaining contents of his bag produced the file folder he was looking for. "Ah, here we are."

Victoria opened the folder and studied three photographs of the crime scene. The crowded room appeared to be square with tall, double-hung windows on all four walls, obviously a tower room of some sort. Bright light flooded the chamber and glinted off the window facing the sun.

"The room looks cluttered. Does that indicate a struggle occurred?"

"No struggle. Alec said the room was always a mess. The wife was an artistic type. Not one to mind a little chaos. He said he used to tease her about it because she was always losing things, only to find them again beneath it all."

59

The next photo showed a woman slumped over a draftsman's table. Her head lay pillowed against her arms and her face was thus obscured. Her long hair hung down her back in casual disarray.

The last photograph was the only one to suggest the gruesome nature of what had transpired in that tower. Cameron Curtis Langley sat back against an upholstered wicker chaise lounge. He was a handsome man even in death, with delicate features—a fine slender nose, thin mouth, and pale, heavy-lidded eyes. His fair hair curled against his brow and hung past his collar.

A dark stain, like a terrifying halo, encircled his head where it lay against the light-colored upholstery. She strained her vision to search into his pale, seemingly lashless eyes, trying to absorb some tiny vestige of the man's last view as he stared out so blankly. What had he felt at that moment? Fear? Anger? Desolation?

"May I keep these for study?"

"All right, though I may need them back at some point."

"Does Mr. Ingersoll have any thoughts or theories about how they died?"

"He thinks it was either a double suicide or a murder-suicide."

"If the latter, who killed whom?"

Oberholtzer shrugged. "The sequence of death was too close to call. I think that question torments him most of all."

The privacy of their meeting was suddenly invaded by what could only be a newspaper reporter.

The tall, skinny young man had not even bothered to remove his derby hat before forcing his presence upon them. His clean-shaven face was peppered with freckles, giving him a youthful appearance. He could not have been more than twenty-four.

"Nick Faraday, *Chicago Tribune*," he breathlessly announced.

"Mrs. Woodhull, may I ask your reaction to Mr. Theodore Til-ton's testimony yesterday in Brooklyn regarding his relationship with you?"

"What testimony was that?" She resented the constant harass-ment of the press during the Beecher trial. It was said that the Associated Press alone had assigned thirty reporters to the case and she could certainly believe it.

Before arriving in Chicago, the *New York Tribune* had hired a coach filled with its reporters to literally chase her from one speaking engagement to another throughout the Midwest.

"Sir," intoned Mr. Oberholtzer sharply, in his best courtroom voice. "This lady and I are engaged in a *private* conversation and I will thank you to—"

"He testified that he *deeply regretted* his involvement with you, Mrs. Woodhull," said the reporter, ignoring her stern tablemate who now hopped up to retrieve the manager.

Anger surged through her veins, causing her hands to clench and her heart to pound. *Regretted his involvement*, did he? What part of it? The three months he lay in her arms every night in loving passion orchestrated to his own badly composed poetry? Or the months he spent writing her biography, delving into the most intimate realms of her memory, mining her tragedies and triumphs for his own advancement?

"You may quote me, sir: 'Mr. Tilton will make a fine man someday *if he ever grows up.*' "

The reporter eagerly transcribed her words just before the proprietor of the restaurant grabbed his elbow and unceremoni-ously ejected him.

Victoria took several deep breaths to calm herself. Allowing the press to bait her into a temper should have been beneath her by now.

When Mr. Oberholtzer returned to his seat, she asked, "Do you think he recognized you and will guess at our connection?"

"Dear Lord, I hope not. Since he did not mention my case, we will assume our mission is still unknown."

"I should like to tour the Ingersoll home and the exact location of the tragedy if I might."

"We can do it this afternoon, if you wish. I'll arrange for my carriage to pick you up after you've finished your interview with Alec. It's a nice house over on Prairie Avenue. Oh, one more thing before I forget. You might wish to transfer your lodging to the Sherman House, Mrs. Woodhull. Much more convenient to the courthouse and the jail where we will be meeting with my client. It's just a short trip over the Clark Street Bridge and three blocks north."

"I prefer to stay at the Palmer House. Particularly now that it has been so spectacularly rebuilt. They claim it is the most *fireproof* hotel in the nation." The city of Chicago was now synonymous with fire.

Oberholtzer laughed once more. "Can't say I blame you on that score."

CHAPTER EIGHT

Flynn sat at the counter in her father's bookstore and sipped her morning coffee. The shop's computer keyboard lay at her fingertips. She refused to open the Internet connection because she would once again be sucked into Auction-land and away from her assigned morning routine of cataloging new books into the inventory.

In an antiquarian bookstore, this was a labor-intensive task. She had worked part time at a bookshop (that sold only new books) while she was in college and knew that drill pretty well. She had been disappointed that so little of her experience had transferred to her dad's situation.

Instead of simply checking off the books that had been delivered—which resulted in all the information being entered into inventory automatically as a part of their integrated ordering system—she had to carefully examine each book, note all publishing details about it, then describe and grade its condition in exhausting detail. This was exacting and time consuming. Often, research was required. Consultation with published bibliographies was necessary on highly collectible titles. Sometimes it was interesting, but more often she found it tedious.

Her dad had been summoned to a private sale the previous day and had made quite a haul. Four banker's boxes filled with first editions collected over the last several decades by a recently deceased lawyer. A friend of one of Dan's former partners had recommended him to the surviving family.

She frowned when one of the boxes contained four books by David Holloway. Her dad had stuck a yellow sticky note on them: "You're the expert on these!"

Yeah, she was an expert on the works of the late, great David Holloway, for whatever that was worth. A copy of *Mountain Daylight Time* sat gleaming in its gold foil dust jacket.

When opening the volume, the spine gave that audible *crack*, suggesting that the book had rarely been opened. The pages were pristine, as one would expect. The novel had pretty obviously never been read by its owner and was thus in excellent condition. And, of course, it was only twelve years old. She flipped the book open to the copyright page and deliberately did not cast a glance to the dedication that sat opposite.

Yes, a first edition. All the identifying information was there. She turned to the title page and found David's signature and the date of his signing. A chill snuck along the back of her neck to see his nearly illegible handwriting again.

A signed, first edition in this well-cared-for condition would be worth some money. The deceased book collector had known what he was doing. He had protected the fragile dust jacket in a nice, shiny Mylar sleeve just like the pros recommend. He had gotten the signature of the author with no personalization, which would have hurt its value unless the person he was signing it to was a celebrity in their own right or connected to the author in some way.

She read the first sentence: *"Too much of a good thing is rarely a good thing but just try getting someone to understand that before it's too late."*

She smirked at this. She could remember him actually saying that fifteen years ago. Dwelling on thoughts of David, and worse, David and Barb, was never healthy. Some scenes look best in the rearview mirror.

She hadn't read the book in many years and wondered if she would appreciate it more with age. It was a simple story of love and betrayal set in a more innocent time, with the all-important double-cross that gave the story its teeth:

A world-famous scientist [read: novelist] and his equally renown artist-wife [read: poet-wife] spend the summer away from their college teaching chores to focus on their real work. They repair to their oh-so-perfect cabin in the mountains. [Well, not really a cabin. Actually, a condo in the Rockies that was profitably rented out during the ski season.]

The celebrated couple brings with them a promising young graduate student to help organize the scientist's recent, ground-breaking research and assist him in writing it up for journal publication. The young woman is thrilled by the opportunity to work with this glamorous couple. Though her "work" seems to involve more dishwashing, grocery shopping, and vacuuming than furthering the cause of science or art, the eager, naive student does not complain.

The young woman happily tolerates her unplanned domestic servitude because she is passionately, hopelessly in love with the scientist and would do anything to be near him.

According to Chapter One, that is.

Flynn groaned and massaged her face with her hands. She decided to grant herself a break from cataloging and grabbed the feather duster to take glancing blows at the many oak bookshelves.

She found an elaborate spider's web in the corner of the door into the children's room. The spider was in the grisly process of pulling a trapped fly to one end of the web. She chuckled with the possibility of telling a child customer that this might be "Charlotte" of the famous "Web."

Unsentimental about spiders, Flynn quickly obliterated the

web. She searched the floor, hoping to step on the spider, but couldn't find it.

She returned to her post at the cash wrap to resume her weary task. She eyed the Internet button on her keyboard. She needed to go back online to look up prices for the newly acquired books anyway. Surely it would not hurt to take one *little* peek at the eBay auction.

No surprises there: The bidding had topped out at two grand even and sat currently with WOODHULL28. It seemed that ORDLAW, otherwise know as Mr. Matt Holtser, had folded, true to his word.

So there was no harm in contacting him then, right? She might just as well find out what he knew.

She emailed Holtser and told him she would be happy to meet him and show him the photograph. She added at the end of the message:

> *I would love to hear more about your writing project involving this old photo, if you wouldn't mind.*
> *Sincerely yours, Flynn Keirnan*

Her dad would not approve of her giving out her real name, but she had liked the sound of this Holtser guy's email "voice" and wanted to be equally friendly. He seemed so much nicer than that snippy WOODHULL28.

She hit SEND and then resumed her weary task of cataloging.

Less than fifteen minutes had passed before she heard the familiar *ping-ding* of her *New Email* announcement. It made her jump and yet she was relieved to have a legitimate distraction.

> *Hi Flynn (sounds a little friendlier than Westonbookgrrl):*
> *Thanks for answering my last "e." I have to confess I am not a professional writer. My day job is that of assistant general*

*counsel to a medium-sized insurance company (and yes, it is as
boring as it sounds)—*

Flynn had to smile that her father had been right about the
lawyer bit. She would have a good time kidding him about his
psychic and/or detective powers.

*—but I am currently working on a labor of love. I am writ-
ing a book about my great-great-grandfather who was also an
attorney here in Chicago, way back in the nineteenth century.*

*He got involved in a famous murder trial that the news-
papers of the day called the "Free Love Murders" (by the
Chicago Times) and "The Prairie Avenue Massacre" (by the
Tribune)*

*Ah, you just gotta love our industrious Fourth Estate. . . .
Anyway, it sounded so juicy, I couldn't resist.*

*When my paralegal, who is a rabid eBay addict, came across
what seemed to be the name of one of the murder victims in an
auction of an old photograph, she called me just in case.*

*She was right and then some. Your photo is not just a portrait
of Medora Lamb, one of the victims of the Free Love Murders,
but also includes the other victim, Cameron Curtis Langley, and
Medora's husband, Alec Ingersoll, who was charged with killing
them both. The husband was the client of my gr.-gr.-grandfather.*

*I really felt like I had won the lottery when I saw that picture.
I mean, wouldn't it make a great cover for my book? If it ever
gets written, that is.*

*I can be on a plane first thing tomorrow morning. Can we
meet?*

Best regards, Matt

CHAPTER NINE

Testimony of Grace Harrigan, examined by Mr. Lynch for the State.

Miss Harrigan: My name is Gracie Harrigan. I'm 19 years old and I worked for the Ingersolls as a housemaid. I helped out in the kitchen, too.

Lynch: How long did you work for the Ingersolls?

Harrigan: Less than a year. I came last summer, just before they lost the baby.

Lynch: Did you live in the house?

Harrigan: No, I was just a day-wager. I live with my parents.

Lynch: What were your duties in the household?

Harrigan: Oh, anything Mrs. Teller put me to. Mrs. Teller was the housekeeper. I made up the beds in the mornings and washed up after the meals and so forth. I also helped Miss Lamb—that is, Mrs. Ingersoll—with her work.

Lynch: How did you help her with her work?

Harrigan: I fetched water so she could mix her chemicals for the photographs. It was a long haul up those stairs. But I didn't mind, see, 'cause it was fascinating, seeing her make the pictures. Kind of like magic. Then I cleaned up afterward. She promised to take a picture of me someday, but I changed my mind.

Lynch: Why did you change your mind?

Harrigan: Well, after I saw Mr. Langley get his photo taken, I was afraid she might ask me to take my clothes off.

[Laughter in the courtroom.]

Lynch: Describe the photographic session you witnessed involving Mr. Langley and Mrs. Ingersoll.

Harrigan: She took lots of pictures of him.

Lynch: I refer to the incident in which the gentleman did not have all his clothes on.

Harrigan: Oh, yeah, well, I went up to the tower room one day—it was last fall—to ask Mrs. Ingersoll if she needed anything more before I left for the day. I went in and he was . . . uhm . . . undressed, so I said, 'Scuse me please,' and turned to leave, but Mrs. Ingersoll told me to stay. She wanted me to hand her something.

Lynch: What was Mrs. Ingersoll doing when you entered?

Harrigan: Fussing with her camera. She was underneath the big black cape that lets her look in the back of the camera.

Lynch: What was Mr. Langley doing?

Harrigan: Sitting on the floor with lots of pillows and drapes around him.

Lynch: They were not in any sort of embrace?

Harrigan: No, sir. He was just posing for the camera.

Lynch: What did Mr. Langley do when you entered?

Harrigan: He covered himself with one of the pillows enough to be decent and sort of laughed, embarrassed-like. Mrs. Ingersoll told him to stay still. And he said, "Yes, sir!" like he was in the Army.

[Laughter in the courtroom. Judge calls for order.]

Harrigan: He was funny like that. Always making smart remarks and joking, but never in a mean way.

Lynch: Did you observe the three of them together at any time? The Ingersolls and Mr. Langley?

Harrigan: Yes.

Lynch: Were they a congenial group? Harmonious?

Harrigan: Yes. Mr. Langley's coming to live with them cheered them right up. They were sad, you see, after losing their baby. She would hardly get out of bed some days, though I don't think she was ill. Just lay around weeping.

Mr. Ingersoll worked more and more. I didn't see him much. He often left before I came to work in the morning and didn't come home 'til after I left. Then Mr. Langley came and everything changed. Mrs. Ingersoll was happy and started working in her studio again. And Mr. Ingersoll came home earlier and didn't miss a single supper after that.

Lynch: What was your reaction to the scene you saw with the postman on Tuesday, March the second?

Harrigan: I didn't see the bodies. I'm glad of that. I was shocked by what happened, but not really surprised, I guess.

Lynch: You weren't surprised to learn that a double murder had occurred?

Harrigan: Well, they had it coming, didn't they?

Mr. Oberholtzer: Objection, Your Honor. The witness's opinion is not—

The Court: Sustained.

Lynch: Your Honor, I want to ask the witness why she believed the two deceased "had it coming."

The Court: I'll allow it, but only if her opinion is based on fact, not speculation.

Lynch: Why did you believe Mr. Ingersoll had a motive to kill his wife and friend?

Harrigan: Well, the pair of them was involved . . . since Christmas at least. That was when they all started being quite free about it. So maybe it started earlier.

Lynch: What do you mean by "involved"?

Harrigan: You know.

Lynch: Miss Harrigan, I assure you that the jury does not know and must be made aware.

[Witness hesitates.]

70

Lynch: Do you mean that Mr. Langley and Mrs. Ingersoll engaged in criminal conversation?

Oberholtzer: Objection. Leading the witness.

The Court: Sustained.

Harrigan: [To judge] I don't understand, sir. What sorts of conversations are criminal?

The Court: Criminal conversation is a legal term meaning that two parties engaged in some sort of illicit sexual intercourse. Contrary to law and convention.

Harrigan: Like adultery?

The Court: Yes.

Harrigan: Oh yeah. They did a lot of that sort of conversing, then.

[Laughter in the courtroom.]

Lynch: No further questions.

The witness is cross-examined by Mr. Oberholtzer for the defense.

Oberholtzer: On what facts do you base your *potentially libelous* assumption that the two persons under discussion were engaged in an illicit affair?

Harrigan: Everybody knew about it.

Oberholtzer: I'm asking for facts, Miss Harrigan. Not gossip. Do you have any facts to offer?

Harrigan: Like what?

Oberholtzer: Did you ever see the two parties kissing, for example?

Harrigan: No.

Oberholtzer: Hugging?

Harrigan: No.

Oberholtzer: So you have no definite evidence that the two individuals were anything more than friends?

Harrigan: She saw him naked, now didn't she?

[Much talking and agitation in the courtroom. Judge calls for order twice and threatens to clear the room. Order restored.]

Oberholtzer: And you believe that posing for a photograph constitutes adultery?

Harrigan: I'm the one who made the beds each morning. They all had their own rooms. Sometimes one bed hadn't been slept in. Sometimes another. They were doubling up somehow, weren't they?

Oberholtzer: Was there some pattern to these sleeping arrangements?

Harrigan: Not that I could tell. I wondered if maybe the gentlemen just flipped a coin for her.

Lynch: Objection.

The Court: Sustained. Strike that from the record.

Oberholtzer: Please confine your remarks only to the facts, Miss Harrigan, not your speculation.

Harrigan: I asked Mrs. Teller what she thought about it and she told me to keep my mouth shut or I could look for other employment.

I didn't want to lose my job. The pay was good and the Ingersolls were not hard to work for. Mrs. Ingersoll, she wasn't what I'd call friendly but she was easy to please. She didn't seem to care if the house was a mess or not. She never really seemed to notice.

And Mr. Langley, he was so nice. He always had something pleasant to say.

Oberholtzer: Miss Harrigan, if you will permit me to say so, you are an attractive young woman.

Harrigan: Thank you, I guess.

Oberholtzer: Did either of the gentlemen of the household ever make any inappropriate remarks or suggestions to you?

Harrigan: No, sir. They were always perfect gentlemen. I wouldn't have stayed otherwise. I don't need that kind of trouble.

Oberholtzer: Do you recall a burglary of the Ingersoll residence prior to the deaths of the parties?

Harrigan: Yes, sir.

Oberholtzer: Describe what you remember.

Harrigan: I came to work on a Wednesday, like always after having Tuesdays off. I was told to go up to the tower room and clean up as there had been a robber in the house who had made a terrible mess of Mrs. Ingersoll's photographic studio. We were all upset about that, of course.

Oberholtzer: Did you have any idea who might have done such a thing?

Harrigan: No, but they had a strong suspicion about Mr. Langley's friend who came to call just a few days earlier.

Oberholtzer: Mr. Jackson Hurley?

Harrigan: I think that was his name, yes. I answered the door that day he stopped by. He was a nice-looking sort of young man with a Limey accent.

Oberholtzer: Do you mean to say that he was from England?

Harrigan: Yes, sir. I liked the way he talked. Kind of musical, but Mrs. Teller said it was a common sort of accent. Like he was from the wrong side of the tracks, so to speak. Cockney— that's what she called it. She said that English *gentlemen* don't talk that way and that she couldn't understand why so fine a man as Mr. Langley would have reason to know someone as common as Mr. Hurley.

Anyway, he came to the door asking for Mr. Langley and he said, "Tell him Old Jackie wants to see him."

Then Mrs. Ingersoll came to the door with Mr. Langley and Mr. Langley did not look happy to see his friend at all and didn't even introduce Mrs. Ingersoll to him. He just hurried out onto the porch and spoke in private to the man, then he came back in, but you could see that he was upset and bothered. His cheeks were redder than blazes. He had the sort of complexion that lit up with any emotion. Couldn't hide his feelings if you paid him to.

After the break-in, Mr. Ingersoll and Mr. Langley talked about whether it might have been this man. Mr. Ingersoll talked to both me and Mrs. Teller and asked what Mr. Hurley had said when he called and if he had come back or been seen hanging around.

I was in the studio when the police came to investigate the robbery. I helped Mrs. Ingersoll remember where everything was and what all was missing.

Mr. Langley did not mention this man, Mr. Hurley, to the police, even though that's who they were certain had done the deed. Afterwards, Mrs. Ingersoll asked them why they didn't talk about their suspicions to the police.

Oberholtzer: Did you hear Mr. Langley say why he didn't want to tell the police about Jackson Hurley?

Harrigan: Not really. He just said, "I can't bear to have New York happen all over again." Mrs. Ingersoll dropped the subject and Mr. Ingersoll patted Mr. Langley on the shoulder in a kind sort of way, like he sympathized.

CHAPTER TEN

Saturday, April 24, 1875

The requested barber had transformed Alec Ingersoll's appearance drastically from that of his first interview with Victoria.

"You look much younger without a beard, Mr. Ingersoll," she said. Victoria could not help but notice he looked quite handsome as well, but she did not remark upon this.

He grinned and self-consciously massaged his newly clean-shaven cheeks. "I feel like a new man. I've worn a beard my entire adult life. I'd forgotten what I looked like without one. I'm glad it's gone now . . . I think."

She and Ingersoll sat in a room called "The Cage," an iron-barred apartment in the jailhouse reserved as a place for attorneys to meet with their clients. The nice, clean room at the courthouse had been unavailable because it was the weekend.

Even though the jailhouse was new, the unmistakable stench of a prison filtered through like a missive from Hell. The inevitable memories of her numerous incarcerations in Ludlow Street Jail in New York after the publication of the Beecher scandal surged back and sickened her, but she tried not to show it.

"Did you meet your wife before you met Mr. Langley, or after?" asked Victoria.

"Oh, I knew Cam since our teenage years. We both got drafted in the last year of the War. Two scared eighteen-year-olds, I can tell you. Little good to the service of the Union, I imagine, looking back now. We were assigned to share a bunk bed and had little choice but to become fast friends." He smiled at the memory.

"After the war ended, we decided to go to Europe together. I wanted to study painting, but my grandfather—he raised me after my parents died—convinced me I needed to find a more practical—that is to say, financially rewarding—outlet for my artistic impulses and wrangled me an invitation to study architecture at *l'Ecole des Beaux Arts* in Paris.

"Cam dreamed of becoming a writer and thought a tour of Europe would be inspiring, so he came with me. Such high-minded ambitions! I'm ashamed to say we frittered away our time there, traipsing from country to country like a pair of vagabonds. All we studied was the local wine and beer of each village. Those were wonderful times. So much fun—well, except for getting robbed and beaten by Gypsies outside Rome! But anyway, I didn't get back to Paris in time for the start of the fall term. I was just a few days late but they informed me my slot had been given to the next name on their lengthy waiting list. I was out of luck.

"We continued our traveling party until two dreadful things happened: My grandfather found out about my dismissal and cut off my allowance. And then, even worse, Cam's father died and left only debts behind, making Cam the sole support of the Gems."

"The Gems?"

An embarrassed but fond smile crossed the paleness of his newly revealed face. "Cam's sisters. The three Misses Langley have the unlikely names of Garnet, Sapphire, and Opal. Cam used to refer to them collectively as 'the Semi-Precious Gemstones.' 'The Gems,' for short. They don't know we called them that, mind you. It was sort of a sarcastic joke between us."

Victoria smiled with empathy. Coming from a family of seven, she could easily imagine such nicknaming high jinks.

"Poor Cam," Ingersoll said. "He often lamented that he could never afford to get married as long as he had the Gems to support. I used to tell him he should spend all his free time playing matchmaker and finding husbands for those freeloading harpies—" He stopped and seemed distressed.

"Oh, I shouldn't talk about them like that. Please don't write that down. They were kind to me for many years. Even now, little Garnet testified on my behalf at the trial. She sends me letters almost every day, assuring me she believes I'm innocent. She must be the only person in the world who does. Her two sisters certainly don't. They would happily spring the trap on my gallows, I'd warrant."

"Your lawyer believes in your innocence, Mr. Ingersoll. I had a lengthy talk with him this morning and I can assure you of that."

He nodded. "Frank has been good to me. I hope I will have the money to pay him. I don't know if I will, when this is finished."

"Now where were we? I believe you and Mr. Langley had been forced to curtail your European adventure . . ."

"Yes, we returned to New York in . . . it must have been the spring of '67. We found a bachelor apartment on Eleventh Street, just off Broadway. A convenient location, but a miserable apartment. A one-room affair, meant for a single party, but we were so broke we had to share it. We didn't mind, though.

"We both wanted to be independent of our relations and live like young gentlemen in the city. Of course, in my case, I didn't really have a choice. My grandfather wouldn't speak to me after the stunt I'd pulled in Europe. I couldn't blame him. I had foolishly squandered the opportunity of a lifetime.

"I did want to become an architect, though, just to show him I *could*, if nothing else. I got myself hired as a draftsman for a large firm—Bender, McDonough, and Hughes. You've heard of them, perhaps?"

"Why, yes. I believe they designed the building first housing my brokerage on Broad Street."

"You and your sister were the lady stockbrokers, weren't you? I remember it now. Quite a splash you made on old Wall Street. Vanderbilt was once your client, wasn't he? He believed in the Spirit World, too, right?"

"He professed to."

"I heard it that he and your sister were—"

"Let's return to *your* story, shall we?"

He nodded, properly chastised for his attempt to gossip. "Mr. Hughes took a liking to me and my work and began to serve as my mentor, carefully steeping me in the many facets of the profession, involving me in all the countless decisions he had to make in a day.

"I needed more math so he advanced me money to take a night course at the university. It was a mutually beneficial relationship in that he was slowly losing his eyesight. He did not want the firm to find out just yet, so I became his eyes for him. The education he gave me was priceless.

"And as I mentioned, Cam longed to be a journalist. He got a job with the *Herald,* writing obituaries."

"I suppose all young reporters begin that way."

"I'm sure they do. Funny thing was, though, Cam *excelled* at it. He had the heart of a poet and a gentle manner that bereaved people adored. His obituaries were matchless. Soon undertakers throughout the five boroughs were recommending him to their clients. People read his obituaries whether they knew the deceased or not. They were . . . entertaining, if you can imagine that.

"Cam always kept a sense of humor about his work though. Never took it too seriously, despite his success. He used to call the folks he wrote about his 'Dearly Departeds.'

"He eventually became so popular the various papers began to bid on him. By the time I left New York he was making almost as much money as I was. Of course, supporting the Gems kept him broke."

Victoria nodded in sympathy with the late Mr. Langley. She had supported as many as sixteen family members over the last decade—a father, a mother, sisters who can't seem to stay married, sisters who marry men uninterested in supporting themselves and only too happy to delegate the task to her, plus an inebriate former husband too ill from drugs and alcohol to manage himself, and then there were her own and everyone else's children in the bargain.

"We enjoyed the art and culture New York had to offer us. Our European sojourn did not make snobs of us. If anything, it gave us a whole new appreciation of what we have here in the States."

"That's a surprising statement, sir," Victoria said. "Everyone I know in New York seems to worship all things European, as though nothing has any value until it is at least two hundred years old."

"Mired in the past. That's what all of Europe is. The 'New World' is just that—new and brilliantly original. The future of mankind lies on these shores. That is why I found the opportunity to practice my career here in Chicago so exhilarating. They are willing to entertain new and daring forms, designs that have no antecedents.

"Dora thought that too. She liked the work I was doing here. Possibly the only thing she liked about Chicago. Breaking with the past strictures had formed a part of her own artist's journey. You mentioned yesterday her arrest at the instigation of Mr. Comstock. That certainly triggered special memories for me.

"That was the night we met her."

79

CHAPTER ELEVEN

C.C.L. Notebook
January 1873

The cold rain commenced just as they left their flat. The temperature hovered near forty. They argued briefly over whether to pool their money for a hack to the art gallery on Nineteenth, as that was their destination. They were both a week from payday and had little cash to spare.

"I don't want to meet her looking like a drowned rat," said Ingersoll, ever conscious of his appearance when ladies were concerned.

"We barely have enough money between us to buy dinner," said his flatmate, Langley. "If she's destined to fall in love with you, she'll surely overlook a wet hat and coat."

"My clothes are already so shabby I hate to go out in the daylight. I can't afford to lose whatever advantage I may have left to an inopportune fall of rain."

With that, Ingersoll waved frantically at a passing hack. Amazingly, for the weather, the cab slowed to meet them where they stood on the sidewalk.

"Where are you young gentlemen headed on this watery night?" said the lone occupant of the hack who had agreed to share his coveted dry space with them. They gladly climbed in.

The small candle lamp lit the face of their benefactor. He sat opposite them, wearing expensive tweeds and swaddled in an enormous plaid neck scarf. Tiny spectacles sat perched upon the bridge of his long and distinguished nose. Bright white hair spiked out from under his fine beaver hat as though the topper had tried to contain the unruly mass, but was unequal to the task.

The comparative warmth of the coach soothed their wet faces in a congenial relaxation, allowing them to sigh with relief as they inhaled the pungent odor of wet wool and the sweet aroma of their host's pipe tobacco.

"Mr. Reid," said Langley, recognizing the publisher of his newspaper, the *New York Herald.* "You are our savior."

"Indeed," echoed his friend. "A thousand 'thank you's' would not be enough."

The older man grinned and waved off the gratitude. "You're one of my employees, are you not?"

Langley blushed. "Yes, sir. Cameron Curtis Langley. I write obituaries for your paper."

He could not believe a man as busy as Mr. Whitelaw Reid could possibly know all his employees by sight. The gentleman not only owned the *New York Herald,* but had assumed control of the *Tribune* as well when its former publisher, Mr. Greeley, took ill after his unsuccessful run against Grant for the presidency the previous November.

"Ah . . . that's it. I knew I had seen your face before. An important job, obituaries. Probably half the reason most people buy our paper each day."

"To make sure they're not *in* his column," quipped a jovial Ingersoll.

Langley frowned at his friend to silence him. He was too uncomfortable in the presence of his boss, or rather his boss's boss, to crack jokes, but Whitelaw Reid tossed back his head in an amiable laugh.

Ingersoll nudged Langley for an introduction. "Mr. Reid, allow me to present my friend, Alec Ingersoll. He's an architect

81

with a firm downtown."

The appropriate hand shaking and nodding ensued, then Reid pressed on, "You two have not answered my question yet."

"We're going to an art gallery," said Langley.

"What a laudable use of your time," said his publisher.

Langley had to grin. "We are actually going to see the artist more than the art."

"My future wife," said Ingersoll.

"You're engaged? Well, congratulations."

"He's never met her," said Langley, grinning now. "He thinks that once she meets him, she will *want* to marry him."

"That's positive thinking for you," said Reid with a bemused chuckle.

Now it was Ingersoll's turn to blush. He looked out the small carriage window and pretended attention to the scene outside, though the wet and the cold had fogged the glass to a degree that little was visible, even under the brightest streetlight.

"My friend Alec here falls in love faster than the weather changes."

"When I was your age, I'm sure I did, too."

"Would you like to come with us, Mr. Reid?" said Ingersoll. He ignored the hard nudge Langley had delivered to his ankle to criticize the invitation.

Surprisingly, Whitelaw Reid considered the offer.

"Well . . . I was dining alone tonight and not much looking forward to it, really. My wife is in London at the moment."

"Then you must come," said Ingersoll. "We'll have a grand time. Three 'bachelors,' out on the town."

Langley gave him a reproachful look. He knew precisely what his best friend was up to. Arriving at the gallery opening of an unknown artist with the publisher of the city's largest newspaper in tow would greatly aid Ingersoll's pursuit of the lady, especially if it enhanced her reputation in the bargain.

"So what great artist will we be meeting tonight?"

"Her name is Miss Medora Lamb," said Ingersoll. He pulled a paper flyer from his coat pocket and handed it to Reid.

The older man shifted his eyeglasses down his nose to bring the invitation into focus. " 'They were naked and they were not ashamed . . .' Hmmm . . . well, the artist has managed to intrigue me from the title alone."

"The paintings are Biblical in nature," said Langley hurriedly. He feared his employer might be offended by the provocative nature of the exhibition's title.

"This wouldn't be Betsy Lamb's granddaughter, would it?"

The young men both shrugged.

"I know Betsy and her husband only slightly. She's a cousin to my wife's mother, I believe. They were just sick about how their daughter turned out."

The older man continued when he saw the inquiring looks on the faces of his two companions. "The girl ran off to join the Oneida Community. This must have been twenty, twenty-five years ago. Gave birth to a daughter there. Betsy and her husband fought for custody of the child. Didn't want the innocent girl raised up in an atmosphere of such immorality."

Neither Langley nor Ingersoll had heard of the great social experiment going on to this very day in upstate New York, but both were riveted by the term "immorality."

"Betsy got her granddaughter, all right, but I hear she was a handful. Wonder if it's the same family?"

The hack jolted to a stop before the Shelton gallery. Reid paid the fare as his two young companions held umbrellas aloft to shield him from the chilly winter rain.

A short, plump man whom they would soon learn was Mr. Shelton, the gallery owner, ran out to greet them the moment he recognized their esteemed traveling companion.

"Mr. Reid," Shelton called. "I am so honored by your presence, sir."

They entered the brightly lit interior of the small, crowded gallery. Its hissing gaslights competed with the low murmur of the milling crowd, many of whom were stylishly attired, while others sported the more eccentric garb of the art world, threadbare, but with an original and occasionally exotic flair.

Those not angling for a glass of free Bordeaux gravitated toward one large painting in the back of the gallery. Only the top third of it was visible above their heads, but the art lovers parted like the Red Sea to make way for Whitelaw Reid and his entourage.

When the three "bachelors" beheld the painting in question, their eyes collectively widened to behold it: Before them stood a romantic rendering of Adam and Eve in Paradise and both were unblushingly unclothed.

"Wonder who posed for that?" Ingersoll whispered to Langley. Both men's attention fastened on Adam. He displayed his anatomy exactly as God made him, every detail intact. Whereas they had seen many paintings of nude women, they had never viewed so frank a depiction of the male form; and to think that the artist was a young woman—an unmarried young woman!—no wonder there had been so much scandalized publicity about this art show.

"Medora, come here, my dear," called the gallery owner to a small and beautiful dark-haired woman surrounded by admirers. "There's someone I want you to meet."

She looked like a young queen holding court, so self-possessed was she in the face of such attention. She responded to the man's order and disentangled herself from the adoring throng of well-wishers.

"Mr. Reid, allow me to present the artist, Miss Medora Lamb."

She smiled and nodded charmingly as she took Mr. Reid's hand.

"You're creating quite a fuss tonight, young lady," said the publisher.

"For the life of me, I don't know why," she said with a modest tilt to her pointed chin.

They were about to converse further when a great commotion rose up at the door of the gallery. The owner dashed off to see what the matter was and Mr. Reid followed him, ever a newspaperman, curious to the bone.

This left the three young people to converse for the moment.

"Ingersoll and Langley, at your service, Miss Lamb," said Ingersoll with a courtly bow.

"He meant to say, '*Langley* and Ingersoll'," corrected his friend mischievously.

"Are you a law firm?" asked Miss Lamb, her dark eyes sparkling with amusement.

"Good heavens, no," said Ingersoll.

"Banish the thought," said Langley.

Both were in top form tonight, and neither had even taken the precaution of fortifying their courage with alcohol.

"That's too bad," she said with mock disappointment. "I may need a lawyer before this night is over. There's a nasty rumor making the rounds that I might be getting arrested."

"Then I shall undertake the study of law immediately," said Ingersoll.

Langley grinned at his friend's shameless flirting. Before he could open his mouth to second the sentiment, Medora Lamb's fear came true.

"Take her into custody!" commanded a portly young man of twenty-nine years. The two policemen at his side advanced toward Miss Lamb.

Langley and Ingersoll blocked their path to the young woman.

"Out of the way, gentlemen," said the large man. "I have a warrant for this woman's arrest."

"Who the hell do you think you are?" said Ingersoll. He looked to be spoiling for a fight. No doubt he wished to impress the object of his affections with a manly show of strength, or at least bluster.

"My name is Comstock and I have sworn out a complaint to stop this obscenity."

"How is this your business?" demanded the gallery owner. "I doubt you were even invited here tonight."

"I am head of the Committee for the Suppression of Vice of the Young Men's Christian Association. My assistant received this degrading piece of trash in the U.S. Mail." He held out the same invitation Ingersoll had shown to Reid in the carriage.

"This alone constitutes a violation of federal law prohibiting use of the postal service for the distribution of obscenity. I intend to file charges in Federal Court first thing tomorrow morning, but for now, I have a bench warrant from the local court charging this woman with the promotion of obscenity."

Medora Lamb was then escorted out to a waiting police wagon headed for lower Manhattan and the infamous "Tombs," leaving an outraged Ingersoll and Langley to stand on the sidewalk in the icy night's rain. Both would never forget the extraordinary look on Medora's face as she was ushered away by the police. The streetlight caught her terrified features for only an instant. The precipitation glistened like teardrops on her delicate, heart-faced face, which now flushed bright with the emotion of a young girl caught up in a childish game gone terribly wrong.

Whitelaw Reid stepped up behind them.

"I must repair to my supper, gentlemen," he said. He pulled his wallet from his breast pocket and began to thumb bills as he counted them. He held out a plump stack of cash. Two hundred dollars, at least.

"This ought to be enough. Go bail her out, young sirs. You'll be her knights in shining armor tonight, I'll be bound."

"Mr. Reid, this is so wonderful," Ingersoll sputtered.

"Thank you, sir," said the equally astonished Langley.

"I'll expect you to file a full story on this incident by the second edition at the latest, Mr. Langley. Good night and good luck to you both, on all counts."

"Isn't she the most extraordinary woman in this city? In this world?" said Ingersoll as they collapsed onto their unmade bed and reveled in their adventure of the last twelve hours.

"Certainly in this city," said Langley.

Ingersoll sat up, indignant at this perceived slight to the woman of his dreams. "Who is more extraordinary, then?"

"I don't know. The 'whole world' seems like a pretty tall claim. That's all."

Ingersoll frowned. "Don't you have something you should be *writing?*"

Langley did not need to be reminded of the assignment—the crushing responsibility—his publisher had placed upon him. He tried to think of it as an opportunity rather than a burden, but the prospect of writing his first real news story terrified him.

He rose from the bed and sat himself down at a little table next to their one and only window. He pushed aside the dinner dishes and glasses, with their shrivelled remains of a previous meal, to clear enough space to write.

"Do you have any paper, Alec?"

Ingersoll had already dozed off and issued only a muffled groan at the sound of his name.

Langley reached over, opened his friend's portfolio, and pulled out a clean sheet of drafting paper. Ingersoll's generous firm gave him endless supplies of top-quality paper, pens, pencils, the finest rulers, and any other drawing implements that money could buy. It must be wonderful to be so valued by one's employers.

He then gathered his pen and ink bottle from the window ledge. Though it was only ten in the morning the sun had already deserted the window. It did not stay past noon on the longest day of summer. In winter, they barely caught a glimpse of it.

Their apartment—a grand name for a single room—sat below street level. The lone window opened onto a brick stairwell. Only the feet of passersby on the sidewalk above were visible. He propped his unshaven chin up and watched the busy boots and wool skirts hurry by. Without realizing it, he started to count them, the pounding steps, gliding steps, the occasional perambulator pushed by a young mother or a baby nurse. The passage of a strolling merchant pushing his cart made Langley hungry, though he could not see what sort of fruit or vegetable the vendor carried.

He wondered why he should be hungry when he had only a couple of hours earlier consumed the largest, most lavish breakfast he could remember ever eating. Steak, eggs, fried potatoes, and onions. Even fried oysters. Such thrilling extravagance.

He could not escape the feeling that, in meeting Medora Lamb, he and Ingersoll had entered into an exotic new world: a heightened reality, a fresh and thrilling dimension in their lives that would make their past grow pale and meaningless in comparison.

He sighed and tried to concentrate on his task. He reviewed the facts he had tried to file in his head, most of which were distressing. Though the proper name for the giant building was "The New York Halls of Justice and House of Detention" it had squarely earned the nickname "The Tombs." The stolid ornate columns of its facade had been inspired by an ancient mausoleum.

"What is this dismal fronted pile of bastard Egyptian, like an enchanter's palace in a melodrama?" Charles Dickens had written of the place four years before Langley's birth.

But the funereal theme referenced more than its architecture. Having been built on the site of a swamp, the underground walls wept moisture all seasons of the year. The dampness created an almost perceptible miasma of doom.

The rank stench of unwashed bodies and open pit privies was revolting even in the cold. Over it all lurked the faint odor of gunpowder and the machine oil used to lubricate guns. He had not encountered that unsavory smell since his soldier days, but he recognized it instantly.

The milling policemen with their prisoners and other assorted characters who wound up facing the prospect of imprisonment in the breech of an icy cold New York night completed the hellish tableaux.

Night court, held on the Centre Street side of the building, was equally strange and otherworldly. The weak gaslight gave everyone a feverish pallor and cast unflattering shadows on their strained faces. Ingersoll shouldered his way around, as if he knew what he was doing. Several assumed he was the young lady's attorney and he did nothing to disabuse them of the notion.

Miss Lamb was visibly frightened by the proceedings and could barely voice her answer when asked how she pleaded to the charges against her. She looked so delicate and small surrounded by all these gruff men. Where were her parents? Did she have parents? Was she really Betsy Lamb's granddaughter?

She needed protectors. Thank God he and Ingersoll were here. Thank God Mr. Reid had given them money.

Then there was the unsavory delight the young Mr. Com-

stock seemed to take in persecuting poor Miss Lamb. His pomp-
ous manner was off-putting to begin with, but his absolute
certainty that the Almighty Himself had set the course of the
evening was disturbing in the extreme. How he flattered himself
in his role of the complaining witness.

Miss Lamb's paintings were shocking, that was certain, but
dangerous? That was Mr. Comstock's implication, the purported
reason for his crusade.

When they paid Miss Lamb's bail and she was released, her
gratitude to her two champions had been overwhelming. Ingersoll was in ecstasy during the hack ride to the restaurant for
their four A.M. breakfast.

"I'll repay you, gentlemen," she had said.

"Nonsense," said Ingersoll, always generous with the money
of others. Neither of them had told Miss Lamb that the bail
money had come from the publisher of the *New York Herald.*
"Aiding a lady in distress was our pleasure. Right, Cam?"

"No, I must repay you. I'll find the money somewhere, even
if I have to ask my grandmother for it." Her animated face
turned fretful. "My grandmother is going to . . . going to . . .
oh, I hate to think what she will do when she finds out about all
this. She'll probably take my studio away."

"You have a studio?" said Langley, though Ingersoll nearly
said it, too.

"It's nothing much. Just a room, really. On West Nineteenth.
Three floors above the gallery, actually. But it has a lovely
northern window, plus a skylight. I love the place most of all
because it's mine."

The two young men exchanged faintly scandalized glances. A
young woman with her own artist's studio in the city? Imagine
it. Of course, that a young woman would ride in a public taxi
with two men she had just met and that she would breakfast
with them unchaperoned was indication enough that Miss Lamb

was a true bohemian and scoffed at convention. Why then should an art studio come as a surprise?

Ingersoll had been in top form, ladling out the flattery and dishing up the charm to impress their new friend. But then, he had gained a lot of practice in this sort of thing during the last couple of years.

His superiors in the architectural firm that employed him must have considered him destined for far loftier heights than the lowly draftsman apprenticeship for which he had been hired. That is, if one were to judge from the number of dinner parties to which he had been invited and seated next to every marriageable young lady remotely related to one of the firm partners.

Ingersoll basked in the attentions of these often attractive and frequently well-monied daughters and nieces and cousins once removed.

"It's keeping us well fed," he told Langley, whom he always insisted be invited to these dinners as well. "If my senior partners wish to act as disgracefully as pimps, well, let them."

Langley finally tore his gaze from the traffic of the sidewalk and stared down at the empty piece of paper beneath his elbows. The blankness of that page threatened to rise up and slap his face. He massaged his aching temples.

CHAPTER TWELVE

Saturday, April 24, 1875

"Cam never filed that story," said Ingersoll. "It was a priceless opportunity for a man in his position. That he failed at this seemed to disappoint me more than him, though. He quit his job at the *Herald* to avoid being reproached for his failure and took a similar position at the *Times*."

Ingersoll sighed with sadness before continuing. "I suppose I imagined that every man was as consumed with ambition as I was. I couldn't believe he would let such a chance go by. Was he afraid of failing? Overwhelmed by the assignment? I badgered him about it and now I regret that. Looking back, it was cruel of me perhaps. I was just trying to help him. Oh well, it's long over. Anyway, the three of us, Medora, Cam, and I, were inseparable from that night forward."

"What prompted you to come all the way out to Chicago?"

He hesitated before answering as though he were inventing what to say. This called Victoria to question the veracity of whatever might follow.

"The firm here made me an incredible offer. I was moving along well in New York, but the opportunity here . . . a partnership at my age . . . I couldn't afford to pass it up. So much building going on here after the fire. And with a baby on the way—"

"You and Medora had a child?" Mr. Oberholtzer had not mentioned the existence of a child of the marriage.

"A little girl. Died a few hours after her birth, I'm sorry to say." He glanced away, the memory obviously still painful, but suddenly he smiled and said, "They let me hold her. Well, actually the doctor tried to talk me out of it, but I insisted. I'm glad I did, though. She was so tiny. And *light*. If I hadn't held her for those few precious minutes, I might not have believed she ever really existed."

Victoria reached across the table and patted his hand.

"I don't think Dora ever held her. The doctor gave her laudanum to ease her pain and make her sleep. He knew right away the child would not last the night. He said she arrived too early. Her lungs weren't ready for the world, he said. We told Dora about the baby when she woke up the following morning. She was so melancholy she could not attend the funeral. Well, it wasn't a real funeral. More of a simple graveside service. Such a tiny little coffin . . ."

His voice broke and his eyes filled with tears. He blinked them away and swallowed hard. "Sorry."

"Don't apologize." She liked him a little better for this show of tender emotion.

"She wouldn't speak of the child after that. Wouldn't even help me name her. We had to put something on the little gravestone. I wired Cam for help. He was always so good at that sort of thing, you know. His professional dealings with grieving people made him so compassionate. Maybe it went deeper than that, come to think of it.

"He was good at helping people who had suffered some misfortune or loss. Even when we were just youngsters, during the war. Boy soldiers. Anyway, he wired me back and suggested I name the baby after my mother. So I did. Eleanor. 'Eleanor Ingersoll'—it didn't really roll off the tongue. Guess it doesn't really matter, does it?"

She offered a smile, not knowing what to say.

93

"Then Cam wrote the most beautiful obituary. I wasn't even planning to place one in the paper, but when I read it, I did. He made her seem real. Like her tiny life, however short, had mattered."

Ingersoll stared at the empty tabletop. He looked near tears again, though he would not allow them and pressed his thin lips together. The high polish of the table reflected his sad and weary face.

"I wonder," he said quietly, "I wonder who wrote *his* obituary?"

CHAPTER THIRTEEN

Flynn was late to meet the lawyer from Chicago. She had to drive Brody to an orthodontist's office in downtown Kansas City, then they got stuck in a traffic snarl on the long drive back to Weston. An injury accident on the narrow county road had backed up cars for miles. By the time she dropped her son off at the high school, she was more than an hour later than Matt Holtser's projected arrival time.

She couldn't find a parking spot on Main Street closer than a block from the bookstore. She hurried down the sidewalk, then slowed her pace to catch her breath. No need to meet him looking frantic and panting.

Once composed, she carefully glanced in the side panel of the shop's big bay window to see if he was there. Her dad was engaged in a lively conversation with someone. She could only see the man's back. He was medium height, average build, dark hair, neatly trimmed. Over his shoulder hung an upscale leather version of a messenger bag. His clothes were standard-issue business casual—blue sport shirt and khaki slacks. If he were a crazed stalker or serial killer, at least he was a well-groomed one.

Then there was the matter of his feet. Instead of loafers or something similar, he wore expensive-looking white running shoes. She liked this odd touch. Kept him from looking too lawyer-yuppie-geeky and suggested he tried to keep physically fit.

Flynn caught herself mid-thought. Why was she sizing this guy up? They weren't going on a date, for God's sake.

She watched the two men a moment longer. Whatever they were talking about was certainly amusing her father. He was smiling broadly and nodding frequently.

Then she saw what they were discussing: Her dad was holding that copy of David's book, *Mountain Daylight Time,* the one she had cataloged the day before. She hoped this didn't mean Matt Holtser was a Holloway fan. She did not want to have to deal with that.

She unconsciously hugged her shoulder bag that now carried her precious photograph and entered the shop.

"Sorry I'm so late. Got tied up in traffic."

The stranger turned to greet her with a pleasing smile. He was much younger than she expected, in fact, maybe younger than she was. Probably thirty, but not much more.

"Flynny, this is Matt Holtser. Matt, this is my daughter."

Matt shook her hand. "I'm pleased to meet you. May I call you Flynn?"

"Honey, you won't believe this but Matt works in the same legal department as the son of my old college roommate."

Matt shrugged with an awkward grin. "Six degrees of separation, I guess."

"In the legal world, I think it's a lot less than six," said Dan.

"I hope my dad hasn't been boring you with lawyer war stories." She gave her father a teasing wink.

"I told a few of my own," said Matt.

"I'm sure you and Matt are anxious to talk about this photograph and all. Why don't you two grab some coffee at the café? It's just three doors down from here, Matt."

Here was her father who had not even wanted her to answer this guy's emails, shoving them together? Matt Holtser must be Charm Incorporated to cast such a spell on the old man. Flynn and Matt exchanged embarrassed smiles and headed out the door.

"Dan and I didn't spend the whole time talking about the law. We mostly talked about you."

Her father only let a few close friends call him "Dan," more casual acquaintances had to settle for "Daniel." Obviously, Matt had managed to join this select circle in less than an hour. "That must have been even more boring than war stories," she said as they entered the café. The place was nearly deserted but for Betty, the owner, who sat next to the counter going over some paperwork.

They took a seat in the sunny front window and glanced at the blue plastic menus.

The shabbiness of the little café suddenly embarrassed Flynn. The building housing the restaurant was built in 1847, but this place had not seen a renovation in decades.

"Not exactly Starbucks," she said, though she had never apologized for Weston to anyone before.

"Hey, *better* than Starbucks. I don't have to stand in line to order. Plus I've never been a coffee snob. If it's hot, I'm happy. How's your auction going?"

"Last time I checked, it was still stalled at $2,000."

"Sorry I had to drop out."

"That's okay. I understand."

Betty walked over and filled their mugs. She tried to talk Matt into ordering pie, but he declined. She didn't push any pie on Flynn, which made Flynn wonder if she were invisible. She knew she was quiet; she'd been born quiet, and would probably die quiet. The only time she escaped her mantle of natural shyness was in her classrooms. The unequal balance of power brought out her hidden self-confidence. She had only realized recently how much she liked teaching. She had previously considered it boring drudgery, an easy paycheck and not much more. Now, after her several-month hiatus, she found herself thinking about it more and more.

"Well, I suppose you're anxious to see the photograph," she said.

A couple of patrons entered the café. They took seats on the far wall, but openly surveyed Flynn and Matt. Flynn felt the hovering quality of a small-town society, the need to keep tabs on everyone's business.

"And I have the promised information for you," Matt said. He pulled open his messenger bag and rifled through his contents. "I don't know why but I feel like this is a Mafia 'sit-down.' "

"No need to fear. I stopped carrying a gun years ago."

He laughed and Flynn was flattered. She pulled the photograph from her satchel. She had placed it in a plastic sleeve and secured it between two sheets of sturdy cardboard.

The pair eyed each other cautiously as if to say, Who goes first? Matt held a thick batch of papers held fast by a large, metal alligator clip.

"I'll show you mine, if you'll show me yours," he said.

Flynn cracked up and the tension evaporated. "I haven't gotten that offer since kindergarten."

"This is a partial trial transcript," he said. "It's from the spring of 1875. My great-great-whatever-grandfather is the attorney representing the defendant. His name was Franklin Oberholtzer. My aunt got interested in genealogy a few years back and told me about him because we always thought I was the first lawyer in the family."

"Your name is so similar."

"Yeah, apparently they changed it during World War I because of all the anti-German sentiment. I guess they thought 'Holtser' sounded more Anglo-Saxon, but I'm not sure they really succeeded.

"Anyway, this murder trial involved a big scandal. Front-page news. Now Chicago is home to countless murders, but this one grabbed the headlines because the people all lived on Prairie Avenue."

"I think I've heard of that street," said Flynn.

"Yeah, it's really famous. Everyone who was anyone in the late nineteenth century wanted to live there. All the big names built homes there—Pullman, Marshall Field, Armour, the meat guy. The elite started out on Michigan Avenue, but it took a hit with the Great Fire of 1871. They all headed for Prairie Avenue when it came time to rebuild.

"It was a nice part of town back in the day. Unfortunately, it faded out in the twentieth century. The neighborhood went way downhill and a lot of the grand old houses were bulldozed."

She carefully opened the cardboard and pulled out her treasure. Matt grinned as he studied it for several moments. "So who killed who?" Flynn said, knowing as she said the words that she probably should have used "whom." The decade she spent teaching English Comp to one wave of shockingly undereducated college freshmen after another was not easily shaken off.

"I'm going to have to guess a little because I have never seen any pictures of the people involved, but I know from newspaper accounts that the defendant, Alec Ingersoll, was dark haired and had a beard."

He turned the photo around to face her.

"This guy must be Alec. He was accused of murdering her, his wife, that is, and him, the blond guy who was supposedly his best friend."

"So I assume the wife was getting it on with the friend."

"Oh, it's way more complicated than that. They all lived together in this big, fancy house in some sort of radical *ménage a trois* if you believe the servant's gossip in the trial transcript."

"Wow, you got my attention now. Does the house still exist? I'd love to see it."

"Yep. I got lucky on that one. It managed to survive the wrecking ball somehow. A lot of well-heeled types are re-gentrifying old Prairie Avenue and renovating the few mansions and townhouses that are left. I guess this was one of the fortunate few. I want to get inside it sometime. I tried contacting the new owners last week, but they were out of town. Maybe I'll try calling them again later tonight."

Flynn stared into the three faces and imagined personalities for them while Matt chattered on with obvious enthusiasm for his topic.

When he paused to take a sip of his now cool coffee, she could not help but ask, "So did he do it?"

Matt laughed. "I wish I had a simple answer to that."

CHAPTER FOURTEEN

Saturday, April 24, 1875

Oberholtzer picked up a discreetly veiled Victoria from the jail-house in order to transport her to the Prairie Avenue home of the Ingersolls. On this bright and pleasant afternoon he brought with him an unexpected guest.

"May I present my wife?" he said as he took Victoria's hand and pulled her up into the well-appointed carriage.

A flushed and florid woman in her middle years smiled nervously and thrust her gloved hand in her guest's direction the moment she was seated.

"How do you do, Mrs. Oberholtzer?" Victoria said. She returned the woman's smile and shook her hand.

"A pleasure to meet you, Mrs. Woodhull. When Franklin told me about you, I just insisted he introduce us." Her words gushed out in a stilted, rehearsed fashion. "I already know that we have something in common."

"I imagine we have many things in common, Mrs. Ober-holtzer."

"I support the cause of women's suffrage."

Victoria wondered if her true role was that of chaperone. Whether to safeguard her host's reputation or to satisfy a jealous wife that the notorious proponent of Free Love was not going to swoop down upon her poor husband and seduce him on the grounds of the murder scene, she could only guess.

"And what a worthy cause that is, indeed." Victoria hoped

her relaxed manner would put the woman at ease on all scores. Often women such as this—ladies of sheltered background—tended to actually fear a meeting with her. Once they realized that she was neither the fire-breathing dragon nor the man-stealing siren the press or their local pastor has led them to believe, they were usually reassured.

Just enough April sun shone in the carriage windows to highlight Mrs. Oberholtzer's scarlet cheeks to indicate Victoria still had some ways to go before the lady might feel comfortable taking tea with her. Unfortunately, they did not have time for such niceties.

"Still no verdict, I take it?" Victoria asked Oberholtzer.

"Alas, no. The jury has adjourned for the weekend. They resume their task on Monday morning."

Victoria used the remainder of the journey to make the usual, meaningless small talk with Mrs. Oberholtzer, inquiring after her children—their ages, names, welfare, and so forth—as if such information could possibly be important, given that their paths would likely never cross again.

The husband seemed to glow with pride whenever his wife spoke, which touched Victoria a good deal. He did not appear as bored with their "ladies' talk" as most men often claimed to be. Whether he feigned his interest or genuinely felt it, she was gratified by his demeanor. Dealing with the legal profession could often be either boring or stressful. Mr. Oberholtzer happily proved to be neither.

"Would you like to see the Massacre Tree, Mrs. Woodhull?" the lawyer's wife inquired.

"The what?"

"We are about to pass a local landmark," said her husband. "Prairie Avenue was the site of the 'Fort Dearborn Massacre' back at the beginning of this century. During the War of 1812, actually. Indians fighting on the side of the British did the deed.

"That large old tree there marks the spot. No reason you should have known of it unless you were a school child here. Some of the local papers had the nerve to compare this recent tragedy to that old one. Calling it the 'Second Prairie Avenue Massacre.' "

He frowned as if to say, What can one do about the press?

"Tasteless," sniffed Mrs. Oberholtzer in agreement.

They pulled up in front of the Ingersoll house, an impressive two-story structure with a square tower looming above the first two floors. Victoria realized she had already viewed the interior of that tower in the death scene photographs.

The structure reflected the fashionable Italianate style and carried the signature Mansard roof. Victoria noticed that most of the dwellings on the charming street reflected the Second Empire, a testament to just how fashionable these well-moneyed Chicagoans were. What caused amazement to a first-time visitor such as she was just how new all the houses seemed to be. Many were still under construction. The elm trees lining the graceful and wide street were mere saplings, obviously planted within the last few years.

A generous lawn surrounded the house. The grass grew out of control in its owner's absence, in stark contrast to the carefully groomed appearance of its neighboring lawns.

The lawyer and his wife led Victoria up the stone steps to the covered porch, which spanned only the front doors and the south end of the house. That porch roof in turn became a charming balcony to the floor above. Double doors from a room on the floor above opened out onto it.

A policeman was posted at the door. He nodded in recognition of Oberholtzer. No doubt the luckless house had become an attraction drawing the morbidly curious who might ransack the premises looking for grisly souvenirs, in addition to the fine appointments the mansion no doubt possessed.

"Alec was just renting this place," said his lawyer as he unlocked the large mahogany double-doors and ushered his wife and guest inside. "He married in haste and needed a house in a hurry."

Mrs. Oberholtzer leaned close and whispered, "A little bundle of joy on the way prompted the marriage."

"Now, Dottie, please. We don't need to gossip."

"It's not gossip, dear. It was court testimony after all."

"I'm afraid my wife is correct on that score. Mr. Langley's sister testified to that effect."

"Oh, yes, you mentioned that she testified. I was curious about that."

"Actually, she was one of my defense witnesses," said Mr. Oberholtzer, looking discomfited by the admission. "I had to introduce evidence that Medora Ingersoll had a history of suicide attempts and since Alec wouldn't testify, well. . . . Anyway the little dear contacted me and offered herself, said she wanted to help in any way she could. Came all the way out here by herself."

"The sweet thing had never left the state of New York prior to this," said Mrs. Oberholtzer. "She has been residing with us for the duration of the trial. She believes absolutely in Mr. Ingersoll's innocence."

"When did the Ingersolls get married?" Victoria asked.

"A year ago last February," said Oberholtzer. "Alec had only been in town since December. He was living at the Y.M.C.A. then."

Victoria inwardly cringed at the mention of the Young Men's Christian Association, it being the employer of her arch nemesis, Mr. Anthony Comstock.

"He certainly changed his surroundings for the better," Victoria said as she gazed around the beautifully decorated front hall.

"Howard Mallory—that's one of Alec's senior partners—told me Alec up and asked for a week free to return to New York without giving a reason for the trip. Just said it was critically important. He came back the following Monday a married man.

"He spent the next week looking for a place for them to live. The owners of this fine house happened to be leaving on a two-year tour of Europe and wanted someone reliable to live here in their absence to look after the house. A friend of Mallory's, you see. With his reference, Alec was able to rent this place, furnished and all, for a song."

That explained a small mystery for Victoria. The moment she viewed the grandness of the Ingersoll residence and the excellence of its neighborhood, she wondered how a young man, however successful in his career, could manage such extravagance when he had told her that his remaining family had disowned him.

"I don't think he ever told his wife he was merely renting," said Mrs. Oberholtzer. "We invited them over to dinner right after she arrived and she said something to me that indicated she thought they owned the place."

"If he was trying to impress his new bride," Victoria said, "he must have succeeded."

A magnificent marble fireplace graced the far wall of the high-ceilinged room. Two carved lions guarded either side of the firebox. Their shiny, rose quartz heads caught the afternoon sun. The room smelled musty and needed a good airing. A fine mist of dust particles also caught the shafts of window light.

Oberholtzer led the ladies to the central staircase, pointing out on the way the direction to the kitchen, back parlor, and servant's quarters, but they did not view them. Instead, they ascended to the second floor.

There, four commodiously sized bedrooms lay, two on each side of the stair.

"This was Alec's room." Oberholtzer gestured to the first room on the left.

She peered in and saw a lavishly decorated bedroom. An enormous, darkly stained headboard loomed over the large bed and dominated the south wall between two tall, narrow bay windows, each housing their own window seats. She peeked in a side door to see an elegant bath with an enormous, gleaming copper bathtub.

The lawyer and his wife continued down the hall and pointed into the second bedroom. "This was her room."

"Mrs. Ingersoll's, you mean?"

"Yes, they didn't see fit to sleep together. That tells me a little something about the marriage. Newlyweds with separate bedrooms? What's the point of being married, eh?"

"Oh, Frank, hush," said his wife with a chiding tone of modesty.

"It's an interesting point," Victoria said, not one to blush about a discussion of the intimate aspects of marriage. Indeed, she now made the lion's share of her living giving speeches on the very topic. "The Human Body as a Temple of God" was her current, most popular presentation.

Medora Lamb's bedroom looked decidedly more feminine than that of her husband, but since the couple had moved into the house furnished, it made judging the interiors more difficult. How much of the decoration reflected the Ingersolls' tastes versus those of the home's actual owners?

A magnificent canopy of glistening silver-white silk arched over Medora's bed. The sweet froth resembled an ethereal mist. What a pleasant place to sleep it must have been, as though one had slept out of doors and beheld a sky full of delicate, shimmering clouds upon rising.

The side of the chamber facing the street sported the double doors that led to the balcony that she had viewed from outside.

Several paintings hung on the walls and several more sat on the floor propped against the walls as though the occupant of the room had never quite gotten around to hanging them.

As one painting featured an impressionistic likeness of Alec Ingersoll, she asked, "These paintings are the work of Medora Lamb?"

"Yes," said Oberholtzer in a clipped tone, transmitting his dislike of the late Mrs. Ingersoll.

They returned to the hall and crossed to the other side to examine the last two rooms on the floor.

"Here resided the snake in the garden," said the lawyer as he opened the door of Cameron Curtis Langley's room.

His wife tittered at his remark, though Victoria did not find it humorous.

"He was best man at their wedding," said Mrs. Oberholtzer, leaning in close to Victoria as though what she had to confide was some sort of secret to be kept from the outside world.

The room was more sparely furnished than the other two, as befits a houseguest, perhaps.

"How long did he reside with the couple?"

"He moved out here from New York at the end of last summer. He worked for a newspaper and lost his job. Alec invited him to stay here until he got back on his feet, though I don't know of him looking for a job while he lived in Chicago."

"Mrs. Ingersoll told me he was writing a novel, dear."

The lawyer snapped his fingers and nodded as his memory was refreshed. "Yes, yes, that was the story."

"Story?" Victoria said. "Do you not believe it was the case?"

"Damned if I know what he was up to besides seducing his best friend's wife. The police never found any such manuscript." He led them on to the final bedroom. "This last room was to be the nursery. A sad loss for the couple. Alec took it hard."

They entered the nursery and Victoria's lips parted in

astonishment. One whole wall bore a marvelous and fanciful painted mural. A colorful fairytale forest was represented, filled with animals, trolls, fairies, and such. Three human figures were represented in the giant work.

A woman with long, dark hair stood on the ground and held the strings to two kites sailing above her in the bright blue sky. Each kite was adorned with the likeness of a man. The dark-haired, bearded man was undisputedly Alec Ingersoll. The second kite bore a resemblance to the blond Mr. Langley, though his smiling visage looked a good deal more handsome in the painting than it did in the grisly death photograph.

"That's her," said the lawyer, pointing to the picture of the woman flying the kites.

Victoria studied the portrait more closely. Medora Lamb had a piquant face, all points and angles. Not attractive in the soft feminine way. Not pretty like her own sister Tennie, who was blessed with all the features so highly prized: large, child-like eyes; abundant, wavy, fair hair; full lips; and a delicate button of a nose. No wonder men made fools of themselves in her presence!

Medora Lamb, on the other hand, possessed a pointed nose and a chin to match. Her flaring nostrils arched at an angle echoed in her broad jawline and dark eyebrows. In the painting, her thin lips did not smile.

"She painted this, I take it?"

"She and Alec both did. He told me they used to work on it in the evenings after supper. All the long spring and summer of waiting for the baby to come. He seemed to brighten when reminiscing about it. They were both accomplished artists. I suppose they would come up here and paint together and dream about the future."

"One item puzzles me," said Mrs. Oberholtzer. "How did they plan to explain the painting to the owners of the house?"

Her husband chuckled cynically. "I imagine the mural was her idea and he couldn't find a way to talk her out of it unless he told the truth about not owning the house."

Victoria meditated for several moments on this grand painting and the odd representation of Medora Lamb flying her two kites—Alec and Cameron—in the air. A rather bold statement of her mind to place on the wall of her child's future bedroom. A strange woman indeed.

"If the baby hadn't died," said Mrs. Oberholtzer, "perhaps none of this would have happened."

"How so?" Victoria asked, curious at the woman's speculation.

"Alec invited that man to come stay with them to cheer her up after the loss."

Her husband made a cynical "harumph" at this.

"I guess Mr. Langley overdid it," Victoria said without thinking how shamelessly out of place her humor would be.

The lawyer laughed loudly at her thoughtless joke and even his wife smiled as she blushed.

"Seriously, though, she was not really happy here long before they lost the child," said Oberholtzer.

"She didn't like Chicago," said Mrs. Oberholtzer. "Thought it was too windy. And too . . . uncivilized. Lacking in culture, I guess. She could be quite rude about expressing her dislike of the place. You would have thought she could have had the courtesy to keep her opinions to herself when she was in the company of those of us who love this city—"

"Now, Dottie, let it go."

"I'm sorry, that's just how I feel."

"Well, it doesn't matter now, does it? So, ladies, are you ready for the final room? I should say, the final *resting place* of two of those three individuals."

"Lead the way, sir."

"Dottie, are you sure you want to do this?" he asked his wife in kind terms.

"Yes, dear. I'll be fine. It's all been cleaned up, hasn't it?"

"Not completely."

Dottie Oberholtzer tossed Victoria an uncertain frown over her shoulder as they followed her husband up the winding staircase that led to the tower room.

"This tower was her photographic studio," said the lawyer. "She called that closet behind the stairs her 'dark' room. That's what photographers call the room reserved to use the chemicals to develop the plates and make the pictures."

The room looked to Victoria much as the police photographs presented it. Still, it seemed bigger than she expected. The chaise lounge upon which Cameron Langley died still carried his bloodstain. Mrs. Oberholtzer grimaced when she saw it and quickly marched to the opposite side of the room.

"Do you sense the presence of any spirits, Mrs. Woodhull?"

"Not yet, Mrs. Oberholtzer." She walked slowly around the room, touching various items, sniffing the somewhat repellant odors particular to the photographic profession.

"Where are her photographs, by the way?"

"Stolen."

"What?"

"All of them were stolen. Prints, plates, the lot. Not a single one has surfaced."

"When did that happen?"

"About a week before the murders. The house was broken into one morning when no one was home. Her photographic equipment was stolen along with some silverware and candlesticks. A brooch of small value, save sentiment, and Mr. Langley's pocket watch. The authorities didn't know what to make of it. They kept a look out on the pawn shops in town, certain that the camera or the watch would show up there, but they didn't. Alec had all the locks changed and bought a gun for Medora to keep next to her bed."

"Was that the gun that—?"

"Yes, that was the gun that killed Cameron Langley. Of course there was much discussion about whether the two events were linked. I tried to play it up during the trial. The prosecution wanted to characterize it as a mere coincidence."

"I have never believed in coincidence," Victoria said.

When she caught the view out of the eastern window, she had to gasp. Before her spread a magnificent view of Lake Michigan in the distance.

Mr. Oberholtzer joined her in admiring the vista.

"You can see more than fifty miles from this window. Over there, down and to the right, that's where all the money is made."

She followed his gaze and saw a large collection of rail lines running next to what she presumed must be the fabled stock-yards.

"The view of the lake is fabulous," she said.

"Alec said this tower was his wedding gift to his wife. Being an artistic type, she loved being able to see so far into the distance. She did some photographs of the various landscapes from up here. Too bad they are all gone now."

Victoria returned to the wooden drafting table over which Medora Lamb Ingersoll had been found collapsed. She placed her hands upon it, palms flat, and closed her eyes, hoping for some sign.

None appeared, yet her mind was made up nonetheless.

"I would greatly like to conduct the séance in this room. We can form the spirit circle around this very table. Is there any way Mr. Ingersoll can participate?"

"Not unless the jury acquits him or the prosecution suddenly agrees to a bail. The latter is not likely and the former—well, who knows?"

"May I participate, Mrs. Woodhull?" said his wife.

"*Dottie*—" said her husband.

"Please, Frank. I've never attended a séance before."

"I have no objection, Mr. Oberholtzer. Would you like to join us also?"

"I don't think you would want nonbelievers in your circle, would you?"

"It shouldn't spoil things. As long as you are not too violently opposed to the proceedings. A group of four or six is about right. And, if possible, an equal number of each sex."

"What else will you be needing, Madam?"

"Let's see . . . some sharpened lead pencils and some paper to write on—"

"To write down the spirit communications?" asked Dottie Oberholtzer eagerly.

"Yes, it . . ." She found herself suddenly preoccupied with the strangest thoughts. "Who did you say discovered the bodies? Mr. Ingersoll?"

"Yes," said Oberholzer. "He was the first to arrive, then later the postman."

She turned to survey the murder scene once more before taking her leave. Something was not right. She ran her hands over the table once again and then returned to the chaise lounge, lightly touching the bloodstain.

"Only one person died in this room," she said.

"No, Madam," said the lawyer, "I can assure you that both victims were found—"

She cut him off with a backwards wave of her hand and repeated with a chilling, otherworldly certainty, "Only one person died in this room."

Chapter Fifteen

"You invited him out to dinner? I guess that means you don't think he's a 'dangerous flake.' "

"I liked him," said Dan Keirnan as he counted the change in his cash register, a prelude to closing out for the day. "He asked me where he should eat dinner and I felt sorry for anybody having to eat alone. I told him we'd take him to Fensters. I think that's a better choice than Border Wars, don't you? The service is a little more consistent. And Clancy's Bar is just, well . . . maybe we could end up there for a nightcap."

Flynn sat down behind the counter and sighed. "Well, I can't be there. This is Monday and Brody has to be driven to his guitar lesson at 7:30."

"Oh, that's right. Well, I'll just stay for drinks, then *I'll* drive Brody. You two can stay for dinner. Put it on my credit card though. It's my treat."

"Is this a fix-up? If it is, I'm going to be mad—"

"Oh, Flynny, what you do with your life is your business. He's just a nice guy from out of town. And you two can talk about the photo." He walked to the door, turned the bolt lock, and flipped the "Open" sign to "Closed."

"Well, he's probably married."

"He didn't mention it," said Dan.

"Or gay. He's staying at that Victorian B&B down the street. What does that tell you?"

"It tells me you buy into stereotypes, little missy. Never

thought I'd have to tell my headstrong rebel of a daughter to be more liberal."

They both began to grin. "Point taken, Counselor."

Flynn was still not convinced of her father's motives. "If this is a fix-up, I hope he's married *and* gay. That would teach you."

"Who am I to judge?"

Flynn wanted to let him have it for that remark. He and her mother had been plenty judgmental when Brody came along fourteen years ago.

"I just care about you, honey," he continued. "You haven't been on a date since you moved here."

"So? Maybe I'm not in the mood. It's not like I lived like a nun all those years in California."

Dan made a frantic, theatrical shiver. "Stop right there. Don't make me imagine things a father never wants to imagine."

"Don't worry. You're not going to hear the intimate details of my sex life. I'm saving that for my memoirs."

"Thank God. Hopefully, I'll be long dead by then. But seriously, I hate to think of you being alone. At your age."

"I haven't been alone all the time. Have you forgotten Sam?"

"The drug addict?"

"That wasn't his fault. They were prescription painkillers. He was a professional skier."

"Who stayed stoned years after he recovered . . ."

"What about Randy? I suppose you hated him too."

"The deadbeat?"

"Oh, you are so unfair. He couldn't help it that he didn't get tenure—" she halted mid-sentence, not wanting to go down this tired road again. She shifted strategies. "Dad, have you ever considered the fact that maybe we're only entitled to one great love in our life? And maybe I've already had mine?"

"Brody's father?"

She didn't answer. "Maybe American lives really don't have

second acts."

"Says who?"

"F. Scott Fitzgerald. Your favorite Greatest Dead American Writer."

"Well, if he said that, he's not my favorite anymore."

"Give it a rest, Dad. It's not my fault all the good guys like you are already taken."

She leaned over the counter and gave him a kiss on the cheek.

He chuckled and pulled off his glasses. "Just promise you won't be too hard on poor Matt. He's an innocent bystander in our little war."

"He's safe. Well, pretty safe. And, for the record, I like him too. He seems nice."

She had no more than spoken when the gentleman under discussion was heard tapping on the glass of the bay window.

Dan waved at him and grabbed his jacket.

They strolled along the nearly deserted sidewalk and headed for Fensters, a nice little restaurant and one of the few in town open on a Monday night. Flynn trailed behind and watched the two men chat away. More than once, Matt glanced back over his shoulder, looking for her. She quickened her pace to catch up when they reached their destination.

The restaurant was located in a converted house dating from before the Civil War. A stone walkway and tiny garden separated it from the narrow side street where it dominated its short block.

Each large room on the main floor now served as a dining room and most had fireplaces. Very few tables were occupied that night since the tourist season had not kicked off yet.

"Table for three?" asked Mr. Fenster, their cheerful host.

"Yes," said Dan, "but I'm afraid I won't be here for dinner, just appetizers."

"Oh, Dan, you're not staying?" said Matt.

Flynn felt mortification burning her from the inside out. She pitied Matt Holtser. He was undoubtedly thinking he had been duped into a blind date of sorts.

They sat at a candlelit table in the window, entirely too intimate for a business dinner, but Flynn said nothing. After they had placed their drink orders, she opened with:

"Well, Matt, do you stay in B&Bs a lot?"

Her dad shot her a warning look and she tried not to grin.

Matt looked up from his menu and said, "Actually, this is my first time. A bed & breakfast virgin, I guess. That little hotel down the street was closed for renovations, according to their website. I've always been kinda leery of B&Bs. I'm not sure I'll be comfortable eating breakfast with strangers." He dropped his gaze back into the menu.

Dan gave his daughter an I-told-you-so smirk. She decided to behave herself for fear he would invite their visitor to breakfast as well.

"I take it your wife doesn't like them either?" said Dan.

"Not married. Not anymore." He again went back to studying his menu.

Flynn mouthed the words, "Smart ass."

Their drinks arrived. Flynn had gone with a single glass of wine, nothing fancy, just the house wine. Matt picked an imported beer and her dad had followed his lead. The two lawyers engaged in shop talk—nearly putting Flynn to sleep— until 7:15 rolled around and Dan made his excuses to leave.

As soon as Matt sat down again, he announced, "I've got major news."

"About what?"

"Our photo friends. After we left the diner this afternoon, I managed to get in touch with the lady who owns the house."

"The murder house?"

"Yeah, only she didn't even know about the murders. She and her husband bought the house at a tax sale a few years ago for twenty grand. They plan to fix it up and flip it, I assume. At that price, they can't possibly lose money."

"Hope you didn't ruin her day, telling her about the murders."

"Not at all. She actually thought it was cool. Here's the beauty part: She knew all about the three people—Alec and Medora and Cameron. She just didn't know about the murders."

"But how on earth?" said Flynn, now on the edge of her seat. And she thought this was going to be a boring, awkward evening that was over before nine.

"When she and her husband were remodeling the upstairs rooms, they found an old notebook hidden behind the wainscoting in one of them."

"Oh, this is just like a Nancy Drew novel," Flynn said with a grin

"No shit. Anyway, this notebook was bound in red leather and had the initials *C.C.L.* stamped on the front."

"Cameron Curtis Langley!"

"Correct! Miss Keirnan advances to the lightning round."

Flynn laughed in a pleasing stew of embarrassment and flattery. This Matt Holtser was either the most charming extrovert she had ever met or he was maybe actually flirting a little. As the buzz from the wine comfortably settled in, she decided she didn't care which. She ordered a second glass as their main courses arrived. Matt had chosen the steak—always a safe bet in the Heartland. Flynn tried the salmon.

"The lady said there was one thing really odd about the notebook. She couldn't tell who wrote it."

"It wasn't written by Langley?" Flynn got serious again, happy to be back on subject.

"No, the notebook talks about all three of them—Ingersoll and Medora Lamb and Langley, but Langley is referred to in the third person, so it wasn't a diary or journal."

"But I guess the notebook didn't mention the murder or she

would have known about it," said Flynn—and realized even as she spoke how stupid the remark was, considering two of the three people in the notebook had likely died after it had been hidden.

"She said the book talks about a romantic triangle. Sex is kind of hinted at but not explicitly. I guess that's in keeping with the Victorian prudishness of the day. Do it but, for God's sake, don't talk about it."

"Damn," said Flynn in mock disappointment. "I was hoping for a hot read."

"Me, too!"

They both laughed, perhaps a bit too loudly. The diners at the two other occupied tables turned to look at them.

They exchanged the guilty glances of chastised children. Flynn thought, Uh-oh, now I'll be the star of Main Street gossip for the next several days. Being a slow week, the notoriety might even last into the weekend.

Some of the locals already regarded her as a slightly scarlet woman, given her never-married motherhood status. The twenty-first century may have shown up on the calendar but most residents had moral codes straight out of 1950.

"Oh, and I've done you a favor on your auction, Flynn. The lady wants to start bidding on the photo. She thinks it ought to be in her house, given the circumstances."

"Hey, thanks. I didn't really want that "Woodhull" person to win. He or she was kinda rude. I was miffed."

"Miffed?" Matt Holtser raised his black eyebrows and chuckled at her choice of words.

This from a guy who says "yikes"?

"It would be nice for the picture of those three people to be in that house, I guess," Flynn said, sliding back into a more contemplative mood. "Since two of them died there. Did the lady mention any ghosts?"

"No, but I bet she starts thinking she sees them now," he said.

Eventually, the teenage waitress came by with the inevitable question: "Did you folks save room for dessert?"

Matt and Flynn looked at each other questioningly. He shrugged as did she.

"Maybe coffee?" she said.

"Sure."

They were now the only diners left in the place, making the dinner even more oddly intimate. Her discomfort increased exponentially when Matt innocently steered the conversation into much more personal waters.

"Dan told me you knew David Holloway."

She inwardly groaned but answered him with a modest nod.

"And he said that you actually worked with him?"

Oh, great, another Holloway junkie. She could tell by the worshipful enthusiasm in his question.

"I was a research assistant for him one summer. I had just started grad school. Actually, I lived with him and his wife that summer. They had this vacation home in Colorado where they always spent their summers."

"She was a poet, right?"

"Yeah. Barb Yost."

"You actually lived in the same house with David Holloway." He shook his head slowly, amazed.

With a knowing smile, Flynn stretched her hand across the table. "You can touch me if you want."

He laughed and flushed in embarrassment. "Sorry, sorry. He's just always been a big hero to me."

"I'm teasing you. My sense of humor is warped. It slides by most people unnoticed. And don't apologize. I understand totally. He meant a lot to a lot of people. In college, I was a total Holloway maniac, myself."

More like a Holloway groupie, she thought sourly, but we're not going to go *there*.

"Well, I'm sorry just the same. I started reading him in high school, maybe even middle school."

"You were precocious," Flynn said. She had to admit she was impressed. "Which one did you start with?"

"Benchmark."

"That's where just about everyone starts. That was the one that sold the most. If you added all the other books together, they wouldn't even number half of *Benchmark* in sales. He used to jokingly call it his retirement plan. I don't know what the royalties were, but I know that he didn't really need a day job. I think he kept up his teaching career because he wanted to stay constantly busy. Today, we'd call him a workaholic. He only slept four or five hours a night."

"Just like Bill Clinton," said Matt.

"Something like that, I guess."

Matt continued on his Holloway rift. "My favorite was *Post Rock Country*. That book made me feel good about growing up in the Midwest. I was born in a little town about an hour outside Chicago and I spent my whole childhood deeply embarrassed of that fact until I read that novel."

"But it took place in Kansas," she said.

"Rural Illinois, rural Kansas—big diff."

Flynn laughed. "Now you're talking like a 'coastal.' That's what David used to call the people who lived on either coast."

"The ones who call this 'flyover country.' "

"Exactly. For the record, even David hated living in Iowa those years he taught at the Writer's Workshop. The winters were too cold and the summers too hot and steamy."

"I'm with him on that one," said Matt. "I have to admit Chicago weather is a challenge at times. My mom moved me and my brother to Dallas after my folks got divorced. I only moved back to Chicago three years ago."

"The weather requires more stamina than I've got. I was glad to leave the Midwest. As soon as I finished college, I headed for the Left Coast."

"Yeah, Dan told me you were an English professor there."

My God, but Dad is a blabber mouth, she thought. "Not a professor, just an instructor. I never got on the tenure track. I didn't like the departmental politics. I just wanted to pick up a paycheck and have enough free time to raise my son."

She took one last sip of coffee, then decided to add, "For what it's worth, Matt, *Post Rock* was David's favorite, I think. He never thought *Benchmark* was his best work, even though that's the one he'll be remembered for."

"Really?" He grinned with pleasure.

"*Post Rock* was my favorite, too."

Flynn spent half the night reading the trial transcript of *The People of Illinois vs. Alec Ingersoll,* which Matt Holtser had given her. The various testimonies were both confusing and fascinating. No wonder Matt wanted to write a book about his ancestor's involvement in the case.

Before surrendering to sleep she took one last look at the photograph. She focused with renewed interest on the ghostly faces of the two young men and the odd expression of the young woman; they now not only had names, but had grown the hints of personality and context.

She fell asleep wondering why the woman looked alive but the two men did not. According to the trial transcript, the images of Medora and Cameron should have appeared as ghosts. Only Alec Ingersoll survived the wreckage of their misbegotten experiment in love.

CHAPTER SIXTEEN

Sunday, April 25, 1875

"Cam and I spent every spare moment of the following year in Medora's company," said Ingersoll.

Victoria Woodhull could tell by the almost dreamy look in the man's eyes that these memories were cherished ones. That look had been noticeably absent when he reminisced about his marriage. How curious that he would treasure his courtship days more deeply than his wedded ones.

She now realized she may have pegged him wrong from the start. She initially believed him to have been the outraged cuckold who would stop at nothing to avenge his damaged pride. A different flavor now formed on her palate, though she could not completely identify it yet.

"I proposed to Medora in New York in December of '73, just before I moved to Chicago. We married two months later and she joined me. I'm afraid she wasn't very happy out here in the West. Missed New York and her arty circle of friends back there."

"Surely that's understandable." Victoria could imagine that to a young woman raised in the comfort of New York society, this young frontier town would be a challenge, despite its pretensions to be the next great city of America. If one did not come here with the enthusiastic resolve to make the best of the adventure, the transition would be rude indeed.

"I made sure we had a house with a splendid studio, but she refused to paint anything except a mural on the nursery wall."

"I saw that yesterday. Mr. Overholtzer took me on a tour of your house. The mural was lovely. He said you painted it also."

"Yes, I still paint occasionally." Ingersoll grinned sheepishly. "Cam wrote her with the suggestion she should take up photography. He corresponded with a distant cousin of his in England. They had an aunt who practices photography and has achieved an enviable success at it. Her name is Julia Cameron. Don't know if you've ever heard of her. Cam's mother was a Cameron, you see. That's how he got the name."

"I was willing to try anything, so I went into considerable debt buying her the camera and all the other paraphernalia, even lessons with a local photographer. She became his unpaid assistant for a time. She threw herself into her newest obsession with a vengeance.

"She worked night and day learning the craft. I admit it was quite diverting. I wished that I had had the free time to learn as well, but my duties at the firm kept me continually engaged.

"If I could have been home more, perhaps then . . ." Ingersoll's voice trailed off and his gaze drifted out the nearby window. He strode over to study the scene outside. "That is where it will happen."

She rose to look at whatever scene had so distracted him.

He stared at an open yard between the jailhouse and the courthouse directly to its south.

"Where what will happen?"

"That's where they execute the prisoners. Right there in that little yard. I was made to pass by it every day on my way to court. Have you ever been to Venice, Mrs. Woodhull?"

Why was he discussing Venice, of all things?

He continued before she answered. "There is a bridge over one of the canals that they call the Bridge of Sighs. Prisoners who were condemned to death in the Doge's Palace walked over the Bridge of Sighs to their execution."

He turned to her with the edges of a smile crinkling about his dark brown eyes. "I've decided to call that brick lane there my 'Sidewalk of Sighs.' "

She tried to smile at his bitter humor and was forced to prompt him to continue his story about his wife's new hobby.

"I used to tease her, 'That photographer is getting quite a bargain in you, little wife: A free assistant who's a beautiful woman in the bargain. He will be sad indeed when you must leave his service to enter the ranks of motherhood.' "

Victoria quickly pounced on this remark. "Were you ever jealous of this gentleman? Did you have fears he had designs on your wife, or that she bore more than a professional interest in her mentor?"

He threw his head back in the merriest of laughs at her question. This was the first time she had seen him express unbridled good humor. He continued to smile and shake his head until he was capable of speech again. She did not take offense at his amusement. She had feared her bold inquiry might produce an outraged response and was relieved, nay, gratified to have given the poor man some unplanned cheer.

"My dear Mrs. Woodhull, you must indulge me my reaction to your, no doubt, earnest question. Please don't think me conceited if I tell you that I did not feel in any way threatened. If this gentleman were a secret Casanova, he would fool the entire world into thinking otherwise."

This welcome moment of levity faded quickly as Alec Ingersoll returned to the meat of his discourse.

"I knew Dora was not happy in Chicago, but at least during that period, she stayed busy. When we lost the baby, though, she was dismal all over again. Until Cam came out West to stay with us."

CHAPTER SEVENTEEN

Testimony of Garnet Langley

Examined by Mr. Oberholtzer for the defense.

Miss Langley: My name is Garnet Elizabeth Langley. I'm twenty-four years old and I reside in Brooklyn, New York.

Mr. Oberholtzer: Miss Langley, please state your connection to this case.

Langley: Cameron Langley was my brother.

Oberholtzer: Where were you on March the second of this year?

Langley: At home in Brooklyn.

Oberholtzer: So you were not a witness to the tragic events of that day?

Langley: No, sir.

Oberholtzer: You were acquainted with the defendant, Mr. Ingersoll, and his wife?

Langley: Yes, sir. I feel that I was a good friend to Mr. Ingersoll. He was a frequent visitor to the home of me and my sisters.

Oberholtzer: When did you meet Mr. Ingersoll?

Langley: About 1864, I suppose. Cameron brought him home when they were on Christmas leave from the Army. He stayed with us for about a week. My brother went with him to Europe after the war and when they returned, they took up lodgings in Manhattan together. They frequently dined with us on Sundays after church.

Oberholtzer: When did you meet Miss Medora Lamb?

125

Langley: Well, it must have been about 1873. In the spring of that year. My brother took me to a museum event, the opening of the Cypriot Antiquities exhibit at the Metropolitan. The reception was quite a grand affair since they had moved the museum temporarily to the Douglas Mansion on 14th Street. Oh, I suppose that's not important.

The boys—that's what we always called Cameron and Alec—the boys wanted us to meet Miss Lamb, and she was going to attend this affair also. They were both quite taken with her and had talked of no one else since the night they met her.

My two sisters declined the invitation because they did not really . . . approve of Miss Lamb. Though her grandparents were well-known members of New York society and had raised Miss Lamb from a small child, Miss Lamb's mother was thought to be a somewhat eccentric—no, I mean, an unconventional—person.

Oberholtzer: In what way, Miss Langley?

Langley: According to what Alec and Cameron said, Miss Lamb was born at the Oneida Community.

[talking in the courtroom. Judge calls for order.]

Oberholtzer: And the Oneida Communists was well known for its unconventional views on marriage—or the lack of it. Would that be fair to say?

Lynch: Objection. Leading the witness.

Oberholtzer: I'll rephrase. Tell the court what you and your sisters had heard about the Oneida Community.

Langley: I am no expert on the subject, but Alec told me that the Community practiced what they called "Complex Marriage" in which many individuals considered themselves married to many others. Apparently Miss Lamb did not know the identity of her father because her mother was not sure of this either.

[More talking in the courtroom. Judge calls for order.]

The Court: I am sorry for these outbursts. Pray continue Miss Langley.

Langley: What upset my sisters was not the facts surrounding Miss Lamb's birth—for certainly no child is responsible for the actions of its parents—but Miss Lamb's attitude toward the situation. Instead of being, well, ashamed or at least reticent about the circumstances of her birth, she was actually quite forthright. One might even say proud of the state of affairs. This shocked my sisters and led them to believe she was a young woman of rather questionable morals.

I did not wish to judge her without meeting her, so I, alone, accepted my brother's invitation.

Oberholtzer: What was your first impression of Miss Lamb?

Langley: Well, I confess I did not form a favorable opinion of her. She was quite cool to me when I first introduced my-self—my brother was still arranging to stow our coats at the entrance to the place. But her demeanor changed decidedly once she learned I was Cameron's sister. Then she could not do enough for me.

Such a drastic change of attitude gave me the impression she was somewhat self-centered, that she was a person who pursued only her own interests and had little use for the feelings of others unless they directly impinged upon her own advantage in some way.

Oberholtzer: Did you continue your social intercourse with this lady?

Langley: No. As I said, I did not care for her. I met her on only one other occasion.

Oberholtzer: Yes, that other occasion. Please describe that in detail for the jury.

Langley: Well, it is difficult for me to talk about. In fact, I have never revealed the events of that terrible evening in February of the year previous to the present one, to anybody, including my sisters.

My brother came to our home on a Tuesday night in a terrible state. He had been contacted by Miss Lamb's maid or private nurse or something who had told him Miss Lamb was critically ill and near death and that she had urgently requested to see him.

My brother did not want to attend Miss Lamb without . . . uhm . . . another person, a woman, that is, being present. A chaperone, I guess you might say, and so he beseeched me to accompany him to her bedside.

Oberholtzer: Was this before her marriage to the defendant?

Langley: Mr. Ingersoll was already living in Chicago at this time. He had moved about two months earlier, but they were not married and I had not been told of any engagement.

Oberholtzer: What was the nature of Miss Lamb's illness?

Langley: She would not say at first and insisted on speaking with my brother privately, but he refused to see her alone. He would not compromise either her reputation or his own. This may surprise a good many, judging from the awful things they have been saying about him in the press, but my brother practiced the highest moral standards—

Lynch: Objection, Your Honor.

The Court: Sustained. Miss Langley, you must try to answer Mr. Oberholtzer's question with precision and economy.

Langley: Miss Lamb told us she had attempted to take her own life.

Oberholtzer: Suicide? Did she tell you the manner of her attempt?

Langley: Poison.

[Loud commotion in the courtroom. Judge demands order.]

Oberholtzer: You are telling the court that Mrs. Ingersoll attempted to take her own life by the same means that ultimately ended her life on March the second?

Langley: Well, that is what she told us. She said she had taken a poison of some sort, but it made her quite ill and her grandmother summoned the family physician who gave her some sort of purgative that rid her stomach of the substance.

Oberholtzer: What happened next?

Langley: My brother was shocked to hear this and asked her why she would do such a thing. Again, she would not answer and begged to speak with him in private, but he again refused. He asked her if this action was prompted by Mr. Ingersoll having moved away. She did not answer this but instead she confessed to us that she was with child.

Oberholtzer: With child by Mr. Ingersoll or your brother?

Langley: Mr. Ingersoll, of course! There was no question raised of that issue, I can assure you, sir.

Miss Lamb had worked herself into quite a state by that point. She was sobbing and saying her life was destroyed and that she had no future.

My brother sought to comfort her and assured her that Mr. Ingersoll would be most anxious to marry her if he knew of the situation, which at that point, he apparently did not. He offered to contact Mr. Ingersoll on her behalf.

Oberholtzer: It sounds as though your brother labored to be a good friend to them both.

Lynch: Objection.

The Court: Mr. Oberholtzer, save it for your summation.

Oberholtzer: Sorry, your Honor. What happened next?

Langley: She rambled incoherently on this subject, saying she had spoiled things between them and that he had told her he never wanted to see or hear from her again.

Oberholtzer: A lover's quarrel?

Langley: I got the impression it was a great deal more serious than that. My brother tried to convince her that Mr. Ingersoll would recant his harsh words if only she would do likewise.

She said she had sent Mr. Ingersoll a letter the week before—I presume to inform him of the baby—but the letter had been returned to her unopened that very morning.

My brother was shocked by this as well and suggested that she had sent the letter to the wrong address, but she said that she recognized Mr. Ingersoll's handwriting on the front of the envelope that said, "Return to Sender!"—with an exclamation point.

And then . . . and then she begged *him*—my brother, that is—to marry her instead. I'm sorry, Alec! I'm sorry that you must hear this. Cameron never wanted you to know that. Please forgive me—

The Court: Miss Langley, do not address your comments to anyone other than the jury. Do not require me to hold you in contempt of court.

Langley: I'm sorry. [Witness begins to weep.]

Oberholtzer: What was your brother's response to her proposal?

Langley: He assured her she was not thinking clearly due to the state of her health and that all would look different in the morning.

We left her in the care of her maid and we returned home. He told me on the way home that he was confident all this would be resolved happily. He said he believed that Miss Lamb and Mr. Ingersoll were meant for each other and that their only problem lay in being too much alike. He said the mere fact of that caused conflict.

He told me he planned to contact Mr. Ingersoll immediately.

Oberholtzer: And did he?

Langley: Yes. They were married the week following the night we attended Miss Lamb in her bedchamber. She soon followed her new husband to Chicago, as one would expect.

CHAPTER EIGHTEEN

C.C.L. Notebook
December 6, 1873
Ingersoll entered the room at just after two in the morning, lit a lamp, and sat down at the table to face the sleeping Langley, who struggled to sit while shielding his eyes from the sudden brightness.

"What's happened?"

"Everything," said a jubilant Ingersoll.

"What time is it?" Langley rubbed his eyes and yawned.

"She loves me."

"She told you this?"

"Not in words. Better. She *showed* me how much she loved me."

"What are you talking about? Are you drunk?"

"Only on love."

"Stop talking in riddles. It's much too late . . . or early. I'm not sure which."

"Come to think of it, I need a drink. So do you. Get up, get dressed. Let's go out and tie one on to celebrate."

"Celebrate what?"

"My good fortune! The woman of my dreams loves me, Cam! I'm the luckiest man on earth."

Langley turned skeptical. "Why are you so certain she loves you if she didn't *say* it?"

"Are you not paying attention? I just told you she showed her love. She gave herself to me *body* and soul. No woman like her would do that if she were not in love."

Langley wanted to believe this, but as they were discussing Medora Lamb, he was not inclined to talk in generalities. "What are you saying?"

"What do you think I am saying?" Ingersoll grinned.

"Stop playing coy. Are you asking me to believe that you and she . . . that the two of you were . . . intimate?"

His friend grinned broader and eagerly nodded.

"Actual sexual intercourse occurred?"

"Well, yes, if you insist on getting clinical about it."

Langley was speechless. He stared in disapproval at Ingersoll who had now stopped grinning.

"How on earth did this happen?"

"I can't tell you the details. Not and remain a gentleman."

"You damn well better. You woke me up at this ungodly hour."

Ingersoll's reluctance was entirely a sham. He was dying to share the events of his evening with the one person on earth he felt close to besides Medora. He recounted how they had dined together at Delmonico's, drank considerable quantities of wine, and then walked back to her studio.

"We sat together on the little sofa. The one with all the paint stains on it. I started kissing her and, well, before I knew it. You can imagine the rest."

"Then what?"

"You know."

"I mean *after.*"

Ingersoll shrugged indifferently. "It was kind of awkward. Neither of us seemed to know what to say, so she suggested I go on home. She planned to stay there the night."

"You left her alone?"

"She often sleeps there. She says it's safe."

They sat in silence, each reviewing the shared information,

forming and reforming opinions.

"When will you marry?" said Langley. Since the young lady in question had no father or brother to defend her honor, he decided to place himself in that role.

"Uh . . . well . . . sometime, I'm sure."

"You didn't ask her?"

"No."

"Shame on you, then." Langley pulled on his robe.

"Well . . . well . . . of course we'll be getting married. I mean, that's not open to question."

"When do you plan to get around to asking her?" Langley got up and poured a glass of whiskey from the bottle they kept under the cupboard, a sign he was particularly upset.

"Today. There, are you satisfied?"

"Yes."

When Langley returned from work that evening he found his roommate throwing clothes in his steamer trunk, which still bore the stickers of their European adventure.

His heart soared. Ingersoll and Medora had decided to elope. He hoped he would be invited to attend the wedding, but perhaps that would be impossible now.

"Well, what's all this?" he asked with a broad smile.

"I'm taking that job in Chicago." Ingersoll did not bother to look up, just kept crazily stuffing socks and underwear into the top pocket of the trunk

"But what about Medora?"

"She can go to the devil, as far as I'm concerned."

"What . . . what in the name of—?"

With an angry sigh, Ingersoll sat down on the bed so hard the springs complained. "She turned me down."

Langley gasped, unable to comprehend this.

"It's true." He tried to smile, to defuse the situation, but he was in too much obvious pain to successfully hide how miserable he was. "She told me I was taking it all too seriously. She accused me of being old-fashioned. I swear she stopped just short of laughing at me outright. I guess I know what a complete fool feels like now."

Langley saw the tears Ingersoll blinked back and his own heart ached for his friend's disappointment. In all the years he had known Ingersoll, he had never seen him cry.

Now he regretted insisting upon the foolish marriage proposal. He felt an impotent fury at Medora Lamb's casual rejection of a man who loved her so passionately and completely. He had a sudden, overwhelming desire to throttle Medora's skinny white neck. At the very least, he wished he could shake her until her teeth rattled.

"I . . . I'm sorry." Langley sat down next to his friend and put a comforting arm around his shoulder.

Ingersoll shrugged off the arm and resumed his packing.

"Alec, I really never imagined—"

"You don't have to apologize. This isn't your fault."

Langley had the sensation of falling, that his whole life and those of his friends were falling through the floor and nothing would ever be the same again. This couldn't be happening. This shouldn't be happening.

"Don't you think you're being a little bit hasty, Alec? Sleep on it at least. Maybe if you talked to her in a day or two . . ."

"I do not wish to speak to that lady ever again." He resumed his packing, haphazardly tossing shirts into the trunk. They would arrive in Chicago a wrinkled disaster. "I wired the firm at noon and got an almost immediate response. They even wired me the money for train fare. I leave on the 1:17 A.M. out of Grand Central. At least somebody wants me."

"I can't imagine that you're leaving." Langley could not picture living alone in this apartment. In this city. This was all so abrupt. He loosened his necktie to try and supply some additional air to his constricted lungs.

Ingersoll stopped and sighed.

"Let's go out to dinner one last time, old friend," he said.

"Sure, but won't you even say goodbye to the Gems? They'll miss you, too, you know."

"That's a great idea. We'll hobo dinner off your sisters. Let's go." He seemed to have briefly recovered his spirits, but then he stopped. "Wait a minute. We can't dine at the Gems on my last night in New York. They won't let us drink. And I plan to toast my own future, if I have to."

"We'll stop off at the Anchor on the way to the station," said Langley. "I'll see to it you arrive in your new town with a raging hangover."

"I knew I could count on you." Ingersoll managed a smile.

A choking gloom descended upon Langley the moment his friend's train grumbled to life and began its journey down the frozen track. On the bitter cold walk home from the station—taking Ingersoll out for a night of drinking at the Anchor had left him without hack fare—his mood drifted between despair at his friend's departure and self-directed anger at having occasioned the catastrophe.

The pall never retreated. He avoided Medora for as long as he could, so angry he was at her for the hurt she had caused his friend. She kept contacting him, though, and his aching loneliness wore down his resistance.

The decision to finally see Medora had created a host of confused feelings. The first dilemma being would Ingersoll consider him disloyal for even remaining friends with her since she had broken his best friend's heart so profoundly that he had deserted the vicinity in ill-considered haste?

A short note from his friend put his mind to rest on that

score. Ingersoll adopted a cavalier indifference to the matter in a flavor particular to spurned lovers. He heartily invited Langley to see Miss Lamb in his absence and even wished him well, though his tone seemed sardonic if not downright cynical.

"Have what pleasure you may at her convenience," wrote Ingersoll, "but do guard your heart. Our formerly beloved Miss Lamb is not to be trusted with items that fragile."

With a mixed conscience on the matter, Langley reluctantly renewed his acquaintance. Indeed, he was so lonely in his flat mate's absence he was nearly reduced to visiting his sisters more often than on Sundays. At least they were passable cooks if not challenging conversationalists.

Medora began inviting him to dine with her at least twice a week, but that initially proved problematic as well. Nearly every spare dollar he earned at the newspaper went straight to Brooklyn to support the Gems. When he awkwardly confessed his lack of funds to dine in the type of restaurants she favored, she insisted on covering the expense.

"Don't pull that long face with me," she said on the first such occasion.

"But, Medora," he pleaded, thoroughly miserable, "You must have some sense of just how inappropriate it is for a lady to pay for a *gentlemen*'s dinner."

"*I'm* not paying," she said with that mischievous smirk she adopted so frequently when suggesting something outrageous. "We, both of us, are the beneficiaries of my grandparents' largesse. Simply consider yourself a part of the Lamb family, my dear Cameron."

She was so modern, it frightened him sometimes. This very aspect of her personality had enflamed and entranced Ingersoll. Now that his friend had left the region, Langley found he had no buffer and must weather her whims full force. He lapsed frequently wordless in her presence, never knowing whether to laugh at her wild remarks or seriously consider them.

But in less than two months, his pleasant dinners and theater forays with Medora ceased with the horrible news that turned out to be a suicide attempt. Or so she said.

Although he and his sister Garnet had been thoroughly convinced of its authenticity at her bedside, the more he thought about it during that long sleepless night that followed, the more he began to suspect that she may have staged the attempt for his benefit.

Certain circumstances did not make sense. Where were her grandparents that night? They did not appear to be at home. Would they leave their young granddaughter on death's door to attend a play or dine at a restaurant? Certainly not.

Had she actually taken some potion or pill to rid herself of the pregnancy? Such remedies to this common inconvenience were advertised in his newspaper routinely, though due to the crusade of the odious Anthony Comstock over the last two years, they were forced to invent increasingly imaginative euphemisms for their abortive concoctions.

The men in the advertising department often laughed as they read them out loud. "Restores monthly regularity," was the current most popular claim, though all manner of covert references were used. Langley had to explain what this meant to a couple of his younger co-workers at the paper. He possessed a better acquaintance with the female reproductive system than most single men his age. He did not grow up in a household with three sisters without picking up a few tidbits of overheard conversation. He had even set Ingersoll straight on some of these matters and Ingersoll was the worldliest young man of his acquaintance.

But any mention of means to limit a woman's fertility was strictly banned as obscene by Mr. Comstock. Had not that fiendish persecutor of their dear Medora repeatedly jailed those two outrageous sisters who ran *Woodhull and Claflin's Weekly* for publishing a single article about the Reverend Henry Beecher's alleged dalliance with one of his female parishioners?

Though Langley detested the man for attacking women, he had to agree that promoting in a public newspaper the dangerous and immoral use of such contraceptive products and practices was improper. But jailing people for it? That seemed overreaching.

Had Medora resorted to such extremes? To be a young, unmarried woman expecting a baby was certainly a dire fate, especially since Alec was not on hand to remedy the situation in an honorable manner and the pair of lovers was no longer even speaking to each other.

Had an attempt to prematurely end this "blessed" event been unsuccessful and her sudden proposal to him of marriage been a desperate attempt to save herself from disgrace? Yes, that might be one explanation—one that comforted him more than imagining her so melancholy as to contemplate ending her own life.

At dawn he walked the cold city streets. He marched into the Western Union office and sent the longest, most expensive telegram of his life. Finding the right words was vexing. Telegrams afforded no privacy. He could not simply blurt out the situation to Ingersoll, of course. Decorum forbade discussing a pregnancy in print. His own paper used the phrase "in a family way" when a news story demanded the reference. That was the safest choice.

He was blunt in his insistence that Ingersoll come home immediately and attend to the matter. He sent it off and received a reply at his office two hours later: Ingersoll would be on the next train to New York.

Langley smiled to himself. He had saved the two people he loved most dearly in the world from being victims of their own foolish pride. He was their savior, though they did not know it yet.

And he had saved himself from a marriage he could ill afford, as he had resolved to accept Medora's proposal if she and his friend did not mend their differences and Medora found herself still in need of a husband. He would do it without question, of course, but the prospect of supporting *four* women (plus Ingersoll's bastard!) was daunting beyond measure.

A week had not expired before Alec Ingersoll and Medora Lamb were joined in matrimony in a nondescript ceremony at city hall. Langley stood with his friend as best man and the three dined in grand style to celebrate the occasion. He left them in his little, one-room apartment to embark upon the first night of their wedded life. He headed south to catch the Brooklyn Ferry and spend the night with the Gems.

Alec was on a train the following morning, returning to Chicago to prepare lodgings for his bride. Langley put Medora on a similar train two weeks later and then he was truly alone.

He had never led a solitary life nor wanted to. The walls of his apartment pressed in on him. Any food he ate, when he remembered to eat, might as well have been dust for all the flavor it afforded him.

And then there were his money woes. He was already three weeks behind on the rent. The Gems pressured him to give up his flat in the city and return home to Brooklyn, but he resisted. Living in that house again would be worse than being alone. As a last effort to maintain his independence, he placed an advertisement for a new roommate.

That is how the devil in human form entered his life: Jackson Hurley.

CHAPTER NINETEEN

Testimony of Marta Teller, examined by Mr. Lynch for the State.

Miss Teller: My name is Marta Louise Teller. I'm thirty-eight years old and I was the housekeeper at the Ingersoll residence.

Mr. Lynch: How long were you employed there?

Teller: I was hired right after they was married. Mr. Ingersoll employed me to get the new house ready for Mrs. Ingersoll's arrival from New York. That was . . . February of last year.

Lynch: What were your regular duties?

Teller: Well, the usual sorts of things—running the house, marketing, some cooking. They employed a cook on and off and they dined out often, but otherwise it fell on me. A laundress came in twice a week. A maid of all work, five days a week— Gracie Harrigan. Not a very large staff for such a house, but the Ingersolls never entertained, never had company at all, so it was manageable with so few.

Lynch: Did you live in the house?

Teller: No, I never lived in, which is how I preferred it. I support and care for my elderly parents, you see. They need me to live at home.

I worked at the Ingersoll house from six in the morning until six or seven at night, Sunday mornings off and all of every Tuesday.

Lynch: What was the mood of the household when you first came to work there?

Teller: Mood?

Lynch: What was the temper of your master and mistress?

Teller: They was nice enough. No better nor worse than others I've worked for. Mr. Ingersoll wasn't home much. The Missus was busy with her work, her photography, that is. She was homesick for New York. I got plenty tired of listening to all her moaning and mean-mouthing. You would have thought New York was heaven on earth, to hear her tell it.

Lynch: And after they lost the baby?

Teller: The whole house was mournful, of course. We was looking forward to the little one. Tragic loss. Miss Lamb, I mean Mrs. Ingersoll was bad off, very bad off. But then everything changed.

Lynch: How so?

Teller: Mr. Ingersoll went to New York quite suddenly with no explanation to anyone. Mrs. Ingersoll told me he got a telegram from the sisters of Mr. Langley that said Mr. Langley was either ill or in some kind of trouble—never knew the straight of that, but he dashed off on the next train east, barely taking the time to pack a change of clothes.

He came back a week later with Mr. Langley in tow and sporting a black eye, which he never explained to anyone, at least not to the staff. We prepared the third bedroom for Mr. Langley as quick as we could and he lived there from then on. That would have been end of last summer, beginning of fall.

Lynch: What effect did this houseguest have on the couple?

Teller: Oh, both was happy to see him. Mrs. Ingersoll forgot her grief entirely, like it had never happened. They was all happy together, always joking and laughing, singing in the parlor, playing cards and chess, posing for her photographs.

It seemed like all they needed in the world was each other, the three of them. I don't think they had any other friends, but they didn't seem to want them.

Lynch: How much time did Mrs. Ingersoll and Mr. Langley

spend together outside the company of her husband?

Teller: All the time. Well, Mr. Ingersoll was working, wasn't he? Somebody had to pay the bills.

[Laughter in the courtroom.]

Lynch: So you are telling us that these two individuals had virtually unlimited, unchaperoned time in each other's company?

Teller: Yes, but Mr. Langley—he was treated more like a family member than a guest. It didn't seem so . . . irregular, I guess. In fact, I wondered at times if he was some relation. Like a brother or a cousin. That's how he acted.

Lynch: Did you, at any time, have actual knowledge that Mrs. Ingersoll and her houseguest had become intimate?

Teller: I would say they was always on intimate terms. Like I said, they treated him as casual as family.

Lynch: Mrs. Teller, by "intimate" I mean, criminal conversation. Adultery, if I may speak plainly.

[Witness is silent.]

The Court: Answer the question, Madam.

Teller: I never saw them abed together, if that's what you mean.

Lynch: Domestic servants such as yourself must overhear conversations . . . ?

Teller: Well, once I heard Mrs. Ingersoll up in the studio. I was cleaning the bedrooms just below the tower and her and him—Mr. Langley, that is—was up there and they was having quite an argument. December last, I think.

Lynch: Can you remember what they said?

Teller: Yes, sir. I was quite shocked by what I overheard. I wasn't eavesdropping, you understand. I was just doing my job and I can't help it if they was talking in loud voices for all the world to hear. And it was so rare to hear Mr. Langley raise his voice. He was a soft-spoken sort. Very refined.

142

Lynch: Tell us what you remember of this conversation.

Teller: She was telling him she loved him. This seemed to make him angry, not happy. He told her that now that Mr. Ingersoll was upset and angry with them that none of them could ever be happy again.

Then she said that they should run away together. She said she had money. Plenty enough for them to get back to New York and find a place to live.

Then he says, "But I thought your grandmother cut you off," and she says, "I've got my own money. I've earned it and there's plenty more where that came from."

Lynch: Did she ever say the source of these mysterious funds?

Teller: No, sir. She refused to say. Mr. Langley asked her and asked her and she wouldn't tell him. But it was true. She did have a big store of cash in the bottom of her clothes press.

Lynch: You saw this money?

Teller: Yes, sir. She set me to looking for a brooch she misplaced and that's when I noticed. I didn't mention it to anyone. I didn't want the staff to get ideas. Not that I'm saying they would do something—

Lynch: We understand, Mrs. Teller. You were protecting your Mistress's best interests.

Teller: Her private affairs wasn't no business of mine.

Lynch: On the day that Mrs. Ingersoll and Mr. Langley argued, do you know Mr. Langley's response to her invitation to run away from her husband together?

Teller: He turned her down flat. Said he could never be happy if it meant making Mr. Ingersoll unhappy. He said he would rather die.

Lynch: Did they say anything else?

Teller: Yes, she changed her tune entirely. She stopped pleading with him and sounded suddenly happy. She told him she had the answer to all their problems. He sounded pretty surprised to hear this and all she would say was that the time had come for them—and it seemed she included Mr. Ingersoll in this—that it was time they entered "the next stage."

Lynch: Those were her exact words?

Teller: As I live and breathe. But don't ask me to explain what she meant by that. I don't know. Couldn't even imagine. Frankly, didn't want to imagine what they might be getting up to. Listening to them that day . . . it gave me an awfully odd feeling.

I only work for respectable houses, you understand. I thought I might have to leave and find other employment if things got any more irregular. I didn't really want to. They was so easy to work for and the house was so lovely.

Lynch: Yes, Mrs. Teller, we understand your dilemma. But we must return to that conversation between your mistress and Mr. Langley. How did it end?

Teller: I'm not quite sure. They was coming down the stairs from the tower room and she was saying: "We'll talk to him at dinner." And Mr. Langley says: "He won't agree," and she says—all confident and smiling, "Oh, yes, he will. It's a brilliant idea and the only way we will ever all be happy."

And then they saw me coming out of the room where I'd been working and they both stopped dead in their tracks. They looked at each other kind of guilty-like. Thinking I might have overheard them, then they left the house.

Lynch: No further questions.

CHAPTER TWENTY

Flynn shuffled out to the kitchen and found her father already pouring his second cup of coffee

"Late night, honey?"

"If you mean with your little attorney friend, no, not really. But I am willing to admit that we had a really nice dinner. Lots of fun, very interesting." She pulled the milk from the refrigerator and fixed a bowl of cereal.

"Matt gave me a copy of the trial transcript of the murders of the people in the photo. I stayed up late reading it," she continued. "It was fascinating. Those people seem so real to me. Now they have lives, they have a history."

She joined him in the sunny breakfast nook overlooking downtown Weston. She enjoyed being able to walk to work, one of the little pleasures of her father's new venture that she would miss when she resumed life in the real world.

"There's more info to come, too. Matt contacted a woman who owns the house where the murders took place and she has some sort of journal that was written about the three people."

Brody walked in, grabbed a couple of toaster pastries.

"Morning, Brode," Flynn said.

He muttered some vague acknowledgment as he headed for the door.

"Taking the bus or walking?"

"Walking."

"Did you brush your teeth?"

He stopped before he reached the door. He groaned but returned to the bathroom.

"Such a little ray of sunshine," said Dan.

Flynn reached over and grabbed a section of the Kansas City paper that her dad had placed in his "already read" pile.

Brody returned in a couple of minutes and left the house without another word.

Dan leaned forward and said in a hushed voice. "You can see the top of his boxer shorts."

Flynn looked up. "It's the style."

"You don't care that everyone can see his underwear?"

"Dad, *you're* the only one who cares."

Flynn continued to read the paper and suppressed a smile that kept threatening to overtake her. Messing with her father in this way was embarrassingly fun.

"It's just that . . . it's just—"

"Dad, if he starts shooting heroin, I *will* intervene. Rest assured. But these fashion crazes? I'm not going to sweat it. Like when he got his ear pierced at twelve."

"My grandson has a pierced ear?" He looked horrified.

Flynn shrugged. "Be glad it was his *ear.*"

Dan shook his head as he stared at his sports section.

"Dad, remember when you told me how you were upset at grandpa for bitching about you growing Beatle bangs in college?"

"Yeah, but I wasn't still living at home and—oh, never mind, I guess it doesn't matter." He looked out the window as if he might find an answer lurking out there.

He sighed. "How's the auction going?"

"Moving up again. At $2,500 this morning. Matt found another bidder. The lady who owns the murder house on Prairie Avenue. Now *she* wants the picture."

"Has he made you an offer on the licensing rights?"

"Not yet. He still hasn't found a place that can scan it to the level he wants. I assume he's still here, that is."

"I wish I knew more about licensing images, said Dan. "I want you to get a fair price. I could make some calls, if you like."

"Sure. Thanks. Nice to have a lawyer in the family. Even a retired one."

"Not dead yet."

Flynn opened the shop promptly at ten. Her dad had stopped off at the post office to ship some books he had sold on his Internet site. She picked up the feather duster and made the rounds.

She practically swore out loud to find the stupid spider was back in business in the exact same location as before—the opening to the back room of children's books. Hadn't its brush with death taught it anything?

She once again swished the web away with the duster, but the spider managed to escape to weave again another day. She shook her head, defeated by something that weighed a milligram.

She had resumed her seat behind the counter and had just booted up the computer at the cash wrap when Matt Holtser walked in with a jangling of the bell on the door.

"Well, good morning," she said. "Planning to spend another day in our fair city?"

"Yes, I am. I found a print shop in Overland Park that can make the scan for me. Is that very far away?"

"Forty-five minutes, maybe. I'd like to come with you. I'll drive you, if you want."

"Only if you let me buy you lunch. You and your dad have been so terrific to deal with. I guess we still need to talk about financial arrangements. I said from the start that I'll be happy to compensate you for this."

"Sure, yes, about the amount . . ."

"Yeah, we never got around to discussing it last night. We got sidetracked by my David Holloway fixation."

"Well, I'm not sure what to . . ." Her voice drained away. Talking about money always made her uncomfortable. Yet another reason she was unsuited to the retail profession. Salesmen were born, not made.

"I guess I was planning to offer something in the neighborhood of $500? Would that be fair?"

Flynn's slim, dark eyebrows shot up. "That's a very nice neighborhood."

"You're happy with that price?"

"Absolutely," said Flynn. "For five hundred dollars, I'd throw in a signed, first edition of a David Holloway novel."

"No shit?" His face lit up like a kid on Christmas morning. "I couldn't . . ."

"Yeah, you could. I'm afraid I don't have a copy of *Post Rock Country* in stock right now. We have a couple of other titles though."

She leaned down to reach the books she had cataloged into the inventory the other day but had not gotten around to shelving yet.

"What about *Mountain Daylight Time?*" he said. "I think that's the only one I haven't read. It came out the year I was doing a semester abroad. I just never got back to it."

Flynn grimaced at his choice, but grabbed the copy of the requested title. "Sure, that's fine."

"This is awesome," he murmured, handling the book with the reverence of a true Holloway-ite. "Oh, and I have still more information about our photo people and their twisted little lives."

She perked up at this.

"The lady who owns the house—her name is Ellen—she's offered to copy the C.C.L. Notebook and fax it to me at the Sunshine House. We might have it sometime today."

"That's really nice of her."

"I told her I'd give her a mention in the acknowledgments of my book. And you'll be in there, too, of course."

"Well, great. Full speed ahead. Are you . . . staying past today?" She tried not to sound too nosy, still worried about boundaries, but was so hooked on the Ingersoll story that she did not want to let him slip away until she knew it all.

"I'm on a week's vacation," he said. "I decided that this was the week to get serious about my research. I still have so much to do."

"Old newspapers?" she asked.

"Yeah, the ending of the trial was so murky and inconclusive; I don't really know what to think about it. I've only researched the *Times*. I've still got the *Tribune* to slog through. Their archives are all online, but they make you pay per article. It gets expensive fast."

He leaned on the counter and thumbed his Holloway book, but continued, "I know that Victoria Woodhull was somehow involved in all this. At least, after the fact. That alone adds some celebrity glamour to the case."

"Woodhull? That's the name of the other bidder."

"Yeah, that can't be a coincidence. I wondered if the bidder was a descendant or something."

"Didn't she run for president?" said Flynn, chagrined that she had not been more curious about the bidder's name. It wasn't that common, although there were a couple of cities named "Woodhull."

"Oh, yeah, that and a host of other things," said Matt. "She was way ahead of her time. A real radical. Was a big supporter of Free Love. I'm sure that was the nexus that brought her into the case, but she was also into spiritualism, so maybe this spirit photo of yours is connected in some way."

Dan Keirnan breezed in with another jangle of the door.

"Good morning, Matt. You're up early."

"Hi Dan. I've already run four miles and showered twice, as a matter of fact."

"Well, I'm impressed. You sound very . . . clean."

Matt grinned. "It's that damned bed-and-breakfast thing. I felt like I had to get all cleaned up just to go down to breakfast. Which was tasty, I have to admit. Almost worth making small talk with an elderly couple from Des Moines who collect antique quilts. But then I still wanted to take my morning run and well, you know, the rest is history."

"Matt wants to pay me $500 for the scan of my picture, Dad. I said okay."

Dan nodded. He did not look pleased or displeased.

Flynn knew she should have let him do the research on the licensing issue, but she did not want to string this out too long. "I also gave him the signed, first edition of *Mountain Daylight Time*. I hope you don't mind."

Dan frowned like he *did* mind, but Flynn knew it was not for the reasons Matt would assume. "Yeah, right, whatever. I'll be upstairs."

He made his exit so quickly, Matt looked worried.

"If he doesn't want me to have that book, it's okay, really."

"No, don't worry about it. That's just not his favorite book."

Matt wandered around the store glancing at one shelf, then another. She felt obliged to make conversation.

"Where did you do your semester abroad?"

He poked his head out from the biography section. "Paris."

"Ooo-la-la," she teased.

"I minored in French," He ambled back to the counter looking slightly embarrassed to admit it. "I just took it because it was an easy 'A' for me. My mom's half-French. Grandma was a war bride. She used to baby-sit us when my mom was at work. She had me and my brother fluent before we could read or write."

"*Comme sa va?*"

"*Ca va bien, merci*," he shot back, now smiling. "*Et tu?*"

"Whoa, I'm busted," she said. "I can count to ten and after that—I got nothin'."

"Bet you're a John Stewart fan. Am I right?"

"Are you psychic?" She was amazed at how quickly he picked up on things.

"I just watch too much TV. Since moving back to Chicago, I haven't done much else outside of work."

After the divorce, she surmised. Prurient curiosity made her wonder what the story was on that. She doubted she would find out.

"My son, Brody, was born in France," she said.

"Really? What took *you* to France?"

"I spent several months in Europe backpacking with a couple of my friends."

"You went backpacking in Europe while you were . . . pregnant? Wow, you were adventuresome."

She shrugged in a self-deprecating way. "Or stupid."

"Oh, to be young and stupid again," he said with mock wistfulness, making her laugh. "And Brody's father . . . ?"

"Wasn't along for the ride. Correct. Less said the better."

"Sure, sorry. Uh, where in France was Brody . . . ?"

"Lille. Actually I had planned to come home before he was born, but I didn't know there were restrictions on pregnant women flying back then. They wouldn't take you on a trans-Atlantic flight if you were more than thirty-six weeks pregnant. They stopped me right at the gate. Luckily my friends stayed with me. We tried to get back to England at least, but we didn't try hard enough. Only made it as far as Lille, and unfortunately, none of us spoke French. I could have used a translator. Where were you when I needed you?"

"I would have been proud to help out. Usually I only get to show off my skills in French restaurants. Of course, I'm not sure I'd be worth much as a birthing coach. I'm kind of squeamish."

"We could have blindfolded you."

"Well, there you go. If the situation ever arises again, call me."

They shared a laugh and agreed to meet over the noon hour for the long drive to get the photo scanned. The May weather was so inviting, Matt announced his intention to take his new book to the little park south of the business district. He wanted to read and listen to his iPod until then.

He found a semi-comfortable seat in a gazebo with peeling white paint. The built-in bench was a little dusty and splintery but he was wearing jeans so it didn't matter. He saw several bird nests in the high, peaked roof of the structure. The floor was littered with bird droppings.

He opened *Mountain Daylight Time* to the title page and looked at the signature of his literary idol. He could not help smiling, but also felt a little embarrassed by his obsession. That girl and her father must think he was a dingbat; he always came on too strong. Oh well, did he really care what they thought?

He ran his finger over the scrawl that said "David Holloway," just to try and feel the indentations in the paper made by the pen.

His thoughts returned to the little bookshop. Why had Dan Keirnan grunted over his choice of the book?

He reviewed the dinner conversation of the previous night. At least what he could remember of it. Events had gotten a little hazy after Flynn talked him into switching from beer to wine.

He hoped he hadn't said anything too stupid. He didn't drink much anymore, not since he got into running. He had forgotten how to handle himself while "impaired."

Had he come on to her? Oh, God, he probably had. She was cute and he was a little hammered. A recipe for disaster.

Now he remembered. He—being Mr. Suave (groan)—had invited her to walk him back to that B&B, hint, hint, hint. About as subtle as a boat horn.

She'd turned him down flat, but at least she'd been cool about it. She had that slightly off-kilter sense of humor that he kind of liked and kind of didn't. He couldn't always tell when she was kidding. She'd said something about how she had a policy of not preying upon those who were too inebriated to give a valid consent. He'd called her a true lawyer's daughter. They had both laughed and said goodnight.

He now quickly read the copy on the dust jacket flap. The *Mountain Daylight Time* story focused on a famous scientist and his wife and their relationship with a summer intern who moved in with them.

Hmmm. He now remembered clearly his conversation with Flynn about David Holloway. She had been his research assistant and lived with him and his wife for a summer. That similarity to the book in his hands was intriguing, if not a little unsettling. He had better start reading this book immediately.

He opened it again and thumbed through the front matter. His eyes caught on the dedication page. "For F. K." Gooseflesh blanketed his arms.

Holy crap. Was Flynn Keirnan "F. K."?

Matt stopped by his room at the Sunshine House to drop off his Holloway opus. He still had an hour to kill before returning to the bookstore to meet Flynn for their lunch mission.

The innkeeper, Mrs. Houston, a grandmotherly woman with slightly pink-tinted hair, called to him on his way up the stairs to tell him he had received a very long fax, more than 70 pages in fact. He acknowledged that faxes cost money and yes, she could add an appropriate sum to his bill.

The fax was from Ellen, the owner of the Prairie Avenue mansion—the murder house. As promised, she had sent him a copy of the entire C.C.L. Notebook. He sat on his vintage quilt-covered bed and started reading.

When he saw Flynn's car he was surprised once again.

"Wow," he said, as he admired the little convertible BMW. "I was going to offer my rental car for the trip but, hey, this is . . . this is so-o-o much nicer."

"And you had me pegged as a soccer mom, driving a big van or an SUV, I suppose?"

He continued to walk around the car in unfeigned appreciation. "Well, you did tell me you had a teenage kid. Stereotypes are dropping like flies today."

Flynn beamed with pride. "I came into some money a few years ago and decided I needed a toy. The convertible aspect worked a lot better in southern California's climate. Not so good for Midwestern winters."

"Does your son get to drive this baby?"

"I'm teaching him. He just got his learner's permit, actually. I've told him that if he stays on the honor roll, I'll give this to him when he graduates."

"Wow, you are a really cool mom. When I graduated from high school, I got a car. A rusty, eight-year-old Ford Escort." He made a face to invite pity and she laughed.

They climbed in and headed south.

"I have in my hands something I think you'll like," he said. "The C.C.L. Notebook. The lady with the house—Ellen's her name—she sent it to me this morning."

"That was fast," Flynn said.

"Yeah, I'm going to have to send her some flowers or something."

"You're beholden to women all over the place." She gave him a flirtatious smile.

"I'm not complaining," he said, smiling but looking straight ahead at the road. "Keeping the ladies happy—that can be a full-time job."

"But nice work if you can get it?"

"Absolutely."

He pulled out his phone and began punching buttons. She glanced over to see what he was up to.

"I'm sending Ellen flowers before I forget," he said to answer her curious face.

"That's a great phone," she said, amazed he could do all that without uttering a word.

"It's more than a phone," he said in a tone she knew meant some kind of joke was coming. He lovingly cradled the device against his cheek and whispered, "It's my best friend."

She laughed so hard she nearly swerved the car.

And to think she had feared the drive would be dominated by dead air or awkward, forced conversation.

"Matt, I've got to tell you I am dying to read that notebook. Would you mind driving so I could start on it? I'll tell you where to turn and everything."

"Oh, what a burden, what a hardship," he said with mock agony. "Being forced to drive a BMW sports car? I'll try to soldier through."

She grinned and pulled over to the shoulder of the road.

CHAPTER TWENTY-ONE

C.C.L. Notebook
Spring/Summer 1874
How eagerly we rush to our own ruin, Langley thought. Yet when disaster masquerades as ecstasy, how can we not be misled?

The Devil's hand was clear in his actions. His vile compass pointed the way to Hell, to eternal damnation.

He thought about how he had labored to keep his moral failures a secret from those he loved. Ingersoll had been his redeemer. He had proved to be such a noble and exemplary influence that staying on the decent, honorable course was almost effortless.

But the months after Ingersoll's departure from New York had been one long nightmare of degrading temptation, at least in thought if not in deed. The possibility of disgrace hovered around Langley like a foul miasma.

If only he could have received some forewarning that placing an advertisement for a fellow renter of his dismal basement apartment would actually usher in the architect of his own downfall, how simply he could have avoided it. But fate does not post caution signs and so Jackson Hurley arrived at his office early on the last afternoon of the first week of March.

Langley had placed the ad only the evening before and he was amazed and delighted to have such a prompt response.

The young man looked clean, refined, and sharply groomed

with a well-trimmed mustache and oiled black hair parted down the center with the precision of a draftsman. This attention to appearance befitted his employment as a waiter at Delmonico's, the city's most fashionable restaurant. He had immigrated to New York from England only six months before. Langley found his Cockney accent somewhat difficult to penetrate, but that did not matter.

He appeared to be about the same age as Langley, maybe a bit younger—mid-twenties or so. He lit up a small cigar while they conversed at Langley's desk. Langley wrinkled his nose at the cigar smoke, but did not remark on it. The probability of locating a roommate who did not use tobacco was limited. He would just have to adapt to a future of clothes reeking of stale smoke, already somewhat of a problem due to the large number of his coworkers who smoked at their desks from morning 'til night.

He disliked this circumstance. He had to conduct meetings and interviews all day long with funeral directors and grieving relatives placing obituaries. Often a lady objected to the ever-present cloud of tobacco with either words or actions, but there was little he could do to alleviate their discomfort.

"I dine at Delmonico's occasionally," Langley said.

"Which one, then?" said the waiter.

"The one on 14th." Langley tried to sound casual about this, but he was actually trying to boast a little. The Delmonico family operated four restaurants, but the establishment on 14th was the one most favored by society.

"That's mine," Hurley said with an enthusiasm that felt like a pounce. "Bet you're one of those what takes his midday repast in the Café."

"I've never actually eaten in there. I usually dine with a woman friend so we go to the main dining room." Women were not seated in the Café at Delmonico's, only gentlemen.

"Ah, a ladies' man. I mighta guessed. Next time you come in, you ask for Jackson Hurley and I'll see's ya get the best table there is."

Langley flushed at the prospect of getting a good table at Delmonico's, but then he remembered that he would no longer have that extravagant opportunity. Medora was married and living in Chicago. From that point on he had dined in only the cheapest cafés and dining halls.

"And I'll pay my share of the rent on time or better *and* trouble you not at all." Jackson Hurley's aggressive smile displayed a gold tooth just left of center.

The arrangement did seem perfect. Since the man worked nights, Langley would have his evenings quiet to read or work on his writing. Likewise, he would leave for the newspaper early in the mornings, allowing Hurley to sleep daytimes undisturbed.

He hesitated only a moment, wondering if he should ask for references, but the young man, however unschooled, was of such a genial temperament that he found himself deciding before he knew it.

"Move in any time you like," Langley said, extending his hand.

"You'll not regret the day old Jackie arrived," Hurley said as he vigorously shook hands on the deal. "We'll 'ave some fun, eh?"

"Well, I guess so."

They did have fun. Jackson Hurley was a whirling dervish of activity, not all of it exactly wholesome, but his affable charm made Langley overlook the little shortcomings in his ethics. Like how he frequently pilfered liquor from his employers at the restaurant.

"Nobody's going to miss a little quarter-full bottle of whiskey or that 'alf-empty bottle of wine the couple paid for and never finished. Might as just put it to good use. Right, Old Lang?"

He had taken to addressing Langley as "Auld Lang Syne," which sounded more witty than it was when they were splitting a bottle of well-aged scotch at two o' clock in the morning. Not quite so clever when Langley left his snoring roommate at eight A.M. and trudged toward his office with a splitting headache.

And then spring brought the horse racing to town.

"Let's go make the rent," Hurley would declare every Saturday morning that it did not rain. "Old Jackie and his new best friend are off to bet on the ponies!"

Langley tagged along just for the diversion at first. He had no spare funds available to gamble. Instead, he studied the racing form and made imaginary bets, then kept score on his pretended winnings. They frequented the Union Racecourse in Queens at first, but abruptly switched to Jerome Park in the Bronx.

This change was accompanied by a remarkable uptick in Hurley's betting luck. He had taken to an unusual format for wagering. He would wait for one special race and put all his money on just one horse. His returns were spectacular and the second week in a row this occurred, Langley was in awe.

"I'm letting you pick my horses from now on," Langley said. "You must be uniquely gifted at this sport."

"Yeah, somethin' like that," Hurley said with a smirk and a distant look in his dark eyes.

"But how do you choose? Based on the horse's record or the jockey or the trainer's record?"

"I looks over the names and picks the one that feels the luckiest."

When Langley placed a two-dollar bet on the horse of Hurley's choice and collected over fifty dollars on the investment, he felt almost giddy with delight. *Fifty dollars.*

The following week, when Langley took a flyer and placed all the winnings of the previous Saturday on Hurley's selection, he walked away from the betting window with more than $300 in his pocket. For the first time since moving to Manhattan, he feared getting robbed on the train ride home. At this rate, he might just end up dining again in Hurley's restaurant, like all the other swells.

He pressed his roommate for an explanation of this outlandish success when they arrived home in the late afternoon. Hurley was feverishly changing his clothes in order to get to work on time.

He stopped mid–shirt button and eyed Langley with a cool and calculated half-smile. "I likes you, old darling, and I trust you. But do I trust you enough? That's the question, ain't it?"

"Trust me? I'm not sure I understand."

Hurley chuckled and shook his head. "Innocent as a new hatched chick, you are. Let me think about it. I gotta run now. I'm later than late."

When Hurley returned from work at just past two, Langley woke up immediately. In fact, he had barely slept with the anxious wonder of what secret his roommate was considering sharing with him.

Hurley was bone tired from serving at a large wedding feast and not in the mood to talk at all, but after a replenishing glass of whiskey and a smoke he climbed into bed and decided to satisfy Langley's curiosity.

"I work with a feller whose brother is a jock out at Jerome Park. We alls came from the same corner of the world—we're as good as family, see. So's they let me in on it."

"In on what?"

"The jockeys out there got a little game goin' on. They all agree, one day a week to pick one race and set whose gonna win it. They always pick a longshot to sweeten the take, 'cause they wager, too, on the sly. Now for a certain price they will share that information with those what they trust."

"But isn't that illegal?"

Hurley laughed. "Oh, bleedin' 'ell, do you ever plan to leave the cradle? Of course, it's illegal. Why'd you think I said I needed to trust you?"

"But you gave me those tips for free."

" 'Cause I like you, old dear. Wanted you to have a bit of fun, that's all. You're entirely too gloomy, you know. Is it because your lady friend married that feller in Chicago?"

Langley instantly regretted sharing any details of his life. Hearing it repeated back to him by this disreputable waiter seemed to pollute his precious friendship with Ingersoll and Medora.

"I *can* trust you now, can't I?" Hurley's joshing mood chilled in a way that made Langley nervous.

"Uhm . . . well, of course. I would never say anything. It's none of my affair—"

"Oh, but it is, ain't it? You won a fair amount of cash with my help, now didn't you?"

"But I didn't know—"

"Look, I don't give a damn whether you keep on with this thing or not, but I gotta know that you're not gonna be a snitch. Now, personally, I think you oughta keep on with it. You could use the cash same as anyone. Could help out those sisters in Brooklyn even more, now couldn't you? It's up to you."

"I won't betray you, Jack. I swear it."

"That's my good boy," said Hurley, his broad, gold-toothed grin returning. He reached over and tousled Langley's hair like one does to a child. Then he laughed and put out the lamp.

The British have strange customs, thought a startled Langley.

He resolved not to go back to the track with Hurley the following Saturday. He claimed he had been called in to work. He didn't know if his roommate believed him, since he made a sarcastic remark, "More people dyin' than usual, Old Lang? A war or an epidemic I ain't heard of, maybe?"

The dust settled and their room-sharing continued without incident until the heat wave started in mid-July. Day after day the temperatures climbed into the nineties or more. The humidity kept pace as the city turned into a stinking, muggy caldron.

Hurley said he had never experienced such temperatures in England. He came home one night to their sweltering room and nearly had a fit.

" 'Ot, steamy kitchens is one thing, but *everywhere* like this? 'Ow can you stand it? 'Ow does anyone stand it? At least at work they 'ave ice I can steal when the chef's not lookin'. But this little room, this is worse than an oven! Oh, screamin' fuck, I can't take it anymore!"

He stamped around the room, fanning himself with a newspaper. Langley did not know whether to warn him that August might be worse.

Hurley had already started drinking and if he got any louder, someone might complain to their landlady, especially since their one small window was open.

"Well, bloody 'ell, it's too 'ot to wear clothes!" He promptly began to remove his, all of them. He threw them this way and that, muttering curses with each piece.

"For heaven's sake, Jack, put out the light. People on the street can see in."

"I don't give a good God damn, let 'em look!"

"You can't stand stark naked in front of an open window," Langley hissed. "Have you lost your mind?"

"Probably!" With an angry sigh of defeat to the heat wave, Hurley left the window and headed for bed. Before extinguishing the lamp, he paused and looked down at Langley, surveying him with a disturbing intensity. A faint smirk replaced the unnerving gaze and caused his bedmate even more concern.

Before Langley could inquire, the room vanished into steamy

darkness, lit only by the slender wedge of lamplight slanting through the window from the sidewalk above.

Hurley lay on his side with his head propped up on his elbow. A malicious smile across his face caused the frail light to glisten off his gold tooth.

Langley tried to manage some calming small talk to assure himself the waiter had not lost his mind entirely. "I'm sure the weather will change soon, Jack."

But it already had.

CHAPTER TWENTY-TWO

Cross Examination Mrs. Marta Teller by Mr. Oberholtzer for the defense.

Oberholtzer: Do you recall Mr. Jackson Hurley's visit to the house?

Teller: I certainly do. I knew he was trouble from the start.

Oberholtzer: Just what was it about him that put you on your guard?

Teller: Everything and nothing. I didn't like the way he smiled. And when he left the house, he and Mr. Langley had words out in the side yard. I was in the kitchen with the window cracked open because of the steam from baking the bread. I heard snatches of them talking.

Oberholtzer: Please tell the court what you remember.

Teller: Something about money. He wanted Mr. Langley to give him money or else he would make things happen.

Oberholtzer: What did he threaten to make "happen"?

Teller: Didn't say. Was real coy and grinning. The angrier Mr. Langley got, the more Mr. Hurley seemed to enjoy it. But then he got nasty and started saying things like he had a score to settle with Mr. Ingersoll and it would take a lot to prevent him from doing that.

Oberholtzer: Did it appear to you that Hurley was blackmailing Mr. Langley?

Teller: That word came up. It certainly did. I recall Mr.

Langley saying: "You can't blackmail me now. I have no money, no job, thanks to you!"

And this Hurley says, "Your little friends have money, now don't they?"

CHAPTER TWENTY-THREE

Monday, April 26, 1875

Victoria greeted a new day and still had not received a word from the Colonel. His neglect now worried her. They had never been apart for so long without a single communication. Was he still angry over her decision to stay in Chicago a single week—missing just two other speaking engagements? Was he punishing her for this decision?

If he but knew the interesting material she was gathering for this new story in the *Weekly* he would surely eat his angry words and laugh about his silliness. This story would push the Beecher trial right off the morning breakfast tables of America.

Then a more sinister thought loomed upon her weary mind: Did his silence portend a growing lack of interest in their mutual endeavors, both personal and public? Had his handsome face and vibrant mind captured yet another fair heart?

Or was he visiting his former wife in St. Louis?

Why did she torment herself thus? Was it not she who most famously shouted from the stage of Steinway Hall:

"Yes, I am a Free Lover. I have an inalienable, constitutional, and natural right to love whom I may, to love as long or as short a period as I can; to change that love every day if I please, and with that right neither you nor any law can frame any right to interfere."

Would she seek to deny her husband the same freedoms she claimed and professed to all who would listen? Would she endeavor to claim him as her sole property?

She forced her thoughts to veer away from her personal struggles and contemplate the hellish state of mind Mr. Ingersoll now claimed. His lawyer believed his client longed for the gallows in order to join the two parties he was accused of sending to the other side.

Mr. Oberholtzer had confided that Alec Ingersoll had said, "The State of Illinois, in executing me, will simply accomplish that which I was too cowardly to achieve by my own hand. I should send them a note of gratitude immediately prior to the deed."

She pitied Mr. Oberholtzer. Having a client with no will to live must be frustrating in the extreme. She stood in awe of the gentleman's dedication to his calling to so vigorously defend his client without so much as an ounce of cooperation from the accused man. Nor probably much chance of remuneration. Mr. Ingersoll was spending the last of his personal savings to cover her living expenses in this fine hotel.

Of course, Mr. Oberholtzer's name was much in the Chicago press, giving him a wealth of free publicity for his labors. That alone might offset his lack of monetary compensation in the Ingersoll case.

The lawyer had said he gains hope of his client's acquittal every hour the jury deliberates. The fact that they have now entered their second day must give him ever-increasing optimism. He said he thought this meant at least they are not of one mind in the matter. Some one of them or maybe several have been persuaded by the doubts he tried to raise in the trial.

In organizing her notes and correspondence on the nicely appointed hotel desk, her eyes fell upon the telegram from Mr. Norris, the poor spirit photographer who stood accused of fraud.

As Mr. Oberholtzer was detained this morning on another matter and could not accompany her to the jail to speak with

Mr. Ingersoll until the afternoon, she decided she should call upon poor Mr. Norris and determine the state of his legal complication.

She sent a note via the hotel's messenger service to Mr. Bertrand Norris to request a visit to his studio. She asked him to pick her up in front of the Field & Leiter Store on State Street at eleven o'clock.

One hour later, the gentleman responded by return messenger, saying that he was overjoyed by the prospect and would send a driver at the appointed hour.

This would work out conveniently. She had been longing to do a little shopping from the moment she arrived in the city. Her schedule was usually so tightly organized by the Colonel that she seldom had the luxury of the glorious female indulgence of shopping. She looked forward to it and tapped on her sister's door to invite her along.

"Tennie?" she said in the open hallway, hoping to rouse her if need be. She often slept late whenever their travel schedule permitted.

She glanced about but saw no other guest in the vicinity. She smiled to herself with contentment. The Palmer House was such a splendid venue in which to spend one's time, with its seven stories of exquisite decoration and the finest services to be had outside the city of New York. Who could not love a lodging that boasted every modern convenience including a lightning-quick perpendicular railway? (Some called it an "elevator," but Victoria thought this a strange appellation since the device transported one *down* as well as up.) Every corner of this grand hotel exuded opulence, though the barbershop floor tiled in real silver dollars might have been just a tad extravagant.

After a lengthy and somewhat embarrassing wait in the sumptuous corridor, her nightgown-clad sister poked her nose out of the door.

"Good morning, Vicky, dear."

She was admitted to a chamber somewhat smaller than Victoria's and in much disarray. "Let's go shopping this morning. I'm free until eleven," she said to her sister, who was in similar disarray.

"What happens at eleven? Another visit to the jailbird?"

"No, that's not until after lunch. I'm dropping in to visit the dear man you so cruelly re-named 'Mr. Nostrils.' Why don't you accompany me there as well? It might be fun. He will surely demonstrate the séance techniques he employs to produce his spirit photos."

"I don't know," Tennie said, returning to her bed and lounging upon it. "I remember Mr. Norris from our last visit to the city—was that in the fall of '73, the national convention you presided at? I recall him to be a chatty bore. And a boastful one, in the bargain. Would we have to go about shrouded in those hot veils?"

"Well, yes. I advised Mr. Norris to look for me in my green veil so that he could locate me. It's still important that we keep our visit here a secret. The press thinks we left for Des Moines the day after my lecture."

Tennie groaned in her charming, theatrical way to indicate this was not a burden she intended to bear this day.

"Oh, well, I'll speak with you this evening, then," said Victoria.

"Actually, darling, I have an engagement for supper this evening."

"With whom, may I ask?"

Tennie smiled like she was harboring the most delightful secret. "No one of any importance. Just a charming young man who has promised to take me to tea at four, though we will be served champagne in place of tea."

"So you are abandoning me, forcing me to dine alone

169

tonight?" Victoria pouted at this prospect. Usually, she would not have difficulty seeking out some individual or group eager to rescue her from such solitude, but her current need for anonymity ruled out contacting the local spiritualist or suffrage societies who so often served as her host in a strange city.

"I'm sorry," Tennie said, entirely feigning her contrition. "I'm just so terribly bored."

Victoria rose to depart. "Just promise me you'll be careful."

"Of course. You know I will. Have fun visiting Mr. *Nostrils.*"

Victoria shopped to her heart's content, but her purchases numbered only a few new handkerchiefs. Her dire lack of funds prevented further extravagance.

She loitered about State Street in her heavy green veil and soon detected a public hack with a small, plump man hanging out its window, waving his hat in her direction.

"Mr. Norris," she called with a polite smile and placed her hand in his as he assisted her in entering the small and shabby public carriage. "How nice to see you again."

She had to suppress a giggle when she saw him up close—he did have rather large nostrils.

"I am delighted to see you as well, Mrs.—"

"Shhh." She placed a gloved finger to his lips to silence him before he could say her name in public. She could not be too careful on this matter

"Oh, Mrs. Woodhull," whispered Bertrand Norris with gushing enthusiasm the moment the carriage jerked into motion. "I cannot begin to thank you for your support in my current . . . uhm, difficulty. If you can but give a deposition on my behalf, it might make all the difference."

"Well, I will help if I can. I would like to view your procedure and technique."

She felt he had a good chance of prevailing. Mr. William

Mumler had won a similar case not six years ago in New York City, even though none other than Mr. P. T. Barnum had testified against him. The renowned showman claimed Mumler was producing nothing but humbug and taking advantage of grief-stricken persons whose judgment was clouded by their state of bereavement.

Spiritualists often suffered such tactics undertaken by doubters. Victoria felt sorry for their lack of belief in the spirit world. She knew they would be much happier and at peace if they could but open themselves to the existence of spirits and heed the valuable information they can convey to the living. How she hoped she could soon give Mr. Ingersoll the solace he longed for.

They arrived at "B. H. Norris Photographic Atelier" in just a few minutes. The ground-floor business was situated in an attractive brick building somewhat south of the busy center of the city; far enough south in fact to have escaped the dreadful fire of '71.

The entrance area served as both a waiting room for his customers and a showplace for his photography. She pinned back her veil to examine the premises.

His exhibit included a wide array of *cartes des visite* and traditional cabinet cards. Single portraits and family groups, as one would expect, were in strong evidence. There were also the usual architectural shots of homes, even portraits of race horses posing with their jockeys after a win. One portrait of a little dog was quite cunning and caused her to smile.

An entire wall, however, was devoted to his spirit photographs. These simply took Victoria's breath away. She drew close and studied them with care. They were quite different from other examples of the craft that she had viewed in New York and the regional conventions of spiritualists.

These were in a class by themselves. The clarity of both the subjects and the spirits was unmatched. The level of their artistry and expression of the spirit visitor was nothing short of dazzling. Never had the spirit world shown itself with such stunning lucidity. Each spirit's face or form emerged from a cloudy, ethereal fog. No wonder Mr. Norris was reputed to be the foremost new practitioner of spirit photography to reside outside the city of New York.

The good gentleman interrupted her study of his work to lead her up a flight of stairs to the second floor of the building.

They entered into a large, brightly lit studio room where his subjects sat for him.

"How long have you been involved in spirit photography, Mr. Norris? I had not heard your name in this regard until last year."

"Yes, although I have been a member of the American Spiritualists Association for the last five years, it was but a little more than one year ago that the spirits first manifested themselves to me through my camera lens.

"I have practiced the art of photography for nearly ten years. I pride myself on adapting to the latest scientific methods of the profession, but I was as surprised as anyone when the first spirit chose to grace my humble studio. I considered it a great honor."

And a lucrative one, she thought but did not mention for fear of offending him. She had viewed his price list of services. His charge for summoning the Spirit World started at the staggering sum of fifty dollars! And the price did not include the cost of the prints to be ordered; that was just the sitting fee. Mr. Norris must be the wealthiest photographer in the city of Chicago.

A large bank of windows provided impressive lighting from the noonday sun. Long velvet drapes occupied the opposite wall, providing the traditional backdrop to formal studio portraiture.

"As you can see, Mrs. Woodhull, this is a most ordinary

studio. No tricks here." He tittered nervously, but invited her to step behind the drapery to examine the area. He was correct: there was but a simple and unadorned wall there.

"This is the camera I use primarily for my spirit photographs."

The large box camera with its complicated lens apparatus on the front portion was separated from the back half of the wooden box by an expanding leather bellows positioned on a set of tracks.

He motioned for her to cover her head and shoulders with the black velvet "dark cloth," as he called it, so that she might peer through the camera lens. She did so and beheld an upside-down view of Mr. Norris who cavorted and waved for her benefit in a most undignified manner.

"Thank you, sir," she said as she attempted to remove the cloth from her head without dislodging her hat. She only partially succeeded.

He saw that she struggled to right the hat and guided her to a mirror hung on the wall of a back room where he stored the numerous supplies he employed in his trade.

"You will agree, Madam, that my camera and studio are no different than any other practitioner."

"Yes, I see that, Mr. Norris." She paused to survey the vast and ill-smelling collection of chemicals particular to the profession. Countless bottles and jars sat on open selves near his work area bearing threatening names like sulphuric acid, bichromate of potash, chloroform, ether, crystallized nitrate of silver, and acetic acid as well as more benign items like a bowl filled with fresh eggs and a large ceramic jug labeled "rain water."

"Mr. Norris? What do all these fearsome chemicals do? I know little about the actual process and am curious."

"It requires a great interest in chemistry. I fear most outside our little fraternity would find it tiresome."

"I came here to learn, Mr. Norris."

"Well, the plate is first coated with what we call collodion. That's a mixture of alcohol, ether, iodine of ammonium, and pyroxyline. This forms a base that is then sensitized by a bath in crystallized nitrate of silver, together with water and acetic acid. Silver is our magic ingredient. It turns dark when exposed to light.

"Once exposed to the light, the image is intensified or developed by a bath in pyrogallic acid. This stops the silver from reacting. The unexposed silver salts are washed away and we have our negative image, which is then 'fixed' permanently by using hyposulphite diluted in water. We then have our negative image ready to be printed."

"Oh, my heavens, what a complicated process." Victoria was touched by the animation in the man's face, the dancing light in his eyes, as he described what was no doubt his obsession, his *raison d'etre*.

"What is cyanide of potassium used for?" She remembered that this chemical caused the death of Medora Lamb but she did not see it among his bank of chemicals. "I have read that photographers use that as well."

"Some use it in the fixing process that I mentioned," he said. "A bath of it washes away the unexposed silver salts. It's not currently in vogue, though, as it tends to penetrate the collodion film and disorganizes the stratum of albumen beneath it."

"Excuse me?" she asked, completely lost.

"Causes bubbles."

"Oh, I see."

"I follow the recommendations of Professor Towler almost to the letter." He pulled a volume from his chemical shelf and displayed it to her. The title of the treatise was *Dry Plate Method, or The Tannin Process,* by John Towler, MD. "This little tome rules every step of the modern photographer's protocol."

He looked at the book in his hands and smiled down upon it with a kind of reverence that one would expect to show one's bible.

"Occasionally, potassium cyanide can be employed to clarify a fogged negative, but I seldom need—I'm sorry, I am probably boring you with this minutia. Is there a reason you asked about that particular chemical?"

"Just curious. Perhaps you can tell me about your séance technique?"

"I would be delighted, Mrs. Woodhull. Allow me to escort you back into the studio room."

They passed an enjoyable hour discussing his practices to contact the spirit realm prior to making the photograph. They varied from hers in many ways but she could not fault his procedures. Each medium must adhere to his or her unique gifts. They are God-given and cannot be taught. The one unusual feature of his séance technique was to require the family member requesting the séance to supply a photograph of the deceased that they wished to contact. Norris said his concentration on the face of said person was crucial to his ability to summon them.

They parted with the agreement that she would make a sworn statement or deposition of some sort before the attorneys involved that could be used in Mr. Norris's defense. She could not speak to the process of photography exactly, having no technical expertise in that realm, but she could assert the existence of the Spirit World without hesitation.

He profusely thanked her for her promised support and for granting him this time out of her busy schedule. He assured her his counsel would contact her as soon as possible.

CHAPTER TWENTY-FOUR

Continuation of direct examination of Garnet Langley by Mr. Ober-holtzer for the defense.

Oberholtzer: And did your brother seek another roommate to share his lodgings after Mr. Ingersoll departed for Chicago?

Langley: Yes, a man named Jackson Hurley.

Oberholtzer: Did your brother continue the habit of bringing his roommate to your home for Sunday dinner?

Langley: No, he never introduced the gentleman to us. He said the man was not really a friend of his, but more like a lodger. They shared the apartment as a matter of economy to them both. And he also confided that this man was too common a person to mix in our sort of society. He was not very refined in his speech or manners and he had many questionable habits.

Oberholtzer: How did you learn of these habits? Did your brother speak of them?

Langley: No, I learned of them when . . . when . . . my brother was arrested at the end of last August. [Witness begins to weep.]

Oberholtzer: I'm sorry to ask these painful questions. Your Honor, might we recess for—

Langley: No, sir, I can answer. I want to answer. We received a message from Cameron that he was at the police station in the borough of the Bronx. He had been arrested at the Jerome Park Race Course.

He and this Mr. Hurley had taken to attending many horse

racing events at the various tracks around the city and they were betting on the races. Cameron had never indulged in wagering before. It was so unlike him.

Anyway, he was being questioned in regard to something illegal that had transpired there. This Mr. Hurley had told the police that my brother was responsible. It couldn't be true. He simply would not have done something like that.

Oberholtzer: How was the matter resolved?

Langley: Mr. Ingersoll came and sorted it all out somehow. He indicated that this Mr. Hurley was to blame, that he was threatening my brother somehow.

Oberholtzer: Was your brother afraid of Mr. Hurley?

Langley: Yes, I know he was. They were not on good terms, you see. They had quarreled about Mr. Hurley not paying his share of the rent and my brother changed the lock on the apartment door and placed all of Mr. Hurley's possessions in the hallway.

I heard my brother tell Mr. Ingersoll that Mr. Hurley was "out to get him"—those were his exact words.

Oberholtzer: Was your brother then released from jail?

Langley: He was not in jail exactly when Mr. Ingersoll arrived from Chicago. He had been transferred to Bellevue Hospital for observation.

Oberholtzer: And what caused him to be transferred to a hospital?

Langley: They said . . . they said he . . . [Unintelligible]

The Court: Pray speak up, Miss Langley.

Langley: They said he had attempted to hang himself while he was in police custody. I do not know the details. He would not discuss the matter with anyone.

I think it had to do with some type of blackmail. Or Mr. Hurley wanted to get even with my brother for locking him out of the apartment.

Mr. Oberholtzer to the Court: Your Honor, I wish to introduce into evidence a copy of an outstanding warrant for the arrest of Mr. Jackson Hurley from the State of New York for involvement in an illegal betting scheme at various race tracks in the city and for making false statements against Mr. Cameron Curtis Langley.

Lynch: Objection, Your Honor. I'll stipulate that the warrant is genuine, but Mr. Hurley is not on trial here. Whatever his transgressions in the State of New York, I do not see the relevance.

Oberholtzer: These documents reflect that Mr. Langley had made a serious enemy, whom we have established followed him to Chicago, arriving immediately prior to the date of Mr. Langley's demise.

The Court: I'll take judicial notice of the warrant and allow it for that limited purpose. Objection is overruled.

CHAPTER TWENTY-FIVE

Tuesday, April 27, 1875

The good lawyer Oberholtzer arrived punctually at two o' clock in the afternoon, picking Victoria up from the ladies' entrance to the Palmer House Hotel. He transported her to her next appointment with Mr. Ingersoll for what she hoped would be their final interview. She was now becoming as anxious as he was to perform the crucial séance.

"Learned anything interesting yet, Mrs. Woodhull?" Oberholtzer asked. He drummed his pudgy fingers on the open window of the hansom cab, staring out upon the busy sidewalks of the city as they struggled to the courthouse through the traffic, which slowed to a near halt at the Clark Street bridge. She glanced at the barges and other ships making their way up and down the Chicago River.

"Well, I wish I could tell you I knew the truth of what happened in that house on the morning of March the second, but alas, as even poor Mr. Ingersoll knows not, I am in a likewise state of bafflement."

"My sentiments exactly for the last six weeks of my practice. This is the third day of jury deliberations. The longest of my career to date. The wait is grinding on Alec's nerves, I can tell. I thought I might cheer him with the thought that the longer the deliberation, the more likely we might anticipate a deadlock. He did not greet this in as positive a frame of mind as I had imagined."

"A deadlock?" she asked. "Is that what is known as a hung jury?" He nodded, so she continued her inquiry, "What would happen then?"

"If the judge decides to accept the jury's claim that they cannot and will never be of one mind, then a mistrial is declared. The prosecutor, Mr. Lynch, in his sole discretion, must decide whether to retry the case. If he does not, Alex walks out a free man, though he would bear the possibility of having the charges refiled at a later date. I frankly doubt that Lynch would choose that course. When he comes up for reelection, such a decision might be viewed as a failure on his part."

The lawyer sighed loudly and shook his head. "Poor Alec cried out when I suggested he could be re-tried and have to endure all of that agony again. I honestly believe another go-round in the courtroom would kill him. He claims he is spiritually dead already."

"How was it that Mr. Langley came to live with you and your wife, Mr. Ingersoll?"

He frowned with deep thought as to how to answer this question. "A strange series of events, really. Cam got himself into some trouble. It involved that man, Jackson Hurley."

"The man you thought robbed your house the week before all this happened?"

He nodded. "I got a frantic telegram from the Gems—Cam's sisters, that is. They begged me to come at once and 'save' their brother. Dora and I did not know what to make of this. We both corresponded with him frequently, though Dora had slowed down due to her distress in the weeks after the baby died.

"All we knew for certain was that he was hard up for money and that it was worrying him. His roommate—this Hurley character—was not keeping up on the rent and was in fact borrowing money from Cam, I think. That didn't make sense to

me. Cam was tight with his money and it always went straight to Brooklyn and those damned sisters of his."

He instantly grimaced with contrition. "Forgive my language, Mrs. Woodhull. And please do not report any negative comment I might make about those ladies. I must remember Garnet's recent kindness to me for which I am very grateful. True, she revealed some information that I did not know about my own wife—facts that were very hurtful to me. But she was sincerely trying to help my case. I won't forget that."

Victoria assured him she understood his situation but encouraged him to continue his recollections about the previous fall.

"Cam's money woes increased when the roof of his family house needed major repairs. A storm brought a tree limb down and smashed through Opal's bedroom. This forced her to share a room with Sapphire and Garnet and . . . that was a disaster all on its own." He shook his head with a smile. "You would have to know Opal. She's somewhat . . . cantankerous."

"I am one of seven children, Mr. Ingersoll. I know that siblings can be difficult at times." She did not share her own sisterly grudges that included much more mayhem than any he could imagine from Cameron Langley's spinster relations.

"Well, I know Cam was under pressure to find money for this little problem and he may have—don't quote me on this, as I do not know the truth—engaged in some sort of fraudulent gambling scheme at the behest of Hurley. In any case, someone tipped off the police and Cam was arrested when he tried to collect his winnings. I'm convinced he was an innocent dupe in the whole matter.

"When I arrived in New York, the Gems greeted me with even worse news: Cam had attempted to hang himself in his jail cell. I rushed to his bedside, in the hideous psychiatric ward of Bellevue Hospital, no less.

"He sparingly shared as much of the story as I could pry

181

from him. He was thoroughly demoralized by the matter. I could not understand for the life of me why he did not tell the police that he was feuding with this man, Hurley, and that Hurley had given false evidence against him.

"He seemed terrified of the man and I got the impression that some kind of blackmail was afoot, though how anyone could find a reason to blackmail a man as inoffensive as Cam Langley was beyond me. He even begged me not to contact Hurley.

"I ignored this request, of course, and went straight to the restaurant where he worked. I did not allow him any chance for explanation when I called him out into the alley behind the place.

"After identifying myself to him—I was so furious I did not even fear the consequences of my rash actions—I just said, 'The next time you decide to harm someone, you had better pick a victim who has no friends.'

"I commenced to give him the beating of a lifetime. He must not have been well liked because the few fellow workmates who happened to witness the scene did not come to his aid. In fact, they laughed at his misfortune.

"The odd thing was, Cam was not particularly happy about my actions. He was alarmed, in fact, and kept asking me, 'What did he tell you? What did he tell you?'

"I laughed and said, 'After I broke his jaw, not much!' Ha ha."

"So this man, Hurley, bore you a grudge?" she said.

Ingersoll sighed. "Yes, I suppose so. In any case, the police dropped all charges against Cam, once the complaining witness 'disappeared,' shall we say? That prompted me to invite Cam to come live with us in Chicago. I convinced him he needed to rest for awhile and recover his health—and, between you and me—maybe his sanity.

"He had long been working on a novel, or so he claimed. He would not show it to me or even to Dora, just claimed he was always working on it. I told him he could have the leisure to finally finish it if he resided with us for a few months."

"I'm sure you now regret that decision," Victoria suggested, wondering where next his story might veer.

It was then that he looked her directly in the eye and said with heartfelt emotion, "The odd thing is, I don't. Those first months after his arrival were . . . golden. The happiest of my entire life. The three of us together again. Dora was so happy . . . and I might add, more affectionate to me in—shall we say, a *wifely* sense—than she had ever been before. I trust you take my meaning."

A blush stained his cheeks, still pale not only from his weeks of incarceration but also from the fact that he had just given up his full beard.

"I believe I do, but I should think that you would know, in speaking to me, of all the people in the world, such elaborate euphemism is hardly needed."

"All right, then. Sexual relations between my wife and I increased in frequency and ardor for us both! I dare you to print *that*."

"Don't you feel better now?" Victoria gave him a teasing smile.

"Not really," he said, laughing.

They both shared another wave of merriment, though he continued to blush, modesty forcing his gaze to the floor.

The levity faded quickly as the reason for their conversation returned to them. A sobered Alec Ingersoll continued. "As I was saying, those weeks, those short months were perfection to me. Every day was a gift."

"But it was a false paradise, was it not?"

"I suppose it was, given my reaction to learning that Cam

and Dora had become intimate in body as well as spirit."

"How did you learn of this, Mr. Ingersoll? The servants who testified at your trial seemed to base their suspicions mostly on the nude photographs your wife took of Mr. Langley."

Surprisingly, Ingersoll scoffed at this possibility. "Good lord, no. Indeed not. We were all artists, in one way or another. We thought the human form to be beautiful, not shameful."

"I applaud that notion, sir."

"I think I know your sentiments on that issue. That was one of the reasons I assumed you might be sympathetic to my odd situation. Most are not so broad-minded."

"Please be hesitant to make assumptions about me, Mr. Ingersoll. When a person receives the amount of attention I have, I find often that persons—complete strangers to me—begin to think that they know me or can guess my opinions. But that is simply a figment of their own imagination."

"I apologize then. I'm sure you are right. The public is certainly making assumptions about me, if the newspaper articles and frequent editorials are to be considered."

"So, you say you viewed the nude photographs of Mr. Langley and did not object to them?"

"No, I thought they were excellent. Mrs. Woodhull, I am in earnest about this. I could not have loved Dora Lamb and felt otherwise. In point of fact, Dora posed in the nude for me once in the drawing room of our house. Cam was present. I didn't mind."

"You are broad-minded indeed, Mr. Ingersoll. I'm impressed."

"Of course, I knew we were not in the common herd on this. Hearing our maid, little Gracie, in court, recount her embarrassment at walking in on Dora photographing Cam was an unpleasant reminder of just how different we were. How few in the world at large would understand us. In retrospect, I suppose if we had known the servants were taking notes, we might have conducted ourselves with more discretion."

"So what brought about the end of this sojourn in Eden?"

He drew a long breath and gazed into the imaginary distance as though now far removed from this stuffy room that smelled of wood polish, stale cigar smoke, and the nasty, decaying contents of the spittoon in the corner.

"Now begins the hard part," he said. "I've dreaded this from the beginning, but a bargain is a bargain."

He needed several moments to collect his thoughts before continuing. He poured a glass of water from the pitcher Mr. Oberholtzer so thoughtfully provided for them each day at their meetings. Victoria shuffled her notes and pretended attention to them to give him this time.

"I just wanted to find out what Cam's novel was about. As simple as that. I had no right to the information. But his very secrecy fueled my interest. He would snap the notebook shut whenever anyone came near to him."

"Before even the ink dried?"

"He always wrote in pencil. He liked the portability. He was vain about that notebook, bound in red leather with his initials printed on the cover. He would take it everywhere with him. Out on walks, for example. I used to tease him: 'Taking the novel for a walk, Cam?' Like one might walk a dog. When it wasn't with him on his very person, it was hidden away somewhere.

"Then one day last December, I got my chance. It was early on a Sunday morning. The servants were off and we had the house to ourselves. The weather was shockingly cold, but the sun shown that morning and Dora set up a wail to be taken ice skating. I told Cam to take her. I had to stay home and work. Some last-minute changes to a house I was designing. The builders would sit idle on Monday morning if I did not revise the blueprints.

"When they had gone, I noticed that Cam had left the door to his room open in his haste to depart and catch up with Dora. There on his desk lay the forbidden volume, open and unguarded, ready to yield up its secrets for any who might pass.

"I could not resist the temptation. And so I read it. It was not really a novel at all! It was an exact rendering of everything that had happened to him in the last three years.

"He hadn't even bothered to change the names. He wrote it in third person like a novel but whole conversations were contained in it verbatim. I know that everything he wrote about me was true so I had to assume that the rest really happened. When they got home, I confronted them and they did not deny it."

He paused and looked into her eyes with a chilling intensity. "If I could now take back that day, I would. Surely living in a fool's paradise was preferable to living in Hell—my present address."

"But you accepted the situation for more than two months, did you not? The testimony of your servants hinted that from Christmas onward, your wife and friend no longer made a secret of their affair."

"Yes, Dora 'negotiated' a peace between us all. She insisted she was not a 'thing' to be owned. I did not quarrel with this aspect. I never sought to be a despot in my own house. I never wished to oppress her in any way that would cause her unhappiness.

"Though Cam immediately apologized profusely for what they had done. Dora apologized *only* for the deception. She claimed she was heartily sorry and felt cowardly that she did not ask for my blessing of the union *before* it was a consummated fact. She quoted fragments of *your* speeches to Cam and I, whatever specific sentences she could turn to fit her own singular agenda.

"And she argued as historical precedent the story of her own mother. Dora was infatuated with the Oneida Community. She talked of it constantly. She told us you would approve, by the way. She insisted we enter into what they call 'Complex Marriage.' " He sighed and shook his head as he sat back in his chair. "It was complex, all right."

"It's true, I have advocated in favor of the system you describe created by Mr. Noyes at Oneida. It appears to me an ideal alternative to the false system of enforced monogamy that our government and laws currently require."

"You advocated it in speeches but never personally lived it. Would that be fair to say?"

"I suppose so," she said warily.

A silence fell between them as he frowned and gazed once more into the middle distance.

"Well, in any case," he continued, "we tried it. At first it was awkward, but my shock wore off as the days passed. They walked on eggs around me, attentive to my wants and wishes, striving to please me at every turn. Eventually I began to accept their claims that my happiness was crucial to them. Of course, I was also supporting them. I don't think that fact was entirely overlooked.

"In time, I gave in to it. I could not hold out forever. It was easier to accept their gifts of love. They labored to make the whole arrangement irresistible to me.

"Especially Dora. I blush to recall all the ways she strove to please me. The average man would die to have a wife so attentive. An Arabian sheik with all his concubines could have envied me.

"For awhile, it seemed to work. The idea, this Complex Marriage of ours, it started to feel more and more natural.

"Truth has two facets, does it not?" he continued. "There are the truths we are willing to say out loud and then there are the secrets that lie in our hearts and are never shared with anyone."

Silence fell between them once again.

"I guess Cam must have destroyed that notebook," he finally said. "It seems never to have been found."

"Your lawyer said the police looked for it unsuccessfully," she said.

"That is good. I half-expected to see it printed in the newspapers, further defiling Cam's memory."

He drew a long, deep breath. "I now wonder if my transgression that day of reading the notebook set in motion their ultimate fates."

"How so, Mr. Ingersoll?"

"I did not murder them, Mrs. Woodhull. They must have ended their own lives or one killed the other and then him- or herself. I just don't know how it all played out. And though I am loathe to admit my culpability, I am certain I am the cause of their desperate actions."

"But they are the ones who transgressed. Why do you blame yourself?"

"It's so hard to talk about. It is so hard for me to admit what I did to drive them to it, even now."

His voice choked with an emotion so deep and dreadful, Victoria shook with anxiety. He buried his face in his hands. His breath came in short hesitations and she knew he must be weeping.

She could not stand by and witness his pitiful outburst with the requisite journalistic distance. Her woman's heart reached out to this suffering creature. She rose from her chair and advanced to his side of the table. She placed her hands upon his shoulders as they shuddered. He accepted the comfort she offered—perhaps the only such gesture he had experienced throughout his ordeal.

He impulsively threw his arms around her waist and buried his face in the muslin of her blouse to sob openly. She stood there quietly, patting his back and smoothing his hair. She thought how like a child he seemed in that despairing moment.

But time did not stand still for Mr. Ingersoll. His lawyer burst in the door without a knock to find them in this awkward embrace. Mr. Oberholtzer paid no heed, but announced breathlessly: "The jury is back!"

CHAPTER TWENTY-SIX

Flynn voraciously read the faxed pages of the C.C.L. Journal while she waited for Matt to get his scan. They had managed to hit the print shop at the height of the lunch hour rush and had waited quite a while until his name was called.

When he disappeared into another part of the large shop with her precious photograph in his hands, she had felt a momentary twinge of separation anxiety. Not that she didn't trust Matt; he seemed like a great guy. He wouldn't steal her precious picture.

Instead, she realized she was forming some kind of weird attachment to the silly photograph, separate and apart from any monetary value it might end up having. She was no longer sure if she owned the photo or if it owned her. The three attractive faces pictured in the fading sepia were so real now, so human, she felt like their guardian. Guardian of their legacy, at least.

"All done," Matt announced twenty minutes later, walking up to her where she sat in the waiting area with its uncomfortable bank of molded plastic seats. He handed back her photographic treasure and she mentally heaved a sigh of relief to have her hands on it again.

"I'm starving," she said. It was now nearly two. "Can I drive us to lunch? I know a great sushi place. Do you like raw fish?"

"I'm so hungry, I could eat raw *anything* at the moment."

"I know I should take you out for barbeque. That's what Kansas City is famous for, but I just haven't had the chance to eat sushi in ages. My son and dad don't like it."

"Then I'm your man."

"Unless you'd rather eat French food," she taunted with a playful smirk. "Just to show off those language skills . . ."

"Drive, Keirnan. Starving men can get ugly."

She drove him to a Kansas City landmark, the Country Club Plaza. They strolled along the streets of the nation's first suburban shopping mall. Sounded cheesy to describe it like that, but since the area had been built in the 1920s it had now taken on a classic, vintage patina. Matt seemed properly impressed with the bizarrely out-of-place Moorish architecture.

"It's pretty at Christmastime," she told him. "They outline all those buildings with lights. It looks like an 'Arabian Nights' fairy tale."

She sensed his eyes glazing over so she knocked off her tour guide shtick.

Arriving in the middle of the afternoon as they were, they had no trouble getting seated at the most elegant pan-Asian restaurant in the city. They chose an outside table on the sidewalk to take full advantage of the unusually pleasant weather—such a rarity on the Great Plains.

Flynn chose a Mojito when the waiter came by for their drink order. Matt picked an imported beer.

"I nearly finished reading the journal," she said as they perused their menus.

"I'm surprised your eyes aren't bloodshot. Faxes can be hard to read generally but this one was really a challenge since the original had been written in pencil," he said. "I want to make my own copy when I see it. Ellen said she'd be happy to show it to me."

"Yeah, it was sort of hard on the eyes. The more I read it, the more I felt sorry for Cameron."

"Why?" He looked surprised by this remark.

"Caught in the crossfire between that crazy husband and wife? That had to suck."

"Cameron was the villain of the story. I don't see how you can feel sorry for him. I mean, he broke The Guy Code. There's no coming back from that."

"The 'Guy Code'?" She smirked at this as she could tell it was leading him into some type of rant, but not the serious kind.

He smiled across the table at her and she noticed for the first time he had a slight dimple in his right cheek.

" 'The Guy Code': Thou shalt not hook up with Thy buddy's girlfriend. It's immutable, since the beginning of time. Guys who dare to break it deserve no mercy."

"Since the beginning of *patriarchy,* you mean."

"Okay, I'll give you that much."

They placed their lunch orders just after their drinks arrived and Flynn noticed that Matt really knew his way around a sushi menu.

"If you want my take on the whole Ingersoll triangle," he said. "Since reading that journal, I'm picking up a strong 'Jules and Jim' vibe. I think that Medora was one crazy bitch. Like maybe *she* killed Langley, then herself. Alec had probably finally had it and said, 'No more, I'm tired of this Complex Marriage shit,' and wanted his traditional marriage back.

"So Langley probably said, 'Okay, fine, I'll leave,' but this Medora didn't want that and just flipped out. It was all one of those, 'If I can't have you, nobody can' murder-suicides. She shot Langley, then drank the cyanide, and poor old Alec had the misfortune to get left to clean up the mess."

Flynn propped her chin on her elbow to digest this. She idly watched the affluent shoppers stroll past, many accompanied by their too-cute-for-words purebred dogs, some wearing little sweaters. Her dad referred to these pampered pooches as "fur children." She smiled at this but sometimes wished she had one.

She loved sitting here at this outdoor café. If not for the brilliant May sunshine beating down, she could almost pretend she was back in Paris.

"The last man standing," she murmured.

"What?"

"I was thinking about our Alec. The last man standing. No real victory in that."

He shook his sadly. "I wonder if anyone's marriage has a happy ending. Mine didn't. My parents didn't. Hell, my dad's on his *third* marital go-round."

"Theirs was a generation that got married a lot," she said.

"Or never learned from their mistakes."

"My parents stayed married for forty years," she said. "When my mom died, I was so worried about my dad going it alone, I moved back here just to keep an eye on him awhile."

The waiter delivered elaborate plates of maki and sashimi, all laid out like tiny works of art. Flynn tapped her glass for another Mojito.

"Your parents are the exception," he said.

"Well, I'm not down on marriage. That's all I meant to say."

"That's probably because nobody's ever broken up with you by voicemail," he said, diving into the array of raw fish with gusto.

"Wow, that's cold. I'm sorry. Are we talking about your ex-wife?"

He nodded and continued to eat, wielding his chopsticks like he'd just flown in from Tokyo. It didn't seem like talking about it bothered him so she continued to probe.

"How long ago?"

"Two and a half years. I'd just moved back to Chicago. See, I got this big promotion and they transferred me to the home office there. It was January. Cait—that is, Caitlin, my ex—was under a teaching contract until summer, so the plan was for her to join me in June. We'd see each other on weekends, you know, that kind of thing. I knew she wasn't crazy about leaving Dallas, but I really wanted to try Chicago. I thought it would be nice to maybe reconnect with my dad." He snorted and rolled his eyes to indicate the father-and-son reunion thing didn't go as well as it might have. "Yet another of my miscalculations.

"Then one day I come home from work and there's this blinking light on the answering machine and a ten-minute message telling me she'd met someone else and maybe she realized she hadn't been ready to settle down yet anyway. Guess that goes without saying—*duh.* Oh, and that it was better to end it now before we'd fucked up a couple of kids like our parents did and we both needed to be adults about this, and blah, blah, blah. *Voicemail.* Like it wasn't important enough to call me on my cell?"

"Well, if it's any consolation, my break-up with Brody's father was so bad I never even told him I was pregnant. I didn't want to see him again *that* bad."

"Whoa . . . he must have been a real asshole for you to hate him that much." His face changed in an instant. "I'm sorry. I shouldn't have said that. Way out of line. Here we are, practically strangers—"

"Sometimes it's easier to talk to a stranger." She chewed the top of her plastic straw.

"You know, it must be. You're the first person I've ever told about the voicemail. It was just so damned humiliating; it knocked me off my feet."

"You seem fine now."

"I'm better. Way better. The first six months, though, I literally marinated in vodka and Red Bull. Not to mention self-pity."

"Vodka and Red Bull?" She twisted her face in horror. "Does that actually taste good?"

"It's not bad at all."

"But the combination—one's a stimulant, the other's a depressant—aren't they at cross purposes?"

"The theory is that the caffeine keeps you awake longer, allowing you to drink more alcohol. It works . . . I think."

"Well, in my professional opinion, it sounds like a real brain fuck."

He shrugged good-naturedly. "Long story short—I snapped out of it one day, got on a big health kick, started running. I'm in the best shape of my life. Emotionally, too, no shit."

"I believe you." The funny thing was, she did.

After their long, slow, very late lunch, Flynn headed them toward yet another restaurant down the street with a nicely decorated patio. This one offered tiki torches and ice cold red wine sangria.

"See, it's practically health food," she said, pointing to the fruit floating in the large, brightly colored ceramic pitcher.

"And Happy Hour pricing. We can't afford *not* to," he said with a wink.

They discussed the next avenue for investigation into the sordid lives of their photo friends. But not before they checked Flynn's auction on his Blackberry. It now neared $3,000.

"Thanks for letting that woman with the murder house in on the bidding. She's keeping pace with WOODHULL toe-to-toe."

"Told you she had deep pockets. You know, I'd really like to talk to that WOODHULL bidder. Find out what her angle is."

"For some reason I thought it was a 'he.' The emails I've gotten have been so abrupt."

"Since reading that journal this morning, I know I've got to do some research on the Oneida Community," he said.

"Yeah, I always thought that was a silverware company."

"Me, too. I know that there were a lot of new religions and utopian experiments in America back then. That's when the Mormons got started, so did the Shakers. They sure had their own ideas about sex and marriage—the Mormons practiced polygamy and the Shakers were totally celibate."

"I guess that explains why one group died out and the other has six million members today." She mused on the fact that the Shakers had at least left behind some pretty decent furniture. Wasn't a total loss.

"This sangria is really good," Matt said as he signaled the waiter for another pitcher plus more chips for their guacamole. "I don't think I've ever had it before."

"I figured if you could handle vodka and Red Bull without throwing up, you could definitely survive wine and fruit juice. Can I use your phone to send WOODHULL a message?"

"Absolutely." They tapped out a brief note to the bidder asking him or her to call Flynn as soon as possible.

"Couldn't hurt," Flynn said as she hit the SEND button.

"I want to know more about the Victoria Woodhull connection. I need to know it for my book research."

They chatted on about the photograph until they ran out of chips and dip once again. The restaurant was now starting to fill up with the dinner crowd.

"Matt, I've got to tell you that I am not in any shape to drive home." Her head was swimming but she was in a terrific mood.

"Honestly, I don't think I am either. What are we going to do? I don't think the restaurant will let us just sit here until we sober up."

Flynn cast her eyes in the direction of their waiter who was staring a hole in them, undoubtedly wanting to fill the table with more lucrative clientele for the evening.

"Yes, doubtful," she said. "It might be safer to rent a hotel room."

"Safer for who?" he said, leaning forward, the dimple edging its way back into his cheek.

"Safer for . . . other motorists? They probably built that hotel across the street just for that purpose."

"Imagine that," he said and they smiled at each other in such a manner that both knew they were no longer discussing safe travel.

Flynn reached into her bag to locate her cell phone. She hoped she would just get her dad's answering machine. This "I'll be home late" message was going to be tricky.

"What happened to your policy of not taking advantage of the alcohol impaired?" he asked, with just a hint of a friends-with-benefits-type smirk.

"If we're equally impaired, the policy is suspended."

"Good enough for me." He waved at the waiter. "Check, please."

CHAPTER TWENTY-SEVEN

C.C.L. Notebook
Autumn 1874
Ingersoll lived in a mansion! To think how high he had risen in the world with such amazing speed dazzled Langley. When they arrived at the house on Prairie Avenue on that bright September day, Langley had sat still in the hack, staring at the grand residence.

He thought they might be stopping by the house of one of Alec's clients for some business purpose, or perhaps he had stopped at this address to point out a home he had designed. Many large houses were in various states of construction in both directions on the elegant street.

"Did you design this house, Alec?"

Ingersoll had alighted from the cab and turned to him with a proud smile.

"No. I did participate on that one down there," he said, pointing to a tall home on the end of the block that was currently being bricked by a large crew. "Come on, get out."

"You mean . . . this is *your* house?"

"Why else would we have stopped?" He paid the cabbie. "On Saturday, I'll take you and Dora out for a drive. I'll hire a rig and show you both several of my projects. Dora's been asking to see them since before the baby—"

He watched his friend cut short his sentence to avoid a still-painful topic. Langley wanted to say something of comfort, to at last deliver his condolences in person. He felt like a selfish monster not to have mentioned the lost child in the whole previous week they had been together.

Before he could summon up the appropriate words—he who was, after all, a professional at dealing with grieving family members—he heard a familiar voice call out from the front porch.

"Cameron! Is it really you?"

Medora came running down the front walk. She wore her habitual ticking-striped blue and white work smock. Her dark hair hung in haphazard schoolgirl plaits over each shoulder. Dear Medora: never one for fashion.

Langley felt an overwhelming surge of joy to see her. She jumped into his arms and he swung her around, planting an off-center kiss on her forehead.

He threw a glance over his shoulder to Ingersoll and said, "I've never kissed a married woman before."

"Don't make a habit of it," said a grinning Ingersoll. He motioned for Langley to help him with the heavy trunk.

Medora approached her husband to place a welcome kiss upon his face, but stopped with concern. "What on earth happened to your eye?"

"I had to rescue Cam from pirates." He flashed a look at Langley to indicate they were not going to reveal the events that produced the blue and purple streaks under and over his left eye. Jackson Hurley had managed to land one solid punch before Ingersoll had thrown him to the ground.

"Pirates? Hmmmm," said Medora, who picked up her husband's traveling valise to follow the two men as they hauled the trunk up the front walk.

"I hope this will be adequate, Mr. Langley," said Ingersoll with a grand gesture as he opened the door to Cam's new bedroom.

They jointly lifted the trunk and carried it in, setting it at the foot of the bed.

Both men were winded by the exertion and mopped their foreheads with their handkerchiefs.

"We're a long way from the Eleventh Street basement, don't you agree?"

"This is amazing," said Langley, shaking his head as he marveled at the splendid decor. "This is larger than . . . than our entire old apartment."

"I think you'll be comfortable here," said Ingersoll with undisguised pride at offering such luxury to his oldest friend. "Mrs. Teller has agreed to stay later tonight to serve us a special dinner to welcome you."

Langley walked around the room to admire the scrolling burgundy wallpaper, the richly carved wainscoting, the marble fireplace interestingly placed in the corner of the room. He peeked out the heavy draperies to see the view from the tall windows. Though the room faced Prairie Avenue, he did not worry that the clatter of carriages would disturb his slumbers. The house sat at an elegant distance from the brick-covered street.

"Wait until you see the billiard room. I've taught Dora how to play. The three of us will have a round after dinner."

"A house with its own billiard room? And a library, too, no doubt."

"Of course," said the beaming Ingersoll. "You will have the perfect solitude to write your grand literary masterpiece."

"Oh, that," said Langley, blushing. "My foolish scribblings, you mean."

Langley sat down on the bed and smiled at his friend in quiet amazement. He realized then just how tired he was from the long train journey.

Ingersoll clapped his hands together. "Well, I'm going to

wash off this train dirt and get dressed for that supper Mrs. Teller has promised. You will love the bathroom, by the way— hot water piped up directly from the kitchen. Pure heaven. See you directly."

"Alec," Langley said to his friend before he departed. With a heartfelt tone he added, "Thank you . . . for all of this. You saved my life."

Ingersoll shook his dark head with a smile, his teeth gleaming white from his bearded face.

"You're home now, Cam."

Langley fell into the embrace of a brief and refreshing nap. He had not bothered to remove his shoes or jacket, nor did he pull down the elegant brocade of the bed covers. When he awoke, he decided to explore.

It was certainly the grandest private home he had ever been able to ramble at liberty. It rivaled the townhouse of Medora's grandparents, though it was much more modern.

He first poked in the bedroom next to his. The sight made him wince for his friends' pain and loss, for it contained a fully furnished nursery. In a bright corner of the room he saw a cradle draped in gauzy fabric and adorned with small silk roses.

He closed the door quickly and moved on to the rooms on the opposite side of the central staircase.

He gently knocked on the first door and, hearing no sound, tried the knob. It opened and revealed another richly decorated bedroom. He saw some of Alec's traveling clothes on the floor.

He wandered in, wondering what had become of his host. A door stood half open connecting the chamber to another room. Was it a dressing room? Perhaps Alec could be found in there.

He pushed open the door only to behold a sight that turned his pale cheeks twelve shades of scarlet! The room was filled with steam and mirrors and held a large copper bathtub encased in carved walnut. In the tub sat not only a wet and soapy Alec, but Medora as well! Her dark cloud of hair sat on top of her head like a rich chocolate soufflé.

"Oh God!" Langley screeched as he hastened to slam the door, but not before Alec lobbed a wet sponge at his head.

"I'm so sorry," he called through the closed door.

But Alec laughed as though this were the best joke of the week.

"Peeping Tom!" Medora shouted between giggles.

He walked back into the hall with a single thought: Alec Ingersoll was the luckiest man on earth.

They sat together waiting to be served in the long and elegant dining room at a table built to accommodate twelve. The ornate, coffered ceiling soared fifteen feet above their heads.

A bank of tall, shuttered windows lined the side of the room. It gained its evening light from three grand gasoliers above the table. Not enough light to fully appreciate the highly polished burled wood paneling.

Medora had deserted them momentarily to discuss something with the housekeeper-turned-cook for the evening.

Ingersoll, who sat at the end of the long table as befits the host, apologized to his guest for not employing enough servants to adequately run such a fine house.

"As a junior partner in the firm, I am afraid I do have my limits," he said.

"Knowing the details of my prior dwelling and the house I grew up in," Langley said with a grin, "you must know that I would not notice the lack of servants, much less require them."

"My wife is a different story," said Ingersoll, with fading humor.

"Well, I suppose it's only natural. Given the environment of her youth. Few enjoy that kind of privileged upbringing. But children take everything for granted, good or bad, don't they?" Langley leaned in close from his seat at Ingersoll's right and whispered with a glittering eye, "Do all wives wash their husband's hair? Is this a benefit of marriage I had not heard about?"

"One of many!" Ingersoll laughed. "But seriously, that was the first time ever. Her idea. Surprised the hell out of me."

"But in a good way," teased Langley.

"Yes, in a good way." Ingersoll raised his glass for a mock toast. Their glasses met in a loud clink and a splash of dark crimson hit the heavily embroidered white table cloth. They were already well into their first bottle of wine and had not eaten a morsel since the meager egg sandwiches on the train, hours before.

When they saw the stain, they both made guilty faces like little boys who were going to receive a scolding from their mother.

"Mrs. Teller won't be pleased," Ingersoll whispered.

"Alec, as the master of the house, I don't think you have to whisper." Langley sat the bottle of wine down over the stain as though that cured everything and they both dissolved into tipsy giggles.

"Oh, you're right," he said and they laughed even harder.

Medora returned from the kitchen. "What's so funny, you two?"

"Nothing," said her husband. "I am just so blasted glad to be off that train and sitting in my own dining room again with my two favorite people on earth."

"I believe that very fact deserves a toast," said Medora. She pushed her glass toward Ingersoll who poured what was left of the bottle into her glass: less than two ounces.

She studied the paltry serving, swirling it with a warning

smirk. "I can see the two of you are already misbehaving. It's going to be an interesting night."

One beautiful autumn day followed the next and Langley was convinced he was living in a dream. Only the steady stream of letters from the Gems reminded him of his old life in New York. Ingersoll was sending them some money, though he would not say how much. Langley insisted he keep an account so that he could repay him once he started working again.

He sometimes missed his old job at the *Times*. Not the work itself so much as the lunch breaks he used to enjoy in the little park across the street from the Times Building on Printing House Square. Though the noisy chaos of traffic on Park and Spruce surrounded him, he managed to ignore it and gaze at the fine bronze statue of Benjamin Franklin who benevolently looked down on all the producers of the written word, himself among them.

Franklin was so wise. Langley thought he was easily the most intelligent man in his own—or any—century. Just contemplating his wit alone made Langley sigh with hopeless envy.

Franklin would have known how to deal with the Medora Question. That was what he had named his new dilemma.

Ingersoll and Medora were possessed with so much life force that living with the two of them under one roof was exhausting. He never got bored, to be sure, but sometimes he just wished there could be the tiniest fraction of tranquility added to the daily business.

And they both had such amorous natures, they could not hide them, or maybe they just did not trouble to. He was more family than visitor, they insisted on countless occasions. Sometimes their animal spirits so overtook them, he became uncomfortable. He did not categorize their actions as deliberately rude, more like thoughtless.

Only last week he had retired for the night, but found himself wakeful. He had pulled his clothes back on. (Though Ingersoll and his wife felt free to wander the house in their dressing gowns whenever servants were not present, Langley did not do likewise.) He went downstairs to see what might be tempting in the kitchen. Warm milk was always the panacea for sleeplessness when he was a child.

He saw the drawing room was still fully lit so he stopped by there. "Still up, Alec?"

Ingersoll was sprawled prone on the Turkish carpet, propped on his elbows, vigorously sketching in charcoal. He did not look up when Langley entered the room.

Langley stopped cold when he saw the subject of his friend's drawing. Medora posed, quite nude, in front of a blazing fire. She had struck a pose that made her appear to be hiding behind, or really beside, one of the magnificently carved rose quartz lions. They had been imported from Italy.

Langley hesitated in confusion.

"Stay or go," said Ingersoll, still without looking up. "Don't just stand there."

"You don't mind if I stay?" He looked first at Ingersoll and then in the vague direction of his model.

"It's up to Dora," said her husband in a disinterested monotone. His artistic work so absorbed him, he seemed oblivious to anything else.

"Why should I care?" she said. "He's seen me naked before, haven't you, Cam?"

"He has?" said Ingersoll, finally breaking his concentration, but more curious than shocked by the possibility.

"I have?" said Langley in confusion.

"He saw that self-portrait I did last year."

"That didn't look very much like you," said her husband. "No offense."

205

"It was *meant* to be abstract. It was my *impression* of myself."

Langley had faced mockery from his former roommate on the subject of his prudishness. He would not get that opportunity tonight. Langley would behave as though nothing whatsoever was out of the ordinary. He could be just as sophisticated as they were.

Toward this end, he casually picked up the copy of *Harper's* new monthly magazine he had been reading earlier and found a seat that faced Ingersoll in the center of the room, placing the fireplace at his side. He watched his friend earnestly craft the picture, which focused more on the lion than the damsel or nymph or whatever Medora was supposed to represent.

Watching Ingersoll draw reminded him of their youthful trip to Europe. He had watched him spend countless hours sketching, though his subjects there tended to be Medieval churches and mountains reflected in lakes, a far cry from his present subject.

Langley stole glances at Medora. How could he not? Her creamy white skin contrasted gently with the polished red- and pink-veined stone. The fire glowed amber on the edges of her silhouette. The stone lion raised one paw as though offering to shake a visitor's hand.

She had placed her own delicate hand upon it. Her slender limbs were tucked under her sideways. Her abdomen gracefully curved toward the beast and looked smoothly unmarred by her recent maternity.

Her long dark hair hung loose about her shoulders and shielded at least one of her breasts from view.

Ingersoll sat up and stretched his back. He then placed his drawing slate with its papers across his lap. As he worked on a tiny detail he bent to blow the excess charcoal dust away, then used his handkerchief to remove an errant smudge. He whispered curses at himself in the process.

"Mrs. Teller does not approve of you using your handkerchiefs for your drawing," said Medora. "She says you should use rags instead. She can't get the ink out the ones you use at the office."

"Mrs. Teller can go to the devil," said her once again absorbed artist-husband.

Medora grinned at both him and Langley, "I'll tell her you said that."

Ingersoll looked up and threw the offending handkerchief at his wife. She dodged and the balled-up cloth landed in the firebox behind her.

Medora tried to retrieve it, but the cotton had already caught fire. She yelped as she dropped the flaming handkerchief on the hearth stone and scooted sideways to remove her naked skin from the danger.

Both men jumped up and hurried to her rescue. Langley stamped out the little fire and Ingersoll tossed the ruined cloth remnants into the firebox. The parlor fireplace was the only one in the house to burn wood, all the others used coal.

They watched the handkerchief dissolve into crumbling, dancing embers. Medora sat under one lion, hugging her knees to her chest—a show of modesty at last? Langley knelt next to the other lion, now feeling awkward all over again. Ingersoll crouched in the middle on one knee.

He looked at Medora and said with a tired sigh, "I guess its time for bed. I have to get up in—what—four hours?"

His wife wrapped her arms around his neck and, as he stood up, he lifted her into arms and briefly kissed her. As he carried his lovely burden toward the sliding pocket doors of the parlor, Langley heard him murmur, "Are you sleeping in my room tonight, little wife?"

"If I do, you will get even less sleep," she teasingly warned.

"I'll sleep next week," he said as he bore her up the stairs.

Langley sat down and leaned his own tired head back against the cold surface of the rose quartz lion. They hadn't even wished him goodnight.

"Don't worry, I'll put out the lights," he called after them with a sour expression, but he knew they probably did not hear him.

Medora and Ingersoll were both artists, Cam endlessly reminded himself. Neither gave a hoot for convention, though Ingersoll said he was forced to suppress his views considerably at his office, consorting with his much more conservative senior partners and their still-more conservative clients.

Ingersoll posed the question one evening at dinner: Did having money automatically make one become more conformist?

Medora said that her grandparents would be examples to support that claim, but then what about her own mother? Not a shred of convention in that corner.

The subject of Medora's mother had been popping into the conversation with noticeable frequency, always at Medora's introduction.

This usually provoked a debate on the controversial Oneida Community where Medora had been born. She idealized the concept they called "Complex Marriage."

"How can you support a plan that means a child grows up never knowing the identity of its own father?" Ingersoll would counter during such discussions. Langley would inevitably agree.

"But that's the brilliance of it," she would insist. "A woman would no longer be the *property* of a man. She would be herself alone, a truly free and independent person."

"Not fair to the child. A child needs the love and guidance of both its parents," said her husband.

"The child would be loved and reared by the *whole* community. The child would experience *more* love, not less. I can

208

personally vouch for this."

"How would you know?" he persisted. "You were but three years old when your grandparents brought you to live with them."

"When my grandparents *kidnapped* me . . . leaving my poor mother to die of a broken heart.

"Your mother died of consumption, Dora." He turned to Langley and made a face to indicate they would never win this argument.

"Well, a broken heart didn't help," said his wife.

Complications multiplied exponentially when, one bright morning in October, Medora told Langley that she loved him. She announced this plainly over the remnants of breakfast. The sunlight streaming in the tall Eastern windows made the frothy outline of her abundant hair glisten like a halo, but he did not think her very angelic at that moment.

Her husband had already left for work and—it being Tuesday—the servants were off. They had the pristine October day and the whole cavernous house to themselves.

"You shouldn't say that," he said.

"But I feel it."

"You still shouldn't say it."

"So you are asking me to be a hypocrite?"

"Maybe." He stared at her for several seconds. "I don't want you to say something you will later regret."

"I've always loved you. You know that."

"But you married Alec."

"I love him, too," she said. Her pointed face twisted in confusion and she sat back in the enormous dining chair that dwarfed her small frame. She had not dressed her hair yet—she seldom did before breakfast—and she twisted a long lock of it around her index finger.

At length, she sighed. "We should never have gotten married."

"I don't understand this conversation in the least."

She sat forward again and resumed her attack. "Do you know what he said when he proposed to me? The second time, that is, but the first wasn't much better. He walked into my grandparents' front parlor and, without even sitting down or saying hello, he said, 'Cam says we need to get married. What is your will?' "

"I agree that is not very romantic." Langley got an awful feeling in the pit of his stomach. He now wished that he had not intervened, nay, meddled in their affairs that morning now nearly a year ago when he had insisted that Ingersoll propose marriage the morning after he had first spent the night with her. Langley had believed—misguidedly or not—he was defending her honor.

But if he had kept his opinions to himself, perhaps the couple would have gradually reached an appropriate agreement as to their future together and matters would not have gone so horribly awry.

"I burst into tears when he said that," she continued. "My nerves were in shreds anyway. I was not feeling well at all and I was . . . well, quite frankly, I was a coward. Facing the unbridled fury of my grandparents alone was just—"

She sighed and shook her head. "They would have turned me out with barely a change of clothing to my name. They cut my mother out of their lives and never looked back. They would have done the same to me."

"Alec loves you to pieces, Medora. You must understand that he was still smarting from your first rejection of him when he came back. He's a proud man. He doesn't take rejection gracefully. He never has. And when he thought that you didn't love him, he couldn't stand it. He ran away so fast it made my head spin."

"But, of course, I loved him," she said. "Wasn't that obvious? Why would I have given myself to him if I did not? What further proof did he need above that? It was 'marriage' I rejected, not him."

"Well, Medora, you did not make that distinction very clear to him that day."

"I suppose not." Her features drew up in a childish pout.

"What are you saying? That Alec didn't want to marry you? That he just felt obligated?"

"I don't know. We tried to make the best of it, but neither of us was really very happy at first. I think we both just . . . pretended."

"That's not what I've witnessed in these recent weeks. The two of you seem as happy as a couple could be."

"But Cam, that's because you're here. We were both so happy you decided to live with us. Suddenly, it was like all the problems of this previous year had vanished and it was the three of us again."

He sighed. "The 'good old days,' as the saying goes."

"The best old days in the world," she said with a wistful smile. "If you were to leave, I don't know what would become of us."

Langley heard the implied threat in her words that morning. It weighed heavily upon him, like his clothes had been transformed into chains. He dragged them with him even in their liveliest, most playful moments.

In the days that followed he watched the interplay between Medora and Ingersoll as though through a secret window, worrying that if he said or did the wrong thing, he might destroy their newfound happiness. He did not relish this tightrope walk through his friends' lives, through his friends' marriage.

But sometimes he was lonely being the outsider, the forgotten one. He wanted to share their happiness. He wanted to experience that exuberant confidence that Ingersoll so effortlessly projected and that captivating life force that was Medora.

If becoming closer to her in the way she wanted meant he could enter into that charmed orbit, the temptation became increasingly irresistible. Perhaps she would not want everything, just some affection. They would not be lovers, but rather loving friends. He would exercise discretion, even if she did not.

And somehow Ingersoll would benefit from this, even though he did not know of it. His wife would be more attentive to him, not less. He would see to it that Ingersoll was the most beloved husband on earth. Ingersoll's joy would increase a thousandfold and he would never know that this was his dearest friend's gift to him.

The following Tuesday arrived and once more he was alone in the big house on Prairie Avenue with his winsome temptress. The moment he even hinted that he might have weakened his resolve she took the lead.

He had little experience with women in this arena—actually no experience at all—and he could not believe just how rapidly matters could get out of hand. His idea of them becoming "loving friends" quickly dissolved.

With Medora in his arms inside the gauzy tent that was her bed, it was almost as though he had *become* Ingersoll. With every panting breath, with every pounding heartbeat, he was one step closer.

He could gaze down upon Medora's face mere inches from his own, just as Ingersoll did in such private moments. He could feel her soft breath on his own cheek, the same breath Ingersoll felt each time he embraced her. Every inch of her intimate geography was now touched, known, possessed by him, just as it was by Ingersoll.

Sharing Medora's bed was nothing short of thrilling. How did Ingersoll act so casual about this? How could he be anything less than the happiest man on earth?

But then Ingersoll was so sophisticated he seemed to take everything in his stride as though it were his due in life. (Yet another source of poisonous envy Langley must struggle to keep in check.)

But Langley's euphoria faced an inevitable expiration. Soon the doleful chime of the hall clock announced the hour when Medora's rightful husband would return. With each low *gong* echoing in the hollow of his ear, rationality returned that he and Dora had not sailed closer to heaven but had in fact damned themselves to Hell.

Remorse made him a coward. He announced he felt ill with a headache and needed to rest in his room rather than take dinner with them. As he lay in his pretend sick bed, their voices drifted up the stairs from the dining room. He could not discern the words of their animated chatter, but their laughter was frequent, their silences rare.

One Tuesday followed another and their troubling, exciting adventure continued. Passion conquered reason every time and guilt was momentarily repressed.

Not that all was perfect in that sphere. He frequently found himself inadequate to the task she expected, which confused them both. Remarks by Medora seemed to suggest that Ingersoll never suffered these inconveniences. Yet another painful reminder of his inferiority to his friend, his idol.

Thanksgiving approached and a discussion ensued as to whether Langley should visit his sisters. He wished that Ingersoll and Medora could accompany him, but knew they would not be issued a similar invitation. Even though Garnet was the only one to know that Medora had been with child on her wedding day—and she promised she would never share this information with their sisters—he knew his two older siblings still considered Medora socially unacceptable and the marriage itself a serious error in judgment on Ingersoll's part.

Medora expressed a strong desire to return to New York State and visit the Oneida Community. Ingersoll said, "Out of the question," so his wife departed the room in an angry huff.

That unpleasant scene was followed by the moment Langley dreaded most.

Ingersoll turned to him with a gaze as pointed as a shard of glass to say, "All her prattle about 'Complex Marriage' and the Oneida Perfectionists is starting to make me nervous. I don't have anything to fear on that score, do I, Cam?"

"Whatever do you mean?" He forced a smile and hoped he did not look as nervous as he felt.

Ingersoll narrowed his dark eyes and angled his bearded chin ever so slightly in Langley's direction.

"Does she seek to practice what she preaches?"

The obvious accusation in his tone made Langley swallow hard though all his saliva had vanished. His muscles tightened to a painful degree and his nerves felt like burning wires.

"Alec, I consider you my brother in all but blood. I could never harm you, nor even imagine harming you."

"Brothers, yes." Ingersoll relaxed and lounged back in his chair. "Nature denied us brothers and so we found each other to remedy the deficit. I'm sorry I asked. It was foolish of me."

Langley returned his friend's warm smile and inwardly sighed with relief. If Ingersoll could but know that he, Langley, was striving to increase his friend's happiness by saving his marriage—but how would he ever explain that to him? To anyone?

CHAPTER TWENTY-EIGHT

Wednesday, April 28, 1875

Victoria lay in bed though she knew morning had arrived by the slender thread of sunlight that had found the break in the heavy, brocade curtains that otherwise darkened her room.

Her mind spun back to the astonishing courtroom scene of the previous afternoon.

When Mr. Oberholtzer had interrupted what she thought might be her final interview with his client to announce that the jury had returned, she had carefully replaced her veil to follow them to the courtroom.

Poor Mr. Ingersoll had looked pale as milk as he joined his lawyer on the journey to learn his fate. The hallways of this temple of justice dissolved into chaos as news spread like a prairie fire that the "Free Love Murder Trial" was about to be resolved.

Reporters raced along beside Lawyer Oberholtzer. Their efforts to elicit a comment were so audacious and intrusive that the policeman charged with guarding Mr. Ingersoll threatened to strike them with his nightstick to fend them off.

She noticed that they did not even bother to question the prisoner, knowing from several weeks experience, no doubt, that the stoic and dignified young man had not and would not speak to them.

Every spare body in the Cook County Criminal Courthouse tried to cram into the appointed room. Only the slight wave of

Mr. Oberholtzer's hand, signaling the marshals at the door, allowed Victoria entrance over so many others in the clamoring throng. She was ushered to a seat directly behind the bar of justice and in immediate proximity to the defense table.

He made a similar move to admit another woman who in turn sat next to her, though she did not seem aware of her presence. Victoria wondered who she might be. She looked to be about five-and-twenty years of age, comely in appearance though dressed severely in black taffeta with little ornament to her attire, probably a mourning gown. She wore her fair hair pulled back in tightly coiled braids at the back of her head and a small, not particularly fashionable hat, also black, sat perched atop her head. She clasped her gloved hands tightly in her lap and pressed her lips together as she stared fiercely at the back of Mr. Ingersoll's head.

So many persons in one room caused the April air to ripen and warm to an unpleasant degree. Electricity fairly crackled in the air as all rose for the judge's arrival.

The twelve men of the jury looked hot, tired, and distinctly ill-at-ease.

"Gentlemen of the jury, have you reached a verdict?" said the presiding judge, the Honorable Charles W. Crandall, a plump man in his middle years. He sported luxuriant side whiskers and a small mustache with his graying, thinning hair combed straight back from his broad forehead. Pince-nez spectacles perched on his upturned nose.

The foreman rose and answered in an uncertain voice, "More or less, Your Honor."

Judge Crandall frowned at this odd response to a question requiring a simple yea or nay.

Mr. Ingersoll exchanged a bewildered glance with his attorney.

Certainly everyone else in the room shared his feeling of

confusion. The clerk of the court took the sheet of paper from the hands of the foreman and transported it to the judge.

The judge read its contents and made a sour, disgusted face. He handed the paper back to the clerk.

"The defendant will rise."

Mr. Ingersoll did as he was told, but he could not keep his gaze focused on the twelve men who had decided his future. His breath came quickly and he looked still paler.

"Read it," the judge instructed the clerk.

"We, the jury," began the clerk in a level and lifeless monotone bred from reading countless verdicts. "In the matter of the People of Illinois versus Alec Ingersoll, on the charge of murder in the first degree of Mr. Cameron Curtis Langley, find the defendant—"

Everyone in the room seemed to simultaneously hold their breath . . .

"Not guilty."

The gasps and cries of the assembly rung out. The judge pounded his gavel for silence.

The young woman next to Victoria pressed her hands together in an attitude of prayer beneath her chin. Her lips silently moved as she shut her eyes tight, though tears forced their way out despite her efforts to contain them. Was she sending a prayer of thanks to the Almighty? What was her connection to this case? She and Victoria were the only females present.

Once order was restored, the clerk continued his task. "On the charge of murder in the first degree of Medora Lamb Ingersoll, we have not been able to reach a unanimous verdict and must regretfully report to the court that we are hopelessly deadlocked."

Even more chaos ensued; everyone looked about wondering what might happen next. Poor Mr. Ingersoll grasped the edge of the counsel table for support. He looked nearly unhinged by this pronouncement.

When order was successfully restored—but not before the judge threatened to clear the courtroom—Mr. Ingersoll was told he could resume his seat.

Judge Crandall tapped the fingers of his right hand upon his desk and rubbed his left upon his chin as he debated what to do. Several long and agonizing minutes passed before he spoke. Finally, he sighed and sat forward to make his remarks:

"In ancient days, it was said that a judge could place a jury in an oxcart and refuse to release them until they reached a unanimous verdict."

"Oh, dear God," whispered Lawyer Oberholtzer under his breath.

To answer the question posed on his anxious client's face, he whispered further, "No mistrial today."

Victoria looked to the prosecutor's table and beheld Mr. Jeremiah Lynch in more detail. A lean and tall man, even seated, his solemn, clean-shaven face now bore a creeping smile to replace the silent fury it wore after the "not guilty" verdict had been recited. He even cast a surreptitious look of victory over his shoulder at Mr. Overholtzer.

"In more recent times, judges have been given the discretion to deprive the jurors of food, water, sleep, even warmth in the winter," he continued. "But you, the good and reasonable gentlemen of our jury, need not fear such brutal coercion. I have no oxcart waiting on the street outside."

Some members of the jury smiled nervously at this.

"That being said, I must remind you of the importance and desirability of reaching a verdict in this case, provided, of course, that you can do so without sacrificing your scruples or personal convictions. You all took a solemn oath to this effect. I commend you for your ability to have reached a verdict on one of the charges and am therefore confident that you will be able to complete your task successfully.

"I therefore ask you to retire now, once again, taking as *much time* as is necessary for further deliberations upon the final issue submitted to you for determination."

With that, the judge and jury left the courtroom and the scene returned to its previous hectic state.

"Well, we're halfway home, my boy," said Mr. Oberholtzer to his client. "We can always pray they are deadlocked in your favor. Mr. Lynch over there has no right to gloat yet."

But as surely as he spoke a reporter shouted out from behind them, "Mr. Oberholtzer, is it true that all hung juries sent back to deliberate return a guilty verdict?"

"I've never heard that," he answered with a rueful wave of his hand, but his doleful countenance betrayed the opposite belief.

Mr. Ingersoll turned his attention to the young woman standing next to Victoria.

"I'll be all right, Garnet. Please don't worry about me."

Tears now ran freely down her flushed cheeks.

"Oh, Alec," she whispered as the officers pushed him toward the door to take him back to his cell.

So the concerned young woman was Garnet Langley. Victoria should have guessed that, remembering now Mr. Oberholtzer's comment that the lady had been residing with him and his wife during the trial.

She now appraised the girl's face with a different eye and saw a glimmer of resemblance between her and her late brother, thinking back more on the fanciful portrait from the mural wall of the Ingersoll nursery than the grisly photograph of the murder scene. She desired to introduce herself to her, but dared not reveal her identity in so public a place, rife with the local press corp.

★　★　★　★　★

A light tapping at her hotel door forced Victoria from the swirling thoughts of the previous afternoon to the present.

"Vicky, it's me. Open the door," came a most familiar and welcome voice.

She pulled on a dressing gown and opened the door. A similarly clad Tennie, bearing an armload of newspapers, hurried inside.

"If you've come to apologize for leaving me to my own devices for dinner last night, I have already forgiven you. Mr. Nostrils, as you so 'charmingly' call him, bought me dinner right here at the hotel." Celebrity may have its drawbacks but it was always good for a free meal.

"Well, he should be awfully happy you have agreed to support his case," said her sister, though she looked almost nervous as she sat down in a chair by the small fireplace with her bundle. "He'll owe you more than a fine meal when you win his case for him."

"What is it, dear? What brings you here at this hour?"

"I need to talk to you before you read the papers this morning."

"Oh, if it is about Mr. Ingersoll's acquittal in the death of his friend, Mr. Langley, I know all about it. I was in the courtroom when the verdict was read."

Victoria yawned and sat back down on her bed. She debated what to order for breakfast.

"He didn't kill him?"

Victoria shrugged. "Either the jury believed that the poor man took his own life or they decided that Mr. Ingersoll did dispatch him and—"

"—the no-good bastard had it coming?"

"Who knows?"

"That's not what I came to talk about, Vicky."

She wore her guilty-little-girl face. Victoria felt a qualm of apprehension.

"Promise you won't be too angry."

Victoria jumped up and confronted her. "Tennie, what have you done?"

Tennie hugged the newspapers tightly to her breast. Victoria feared she would smear ink on her lovely pale blue wrapper. It featured such exquisite tea-stained lace accents. "I had dinner last night with a nice young man . . ."

"Spare me the details of your amorous conquests. How would this concern me?"

"We had a lovely dinner and he bought champagne . . ."

"Oh, for heaven's sake, out with it."

"I may have said some things that were somewhat indiscrete. He knew you were staying here. I didn't have to tell him that. He just wondered why we stayed on in Chicago when you were scheduled to speak in Akron and Indianapolis this week."

She could see where this was heading. Only a reporter would have known that much about their movements. Probably someone from the Eastern press wanting more quotes about the progress of the Beecher trial, which she had been too occupied to follow this week. "What did you tell him?"

"Oh, a few things . . . like . . . maybe that you were helping Mr. Ingersoll and that you had an exclusive interview. And . . . that you had agreed to conduct a séance to learn the actual manner of those people's deaths."

"Great heaven almighty! Did you leave anything *out?*"

Her sister made a pretty grimace and whispered, "Not much."

Victoria sighed and shook her head. "Which paper?"

Tennie's words came out the mere squeak of a mouse, *"Chicago Tribune."*

"What was his name?"

She shut her eyes tight in the effort to recall the name.

"Nick . . . something or other. It's listed in the byline."

"I think I know the one. Tall, lanky fellow with freckles?"

Tennie nodded.

"He accosted me the other day in a restaurant while I was breakfasting with Lawyer Oberholtzer. He baited me over the cruel remarks Theodore was making about me on the witness stand back in Brooklyn."

"You mean the 'wit-*less* stand' in the case of our Mr. Tilton."

Instead of smiling at her sister's little joke, Victoria's thoughts returned to her immediate problem and she shook her head sadly. "You realize, don't you, that you have just ruined any chance we have of peace and quiet. And I was so enjoying it."

"Oh, don't cry Vicky." Tennie threw down her newspapers and rushed to her older sister's side, kneeling at her feet. "I can't bear to see you sad. And look on the bright side. This advance publicity will make everyone even more anxious to read your article when we publish it."

"That doesn't change the fact that our brief sojourn out of the public gaze is now over. Does anyone care that I am sick unto death from all these travels? One cold train car after another. Never sleeping well. Irregular meals, most barely worth eating. This has been the only decent hotel we've stayed in all year."

"We do what we can." Tennie cried now also. "The Colonel and I do try so hard to make your life easier. We'd give speeches, too, if anyone would pay us. But you are the one people long to hear speak. You are the only one blessed with that gift."

"I know I should not complain. I have been blessed in many ways. And I am grateful for it. And I know you both work diligently. It's just that these last two years—"

"I know, darling, I know." She patted her shoulder and kissed her cheek. "Uhm . . . while we're on the subject. I got a wire from the Colonel yesterday."

"He's speaking to you and not me, *his own wife?*"

"I guess that means you're still quarreling. Anyway, he wanted to know if you were going to make that stop in Terre Haute? If so, I'll need to leave today to meet him there for the advance work."

Victoria's tears of frustration gave way to a simmering anger. She wiped her wet cheeks and sat silently composing herself for some moments.

"So you are going to abandon me to swim alone in the shark pool of reporters who will accost me now? You, who created this little crisis. And I was so close to completing my work here with Mr. Ingersoll."

Tennie stood again and wrung her hands as she always did when anxious. "I suppose you can cancel Terre Haute. But, Vicky, we are so stressed for funds. Your speaking engagements are all that keep us these days. The *Weekly* hasn't made money since the Beecher Scandal issue."

Victoria drew a deep breath of resolve. "Go on to Terre Haute. I'll manage somehow."

"Oh, thank you, darling. You're as noble as a saint. And . . . maybe you should consider writing the Colonel? Mend a little fence—?"

"When *he* wants to apologize, he can contact *me!*"

Tennie issued a long and theatrical sigh.

Their stalled conversation was interrupted by a sharp knock on the door. They both looked at each other with surprise.

"It's too early for the maid. Surely the hotel wouldn't let up just anyone and advise them of my room number." Victoria approached the door warily and called through it. "Who's there?"

"Room service, Missus. Your breakfast."

She turned to her sister in confusion. "I haven't ordered yet."

She opened the door and a young man wearing a Palmer House uniform stood bearing a tray with the usual coffee service and covered plates, plus the always welcome fresh flower in a small vase.

"Where do you wish me to place it?" he asked.

She indicated the small table before the fireplace where Tennie had resumed her seat.

"I have not seen you before," she said as she reached for her bag to find a coin for him. He had jet black hair, heavily oiled, and a gold tooth showed itself every time he smiled, which he did a great deal of. Nice to have such a cheerful wait staff.

"Are you from England?" Tennie asked.

"Indeed, I am, Ma'am."

"It's 'Miss.' "

"My apologies."

He looked from one sister to the other, grinning but with an almost malicious edge. Victoria handed him a nickel and wished him to leave as soon as possible.

"I could tell by the way you talked," Tennie continued, unable to stop herself from flirting. Coquetry was so much a part of her nature, Victoria did not think she even knew she was doing it. "I'd like to live in England someday, I think."

"I much prefer the States, Miss. The 'Land of Opportunity,' as they say."

"Tennie, this man is busy. We must not detain him."

"Well, I must leave you now," Tennie said, pretending to sound sad. She flounced out the door as Victoria sat down near the fireplace to peek at the food.

The grinning, gold-toothed waiter did not pocket his tip, but rather flipped it in the air and caught it as though playing a game of Heads or Tails.

"I'm sure you must be going," she said to him sharply.

"Quite the contrary, Mrs. Woodhull. I got all the time in the world."

Such impertinence! No man would stay employed by Potter

Palmer and speak so freely to a female guest.

"Do you really work for the Palmer House?"

"As a matter of fact, I don't. A bloke loaned me his uniform with a little old-fashioned encouragement."

"Are you a reporter? Because if you are, I have nothing to say to you!"

"My name is Jackson 'Urley. I trust that name is not unknown to you."

She drew a sharp breath. Annoyance at having her privacy invaded gave way to alarm. Instinctively, she reached for the vase and pretended to sniff the flower's fragrance. She was determined not to show fear. That always worked with dogs at least.

"You're wanted for questioning by the police," she said in an even tone.

"Too late for that, eh? Trial's over, ain't it?"

His confident manner caused her even more distress. She gripped the glass vase tightly.

"They say in the papers that you're writing a story all about those awful murders," he said. "That you interviewed the murderer 'imself. Well, I'm 'ere to tell you that you don't know the whole story by 'alf unless you talk to old Jackie now."

"What information would that be?"

She mentally calculated the distance to the door, but he stood between her and that longed-for destination.

"Lots of information. I 'appen to 'ave known Mr. Cameron Langley quite well. We shared a flat back in New York and I know things about 'im that nobody else does. The stories I got could knock your socks off."

"What sort of stories?"

"The best kind: *scandalous* stories. Worse than anything they've put in the papers so far. Might even shed some light on what really 'appened."

"What do you want to tell me? Hurry up and then leave here!"

"Nothing is free in this life, Missus. I'll give you my information for the sum of . . . $500."

"I don't have $500."

"Well, maybe somebody else does," he said with a casual shrug. "I'm sure one of them other reporters would pony up for my story if you won't."

"No, don't do that. I'll find the money somehow."

"I'll be at the Pier at two o'clock, sharp. In the alley behind a tavern called Lady of the Lake. It's on River Street between Wabash and Michigan. Don't tell the police or you'll be *very* sorry."

"I won't come alone. I'll have to bring someone. Mr. Ingersoll's attorney? He'd have money, I'm sure."

He thought this over for a moment. "All right. Bring 'im. Nobody else, though." He made for the door and said with a cheery air, "Good day, Madam."

"What are you going to do?" Tennie asked as Victoria watched her pack her traveling valise.

A maid was at work making her bed on the other side of the room so she did not speak too loudly for fear the girl might be eavesdropping.

"Well, I want to talk to him, but I won't go alone, of course. I told him I'd have to bring Mr. Oberholtzer with me. I've already sent him a message. This man might have information that could exonerate poor Mr. Ingersoll."

"How can you say 'poor Mr. Ingersoll'? You said the jury just thought he was justified in killing that man. It still means he's a murderer."

"That's only what others are saying. I'm not at all certain anymore. I am very inclined to believe in his innocence. I would love to know what actually happened."

"Well, I've been thinking about that little problem I created and I believe I might have a solution for you, darling. This will certainly throw the reporters off your trail and you'll be at liberty to pass as an ordinary citizen once again."

"I'm willing to try just about anything," said Victoria.

"What if a lady wearing your clothing and your favorite veil—which, unfortunately, our Mr. Faraday described in detail, sorry once again—were to accompany me to the train depot, arm-in-arm, and we would depart for Terre Haute, bidding hale and farewell to all our little reporter friends? The false Vicky would get off the train at the first stop, of course, and catch a return back into the city."

"That's simply brilliant!"

Tennie stuck out her bottom lip. "Am I forgiven for my little blunder?"

Victoria teasingly frowned at her. "Almost."

They turned their attention in unison to the young maid now smoothing the bedcover.

"Girl, come over here," said Tennie.

"Yes, Miss? Is everything to your liking?"

The wide-eyed girl looked fearful that she had erred in some way.

"Just stand still for a moment." Tennie pushed her sister up next to the girl. Victoria was of similar build but an inch or so taller than the maid.

"I have some boots with a slight heel to them," said Tennie as she surveyed the two women with a critical eye.

"I don't understand," stammered the maid. "What do—"

"My dear, have you ever wanted to be an actress?" said Tennie. "Have you ever imagined being famous?"

"I don't understand," she said. "I . . . I'm not the sort that goes about with men—"

"Of course, you're not," said Victoria. "We need your help.

We need you to pretend to be me."

"Yes," said Tennie, all enthusiastic now. "All you have to do is put on my sister's veil and traveling jacket and get on the train with me. We will pay you well for this service."

"How much?"

"Five dollars?'

The girl gasped. "That's more'n I make in a week. When, though? I don't get off until—"

"I'll take care of it," said Tennie. "I will talk to your superior and everything will be fine. Now what is your name?"

"Anna McKee."

"Anna, are you ready to become Mrs. Victoria Woodhull, the most famous woman in America?"

"Oh, Tennie, really," said her older sister.

"It's true, Vicky. You're just being modest. They don't call you 'Queen of the American Lectern' for nothing."

Anna blushed and giggled.

Tennie smiled with glee to see her plan working so beautifully. Young Anna played her role well, keeping her teal green veil modestly in place as they elbowed their way through the waiting throng of reporters who had prowled the sidewalks of State and Monroe since the *Tribune* story had hit the streets before dawn. At least they were staying at a refined hotel where the doorman could be trusted to keep such vultures out of the lobby.

Anna was clearly not used to being the subject of so much attention. The poor girl squeezed Tennie's gloved hand tighter and tighter as they waited for the doorman to summon a cab.

"Mrs. Woodhull? Mrs. Woodhull!" came the ringing chorus from every direction.

"Gentlemen, please," Tennie pleaded. "My sister will speak to you in good time, but now is not that time! Ouch! Someone stepped on my foot. Shame on you!"

Anna placed her hand delicately to the side of her face to shield it from any of the men who pushed in close enough to catch a glimpse of her features through the heavy lace.

The newsmen continued their uproar, heedless of her remarks.

"She is not feeling well," said Tennie, trying another tack, "and you are undoubtedly making her feel worse!"

The doorman placed himself between the ladies and the swarm and helped them up into the hansom cab for transport the few short blocks to the Union Depot.

A couple of the reporters tried grabbing onto the outside of the rig, only to have the driver threaten them with his horsewhip if they did not disembark. He then snapped it over the head of his gray gelding and pulled away from the curb at a smart pace.

"Sorry, gentlemen," Tennie called out gaily to the crowd of two dozen men who now began to recede into the distance.

Anna shook her head slowly and tried to catch her breath. "How do you and your sister put up with that?"

Tennie shrugged. "We're used to it. It's all a part of the game really. To the extent that my sister is famous, she draws bigger crowds to her lectures. Those men play a large role in creating that fame."

Once at the station, Tennie managed to purchase two tickets at the window before the journalistic army arrived in pursuit.

"Oh no," Anna squealed as she caught sight of them and they caught sight of her. She tugged at Tennie's sleeve.

"Our train does not arrive for another ten minutes," Tennie said. "Let's go hide out in the ladies' lounge. They can't follow us there."

They successfully caught their train, but, of course, a few reporters climbed aboard as well.

Tennie kept them at bay by contacting the conductor and

telling him they were being harassed and that her sister was not feeling well. He made the men stay in their own seats and threatened them with ejection at the next station if they did not curb their voices and mind their manners.

As the train reached its next stop on the line, the Sixteenth Street Station, the two women excused themselves to the ladies' washroom in the next car and Anna successfully departed without catching the attention of any of the journalists who had nipped at their heels for the last quarter of an hour.

That is, all the men in the entourage save one who had lingered out of view of the rest. He stepped off the train a moment before it jerked into forward motion. He walked quickly to keep up with the woman in the teal green veil.

He followed her into the station and waited behind a pillar while she bought a return ticket to take her back to the center of the business district.

He watched her fan herself with a section of a discarded newspaper. Then she stepped outside onto the platform to catch some fresh air.

When she wandered nearer the tracks, he drew closer, carefully pulling his hat low to shield his face lest she turn suddenly and catch sight of him. The next train blasted its whistle as it neared the depot, but it did not slow down as it was an express, heading straight north on the closest track.

The milling passersby did not take any notice of the woman in the veil or the man casually nearing her.

"Mrs. Woodhull?" he said softly, but his voice was nearly washed out by the grinding steel wheels of the approaching train. A crack of thunder, harbinger of the coming rainstorm, further added to the din.

She turned in his direction, apparently having heard him above the deafening roar.

Chapter Twenty-Nine

With the summer solstice less than a month away, the sky stayed light until nearly nine. Flynn watched the sun disappear over the Western horizon. She remembered watching the sun set on the Pacific Ocean when she was a little girl. Her dad convinced her that the sea swallowed the setting sun and if she listened very, very closely, she would hear it sizzle.

She heard Matt stir under the rumpled sheets of the bed behind her.

"Did I doze off? I must have." He yawned and stretched. "You wore me out, Keirnan."

She smiled at his mock complaint, knowing he intended it as a semi-raunchy compliment, but continued to stare out the full-length window that stretched across the west side of the room. She looked down to see the cars below now had their lights on. There was still enough twilight to see the diners and shoppers hurrying this way and that, like busy ants.

"Did you think this would happen?" he asked. "You and me, ending up here?"

"Oh, no. If I had planned on this I would have worn much fancier underwear."

"You know, to tell you the truth, I don't even remember your underwear."

"You're right," she smirked, "they disappeared pretty quick."

"But I appreciate the sentiment, all the same," he said. "You know, you shouldn't stand in the window naked like that. People might be able to see in. You don't want to end up on YouTube."

"We're on the twelfth floor. I'm not too worried."

She turned to him with a new thought. "Cameron Langley said that same thing to Jackson Hurley. Do you remember? During the heat wave."

"Yeah, I do. Come back to bed. It's getting lonely over here."

She walked toward him, but her mind was still floating though 1875. "Do you think Cameron was gay?"

"What—you're saying that Cameron was queer for Alec? No. Well, maybe. It's hard to say, given that time period. In any case, the question would be beside the point. The word 'homosexual' didn't even exist until the end of the century. If Cameron was gay, he'd have been the last to think it."

"How do you know all this stuff?" she asked as she slid under the covers next to him.

"Sociology major. Never got to use it until now."

"Sociology, with a minor in French, then law school" she said as he pulled her into his arms. "I'm not sensing a pattern here."

"I don't think there is one. I tend to let the future plan *me*." He started to kiss her, then stopped, "Do we stay the night here or do we have to go home?"

"I *should* go home," she said. "I called them and said I'd be home late, but . . ."

She noticed the mischievous dimple returning to his cheek as he said, "The room's already paid for. It would be such a shame to waste it."

"And it's wrong to be wasteful," she said, pretending to actually debate the issue.

"And you'd be saving me from the trauma of having to eat breakfast with Mrs. Houston and the couple from Des Moines again. Think of it as a humanitarian gesture."

"Well, if I'd be serving mankind, how can I refuse?" They kissed again. She sat up and reached for her cell phone on the nightstand. Another awkward call home was in the offing. "Could we order room service tomorrow morning and eat breakfast in bed?"

"Anything you want is yours."

"Anything?" she said, looking down at him as she dialed home. She playfully arched one eyebrow. "Hmmm."

"Hmmm?" he asked.

"I'm making a list."

CHAPTER THIRTY

Wednesday, April 28, 1875

Lawyer Oberholtzer arrived promptly at one o'clock and met Victoria at the entrance to the Palmer House Writing Room. On any weekday, the place was a buzzing hive of Chicago commerce. Scores of top-hatted and derby-wearing businessmen from every trade and profession met to buy and sell and transact their business beneath the imposing gasolier, with its faceted globes beaming amber light in all directions like a hovering airship of dime novel invention. Victoria despaired that women were not welcome in that room. It would be such an enjoyable place to sit and write.

This afternoon, however, the industrious assembly looked a bit damp. The noontime clouds had now yielded their contents and poured forth. The raindrops tapping on the immense rotunda in the restaurant echoed like distant gunfire even in this busy area.

Franklin Oberholtzer looked breathless and anxious as he hurried to her side. She tried to calm her own nerves by slowly drawing several deep breaths. This trick usually worked in the moments before she was introduced on stage for a lecture. Who knew what sort of audience would be waiting in the alley by the pier?

"Good day, Madam," he said as he drew up along her side. "I came prepared for anything."

He pulled his large raincoat pocket wide and she peered in to see a pearl-handled derringer.

"Oh, dear me," she said, but was glad to have the protection of it. She hoped he knew how to use the thing. "Who's minding the jury watch back at the courtroom?"

"My partner, God love him," he said. "I've brought my own rig so we won't have to bother ourselves finding a cab in this weather, should we need to depart in a hurry. Just hope we won't have trouble finding a place to park it."

"And we are meeting with both Mr. Lynch and the Chief Constable at the courthouse?"

"Yes, they, too, are most anxious to speak with this man, though they hate to admit they might have erred in not looking harder for him before the trial. That acquittal on the Langley murder brought them both up short, to be sure."

They hurried out into the rain-soaked street. A boy held the lawyer's horse for him. He gave the child a coin and helped Victoria into the small buggy. Clear sheeting gave some protection from the storm on the sides of the carriage, but her skirt was exposed at her feet. Oberholtzer noticed this and pulled a bright woolen lap blanket out from behind their seats so that she could protect her garments.

"Alec has requested—no, I should say, demanded—to be present at the meeting, as well."

"That should help, shouldn't it?" she said. "He could no doubt give additional information on this Hurley character."

"I hope so," said the lawyer. "I was surprised by his insistence. He was behaving more like his old self than I have witnessed since the day of his arrest. I attribute all this somehow to your influence, Mrs. Woodhull."

"How so?"

"Don't know exactly, but since his talks with you, I think he has begun to emerge from the fog of grief and shock that has shrouded him from the day he walked into that accursed tower room."

"Well, I'm happy to be of help, though I have worked no magic on him. I do think that talking about one's problems is therapeutic."

"Perhaps so. That poor man was a wreck for the first week of his imprisonment. Could barely utter a word. I had him examined by a physician from the neurological department at City Hospital to see if he was even competent to stand trial. The doctor found him sane enough to meet the minimum standards—which are that he was capable of understanding the charges against him and able to aid in his own defense." Oberholtzer sighed. "I cannot agree with him on that last assessment. The doctor concluded that Alec was just suffering from severe melancholia brought on by the obvious grief. I tried to get the trial postponed until he could recover a bit, but the judge wouldn't hear of it."

"That seems so unfair."

"Indeed. Our Mr. Lynch was even less sympathetic. He said in the papers that 'a murderer damn well better be melancholic.' They edited out the 'damn,' of course."

"I have no regard for prosecutors who are politically motivated," she said with a grim irritation.

"Sounds like you have had many of your own difficulties in that regard," he said. "The Beecher matter, I am guessing."

He could tell by the bitterness etched into her face that she did not want to talk about it, so he quickly returned the conversation to its original course. "Well, I wish to thank you again for this gift, if I may call it such, of returning our Alec to the land of the living. He now actually seems interested in his own fate. Let's just hope he hasn't returned too late for it to matter."

They pulled up to the criminal courthouse and a liveryman

took charge of the lawyer's buggy while they hurried inside at the direction of a waiting constable. He led them to the offices of the Cook County prosecuting attorneys.

Victoria glanced about her and saw the large warren of offices filled with harried lawyers and busy clerks dashing about. Chicago must have an awfully lot of crime to keep so many employed, she thought.

The tapping of that splendid new device called a Sholes & Glidden "type-writer" was also adding to the cacophony reverberating through the halls of Chicago justice. She passed several and cast longing glances at them, wishing she could acquire one for the offices of *Woodhull & Claflin's Weekly*.

Mr. Oberholtzer guided her into the chief Prosecutor's office, which already held, in addition to Mr. Jeremiah Lynch, a tall, mustachioed gentleman who stood at the elbow of Alec Ingersoll himself.

"Alec? Already here?" said Oberholtzer, frowning.

Lynch rose from his desk abruptly and raised his hands. "He's only just arrived, Frank. I haven't said a word to your client. Have I, Ingersoll?"

Ingersoll shook his head.

"Well, thank you, Jerry," said Lawyer Oberholtzer in a voice dripping with sarcasm.

"Hardly recognized him without the beard," said Lynch, chuckling. The tall man at his side was the only one in the room to respond to the prosecutor's attempt at levity.

"Mrs. Woodhull," said Oberholtzer, "This is Mr. Jeremiah Lynch, our prosecutor, and James Barnes, the General Inspector of Police."

"How do you do, Mrs. Woodhull?" said the prosecuting attorney. "Perhaps we should have had a séance instead of a trial."

He chuckled again at his own attempted joke.

She bit her tongue to avoid responding to this taunt and

merely nodded to both gentlemen. She caught sight of Lawyer Oberholtzer squeezing his client's elbow to keep him silent as well.

As she was guided to a chair near Ingersoll, he rose to greet her. She offered him her hand to shake. He took it in both his hands as his wrists were manacled and chained to a leather belt about his waist.

"Jim, is this really necessary?" said Oberholtzer, indicating the manacles.

"If anyone's interested," said Ingersoll, "I had the opportunity to escape from the jail two weeks ago and chose not to. Doesn't that count for something?"

Lynch turned to Inspector Barnes, slightly horrified. "Jim, *again?* That's the third jailbreak since the New Year."

"My department is underfunded," said a defensive Inspector Barnes. "I went before the county commissioners just last week to plead for more money to hire extra staff. We do the best we can."

With a sour expression, Lynch gestured to have the restraints removed from the defendant. He complied and Ingersoll shook out his freed hands.

The group was now all seated except the Inspector who stood at Mr. Lynch's side, hovering like a guardian angel.

"This is the first time I believe I have been asked to investigate a crime *while* the jury is deliberating it," said Barnes.

"How goes that matter?" asked Oberholtzer of Lynch.

The prosecutor sighed with irritation and a put-upon expression. "The jury sent another note to the judge not an hour ago, still claiming deadlock. We told your partner, who said you were already on your way here. Judge Crandall, again, would not accept it."

Oberholtzer shook his head.

"Let's begin," Mr. Lynch continued. He gestured to a young

man with a notebook to enter. "I have asked that this clerk take notes of this meeting so that no one can claim anything improper issued from it."

Oberholtzer nodded his assent to this.

"Let the record here first show that this meeting was requested by the defendant and his counsel," said Lynch.

"Now, Mrs. Woodhull," said Inspector Barnes, "please describe the contact made by this man Hurley."

Victoria told of the morning visit and Hurley's request for money in exchange for information.

"Did he say what sort of information?" asked Barnes.

"I'm afraid not," she said. "If I recall correctly, he said his information *might* shed some light on the matter. He really gave no promises."

"Do you wish to tell us anymore about this man?" the Inspector asked Ingersoll.

"You don't have to answer that, Alec," said his counsel.

"No, I want to," said Ingersoll with determination. "Since Mrs. Woodhull is now involved, I want all of you to understand this man you are dealing with. I think he is quite dangerous and all precautions should be taken."

"Could you be specific?" said Lynch.

"Jackson Hurley was an enemy to both Cameron Langley and myself, but for different reasons. As you know from the trial, he was a roommate of Mr. Langley in New York for six months or so. They had a falling-out—over money, I think. I have strong reason to believe Hurley was blackmailing Cameron. He gave false evidence to the police and got Cameron arrested. I got the matter sorted out and I was furious with this man, Hurley, for what he did to my friend."

Ingersoll paused and looked uneasy. He asked for and was given a glass of water before he continued. "I did something then that was probably illegal."

The Inspector and the District Attorney leaned forward on this remark. Oberholtzer tapped Ingersoll on the shoulder and the two conferred in whispers before he continued.

"I called him out and I beat him up."

Both of the listening men relaxed with a disappointed is-that-all expression.

"I know that sort of thing is wrong but I was and still am glad I did it. The fellow was a thorough-going scoundrel and he had it coming. But that means he had ample reason to hate me and a wish to even the score. That is why he showed up at my house in February, I'm almost sure. The testimony of my housekeeper certainly indicated he was up to no good. And we—that is me and Mr. Langley—were quite certain it was he who burglarized my house the week before . . . before . . ." Ingersoll swallowed hard and looked at the floor for a moment.

Victoria felt a surge of pity for the poor man. He still had trouble putting the tragedy into words.

"Why didn't you tell the detectives who investigated the burglary about this man?" demanded Inspector Barnes. He held a file folder open and was obviously reviewing the record on the matter.

"I wish I had." Ingersoll wiped sweat from his upper lip. "Oh, God, how I wish I had. Cameron didn't want to. This Hurley character had some kind of hold on him. I never figured it out."

"Is it your belief that Hurley had something to do with the deaths of your wife and friend?" said Lynch.

"He's the only person on earth that either of us could label an 'enemy.' I have to wonder," said an increasingly distressed Ingersoll.

"Well, I'm going to post two of my best officers in plain dress in that alley out of sight," said the Inspector. "We'll see what he has to say to the two of you and then we'll apprehend him to question him further. Our time grows short here, gentlemen—

and lady. Mrs. Woodhull, are you still certain you feel comfortable doing this?"

"Yes, I've thought about it a good deal and I cannot imagine that I am in any personal danger from this man. He, after all, gained access to my hotel room this morning, disguised as a waiter. If he meant to harm me, he certainly had the opportunity then."

A uniformed guard entered at the behest of the Inspector to escort Ingersoll back to jail.

Before he exited the office, Mr. Lynch stood up and placed his hands on his narrow hips. "Frank, if I may?" He glanced from the defendant to his attorney and back again. "Ingersoll, why in hell were you not this cooperative and forthcoming *before* you were arrested for murder?"

Alec looked about the room from one face to the next and slowly replied, "I don't know. I . . . I was not thinking clearly, I suppose. In those first days, all I could see before my eyes was the dead bodies of the two people I loved most in the world and the only thought I held in my head was a desire to . . . *join them.*"

Mr. Lynch stared after him for several seconds following his departure. "Well, he may yet get his wish. But for a half-a-moment there, I almost believed he was innocent."

"That's because he *is* innocent, Jerry," said Oberholtzer.

"That's for the jury to say now, isn't it?"

The rain had abated by the time Victoria and Oberholtzer resumed their journey to the appointed rendezvous with the notorious Jackson Hurley.

"What if he asks for his money at the start?" Victoria said.

"I have a satchel containing fifty dollars and a bunch of stuffing. Hopefully that will trick him in to believing you brought his money. I must say, Mrs. Woodhull, you are the bravest woman I have ever had the privilege to meet."

"I just hope I can help. It's all a splendid adventure and a welcome respite from my usual routine. Constant travel can be so wearisome."

They progressed down Water Street after crossing the Chicago River yet again, negotiating the rain-soaked traffic of midday toward the appointed meeting location. Victoria found herself nervously clenching and unclenching the lap blanket that she now no longer needed while the lawyer muttered curses under his breath to the horse and the other drivers competing for space on the busy streets.

They passed Wabash and angled onto River Street at last. It formed a brief diagonal connection between Water Street and the end of Michigan Avenue where the bridge crossed the river again. The lawyer directed his horse into an alley one building up from the tavern called Lady of the Lake. The area was not very pleasant; certainly not a place to which a decent woman would venture alone. Oberholtzer located a young boy of ten or so and paid him to watch his rig.

Where did all these young boys come from? Why didn't they attend school, Victoria wondered, but New York was just the same, never a shortage of street urchins willing to earn a coin or two to run a message or watch a carriage.

The earlier rain had transformed into an ominous mist. A fog horn bawled out its mournful call to the ships on Lake Michigan to help safeguard their passage toward the harbor of Chicago.

"I don't see any officers," said Oberholtzer in a low voice, "but they were not to send ones in uniform anyway. Are you sure you still wish to pursue this, Mrs. Woodhull? No one would think less of you, should you decline."

"No. Let's just get it done and over with."

Arm in arm, they entered the alleyway behind the row of saloons that lined the street before them. No one seemed to be milling about at the moment, the noon rain probably having driven all the "alley rats," as the lawyer called them, into drier refuge. They stopped midway in the alley as far from the trash heaps and occasional privies as possible. Victoria still held a handkerchief to her nostrils to ward off a wave of nausea at the oppressive stench.

"Are we near the appointed time?" she whispered.

He drew out his pocket watch. "Two on the dot."

They stood and waited. Few sounds were heard at first other than the constant low din of horseshoes clopping against cobblestones on the main streets. As more persons began to notice that the rain had abated, laughter, voices, and an occasional song came through the mist from the street side of the establishments.

Both Victoria and her companion jumped like nervous horses when the sound of a back door opened onto the alley. Just a cook throwing refuse into the trash heap.

The cook returned to his kitchen and they both relaxed. She looked east and Oberholtzer kept lookout to the west. A couple of milling sailors could be seen a block away. One bent over and vomited while the other one held his hat. They took no notice of the nicely dressed man and woman who watched their movements.

"What targets we must be," said Victoria in a low voice.

"Indeed, I have no wish to tarry here." He glanced at his watch for the tenth time. "It's nearly 2:15."

"But why has he not come?" she said fretfully, knowing full well the lawyer had no answer.

Both froze at the sudden sound of a scuffle.

"You're under arrest!" came a shout from thirty yards down the alleyway.

"No, no, I haven't done anything, I swear it!" was the frightened answer.

Out from behind a tall pile of boxes, two men—presumably the plain-dressed officers—held a tall, thin, struggling man. One of the constables threatened to strike the man if he did not quiet himself enough to have the wrist irons applied to him.

"Mrs. Woodhull," cried the now-manacled young man. "It's Nick Faraday from the *Tribune*. We've met. In the Dearborn Café—remember? Please tell these officers who I am."

Victoria and the lawyer rushed over to the group.

"Is this the man?" asked the older of the two constables.

"No," she said with disappointment. "He is who he claims to be—a journalist. I've met him before."

She summoned her most condescending scowl for the reporter.

With frowning faces, the two constables unlocked the manacles from Faraday's skinny wrists.

The young man vigorously massaged his freed hands, then adjusted his wool tweed jacket.

"What brought you here then?" demanded the older constable in a threatening tone.

"Just following Mrs. Woodhull. Always a story there," he said with a cocky grin returning, now that he felt himself out of danger of arrest.

"Well, this just tears it," said Oberholtzer. "He'll never show up now. He's probably watching us and laughing as we speak."

"Who is?" said Faraday, his inquisitive blue eyes darting form face to face.

"None of your business," said the constable. "Get out of here before I arrest you for interfering with official police business!"

He gave the young man a rough shove.

"All right, all right." The reporter reluctantly moved on. When he was out of the range of the constable's nightstick, he defiantly added, "The people have a right to know!"

The younger officer shouted a curse in his direction as he retreated.

Once he was out of sight, the little group conversed.

"I don't think there is any need for us to remain here," said the lawyer.

"I agree," said Victoria with a sigh.

"We'll stick around for awhile," said the constable. "Just in case."

"Do you know what Hurley looks like?" she said. "He has black hair and a gold tooth."

"About how tall?" he asked.

"About the same height as you. He speaks with an English accent."

Victoria followed Lawyer Oberholtzer back to the side street where he left his rig. She carefully held her skirts a reasonable distance from the muck, negotiating that fine line between modesty and the vanity of preserving her hems and petticoats. The oppressive sky was now beginning to break up and the smell of the filthy street rose like a foul ghost threatening to smother her.

On the way back to the Palmer House, Victoria assured Lawyer Oberholtzer she would be fine staying alone and that he did not need to send Dolly, his plump, good-natured wife, to come and sit with her.

He guided his rig once again to the ladies' entrance of the Palmer on Monroe. A doorman hurried to help her down. She so enjoyed hotels that afforded female guests traveling alone the luxury of a private entrance so as to avoid unwanted male attention.

Just as she was about to make her final goodbyes to her companion, a young newsboy rushed up to the carriage shouting: "Read it here! Read it first! Mrs. Woodhull found dead!"

"What the devil?" said Oberholtzer.

As one in a daze, Victoria calmly pulled a coin from the little purse she carried at her wrist and handed it to the child in exchange for the paper. The lawyer pulled her back up into the carriage as both knew this evening was far from over.

She spread the "extra" edition of the *Times* on her lap and read the screaming headline:

THE WOODHULL KILLED!

CHAPTER THIRTY-ONE

Flynn yawned and stretched before opening her eyes. For a moment she was disoriented, but when she recognized the sounds of Matt showering in the bathroom she remembered she was in a hotel room on the Plaza.

She smiled to think what an unexpected pleasure yesterday had turned out to be. She immediately felt pangs of regret that Matt would be leaving soon to return to his life in Chicago. She wondered if they would stay in touch. Of course, they would *say* they would stay in touch, it was only polite; but whether they actually would . . . she did not want to think about that now.

She wondered what to order for breakfast. Before she could reach for the hotel phone at her bedside her own cell started braying its vaguely Oriental ringtone. Who in hell would have the nerve to call at this hour? Oh, wait, it was already half past nine.

"Hello? . . . yes, it is. . . . Oh, thanks for calling. I was anxious to talk to you . . ."

Matt heard her conversation and poked his half-shaved face out of the bathroom door with a questioning look.

She nodded at him vigorously while continuing to talk. "That's really interesting . . . yes . . . Could we? Is this a good number to reach you at?"

Matt left the door open and hurriedly finished shaving, then joined her on the bed just as she snapped her phone shut.

"How would you feel about a quick trip to Carbondale, Il-

247

linois?" she said, but couldn't help thinking Matt's devotion to fitness had really paid some serious dividends: even in the unforgiving shock of morning sunlight, he looked terrific. She quickly averted her eyes so he wouldn't catch her blatantly staring.

"That was our WOODHULL?"

"Yep. And you were right, it was a girl. She's a graduate student at the University of Chicago—a neighbor of yours, perhaps? Anyway, she's doing research for her thesis at Southern Illinois University because they're one of just a couple of repositories for Victoria Woodhull's papers. But she's actually bidding on behalf of a Woodhull memorabilia collector. A retired history professor named Blanche Adler."

"I guess that makes sense," he said. He got up and started collecting his clothes from various places around the floor. "I wouldn't think the average grad student would have that kind of coin."

"What do you want for breakfast? I was just about to place an order."

"Whatever you're having. As long as there's lots of coffee involved. Oh, by the way, I stopped at the desk when I came back from a walk and I picked us up a toiletries kit. The clerk gave me such a look—somewhere between a leer and a smirk. I felt so . . . slutty."

Flynn laughed. "You've already been out for a walk? I feel like such a slacker."

Flynn called in the room service order, then shared with Matt the rest of the conversation with the Woodhull girl. "She learned about the Ingersoll murder trial when she came across a bundle of notes in Victoria Woodhull's handwriting. Victoria was apparently going to write an article about Alec Ingersoll and the trial for a newspaper she owned, but apparently she never did. This grad student—her name's Jaime Finch—says she's read all the issues of this paper and the story isn't there."

"Good work, Keirnan. Nancy Drew would be proud."

"Anyway, do you want to come with me to see the archives in Carbondale?"

"Were you actually thinking of going without me? I'm hurt. I'm stunned." He gave her a mock pout before pulling his rumpled sport shirt over his head.

She chuckled at his clowning and headed for the shower.

They both nibbled at their last bits of toast as they simultaneously read Matt's computer screen. They had looked up a biography of Victoria Woodhull on the Internet.

Flynn was immediately smitten. She thought the woman ought to have been considered the patron saint of feminism. She was not only the first woman to run for president, but the first woman to address a Congressional committee, and the first to open a brokerage house on Wall Street—all this in an era when a married woman could not even own a checkbook in her own name.

She ran a radical newspaper with her sister Tennessee Claflin called *Woodhull & Claflin's Weekly,* which promoted equal rights for women and Free Love, and additionally was the first paper in the United States to publish Karl Marx's Communist Manifesto.

And Woodhull also professed to be in constant contact with the spirit world. Hmmmm.

"Does the spiritualism thing strike you as weird as it does me?" Flynn asked.

"I think it probably made a lot more sense in the 1870s than it does now."

"Yeah, you could be right. I read a little bit about spirit photography after I bought the photo and spiritualism was really big back then."

"Well, I just have to go back to Weston and pack up my stuff," he said. "Won't take me any time at all. Should we fly or drive?"

"Driving suits me. I don't think it's more than about six hours or so. We can drop off your rental car by the airport. It's right on the way. And I'll cover tonight's hotel," she said, aware that he had put last night's room on his credit card.

"Don't worry about it. This is all tax deductible for me. I'm researching my book, remember?"

"Uhm, well, okay," Flynn said as she wandered around the room looking for one of her flip-flops.

He packed his laptop computer back into his leather messenger bag and stood up. Then he sat down again. "You know, this room is still paid for until noon . . ."

She looked at his face with its hopeful smile and that faint suggestion of a dimple creasing his cheek and she immediately lost interest in finding her missing shoe.

"Is your dad going to be okay with this?" Matt asked just before they headed into the bookstore. "And . . . uh . . . your son? I guess I don't know the rules for dating women with families."

We're dating? Flynn wondered. "My son's going to probably be a lot cooler about it than my dad. Just a wild hunch, but I doubt he's going to be comfortable with the idea that his daughter spent the night with a guy she knew less than twenty-four hours. He's pretty Old School. Unless he's changed since my teenage years."

"Hey, it's Free Love. Just tell him Victoria Woodhull says it's okay. It worked for Medora Ingersoll."

"Medora Ingersoll ended up dead."

"You have a point," he said, grinning.

"You stay here. No use both of us getting in the line of fire."

"Sounds good. I'm a coward when it comes to facing irate fathers. He doesn't own a shotgun, does he?"

"Get out of here, Holtser."

"I'll go get checked out of the Sunshine House."

Flynn drew a deep breath and opened the door of Weston Books with its clattering jingle to announce herself.

"Hi, Dad."

Dan Keirnan looked up from his computer screen with a frown. "Decided to come home, huh?"

"Dad, I called twice. I left messages."

"That you were going to be out all night with a man you barely know."

Flynn tried a vague stab at humor. "I know him a lot better now."

"Do you think that's funny, because I don't. I could hardly sleep all night for worrying about you."

"But, Dad, I thought you liked him. You were practically shoving me in his direction. Don't complain that you got what you wanted."

"I didn't want you to *sleep* with him," he hissed.

Flynn glanced around the shop. They seemed to be alone. Why was her father whispering?

"Well, prepare to be further enraged: Matt and I are going to take a little road trip."

"What?"

"It's research. Purely academic. It's about the photograph. I've got to find out more. I want to know it all, before I make a final decision on whether to sell it. I have until Monday to call off the auction, before it officially ends. Anyway, I'll call Brody and square things with him."

Two women walked into the bookstore.

"Just be careful," he grumbled before he turned and forged a smile to greet his new customers.

Flynn texted Brody at school to call her on his lunch break. She

Michelle Black

was just about finished packing a quick bag for the trip when he called. Matt sat on her bed and watched as she spoke with her son.

She kept trying to make him understand why she wanted to dash off to a small college town in southern Illinois at the drop of a hat. He was obviously giving her some static. She finally lost her patience.

"Yeah, Brode, but you don't have to be a dick about it. It's a choice, you know?" She looked over and caught a surprised look on Matt's face. "Uh-huh . . . yeah . . . Okay, all right . . . Well, you never know, do you?"

She hung up and seemed happy with the outcome of the call. Then she saw Matt's odd expression. "What's with the look?"

He grinned in disbelief. "You called your son a 'dick.' "

She shrugged. "He knew he was being one. He just likes to yank my chain. Oh, and for the record, he asked if, now that I was 'getting some,' would I be less bitchy?"

Matt laughed in even more disbelief. "It usually works for me."

"You get 'bitchy'?" she teased.

"I don't call it bitchy. Let's just leave it at that." He grinned and kissed her on the cheek.

They walked out and Flynn got in her car while Matt climbed in his rental. He was still amazed by her phone conversation with her son. He didn't know whether he was more surprised by her remarks or the kid's.

After dropping off his rental car, they took turns driving east through Missouri and each spent the off time reading and researching on Matt's computer. He had a data card inserted so that he could pick up the Internet just about anywhere that had a cell phone tower in range.

Matt was curious about the Oneida Perfectionists. "They

were a utopian community in upstate New York that got started around 1840. The founder was a guy named John Humphrey Noyes who came up with, among other things, a concept he called 'Complex Marriage.' Every member of the community was to consider themselves married in every sense of the word to every other member. Forming exclusive relationships was frowned on and broken up by the governing body as being detrimental to the group."

"That must have been to control the jealousy and competition problems," said Flynn.

"I studied cults and utopian societies in a college class and the one thing they always had in common was a complete lack of individual freedom. You basically got with the program or you got out."

Flynn nodded thoughtfully as Matt continued relaying his information on the group that apparently gave the world Medora Lamb.

"Oh, you'll find this interesting, Flynn procreation was strictly controlled; nobody could have a baby without the permission of the group and guess who was expected to take full responsibility for birth control—the *men.*"

"That's gotta be a first in history," she said.

"Wow, this sounds *painfully* politically correct," said Matt as he read aloud: " 'The men were expected to practice a form of birth control called *coitus reservatus*—' "

"I've heard of *interruptus,*" said Flynn.

"This was different. 'Spilling' the guy's seed was considered 'wasteful.' Oneidan males were expected to just, well, not finish, not ejaculate at all. They also called it 'male continence.' "

"I think I'm starting to see why this community never caught on with the general public," she said with a cynical smirk.

"They were apparently experts at it because the group had very few unplanned pregnancies and a low birth rate, comparable even to the present day. You'll like this, though, 'interviews'—that's what they called having sex—lasted as long as an hour at a time, *quote:* 'resulting in increased sexual enjoyment for the female.' "

"Hey, that Medora Lamb was way ahead of her time," said Flynn.

"No shit. Young boys were only allowed to sleep with women who were post-menopausal until they could learn to control themselves. Oh, God, the thought of having sex with someone who looks like my grandmother . . ." He mock shivered. "And as you might guess, the old guys also felt it their 'duty' to initiate the young teenage girls."

"Well, some things never change." Flynn shook her head with a sour expession. "I wonder how many religions have been thought up solely with the hidden agenda of letting old geezers sleep with young girls?"

"More than a few, that's for sure." He continued, "The women wore bloomers—considered very radical—and everybody had their own private bedroom."

"Just like our photo friends," she said with sudden enthusiasm.

"Yeah, but I think the similarities come to an end about there." He continued to pluck information from various websites. "Children were raised communally in a huge nursery so that both parents were free to work at jobs. The community had numerous successful businesses and even employed people from the surrounding cities. They were the most financially successful of all the mid-century utopian groups.

"The party came to an end, though, in 1879 when their leader, Noyes, got tipped off that he was going to be arrested for statutory rape. He fled to Canada in the middle of the night and never came back. The community disbanded except for the businesses they started. Those continued on, independent of the social group."

"So the silverware company really was connected."

"Yep. Originally, at least."

Matt took over driving before they hit rush hour in St. Louis. They grabbed a quick and unattractive meal at a fast-food place off the highway, then headed south through rural Illinois toward Carbondale.

They arrived in the college town just after ten and checked into a little motel near the campus. Flynn was tired from the drive and crashed immediately. Matt was inexplicably wide awake.

He slipped out of bed without waking her, pulled his clothes back on, and went down to the empty lobby with its fake leather chairs and glaring wall sconces.

He wanted to continue reading *Mountain Daylight Time*, but was uncomfortable doing it in Flynn's presence. He knew he did not have any reason to feel that way; she had given it to him, for god's sake, but still, the remarks she made had left him wondering, tantalized by the possibility she was the "F. K." in the dedication, that she was the inspiration for the graduate student in the novel.

It was more than the coincidence of her past association with Holloway and her initials being the same. The remark she had made after reading the C.C.L. Notebook intrigued him in an almost queasy way. What exactly had she said?

That she "felt sorry" for Cameron Langley, that he was "caught in the crossfire between a crazy husband and wife."

Had a very young—and much less cynical—Flynn Keirnan been caught in similar complexity between David Holloway and his notoriously unstable poet-wife, Barb Yost?

Matt had surreptitiously read bios on both Holloway and his wife while they were driving through Missouri earlier in the day.

255

Barb Yost was Holloway's second wife: the young, beautiful trophy wife of his post-Pulitzer years. She had started out as his research assistant prior to their affair, his divorce from Wife Number One, and their eventual marriage. Hmmmm.

Holloway undoubtedly enjoyed the adoration of all those sweet, nubile college girls. He was good looking in his prime and there was the undeniable glamour that attached to a bestselling author. He was known to hang out with Hollywood stars who had portrayed his characters in films based on his books.

Matt entertained a fantasy of Holloway on the college lecture circuit. The guy must have scored like a rock star on tour. Probably could hand his room key to some lackey and tell him which girl to give it to. What a life . . .

Barb Yost died of lung cancer at the tender age of thirty-eight—just seven years ago. Holloway was said to have never recovered from her death and basically committed suicide on the installment plan over the next three years thanks to a prodigious appetite for Scotch. As Holloway, himself, might have put it, "Too much of a good thing is rarely a good thing . . ."

Matt's hyperactive imagination created his own explanation for Flynn's expensive car. She said she had "come into some money" a few years ago. He decided she got a bequest in Holloway's will. Flynn must have been Holloway's muse that summer she lived with him. She must have inspired the character in the book, the alluring, earnest young graduate student.

He had already ruled out Barb Yost as the role model for the character in *Mountain Daylight Time*. She had to be the inspiration for the freaky wife whose artistic success the husband character secretly, destructively envied. Plus, the affair with the graduate student in the novel did not end in marriage, as Holloway's affair with Yost had.

In fact, the further he read, the more he realized just how badly the affair did end. After a shocking night that was alluded to by the characters in the novel but never described, Holloway wrote:

She was up early despite the excesses of the night before. Actually, she hadn't slept at all and had finally tired of trying. She pulled on a tee shirt and her baggy cotton shorts and walked out to the kitchen.

She knew she would have to confront the culinary ruins of the birthday party. He and his wife certainly wouldn't deign to help clean up the mess they'd made.

It was even worse than she imagined. The sink was filled with dirty pots and pans from cooking the risotto and the baked salmon. The dishes sat in crusted stacks, the wine glasses and empty bottles hadn't even made it in from the deck yet.

The half-eaten birthday cake sat on the counter badly listing to one side, its icing now melted and dripping onto the colorful Mexican platter.

She curled her lip at the dried, decaying food that waited for her to attack. She decided to make some coffee first, liquid fortification for the nasty task ahead. She stepped out onto the deck to wait for the coffee to finish brewing. The chilly mountain air helped clear her head.

She was tired but not hung over. She had drunk far less than the others. She now regretted that. Didn't people who drank a lot forget things? That sort of amnesia would have been well worth a hangover, however painful.

The little beep from the coffee maker pulled her back inside to the foul-smelling kitchen mess. She poured a cup, took a quick couple of sips, then headed for the sink. Since the icing on the cake plates had now dried into cement, she debated whether to scrape them or soak them.

The sound of the water in the sink prevented her from hearing him shamble into the room.

"Sorry," he said when he saw her jump slightly in surprise. "Didn't mean to startle you. The smell of that coffee was a siren's song. Couldn't resist."

"Oh, good morning," she said but did not stop her work at the sink. The burnt remnants of the risotto must have been half an inch thick. His wife was the worst cook in the world.

"Everything okay?" he asked as he sat down at the breakfast bar, facing her back.

The sun was not yet up so the lights of the kitchen reflected everything in the room on the window over the sink. She lifted her head from her steamy task and could see him behind her without having to face him. He must have been reading yesterday's paper since she hadn't heard anyone go out to get this morning's edition.

"Sure, I'm fine."

"If last night upset you in any way, I'm sorry."

"It's okay. She said she wanted to do something really special for your fiftieth birthday and I can understand that."

He looked up from his reading, smiling a little incredulously. "She blamed it on me?"

She shut off the water and turned to face him.

"She said it was important to you."

"Shame on her." He chuckled as he shook his head.

"You mean it wasn't your idea?" She felt a sharp, almost painful surge of adrenalin barrel through her veins. Her cheeks flushed hot while her bare arms prickled with gooseflesh.

"She's had her eye on you for months," he said. "She gets these little crushes every so often. Doesn't bother me. It's easier to indulge her than to fight it. I knew she was high-maintenance when I married her so I guess I'm in no position to complain."

He made a vaguely shamefaced smile that said something in between What-can-you-do? and It's-really-no-big-deal.

"Has she known about us? This summer and before?"

He now looked less comfortable. "Well, yes. We have an open mar-

riage. Everyone knows that."

"*Whose idea was it for me to move in with you guys this summer?*"

"*Hers—if you want to get technical, but you know I'm fond of you, too. I'm sure that goes without saying.*"

Fond? Fond? *People are fond of dogs and hobbies. She spun on her heel and turned the water on again full blast. She resumed her scrubbing with a vengeance. The sun was now high enough in the sky to block the kitchen reflection and this was a comfort. She did not want him to see her face as she tried to blink back hot, angry tears.*

"*You okay?*" *he said.*

"*Sure.*"

"*You don't sound okay, sweetie.*" *He left his seat at the bar and sidled up behind her. He started massaging her shoulders. He rested his chin on top of her head.*

"*I just , , , uhm . . . I don't know how to tell you this,*" *she said.* "*You see, I won't be returning to the program in the fall.*"

His hands stopped their motion. "*You're not serious.*"

"*Yes, I've found another program on the West Coast. It's a little better suited to my needs. And they're giving me a scholarship. I just found out about it.*"

"*Which program? Stanford? Because if it's Stanford, I'm going to try and talk you out of it. That damned Marlin is always poaching my best students.*"

"*No, not Stanford.*" *Her mind raced to find another university, another program. It was useless, total brain lock. She stared at the soapy chaos in the sink as though it might yield up a plausible answer to dig her out of this new lie. She bit her bottom lip to keep it from trembling.*

He returned to his place at the breakfast bar. "*I hope you're not leaving because of us. Because of last night. That would be foolish.*"

She turned to look at him and her desperate eyes said, Do you have any idea how much I love you?

259

But his eyes weren't listening.

"Well, good luck to you," he finally said without bothering to look up from his day-old newspaper.

It ended just like that.

She abandoned the dishes and walked straight back to her room to start packing.

Matt snapped the book shut, uncertain what to think. It was nearly two in the morning and he sat alone in the silent lobby. Even the dozing desk clerk had vanished.

He slipped back into his hotel room and undressed as quietly as possible. He looked down at Flynn's sleeping face and once again wondered if she had been David Holloway's lover. That fantasy had initially attracted him—attracted him a lot, but now that he had read most of the novel he realized how little he really knew.

He leaned down and planted a tender kiss on her forehead. She stirred but did not wake.

CHAPTER THIRTY-TWO

April 28–29, 1875

"Back to the courthouse?" Victoria asked Oberholtzer once she had finished reading him the article below the shocking headline announcing her untimely demise.

"No, I think we should go to the main police station. That was where the officer who announced you were dead is located. I am afraid it is in a rather rough part of town. I seem to be giving you a tour of Chicago's worst areas today.

"The station is over on Polk at Wells—the very heart of our vice district. They said that this woman's body was found at the Sixteenth Street Station. That's not too far from there, actually."

A cold, sick feeling crawled through Victoria's veins as she suffered a terrible suspicion of whose body had actually been found, and why she had been misidentified as "Victoria Woodhull."

According to the newspaper account, the woman had fallen or been pushed off the rail platform and onto the tracks below just as an express train was barreling through the station.

None of the witnesses on the fateful platform actually saw her leave it but a scream was heard just prior to the train's arrival. Thus the police theorized that the unfortunate woman had not deliberately thrown herself in harm's way.

Oberholtzer and Victoria arrived at their destination just after four in the afternoon. The traffic was beginning to build for the evening departure from the city's center to the surrounding residential areas. The sun had broken through the clouds and now the chilly April afternoon felt slightly muggy. Once inside the busy police station, Oberholtzer asked to see the Lt. Schultz who was quoted in the newspaper article.

"Are you press?" said the front desk clerk. " 'Cause he's already given a statement about the Woodhull matter."

"I am Franklin Oberholtzer, an attorney, and I am here to introduce Lt. Schultz to this lady, *Mrs. Victoria Woodhull.*"

The clerk's eyes widened and a confused frown gathered on his formerly officious young features.

"I'm not sure I understand."

"Just summon the good Lieutenant, will you?"

"I'll take you to his office."

Lt. William Schultz was likewise dumbfounded after his own introduction to Victoria.

"I . . . well . . . I guess I must say I am relieved to hear you are alive and well, Mrs. Woodhull," he stammered.

"As am I," she said curtly.

"But the woman we found on the tracks—she wore a coat with the name 'Victoria Woodhull,' "

"—embroidered inside the collar," said Victoria. "That was indeed my coat, and my hat, and my veil."

"So you are saying this woman stole your garments?"

She sadly shook her head. "Actually she wore them as a favor to me." With a miserable sigh, she recounted the subterfuge that Tennie had concocted to fool the press corp. The trick had been quite successful with the notable exception of the tenacious Nick Faraday of the *Tribune,* who seemed to have the instincts of a bloodhound when it came to following her.

"Well, that would explain the age problem," the lieutenant said. "The woman's body seemed to be that of a girl of no more than twenty. No offense, Madam, but we were under the impression that the Mrs. Woodhull we all read about in the papers was a . . . well . . . somewhat more mature woman."

"Yes, yes, I am thirty-six years of age. No need to dance around it."

"Do you know the young woman's name?"

"Anna . . ." She had to think a moment. "Anna McKee, if memory serves. She was employed as a maid at the Palmer House Hotel."

"Do you have a motive for the killing, Lieutenant?" asked Oberholtzer. "If killing it was?"

"Well, actually, no. I'm hoping you might help us on that one. One minute she was waiting for the train, the next she was on the tracks. Has anyone made any threats against you, Mrs. Woodhull?"

"No, none of a violent nature. At least not in the last year or so." Her biggest enemy was the Reverend Henry Ward Beecher and those who worked at his behest, but she did not think him capable of violence. Anthony Comstock was happy to torment her with the laws that he, himself, had instigated, but that did not involve a physical threat.

Joseph Treat, once a contributor to the *Weekly,* and now an opponent of her views, had published a scurrilous pamphlet denouncing her with all sorts of libelous invention, but only trying to discredit her, not occasion her death.

"You are a highly controversial speaker, are you not?" said Lt. Schultz.

"True, I've been called every shocking name in the English language at one time or another—such is the price of controversy—but I have never had any weapon but words used against me."

"Assuming the young woman in the morgue is this Anna McKee, would you—I hate to ask this, given the gruesome condition of the body, but would you be willing to identify—?"

Victoria made a desperate face to Frank Oberholtzer, who responded quickly. "Out of the question. Mrs. Woodhull has suffered through an immensely difficult day. Could you not prevail upon the maid's supervisor at the Palmer House to do this unpleasant duty?"

"Yes, that should not be a problem."

Their meeting with the Lieutenant was suddenly invaded by the Chief Inspector himself.

"Inspector Barnes," said a startled Lt. Schultz as he jumped up to greet his superior.

"Good day for a second time to you, Mrs. Woodhull. I heard these reports of your 'demise' and knew at once they were false. The girl's accident occurred an hour before we had our little chat at Mr. Lynch's office, it seems."

"The deceased was wearing Mrs. Woodhull's garments, Inspector. That's why she was misidentified. We must now consider whether Mrs. Woodhull was the actual target of the attack. That is, if she was indeed pushed. It might have been an unfortunate mischance, a wrong step, or perhaps she was inebriated. The autopsy may yield some answers."

The Inspector folded his arms across his chest and sat upon the corner of his subordinate's desk. "It's possible, I suppose. A pity this Hurley character never showed up for that meeting. My officers think he might have been scared off by the arrival of some stupid reporter."

This idea was mulled about between them for several minutes. Ultimately, Inspector Barnes decreed a guard should be placed on Victoria, both to protect her from a possible assailant and to apprehend Jackson Hurley, should he try to make further contact.

"And let's not release any information to the press about this misidentified corpse for at least twenty-four hours," said Barnes.

"If someone did try to kill you, Madam, you might be safer if he thinks he succeeded."

All nodded assent to this plan.

An emotionally exhausted Victoria Woodhull and Franklin Oberholtzer finally headed back to her hotel. She asked only that they make a quick stop at the nearest Western Union office so that she might wire her sister and husband to advise them she was alive and safe, lest they hear otherwise should the erroneous report leave the confines of Chicago.

A large man wearing the uniform of the Chicago Police Department rushed to meet them in tandem with the Palmer House doorman when Oberholtzer pulled his rig up to the ladies' entrance once again. The policeman indicated to the doorman that he would handle the guest and immediately introduced himself as Sergeant Mills.

"How do you do, Mrs. Woodhull? Allow me to assist you in any way I can," he said. He tipped his cap to both Victoria and her companion.

"You'll take good care of this fine lady?" said Oberholtzer, as Victoria stepped down to the sidewalk.

"Absolutely," said the refined-appearing officer. "I've served in this capacity for nearly ten years. Since I left the Army. No one has ever come to harm on my watch, Missus."

"That's reassuring," she said.

Oberholtzer bid her good evening, but did make one request prior to his departure.

"A young person, Miss Garnet Langley, is most anxious to make your acquaintance, Mrs. Woodhull. She has been residing with me and my wife for the duration of Alec's trial. I did not tell her of your involvement initially, but she read it in the papers this morning, like everyone else, and she begged me to set an interview."

"This would be the sister of the deceased Mr. Langley?"

He nodded.

"I would be happy to meet with her. Tomorrow morning, perhaps?"

"May I drop her off on my way to court, just before nine?"

"Yes, fine."

Her uniformed escort took his place at her side as they entered the hotel. They crossed the lobby to reach the stairs, but not without noting the presence of the relentless Nick Faraday of the *Tribune*.

Her blood fairly boiled at the sight of the man whom she now blamed for the events that may have inadvertently resulted in the murder of an innocent young girl.

"Well, if it is not the ubiquitous Mr. Faraday," she snapped as he approached somewhat more meekly than before.

He pulled off his bowler and formally nodded, enduring not only her icy glance, but the slightly menacing presence of her new bodyguard.

"Good evening, Mrs. Woodhull."

"Are you happy with the misery you have wrought by revealing my presence in this city?"

"I was just doing my job, Ma'am, to my best understanding of it. I confess I do not understand why they are reporting your death occurred at noon today, when I know that is not the case."

"Someone tried to murder me, Mr. Faraday. An innocent young woman has now lost her life in my stead. Are you happy now that your journalistic endeavors have gotten someone killed?"

"I . . . don't know what to say."

"Will you at least do me the kindness of keeping my continued health a secret for the next twenty-four hours? The police wish it so to protect me from menace and secure the felon responsible. Can you do me that *courtesy* or do you want another death on your conscience?"

"No, Ma'am. I mean, yes, Ma'am, I will not print anything for twenty-four hours."

A sharp rap on Victoria's door at eight forty-five the next morning brought the expected news that Lawyer Oberholtzer waited for her in the Grand Parlor with his guest in tow.

She was fully dressed and awaiting their arrival. She strode down the stairway instead of using the elevator as she chafed from a lack of exercise. Sergeant Mills was in discreet attendance, making his presence known but not intrusive. He was a true professional at his duty, she could tell.

"May I present Miss Garnet Langley?" said Oberholtzer.

"I'm so pleased to meet you, Mrs. Woodhull," said the young Miss Langley in a high, girlish voice.

She was dressed in the same manner as the other day when Victoria had first observed her in the courtroom. Her fair hair was again tightly bound in a braid at the back of her head. Almost invisible blond lashes ringed her large, pale blue eyes. She carried a flat parcel wrapped in a scarf of some sort.

"The pleasure is mine," said Victoria, taking the young woman's hand and shaking it warmly.

"Well, I must depart for the courthouse, I'm afraid," said Oberholtzer. "Resume my vigil, should the jury make their decision, at last. I will take my leave, with your permission, ladies. Miss Langley, do you need fare for a cab to get home?"

"Oh, no, Mr. Oberholtzer. Your wife has written down the street car lines and I will be able to find my own way."

"All right, then. Good day to you both."

When the lawyer departed, the two women settled into the comfortably upholstered chairs in the Palmer's Grand Parlor. A waiter came by and asked if he could be of service. Victoria and her young visitor requested coffee and pastries.

"I am so gratified that you agreed to meet with me, Ma'am," said Miss Langley. "I have a favor to ask, I am afraid. I know it is presumptuous of me to be asking favors of one I have just met but the circumstances, being so extraordinary—"

"Hush, now, Miss Langley. We need not concern ourselves with the niceties of societal rules. These times are rather more than 'extraordinary,' nay, I would term them dire." The girl placed her curious package on her lap and clasped her gloved hands together at her breast.

"Indeed," she cried. "You understand fully. I knew you would."

The waiter brought the silver tray and poured their coffee in the lovely Palmer House china cups. Every item on the premises bore the proud, wreath-enshrouded Palmer "P."

"Now what might this favor be?"

"Well," said Garnet, setting down her cup. "I would ask that you take me with you the next time you visit Alec. You see, he would not permit me to visit him in the jail. He said it was a terrible place and that I would see and hear things unwholesome and inappropriate for a lady such as myself."

Victoria could not help but chuckle. "I suppose this means he does not think me a 'lady.' "

Garnet made a face of horror at her unintended faux pas. "I did not mean to imply that, Mrs. Woodhull. You are . . . you are more . . . worldly than I. That's all. Alec still thinks of me as a child. A child leading a cloistered existence in a tiny house on a quiet street in Brooklyn. But would such a 'child,' who had never even ridden a train alone before, have traveled one thousand miles to come to his defense and testify in a public court of law?"

"Of course not, my dear. Mr. Ingersoll is fortunate to have friends such as you. I am certain he just longed to protect you, as he said, but it also may be that it hurts his pride to have someone he esteems see him thus. The calamities that have befallen him have not robbed him of all his vanity, you see."

"Perhaps that is true," she said, thinking the matter over. "But I sat through much of the trial, after my testimony was given. Some terrible things were said there. Those vicious servants of theirs made the most awful slanders against my brother. Well, anyway, that is not the point. I simply must see Alec."

"If Mr. Ingersoll is allowed to refuse visitors, how can I help the matter?"

"He won't refuse to see you. I'll simply tag along. Would that be possible?"

"Well, we can but try, can't we? Shall we leave directly for the jailhouse?"

"That would be wonderful," said Garnet.

"Let's send a note in advance, alerting him of our—I mean, *my* impending arrival. Actually I did have one more matter to discuss with him before the séance."

She still wondered what produced Ingersoll's belief that he had done something shocking that inspired his wife and friend to take their own lives. Before he could reveal it, their last interview had been interrupted by the sudden return of the jury that afternoon.

She remained curious because up until that point in his narrative, he had claimed that he had adjusted to the idea of a Complex Marriage and had even begun to enjoy it. What could possibly have changed?

"I am afraid we will not travel alone, Miss Langley. I have a very large shadow at the moment."

She threw a casual glance in the direction of Sergeant Mills who stood twenty yards away, near the large columns at the entrance to the Grand Parlor.

269

"Mr. Oberholtzer told me that the police are guarding you. I will feel doubly safe now."

"I don't think they are guarding me so much as they are using me as bait to try and catch a villain named Jackson Hurley."

Young Garnet's face darkened at the mention of the odious name. "Oh, that horrible man. Mrs. Woodhull, do you think he is responsible for my brother's death? And for the attack on the woman who pretended to be you?"

"Well, he is certainly an unreliable character. Up to no good, as it were."

Garnet's face twisted with worry and she looked on the verge of tears. She finally was able to spit out the words that tormented her: "My sisters are the reason he came here to Chicago."

"What do you mean?"

"He came to our house, looking for Cameron. He claimed my brother owed him money. Opal told him where he was living. In Opal's defense, she did not know as much as I did about Jackson Hurley and the reasons for my brother's arrest. But the damage was done before I could stop her.

"She just said, 'Let Alec Ingersoll deal with him.' She was angry at Alec for convincing Cameron to move to Chicago. She conveniently forgot that if Alec had not rushed back to New York and saved Cameron from the trouble he was in . . . well, anyway, it doesn't matter now, I guess."

"I don't know, dear." She reached over and patted the girl's arm.

Victoria left her to retrieve her traveling cloak and hat from her room. She sighed at the loss of her favorite coat but then immediately felt a pang of remorse at the horrible fate of the young girl who had donned it so innocently.

Sergeant Mills squeezed into the seat next to the driver of the taxi and the two women were off to the jailhouse for their meeting with Ingersoll.

"You have known Mr. Ingersoll a long time, have you not?" Victoria said to make conversation. A chilly sun shown on them and they both pulled the lap blanket over their skirts for warmth.

"Oh, yes, more than ten years," said Garnet. Her face brightened noticeably whenever she spoke of Alec Ingersoll. "I'll never forget the first moment I saw him. I was just fourteen at the time. Cameron was bringing him home on Christmas leave from the Army. I thought he was the handsomest man I had ever seen." She blushed and ducked her head. "I was quite a romantic young girl."

"We all are at fourteen," said Victoria, smiling somewhat sadly. She had thought the same of Canning Woodhull when she was that very age. He was a handsome, twenty-eight-year-old doctor who had cured her of an illness. How eagerly she had assented when he proposed to her. How horribly deceived she had been.

"I remember our mother lecturing us girls before the boys arrived. She said we must be kind to Alec because he was an orphan." She began to giggle at the memory. "When she said the word 'orphan,' I thought of Oliver Twist, not a grown man of eighteen in a military uniform."

Garnet paused, then asked, "Did Alec tell you how he lost his parents?"

"No, I don't believe he did. He just indicated he had been raised by a rather stern grandfather."

"It was a sad story. I am not sure if he ever told it to anyone but me. Cameron never mentioned it. Anyway, they were killed in a carriage accident. Alec was with them. The horse bolted and his father lost control of the rig. Alec was eight at the time and riding in the back. It was open, you see.

"He was thrown free when it overturned. He said he had

some scrapes and bruises but not so much as a broken bone. His poor parents were not so lucky. They were crushed beneath the overturned carriage. All he could see of them was his mother's hand sticking out from under the wreck. He had to wait more than an hour for someone to happen by and help. Can you imagine what that must have been like for a little boy?"

Victoria placed her arm around the girl's shoulders in a sign of sympathy.

"He told me he spent all that time holding his mother's lifeless hand and praying," Garnet continued. "He promised God that he would be a very, very good boy if God would only spare his mother. Then Alec said the most shocking thing—though if you know Alec, you would expect as much. He turned to me with that disturbing, self-mocking smile of his and said, 'I guess God had better things to do that day.' "

"I know the look you speak of. I observed it numerous times over the last few days. The tragedies he has endured have left him cynical."

"I'm afraid so."

Ingersoll had already been moved to "The Cage" for the meeting when the two women arrived at the jail. He rose from his seat at the table to warmly greet Victoria when she entered the barred room. His smile immediately transformed to a look of distress when he beheld her companion entering next.

"Garnet, I didn't want you to come to this awful place."

He nonetheless embraced her and placed a kiss upon her brow.

"Alec, I've never seen you without a beard," said Garnet, looking up at him, but still clutching her mysterious parcel to her breast.

"The awful truth is finally revealed," he joked. He self-consciously rubbed his clean-shaven cheeks. Only long side-whiskers remained to bracket his strong jaw. The vacancy of the beard still marked his skin with its comparative paleness to the remainder of his face.

"I think you look quite fine," said Garnet.

They all sat down around the work table and Ingersoll asked what brought them here.

"Alec, may I attend Mrs. Woodhull's séance?"

"I suppose," he said. "I just wish *I* could."

"Perhaps you will," she said. "The jury will acquit you and then you'll be free and—"

The young woman ran out of words. Everyone felt a bit awkward for a moment.

"Will you be conducting it tonight, Mrs. Woodhull?" he asked.

"I hope so. Mr. Oberholtzer will need to get permission from the police to re-enter your house on Prairie Avenue. I think that the tower room would have to be the best location."

"If I were a ghost, that's where I'd haunt," he said sourly. "Oh, I'm sorry Garnet. My awful sense of humor—you must forgive me. Living with my current felonious companions hasn't improved me in any way. I'm liable to start swearing and spitting on the floor under their tutelage."

"Oh, hush now, Alec," said the young woman, blushing. She was so obviously in love with Ingersoll, Victoria doubted he could do anything to upset her.

"Mrs. Woodhull, what has become of our Mr. Hurley? Do the police have any idea?"

"None, I'm afraid. Though I think the interference of a local reporter yesterday might have frightened him off from our meeting."

"And what was this about you being reported dead? Frank sent me a message last night to assure me the reports were quite false. Thank God."

"Thank God, indeed. Yes, I was not the victim but another

unfortunate woman. My sister and I hired her to wear my clothes to fool the press into thinking that I had left town. I feel so terrible about it. They cannot rule out the possibility that I was the intended victim and she was killed in my stead."

"That's terrible," said Ingersoll, his face wrought with concern now. "Perhaps you should leave the city for your own safety. I certainly never imagined my inviting you here would place you in danger."

"I plan to leave as soon as we have completed the séance, but do not fret for me. They have assigned me a guard."

He sat back in his chair with his arms folded across his chest, somberly considering the new information.

"Alec," Garnet suddenly announced with renewed enthusiasm. "I want to give you something."

She set her parcel on the table and removed the scarf that cloaked it.

"I think this might be the only one of Medora's photographs still in existence," she said.

When Ingersoll looked at the picture, he gasped, then clapped his hand over his mouth.

"Oh, my God," he whispered, staring wide-eyed as though to convince himself of the item's actuality.

"Cameron sent it to me as a Christmas present last December, but I want you to have it."

"Oh, Garnet, however can I thank you for this?" he said, still staring at the picture in wonder. His eyes now glistened with tears.

Victoria smiled at this tender scene. She rose from her seat and walked around the table to get her own look at the photograph that had pleased the grieving man so.

When she beheld it, she was motivated to gasp herself, but for markedly different reasons. She stared at the photograph and shivered with a strange and disturbing confusion.

The picture was a group portrait of the trinity now embroiled in the present tragedy. A traditional portrait of Medora sat in the middle of the composition, while the transparent, disembodied heads of her husband and her lover floated above her, seeming to emerge from spectral clouds.

"Garnet, are you certain Medora Lamb took this photograph?" she asked.

"Yes," she said with a casual confidence.

"I remember posing for this," said Ingersoll, likewise convinced. "She did lots of these. She called them her 'ghosty portraits.' Why do you ask?"

"But how did she take a picture of herself?" said Victoria.

"You can't see her hands in the frame, can you?" said Alec, "Just her shoulders and head. That's because she held the cable release that operated the shutter on the lens in her lap."

Victoria did not follow this technical mumbo-jumbo but pursued her questions. "How did she make your face and Mr. Langley's appear above her like that?"

"Cameron described her method in detail," said Garnet, "in the letter he sent with the picture. He watched her create it. He even assisted. There were numerous steps involved in the process."

"She tried to describe to me how she developed the technique, but I did not fully follow all of it," said Ingersoll. "She discovered it by accident. I know that much. She used to clean the plates for the photographer who tutored her so that they could be reused.

"She did a poor job of it one day and noticed she could still see a faint image. She got the idea to re-coat the plate with the collodion in some areas and not others. When she re-exposed the negative, she had two images, one strong and the other faint. Then she would go in with a paintbrush, using mercury, I think, and add that cloud-like detail. Then she would print the image on the albumen paper."

This was almost incomprehensible to Victoria as she did not have a background in the mechanics of the photographic profession, but the similarity of this "trick" photograph to those of Bertrand Norris's "spirit" photographs was simply too close to be a coincidence.

"What troubles you so, Mrs. Woodhull?" said Ingersoll.

"The style of this photograph is so remarkably similar to that of a local photographer, a Mr. Bertrand Norris—"

"Ah, Norris," repeated Ingersoll. "That was the instructor I hired to teach Dora photography. A silly gentleman. I still smile to think you feared that I was jealous of him."

"Mr. Norris has requested that I give evidence in his favor," she said. "He has been accused of defrauding his customers, claiming he could summon the spirits of departed loved ones and photograph them. I thought his technique seemed perfectly legitimate. That is . . . until I saw this picture. Are you absolutely certain your wife created this?"

"A spirit photograph, you say? Dora never called it that, but she most certainly created that picture you hold. And the subjects of her portrait were all quite alive at its creation," said Ingersoll, grinning. "I can vouch for that."

"But this is incredible," said Victoria, still examining the photograph in disbelief. "This style is unmistakable. Mr. Norris is going to have some explaining to do."

"How curious," said Ingersoll.

"And you say she *invented* this technique?" Victoria persisted.

"Yes," he said. "Is that fool claiming that *he* discovered it? I wish I could sue the bastard. Pardon, my language, ladies."

"I am going to have to confront this man," said Victoria firmly. "I think now that he really is the fraud they claim him to be. Men like him give spiritualists such a dreadful, unwarranted black eye."

She carried the photograph with her as she paced about the little room and tried to resolve how to deal with Norris. She would at least give him a chance to defend himself, but she would inform him that she was more likely to give evidence *against* him than in his favor. Let the consequences be what they may. As the president of the American Spiritualists Association, she had no choice but to expose him.

"I know this picture is very special to you both, but may I borrow it for just an hour or two?"

"Absolutely," said Ingersoll. "That ridiculous man needs to be taught a lesson. To use Dora's cleverness to trick and defraud people infuriates me. I just wish I could accompany you."

Garnet seemed distressed. "Well, it's just that—"

She looked at the photograph with great anxiety. Obviously she did not feel comfortable with it leaving her control.

"Would you accompany me, Miss Langley? I will probably need your knowledge of the photograph's history to refute any defense Mr. Norris attempts to mount. I warn you, he is not going to be happy about this. He's being sued right now and he may even come under criminal indictment."

"Yes, Garnet, please help Mrs. Woodhull. This man needs to be stopped. I never liked him anyway."

The moment came for reluctant farewells. Ingersoll tenderly embraced Garnet and pressed her blond head to his chest.

"I know I asked you not to come, but now I am so glad you did."

"I'm praying for you, Alec." She looked up into his face. "I know the jury will—"

"Hush, now. Don't fret over me. Once I learn the truth from Mrs. Woodhull's séance tonight, I'll be at peace. Let the jury do their worst. Know that I will be at peace and resigned to—"

This was the wrong thing to say. Garnet burst into tears.

"Don't talk like that," she sobbed. "It's bad luck."

Alec threw a pleading look to Victoria over the girl's head, as he tried to comfort her.

"Come, dear," she said and gently pulled Garnet from Ingersoll's arms. "Let's get this nasty business with Norris behind us so that we might prepare for the séance tonight."

CHAPTER THIRTY-THREE

Flynn and Matt waited outside the Morris Library for the arrival of Jaime Finch, the Victoria Woodhull scholar. She arrived only ten minutes late.

Jaime looked like a grad student, no more, no less, in Flynn's estimation. She wore no makeup and her hair—dark blond with one purple streak—was pulled back into a messy ponytail twist. Flynn must have seen a thousand girls just like her on the college campus where she used to teach.

She did not miss them. Ever since crossing the invisible threshold of age thirty-five, these girls had started to seem more like Them than Us. Not exactly sexual competition in that she felt she had semi-retired from that field of battle, but more a silent reminder of what she wasn't anymore and she had trouble letting that go.

But what was "that" anyway? She couldn't define it. It was more than a simple matter of chronology. But, for example, would a guy like Matt have given her a second glance if he had not been tantalized by the possibility she had once been David Holloway's lover?

Granted, that resume was a tad more respectable than, say, being the former groupie of a dead rock star, but she still didn't care to trade on it. She had some pride.

Flynn used her notebook to fan herself. Southern Illinois in May was even warmer and more humid than Missouri. By ten in the morning the air was uncomfortably sticky. Jaime Finch came dressed for the weather, which was to say she wore as little as possible. Her extremely abbreviated cut-off jeans showed off long, slender, albeit pale, legs. A double layering of pastel cotton tank tops completed the ensemble.

Matt looked like he was enjoying the view. Well, why shouldn't he? Jaime was pretty in that Plain Jane, serious-girl graduate student fashion. And she was young. Twenty-two, twenty-three?

All of these arcane thoughts ricocheted around Flynn's brain when she should have been listening to Jaime's spiel on the Woodhull papers and the rules associated with viewing them inside the Special Collections department.

"What do you think, Flynn?" Matt turned to her for a verdict.

"Uhhh." She'd been busted again for not paying attention—a problem that had plagued her since grade school.

"We're going be here more than one day, right? So it makes sense to buy the week's pass rather than pay by the day."

"Whatever happened to libraries being free?" said Flynn absentmindedly.

"We're not students here," Matt explained. "So Jaime, are you going to give us a guided tour of the Woodhull archives?"

"Sure, no problem," the girl said, nearly dropping her world-weary grad school élan. "It'll be fun to talk to a knowledgeable person about Vicky. Doesn't happen much."

"You're on a first-name basis with your thesis subject, I see." He smiled broadly, the dimple showing up again.

Jaime actually smiled back. She even verged on blushing. Matt Holtser was working his magic. That guy could charm a snake if he had to. Flynn hadn't met anyone that charismatic since . . . oh, hell, never mind.

"Well, lead on," he said. "I don't really know that much about old Vicky, as you call her, but she seems to play some sort of role in this murder trial I'm researching. My great-great-grandfather was the defense attorney in the case."

"Oberholtzer?" said Jaime as she and Matt started up the library stairs together. "That's cool."

"Yeah, when we found out from you that there was unpublished information about the case, I was really psyched."

Jaime turned back to Flynn. "So you're the one with the auction, huh?"

"Yeah. That's me."

"Man, you're sitting on a goldmine. The bidding went over four thousand this morning. That bidder from Chicago just won't quit."

"Oh, I forgot to check it," said Flynn.

"You don't even care?" said Jaime. "Maybe you're rich or something but to me, four grand is a shitload of money."

Matt threw Flynn a grin over his shoulder as they entered the library and started the shakedown process to be allowed entrance into the hallowed archives.

"Well, I agree, that's a lot of money," Flynn said lamely, hurrying to catch up with them. She hadn't exactly lost interest in the auction totals so much as she was seriously starting to balk at the thought of parting with her treasure. She did not want to admit this just yet. No reason to have Matt and Jaime thinking she was a loon.

"Well, it's fine with me," said Jaime. "The old gal I'm bidding for is giving me a finder's fee. Ten percent of the final bid. Unless we hit the limit."

"Which is . . . ?" said Matt, raising his eyebrows.

"I'm not telling you." Jaime grinned and waved a scolding finger at him.

"Can you divulge any information about this well-heeled bidder?" he said.

"Oh, sure. She's not trying to be secret or anything. She's just old and doesn't do computers. I'm helping her out. Her name is Blanche Adler, Professor Emeritus Adler, that is. She's retired from her university career, but she was a pioneer in the field of women's studies. She started the first women's history project way back in—I don't know—like, at least 1970 or something."

"And she likes Woodhull, I guess," said Matt.

"Obsessed is more like it. She collects any kind of memorabilia. She wants to start a museum or exhibit or something. I met her last year when I started my research. She's got a ton of knowledge about her. She's helped me a lot."

"I wish I could meet her," he said. "Don't you, Flynn? She sounds interesting."

"Oh, she wants to meet you, too. She lives near here." Jaime then turned to Flynn. "Can I see the picture?"

"I . . . didn't bring it with me," said Flynn.

Matt turned to her with a curious frown. He knew she was lying, but didn't mention it.

The boxes of archival material had already been brought up from their off-site storage location. Jaime had ordered them the previous day after talking to Flynn on the phone.

The three of them sat down at a long table in a glass-walled room and the girl quickly sorted through the contents of the relevant Ingersoll trial material.

"Part of my thesis focuses on why Woodhull suddenly gave up her views on Free Love in 1875 after being the foremost advocate of them for the previous five years. None of her biographers has found a convincing explanation.

"She just up and changed her tune. Beginning with the May 6, 1875, issue of *Woodhull & Claflin's Weekly,* she started writing *anti*–Free Love diatribes."

"That would have been one week after the Ingersoll trial ended," said Matt.

"That's true. I focused my research on everything during the months leading up to that issue. From January until June of that year, the big news was the Beecher trial. It dragged on for more than a hundred days. Beecher and his followers had made life hell for Vicky and her husband and sister ever since she exposed his love affair with Theodore Tilton's wife in 1872.

"Woodhull was financially ruined by the mess and was forced to tour constantly on the lecture circuit after that to make ends meet. She divorced her husband—her second husband, Blood—about a year later. Then, in 1877, she and her sister moved to England. She married this super rich dude and spent the rest of her life—fifty years, in fact—as a country gentlewoman on a big estate. Her sister Tennie did the same. She found a rich husband, too, and even ended up with a title."

"They say living well is the best revenge," said Flynn. "When did she die?"

"1927. She was the only first-wave suffragist to see women in America get the vote. All her contemporaries—Stanton, Anthony, Mott—didn't live long enough.

"The library got a bunch of new material from her estate in England just this year. It had been sitting around in an attic there. That's when I found these notes she made about the Ingersoll murder trial in Chicago."

Jaime pulled a file folder out of one of the boxes. Stuffed inside it was a thick pile of notes on yellowed paper, written in pen and some in pencil. Jaime flipped through them and located one typewritten sheet. She pushed it across the table to Matt and Flynn.

"She started to write an article based on a jailhouse interview with Alec Ingersoll."

Matt and Flynn leaned in and read together the long paragraph beginning with the words: *"Alec Ingersoll is dead."*

The article was not dated though all of the notes carried dates from the last week of April, 1875.

"Well, have fun, kids," said the smart-alecky Jaime.

"Hey, let us buy you dinner tonight," said Matt.

"Sure. I'll call Professor Adler and see if she can join us. Why don't we meet at that vegan restaurant just up the highway on the north side of town? It's called the 'The Garden of Eden.' "

They said their goodbyes and Flynn waited for Jaime to leave the room before she turned to Matt.

"Vegan? Oh, boy, that sounds fun." She made a face like she was going to be sick.

"I'll take you out for a burger afterwards," he said. "Now let's dive in."

They read the notes in date order, Flynn passing each page she finished on to Matt. By three, they were bleary-eyed and nearly finished.

The silence of the research room was suddenly blasted by Flynn's cell phone.

"Sorry!" she said in a loud whisper.

"You're gonna get in trouble," Matt sing-songed. Cell phones were forbidden on the premises.

She shrugged apologetically and left the library to return the call.

"What's up, Dad?"

"I think you might have to call off your auction, honey."

"Oh, why's that?" She held her breath, hoping he would give her a plausible reason for ending it. She desperately wanted to keep the photograph after reading the Woodhull narrative.

"I called up Jason, at my old firm. I don't think you've ever met him—"

"Yeah, yeah," she said, trying to get him to cut to the chase.

"He's a young guy who specializes in intellectual property law. He doesn't think you can sell Matt a license to use the image and then turn right around and sell the photo itself. The new owners would assume they were getting all the rights, including the reproduction rights. You follow me?"

"Yeah, I think so."

"I'm sorry, but I really think you're going to have to choose between selling the photograph and giving the image rights to Matt. In any case, shouldn't you think about transferring it to a bigger venue than eBay? If you got several thousand dollars' worth of interest in it without even knowing what you had, think what you might get at a real auction house with the whole history of the thing known."

"The *provenance*," she threw in casually, feeling a lot more like a pro than she did a week ago. "Thanks, Dad. I think I will end it. Good catch."

She walked back into the research room with a goofy grin on her face.

"Why are you so happy?" Matt asked.

"I just lost four thousand dollars. Or at least I'm going to when I get on your computer."

"I don't get it."

"My dad, being the intrepid legal-eagle that he is, says that I can't sell you the rights to reproduce the photo *and* sell the photo at the same time."

"Oh, shit. He's right. I should have known that. You'd, at the very least, have to make some kind of disclosure."

"I'm glad I found out before I messed it up."

Matt sat silently for a moment. "Flynn, I can't ask you to give up that amount of money. To quote our little friend Jaime, four grand *is* 'a shitload of money.' "

She tilted her chin in a flirtatious way and cocked an eyebrow. "Don't you think you're worth it?"

"Four thousand dollars?" He raised both his eyebrows and slapped the table. "Damn, I had no idea I was that good in bed!"

They both loudly cracked up, earning a disciplinary frown

from the archive librarian.

Flynn whispered, "You could have a whole new career waiting for you."

Matt adopted a mock-dreamy look and said, "Matt Holtser, Professional Male Escort."

"Seriously, though. I may be making a wise investment choice here. If you write a bestseller, think what my photo would be worth then. Look what *Midnight in the Garden of Good and Evil* did for the bird-girl statue on the cover. It spawned a whole bird-girl statue industry. I might have to auction this photo at Christie's or Sotheby's."

Flynn smiled inwardly. She was talking such a good game, she almost believed it herself. And if she flattered Matt in the process, well, that was just icing on an already delicious cake.

Jaime and Professor Adler were waiting for them at the little restaurant when Flynn and Matt arrived.

The young graduate student did not look happy. "Why'd you cancel the auction?"

Flynn guessed this was coming. She felt bad that Jaime was going to lose her finder's fee and wished there was a way she could make it up to her.

"I ran into some legal complications," said Flynn, hoping they would not press her for more details.

"I'm Blanche Adler," said the petite older woman at Jaime's side. She was smartly dressed in slacks and a sweater. She wore her hair in an attractive short cut, but dyed it a surprisingly unnatural shade of dark red, apparently to match the frames of her oversized glasses. She looked to be about seventy years of age.

Matt stepped forward and enthusiastically shook the woman's hand. Flynn joined him in the various introductions.

Throughout the meal, Professor Adler delighted them with

stories about Victoria Woodhull. She tried to illuminate the social climate faced by the individuals caught up in what became the Free Love Murder trial.

"What the 'Free Love' movement in the nineteenth century sought to achieve," she said, "is really the social structure that we have in America today. They wanted liberalized divorce laws—we call it no-fault divorce.

"And they wanted what we now call 'serial monogamy,' inside or outside of marriage. They never advocated promiscuity—that was the biggest misunderstanding. They just wanted the government to stay out of people's bedrooms. But all that has really only transpired in the last thirty years or so. America of 1875 certainly wasn't ready for it and could barely even tolerate a debate on the issue."

"I think there are plenty of people today who still aren't ready for it," said Flynn.

"Yeah," said Jaime. "They're called Republicans."

They all laughed, smugly patting themselves on their liberal backs, but the professor was not so cavalier on the subject.

"You young people aren't old enough to remember it, but when I first started teaching—we're talking early sixties here—Anthony Comstock's anti-obscenity laws were still on the books. They had been quickly expanded in the late 1870s to include outlawing all access to birth control. Those laws didn't finally fall until 1965 when the Supreme Court decided we had a right to privacy."

"*Griswold versus Connecticut,*" Matt chimed in. "I studied it in law school. I think I now appreciate just how powerful Anthony Comstock was. And to think that Victoria Woodhull was his first victim."

"And Medora Lamb," said Flynn.

"Comstock's reign of terror against sex finally ended," said Professor Adler, "but it took an entire century."

CHAPTER THIRTY-FOUR

Thursday, April 29, 1875

When Victoria and Garnet left the jail and stepped out onto Dearborn Street, Sergeant Mills was nowhere in sight. When a nearby officer was asked his whereabouts, the reply came that the sergeant had slipped around the corner to buy some tobacco.

As they waited, Victoria mentally rehearsed what she would say to Norris when she confronted him. That deceitful man! She recalled now how he claimed he "needed" a photograph of the deceased person in order to summon them during the séance-cum-photographic sitting.

She now surmised he re-photographed the requested likeness in order to forge the spirit photograph and thereby dupe his unsuspecting customers—while charging the outrageous sum of fifty dollars for the deceit!

She burned with indignation that he had almost succeeded in tricking her into being his unwitting accomplice by asking her to publicly endorse him. She would make him sorry indeed. She would publicly *denounce* him as the scoundrel he was.

She had no more than thought this than the larger consequences of the scandal dawned upon her. How could she minimize the effect this disclosure would have on all the legitimate spiritualists?

The last thing she desired was to harm the innocent and earnest practitioners, both locally and even nationally. If only she could negotiate a decent resolution without publicly exposing him as a fraud. That would certainly prevent all her brethren spiritualists from being tarred with the same brush, as it were.

Perhaps she should discuss this with him in private. Not having an officer of the law on the premises might actually be an advantage. If she brought Sergeant Mills along at her side, the gentleman would think she intended to have him carted off to jail, forthwith. No need to frighten him so, if a decent and private conclusion could be honorably wrangled. She turned to her companion.

"Garnet, I am anxious to resolve this matter with Mr. Norris. Why don't I go ahead and you stay to wait for Sergeant Mills. He can escort you back to the Palmer House and I will meet you both there. I'd like for us to lunch together. The Palmer House restaurant is the finest in the city."

"But is that wise, Mrs. Woodhull?" asked Garnet. "Is it safe for you to be un—unguarded?"

"I won't be long at this," she said, waving to an approaching hack. "Besides, my would-be assassin thinks I'm dead already. If he reads the papers, that is."

She took the covered photograph from an anxious Garnet and climbed into the hansom cab. She handed the driver the address of the Norris studio though the little trap door in the ceiling.

"No one will follow me," she said to Garnet as the cab left the curb. "No one even knows I'm here."

Bertrand Norris's Photographic Atelier was open for business, but Victoria found no receptionist to greet her. She took a seat in the waiting room and heard the sounds of the photographer completing a sitting upstairs in the studio. A crying baby and a mother and father attempting to quiet it seemed to indicate a family portrait was in progress.

She looked at the "spirit photographs" again with a new eye.

She shook her head with irritation.

Soon she heard a commotion coming down the stairs. The baby still howled inconsolably and the parents mumbled embarrassed apologies to Mr. Norris.

"Think nothing of it," came the booming voice of the photographer. "Next week should work just as well."

Into the room burst the harried father and mother, plus a tyke of about three and, of course, the loudest and tiniest member of the family, all of them decked out in their best attire in anticipation of having their likenesses captured.

They swept past Victoria on their way to the door.

"Next week, give him some cough medicine first," hissed the young father to his wife.

Victoria smirked. Were parents still pulling that trick—dosing their infants with opium-laced baby cough syrup in order to hurry them into slumber?

Mr. Norris waved them out the door and spun to greet the woman in his waiting room. "And what may I do for you on this lovely—"

Norris froze when he saw Victoria's unsmiling face before him. His plump lips parted and his nostrils—which always made Tennie giggle—looked even larger than normal.

"Mrs. Wood—Mrs. Wood—," he stammered.

"Don't believe everything you read in the papers, Mr. Norris," she said, now smiling in spite of her grave mission. She felt a little pang of guilt for frightening the poor man so. "Your eyes don't deceive you. The reports of my death were, shall we say, premature?"

Bertrand Norris did not find her little witticism funny at all.

"Well, umh, thank the Good Lord for that. How . . . how is it that the newspapers could have made such an error?"

"A simple mistake of identity." She did not care to share the details with this man about the whole unfortunate affair.

"What brings you to my humble studio today, Madam?"

He still did not look happy to receive her. Had he already guessed the purpose of her visit? That did not seem likely. "I have a serious matter to discuss with you, sir."

"Well," said Norris, straightening his necktie, "might we adjourn to some more hospitable location? Please step upstairs to my studio room. Much more comfortable seating than this waiting room has to offer."

She assented with a nod and he locked his studio door, turning the hanging sign from "Open" to "Closed." She followed him up the stairs.

She seated herself on the upholstered sofa that was used as a prop in the photographs. Norris remained standing.

"Now, Mr. Norris, I have known you for several years through the American Spiritualists Association and I am always happy to help out fellow practitioners in any way I can."

Norris attempted to smile, though he adjusted his tie once again in a fidgety manner.

"Forgive this long preamble, Mr. Norris. Suffice it to say that I must regretfully withdraw my support for you in your lawsuit."

"And . . . and that's all you came to say?"

Victoria drew a deep breath—now for the hard part. "I have reason to believe that the charges of deception lodged against you are true and I would be remiss in my duties as the president of the ASA if I did not denounce you as the fraud I feel you are."

The color boiled in his plump cheeks now. "I have never humbugged anyone!"

"I am afraid I have evidence to the contrary, Mr. Norris."

"That's impossible," he said. He pulled out his handkerchief to mop his brow and smooth his mustache. "I will sue you for libel!"

Victoria refused to back down, though the threat of yet

another lawsuit would make her poor husband livid.

"Call your lawyers and tell them to do their worst, Mr. Norris. I think a jury will waste little time agreeing with me."

"You have no proof! You can't possibly—"

"Please take a look at this before you continue." She unwrapped the photograph and held it up for view.

Norris's angry face chilled into a look of horror. "Where did you get that? Let me see it."

"No, I can't do that." She protectively clutched it to her breast.

"I want to see it," Norris snapped. "Hand it to me this instant!"

"Do not take that tone with me, sir." Victoria stood up. She did not like the threatening turn this conversation had taken and now wished to withdraw. The man was not behaving rationally—and she should not have been surprised by this. She was, after all, promising to separate him from a lucrative portion of his income and, more importantly, his reputation. Perhaps she should placate him, extricate herself from the present fray, and then alert the proper authorities to this man's misdeeds.

"Mr. Norris, I must ask you to control yourself," she said. "This outburst does nothing to endear you to me. I came here prepared to help you negotiate some gentler punishment for whatever wrongs you may have committed. A quiet monetary settlement to the injured parties and a promise never to practice spiritualism again might avoid an unsavory scandal. No one wishes you to serve a jail term, after all."

The gentleman took a step backwards and tried to regain his composure. He mopped his moist brow once again and placed his handkerchief back in his breast pocket with a small flourish.

"Forgive me, Madam. I have behaved as less than a gentleman and for that I beg your forgiveness. It's just that I am so . . . so wounded by your accusation."

"We can discuss this at length under different circumstances, sir. After you consider your . . . options. I must now depart. You may call on me at the Palmer House later today."

She headed for the door of the studio.

Norris dashed around in front of her and blocked her path.

"Mrs. Woodhull, I beseech you to sit down again." He smiled eagerly. "I cannot bear for you to take your leave without allowing me to make amends for my boorish temper. That screaming infant jangled my nerves earlier, you see. I have no children and very little experience dealing with them. Allow me to make you some tea at least."

"Thank you, but no," she said. "I must be returning—"

"Please share a cup of tea with me, so that we may talk about the matter with cool heads and more composure than I have previously exhibited."

Victoria shrugged wearily, knowing she was showing him more compassion than he probably deserved. "All right. I suppose I have time for a single cup of tea.

Nick Faraday loitered around the sidewalk in front of the Bertrand Norris "Photographic Atelier" and wondered how long Victoria Woodhull would remain in there. Why had she paid a call on Alec Ingersoll and then rushed off to a photographer's studio? It seemed highly curious that she would have such an urgent need to have her likeness taken, given all that had transpired in the last twenty-four hours.

Faraday had only been a reporter for two years but had already developed enough journalistic instinct to know that when circumstances made no sense at all, there was an explanation lurking just out of sight and in need of his ferreting.

He felt that delicious tingle running up and down his spine that some hot new story would soon emerge. He had sensed it yesterday when he had followed Mrs. Woodhull to that alleyway near the river. No woman like Mrs. Woodhull had a rational reason to be in such a place. Of course he hoped today's adventure would not place him at risk for a constable's nightstick on his skull again, as yesterday's had.

A friend on the police force had alerted him to the fact that Jackson Hurley had made contact with Mrs. Woodhull. He now deduced that she might have been trying to meet him there. That would also explain the presence of the attorney for Alec Ingersoll.

He had not originally been assigned to the Ingersoll trial and thus had not recognized Franklin Oberholtzer that morning in the Dearborn Café. How he now regretted not making such an important connection. He certainly knew it now, after an evening spent with Woodhull's attractive—and quite chatty—younger sister.

He had to assume Mrs. Woodhull was in some sort of danger generally, given the murder of that young girl who had been wearing her veil and had stepped onto the train arm-in-arm with Tennie Claflin.

Where was that tall police sergeant who had been guarding Mrs. Woodhull both last night and this morning?

The midday sun made it difficult to see inside the glass door of the studio. He milled around just far enough away so that the occupants of the room inside hopefully did not spot him spying.

He observed Norris suddenly lock the door of the studio and turn the sign from "Open" to "Closed." Faraday became doubly perplexed. Norris wouldn't need to close his establishment to take a photograph, so what was happening in there?

He lit a smoke to pass the time and looked up Twenty-third Street and down again actually hoping that the sergeant assigned to guard Mrs. Woodhull might show up. He would tell him that he ought to be looking into this situation. That might give him the story he craved.

Victoria watched Norris disappear into the workroom where he kept his ill-smelling photographic chemicals and sat back down again on the sofa, placing the photograph on her lap.

The memory of Norris's chemicals triggered a strange feeling deep in the core of her being. The sensation was not unknown to her. She frequently experienced it when the Spirit World was about to make a visitation upon her, but she did not perceive her usual spirit guide.

Feeling light-headed, she grasped the carved wooden arm of the sofa. The scent of almonds filled her nostrils, though she knew from experience that the scents and sensations she encountered while in this state had nothing to do with her physical surroundings, but issued instead from the spirit realm.

The image of a jar appeared in her mind. She tried to read the label on the jar but could not. She saw instead an article in one of the newspapers given her by Mr. Oberholtzer from the trial days. She read the words from the testimony of the coroner's physician: potassium of cyanide was a white, crystalline substance that dissolved in water just like sugar.

Just like sugar.

Victoria stood up, her hands shaking, her breath coming in short gulps. She had to shake off the vision and not succumb to it as she so often did. She must return to full, waking consciousness immediately. She could not handle this situation alone. She would need help. She felt momentarily stronger, she was certain she could manage the stairs now . . .

She turned to leave but Mr. Norris was already standing in the doorway bearing a tray with two cups of steaming, black tea.

★ ★ ★ ★ ★

Faraday leaned against the building next to the door, still hoping the policeman would arrive. The street was not terribly busy. Being so close to the fancy residential area encompassing Prairie Avenue and Calumet Street, it carried little commercial traffic. The horse-drawn street car line was two blocks over. Only the occasional pedestrian walking to or from the street car passed, or the random baby nurse pushing a perambulator to give their little charge some air.

Mothers who were fortunate enough to live on Prairie Avenue did not have to push their own babies around. Faraday wondered what such women did all day—having servants to cook and clean and tend their children. What was left? Gossiping with other idle women of their neighborhood?

Another man soon happened by. He strode directly up the entrance to the studio and tried the door.

"Wot's now?" he said, annoyed to find the door locked at midday.

Faraday tried a gambit. "Did you have an appointment, too?"

"I works 'ere." The man placed his hands on his hips in irritation.

"You're employed by Bertrand Norris?"

"More like an associate," said the man in an English accent.

He did not seem anxious to make conversation and moved on.

When Faraday saw him stride directly into the alley next to the studio, he decided to follow him. This fellow might know a back way into the place and if he did and it was unlocked, Faraday would attempt to enter too. More than the scent of a story drew him on: he worried about The Woodhull. The suggestion that his exclusive report on her had occasioned the death of that maid had stung him more than he was willing to admit out loud.

Sure enough, the man opened a wrought iron-grilled door off the alley and gained entrance to the back of the business.

Norris set the tray down between them on a little table. He held out a cup of tea.

Victoria narrowed her eyes at this despicable man and suddenly he became all the men who had ever oppressed her, her and all her fellow women—Beecher, Comstock, Treat, to name only three of her most recent harassers. The lion in her soul roared, but her words issued as cool as ice:

"Did you offer Medora Lamb a cup of tea that morning?"

Norris looked unnerved. "What . . . what morning would that be?"

"The morning of her death."

"I don't even know that name. Why do you bring it up?"

"You are lying, sir. You knew Medora Lamb quite well. Her husband paid you to teach her the art of photography. But she ended up teaching you a thing or two. Like how to create beautiful, counterfeit spirit photographs."

"I don't know what you are talking about," said Norris, setting the proffered cup back down again.

"Was she demanding payment from you for the technique she invented, Mr. Norris? She had certainly enriched your practice. I know she was getting large sums of money from somewhere. Were you generously sharing your profits with her or was she perhaps blackmailing you?"

"You can't prove that. You can't prove anything!" He jumped to his feet and she did likewise.

"You tried to make certain of that, didn't you? By stealing and destroying all of her photographs and equipment."

"You can't prove that. I was nowhere near that house the day it was burgled. Half a dozen clients can vouch for my whereabouts that day."

"You seem to have that story at the ready. Highly curious that you do, in fact."

"Why shouldn't I? I mean, uh, I—" He took another step back, his face growing redder. "Stop this slander, this harrassment. Don't say anything more or . . . or—"

"Or what, Mr. Norris? You'll poison me too? The circle grows ever wider of the people you need to silence."

"You do not know what you're talking about," said Norris in a suddenly calm voice. He glanced toward the door of the studio. "Let us behave like the lady and gentleman we both are."

"Medora Lamb was no lady, was she?" said Victoria, the thrill of fear exciting her to new levels of daring, not unlike the moments on the lecture stage when hecklers taunted her and she rose to the challenge, responding in kind. "I never met the woman, but I have formed a strong impression of her. I think she was the type who would do anything to get what she wanted. Even destroy the men who were kindest to her."

She paused and decided to switch tactics. "I bet you were kind to her, Bertrand."

"Yes, I was kind to her," said Norris. "I taught her everything. No other photographer in the city was willing to take on a *female* pupil. That haughty young husband of hers, looking down his nose at me. Thought he was superior to everyone just because the newspapers wrote flattering articles about him. And *her*, she thought she was so clever . . ."

"I don't blame you, Bertrand," she said, increasing her feigned empathy when she perceived her gambit had wedged a small crack in his armor. "No one could blame you. She gave you no choice, did she?"

"Indeed, she was impossible," said Norris in an unexpected admission. He took a step toward her. "Now you must give me that photograph, my *dear* Mrs. Woodhull."

"No."

She bolted for the studio door, crashing straight into the looming presence of Jackson Hurley.

"Wot's this, then?" said Hurley, taking her by the shoulders. Hurley's eyes widened, just as Norris's had, when he saw her. "Mrs. Woodhull? As I live and breathe."

Without thinking, he released her, but his large form still effectively blocked the door.

"As *I* live and breathe, you should say. You kept me waiting yesterday, Mr. Hurley."

Victoria's mind raced to comprehend what Hurley's connection to Norris could possible be.

"What are you talking about?" said Norris to both of them. He turned a frantic eye on Hurley. "What business did you have with this woman?"

She instantly sensed conflict between the two men. If she could get them arguing with each other, she might stand a chance of escape.

"Our Mr. Hurley here offered to sell me some information," she said, and then added as a wild ploy, "about you, Bertrand."

"What?" screamed Norris, outraged at Hurley.

"Now, hold on a bleedin' minute 'ere. I did nothin' of the sort, Bertie. And you, Mrs. Woodhull, you spoiled it yesterday, bringing all your little playmates along. Did you really think I was so stupid I couldn't spot a couple o' coppers trying to act like regular folk? Bleedin' pathetic, they was. And that other fella, sneakin' around—never figured out what 'e was up to."

"We have to deal with her," said Norris. "We have to finish what we started."

"Look now, Bertie, this nonsense 'as gotta stop somewhere. This's turned into a lot more than I signed on for. And I 'aven't seen a single farthing—I mean, dollar—yet."

"We have no choice," said Norris. "This woman wants to ruin me."

"Buy 'er off," said Hurley. "All this killin' is way out of my arena. I don't mind a bit 'o mischief, but I'll not risk the noose."

"I can't let her leave here. She'd just try and bleed me dry like the other one did," said Norris, pleading with his uncooperative cohort.

"You do have problems with women." Hurley chuckled at Norris's dilemma. "Look, I didn't mind 'elpin' you out of your first little jam, when you says we can frame Ingersoll for it." He turned to Victoria to explain as if everything he did made perfect, legitimate sense. "Ingersoll 'ad it comin'. Broke my jaw and two ribs, 'e did."

He turned back to the trembling photographer, taking a few steps closer. "But I'm done with it. You're on your own now, old darling."

"How in the world do you two men even know each other?" said Victoria, determined to keep the conversation going, while she slowly edged closer to the door.

" 'E saw me talking to my old mate, Cam Langley, in the yard of that fancy place 'e lived in. Said we might 'ave something in common and 'e was right."

"Did you help him kill Medora Lamb?"

"I've never killed no one," said Hurley, "though I may have helped move a tragic little thing's body to a spot where it looked like her husband might have done her in. If I gets arrested over this Bertie, I'm tellin' it all! The girl, the burglary, the plot to frame that damned husband of 'ers—"

The three desperate people stood looking at each other, running the permutations of this convoluted series of events through their minds. Each trying to calculate a way to gain an advantage, to somehow make it two-against-one, if only for a moment.

But then . . . a new factor burst on the scene:

"Nobody move! I have a gun!"

Nick Faraday appeared in the doorway of the studio. He aimed his jacket pocket out in a woefully inadequate pantomime of a pistol.

"No, you don't," said Hurley, more annoyed than startled.

"Yes, I do," said Faraday.

Hurley folded his arms across his chest. "Let's see it then, sport."

The ruse was so pathetic that even the normally composed Victoria would have felt compelled to laugh if she had not faced mortal peril. Though she had previously felt nothing but contempt for Faraday's dogged pursuit of her, she now was so grateful to see him, she could have planted a kiss on his face.

Hurley rushed at Faraday and the two men struggled. In seconds, Hurley had wrestled him to the ground.

Victoria took refuge behind the prop sofa, still clutching the all important photograph.

Everyone froze, though, when a banging was heard on the glass entrance door below them.

"Open up! Police business!"

Victoria recognized the sound of Sergeant Mills's voice.

"Mrs. Woodhull?" called Garnet Langley from the sidewalk.

Hurley tried to extricate himself from his wrestling match with Faraday, presumably to make good an escape. Faraday, as tenacious as a bulldog rather than a bloodhound, clung to the man's leg and would not let go.

Victoria dropped the photograph on the sofa and rushed to the large bank of windows that overlooked the street. She commenced beating on them with her fists.

"We're up here," she called, hoping the officer could hear her. "Help me!"

"There's a back door," Faraday shouted. "Off the alley."

301

Victoria relayed this information. Sergeant Mills apparently heard her, for he ran in the direction of the alley and disappeared.

Garnet now looked up as well. Victoria violently motioned for her to stay away.

She looked back and saw that Faraday and Hurley continued to scuffle and wondered how to help. And where was Norris in all of this?

She saw him walking to the sofa where she had left the photograph. She beat him to it and once again held it tight against her bodice. He looked at her, oblivious to the two men fighting on the floor and the sound of heavy footsteps entering the building below them. A strangely sad, hopelessness relaxed his florid features.

He stood quite still amid the chaos and with the dignity of a disgraced Roman senator, calmly lifted one of the tea cups from the tray to his lips. He then took a large gulp.

"No!" shouted Victoria.

She rushed over just as he began to violently cough. He fell to the floor on his hands and knees as she reached him.

His coughing and choking stopped as he began to lose consciousness.

"I want to save your miserable life," she cried. She pulled his tie open, then his collar button, lost amid his flabby chins.

"I want Alec Ingersoll to watch his wife's murderer go to the gallows."

But she failed. The poison had begun to take its monstrously efficient toll. The photographer's portly body relaxed into a brief coma and then began to jerk in violent convulsions.

"Halt! Police!" shouted Sergeant Mills, now in the hallway.

Hurley disengaged himself from Faraday's grasp by kicking the poor man in the face. In a frightening burst of strength, Hurley literally rolled Faraday's stunned body at the legs of the approaching policeman. He toppled the tall man like he was a massive human bowling pin. Hurley sprinted over both and ran for the stairs.

"Halt or I'll shoot!"

But Hurley ran and Mills shot.

Victoria heard the sounds of a body falling down the stairs.

She rushed over to help Faraday who sat rocking back and forth on his knees and heels, holding his face, which gushed blood from his nose and mouth.

She offered him her handkerchief.

"I'm pretty sure your nose is broken," she said.

He nodded.

"How much did you hear?"

He pulled the handkerchief away to answer. "Enough that Alec Ingersoll will leave jail a free man before the sun sets tonight."

"God bless you, Mr. Faraday. How can I repay you for this?"

The reporter tried to regain his composure while staunching the blood that gushed from his nose. Ever the newshound, he said, "Let me attend the séance."

"Only if Mr. Ingersoll agrees . . . and I'm sorry, but I doubt he will. Let's talk about this more later."

Faraday dug into his jacket pocket and pulled out a pencil. This had been his pretend pistol.

"Mightier than the sword?" he said. Through all his blood and pain and swelling face, he tried to smile.

Victoria smiled. "Not today, I'm afraid."

CHAPTER THIRTY-FIVE

Thursday, April 29, 1875

A very long afternoon ensued. Victoria and Garnet never got to share that promised lunch in the Palmer House's Grand Dining Room. But neither of them had the luxury of time to notice.

An army of policemen, doctors, ambulances, attorneys, and newspaper reporters arrived at the Photographic Atelier of the now "late" Bertrand Norris. Victoria and Nick Faraday wearily gave one report after another to the various detectives. An assistant district attorney represented the interests of Mr. Lynch.

After hearing their evidence, the young prosecutor sent a messenger back to the courthouse on the run, to suspend jury deliberations pending the outcome of the afternoon's events.

"Mr. Lynch would be most embarrassed if the jury should return a guilty verdict just as this new evidence comes to light," said the fretful young attorney. "Most embarrassed."

"The *Tribune* would not support his re-election," said Faraday, taunting the poor young man. "I can personally guarantee that. Convicting a poor, innocent, grieving widower of his wife's murder. That would not endear Mr. Lynch to the voting public at all."

Victoria watched this byplay with a bemused smile. For once, she was glad the office of district attorney was an elective one.

They were next transported to the criminal courthouse and gave their stories yet again in the form of sworn statements before the judge, with both Mr. Lynch and Mr. Oberholtzer present.

At the conclusion of their testimony, Oberholtzer asked that all the charges against his client be withdrawn.

"I need a little margin of time to sort this all out," said a perplexed Jeremiah Lynch. He asked the judge for a short delay to review all the new evidence in detail, but agreed that the jury deliberations should be further suspended until a hearing on the matter, which was set for the following morning at nine o'clock.

Sensitive to the risk of keeping a probably innocent Alec Ingersoll in jail any longer than need be, the prosecutor did not object to the defendant's renewed motion to release him from custody on a posting of bond.

Thus reporter Faraday's prediction came true: Alec Ingersoll left his jail cell before sunset.

Victoria, Garnet Langley, and Franklin Oberholtzer escorted a stunned Ingersoll out of the jailhouse and transported him to Oberholtzer's home for a quiet dinner, away from public view.

The freed man had little appetite and spoke only occasionally as he struggled to digest instead the revelations of the remarkable afternoon. Every so often he was heard to mumble to himself, "Dora was murdered. I . . . I can't believe it. Dora was murdered."

"But I still do not understand what happened to my brother," Garnet said to her tablemates as Dottie Oberholtzer's maid cleared the dishes.

"No one seems really sure," said Franklin Oberholtzer. "We must content ourselves with the fact that Alec, here, has been acquitted of that crime and can never be recharged with it. We have only the vague and confused comments that the villain Hurley made to Sergeant Mills immediately prior to his death."

"I did not hear these remarks," said Victoria. "I was tending to Mr. Faraday's injuries at the time."

"Mills said that the man denied he ever murdered anyone, just that he had 'helped out' Norris in exchange of money and the promise that they would make trouble for Alec here. He admitted stealing the photographs and the camera.

"Medora went to Norris's studio that morning, he said, and Norris used chloroform to incapacitate the poor woman, then he poured the poisoned liquid down her throat with the aid of a funnel while she was too groggy to resist. This explains the unusual stains the coroner found on her collar and neck.

"Hurley's job was just to deposit her body back at her home and somehow summon Alec to find her. Whether Mr. Langley walked in on him doing so, we'll never know. Hurley died before he could say more."

"I guess that brings us to the matter of the séance," said Victoria. "Providing you still wish it, Mr. Ingersoll."

All eyes at the table turned to Alec.

"I guess so," he said with less conviction than the group would have expected.

"I talked to the Chief Inspector," said his lawyer. "We have permission to go into the house tonight. I said that you and Miss Langley wished to remove personal items, but what we actually do there is up to us."

At a quarter past eleven in the evening, Victoria, Garnet, Ingersoll, and both Oberholtzers entered the tower room for the final time.

Ingersoll looked queasy when he first arrived in the room but insisted he would be all right. His lawyer had entered the tower first, both to light the lamps and to make sure the bloodstain on the chaise lounge was well covered.

The three ladies awkwardly conversed while the gentlemen arranged chairs so that they might sit around the table where

Medora Lamb's body had been found.

Ingersoll looked increasingly ill-at-ease as they sat down together. Victoria asked them to place their hands on the table. His breathing became audible and he could not sit still. Everyone cast nervous glances at him, wondering what was going through his tormented mind.

Just as Victoria closed her eyes to slip into a trance state, Ingersoll abruptly stood up, knocking his chair over in the process.

"I can't do this," he announced. "I'm sorry. I just can't. I know all this was at my own request but now that the moment is here . . ."

He raked his fingers through his hair. Perspiration appeared on his forehead though the room was chilly.

Everyone sat back in their chairs, uncertain what to do next.

"No one says you have to go through with it, Alec," said Oberholtzer.

"We understand, dear," said his wife in a motherly tone.

Garnet said nothing but looked disappointed. She certainly hoped she would finally learn the true circumstances of her brother's death. This séance now seemed to be her only hope.

Ingersoll paced about the room in a distracted fashion.

"If you all would excuse us," said Victoria, "I would like a moment to speak with Mr. Ingersoll alone. If that is all right with you, sir."

Ingersoll turned and reluctantly nodded.

After the other three members of the spirit circle departed, Victoria motioned for him to sit next to her.

"What's really wrong?" she asked as gently as possible.

"I don't think Cameron's spirit would want to speak to me. Or maybe I am too much of a coward to face him."

"But you didn't cause his death."

"I want to believe that. I know Garnet wants to believe that somehow he died a hero's death, perhaps thinking he was 'saving' Dora. Or avenging her. I know he would have been wretched to see Jackson Hurley again. Perhaps he retrieved the gun from Dora's room and confronted Hurley . . ."

"Why do you fear that he did not? Are you still so certain he took his own life? Hurley just claimed that he didn't 'murder' anyone. He might have believed he killed Cameron in self-defense. Not technically a murder, I suppose."

Ingersoll shrugged, but was not convinced. "I realize that theory is *possibly* true, but I still think Cam found Dora's lifeless body and assumed *he* caused her to commit suicide. He then decided he must follow her out of loyalty or guilt or . . ."

"But two bullets were fired from the gun."

"I fired the second bullet," he said quietly. "I picked up the gun and tried to join them in death. I waited for the sound of a passing train to cover the noise. I didn't want the neighbors to hear.

"In the end, though, I guess I was a coward. My arm shook so violently and then seemed to collapse of its own volition. The gun discharged accidentally. The bullet hit the wall across the room. I sat there for I don't know how long, trying to regain my resolve. Then I heard noises downstairs and I realized I'd missed my chance. The next thing I knew, that postman walked in."

Victoria hated to cause the man even more pain but she had to know the answer to her final question. "We were interrupted the other day before you could finish your story. You told me that your 'Complex Marriage' was working. That you had accepted it and even had started to enjoy it. If you can bear to talk about it, I am longing to know: What changed between the three of you?"

"The smallest of things," Ingersoll said with a ragged breath. "After the burglary, Dora was terrified. Completely shaken. I thought buying that gun would make her feel safer. We were all upset, of course, but her losses were the greatest, the most personal. I now wonder if this secret money she supposedly had was also stolen. Maybe that drove her to make new demands on Norris, blackmailing him rather than regarding him as, should I say, a collaborator? I don't know. I guess we will never know.

"Be that as it may," he said, then halted. He began again, but the pain was still raw in his face. "She turned to *him,* to Cameron, for comfort. That she turned first to *him* . . . something inside me snapped. I just couldn't abide it. Jealousy consumed me.

"I longed to hurt her as much as she had hurt me. I set in motion a plan that I can only confess to you now, now that you know that I did not kill her.

"I asked her to come to my room at a certain hour. I then asked Cam to come in a little before. My bedroom and hers were separated by a shared bathroom that was accessible from each of our rooms as well as the hall.

"I spoke to him loudly enough that I knew she could hear. I told him I had something to say, something important to resolve, once and for all. I bided my time and when I saw a shadow under the door to the bath, I knew she was there and was eavesdropping.

"So I started in. I told him I could not go on with the arrangement. That it must come to a stop as quickly as possible or I would go mad. He said he understood and would do anything I suggested. He offered to pack and leave the house at first light if that was my will."

Ingersoll heaved another deep sigh and shrugged. "If I had just said 'yes' at that point, everything might have ended differently. Who knows? Dora would have been upset, of course. Maybe she would have followed him. Then again, maybe not. I will never know. In any case, I think they would both still be alive.

"You see, I didn't stop there, and for that I will always be sorry and forever condemn myself. I knew Dora had heard Cam's response, but I wanted to drive it home to her, to make it utterly clear that his offer was not some empty, chivalrous gesture.

"I gambled on Cam's true feelings for me, his loyalty. I had read his so-called 'novel' after all. So I doubled-down.

"I said with such malicious grace, 'I want you both to be happy. I shall be the one to step away. I will do whatever is legally necessary to secure a divorce. That will leave the two of you free to marry. Your happiness, yours and hers, is paramount to me.'

"Cam reacted exactly as I knew he would and so my greatest act of cruelty was set in motion. He threw himself at my feet—I was sitting on my bed at the time.

"He said, 'No, that is the last thing on earth that I want. I could never be happy if it meant losing our friendship.'

" 'But don't you love Dora?' I said, twisting the knife. 'Don't you dream of marrying her? Starting a family together?'

" 'I love her, of course. What man could resist her? But marriage? No, I never wanted that.'

" 'No?' I said, with feigned surprise. 'Do you mean that if I asked you to choose between us, you might choose me over her?'

" 'I want *you* to have a happy marriage to Dora. That is all I ever wanted. I know that sounds incomprehensible, but it is the truth. Dora told me she would leave you if I did not . . . did not—'

" 'Did not dance to her tune? She's a master at getting her way, isn't she?'

"He began to weep, hugging my legs, burying his face into the folds of my robe and nightshirt. I took hold of his face and held it in my hands.

" 'Cam, my marriage to Dora is gone. She is dead to me. Do

not think that your leaving will preserve that which is already finished. Now, I will ask you squarely, if you had to choose between us and must end all contact with the other party, whom would you choose? *Me or Dora?*'

"He did not hesitate a second. Not even a fraction of a second. 'You, of course,' he said.

" 'Are you sure?'

" 'Yes,' he said. 'Alec, my feelings for Dora are only a pale reflection of what I feel for you. I loved her because *you* loved her. You are the brother of my soul. You always have been.'

" 'So it seems, Cam, that I loved *her* and she loved *you* and you loved *me:* A recipe for disappointment, not a circle of love.'

"At that point I called to her. 'You might as well come out of hiding, little wife. I think you have heard enough.'

"She opened the door but stood quite still. Her lip trembled with the tears that soon would rain down her lovely face, but she said nothing.

"Cam turned to her in horror.

" 'It hurts, doesn't it?' I said to her, savoring every word. 'Not to be first in the affections of the person you love best in the world. Don't worry, Dora, you'll get used to it. *I did.*'

"She melted at that. I think I actually witnessed her heart collapse. I never raised a hand to her and yet in less than five minutes I had destroyed her.

"Strange to admit, but I felt nothing in that final moment. No victory . . . no vindication. What I failed to realize was just how complicated our little Complex Marriage actually was.

"I next looked at Cam's face." Ingersoll paused and seemed almost unable to continue. "I wish I had died before I had seen that look. It remains seared on my memory and haunts my dreams. He was profoundly appalled to learn I had such cruelty in me. And that I was capable of using *him* . . . us—everything we had meant to each other during all the years of our adult lives—as the instrument of my revenge.

"Dora ran to her room. He jumped up and ran after her, but she locked the door against him. He quietly returned to his own room. I never saw either of them alive again.

"He never meant to hurt anyone, you see. I realize that now. He couldn't help it that she loved him more. That was not his fault . . . or hers."

"You once told me," said Victoria, tears filling her own eyes now, " 'We do not choose whom we love, or surely we would make wiser choices.' "

He sadly hung his head.

"Mr. Ingersoll, your remorse is most profound. Anyone can make an error in judgment—"

"Not one as great as mine. I knew in an instant that there was not enough 'Sorry' in the world to mop up the mess I had made."

They sat in silence for several minutes. Then Ingersoll posed a painful question, so painful he dared not look her in the eye: "Are you going to put all of this in your article?"

She knew she could not. The realization of this had slowly taken life over the past week and had reached fruition in the long hours she and the reporter Faraday had spent together giving evidence and speaking in confidence. They hammered out a bargain, but Victoria did not feel at liberty to discuss its terms with Ingersoll at this time, so she gave the second-best reason for her ultimate decision.

"My husband does not wish me to publish this article," she said. "He was opposed to it from its inception as we are still sorting out the repercussions from the last 'scandal article' we published."

"The Beecher matter?" he guessed.

"Indeed. I have now reluctantly agreed with his wisdom on this and would prefer to delay its publication indefinitely."

"At least until after I am dead?" said Ingersoll with a hopeful smile.

"At least." She felt pleased at just how happy she knew she was making him at that moment.

"Mrs. Woodhull, you not only saved my life, but now you are offering to save my reputation as well. This is just . . . I don't know what to say. This is overwhelming."

She grew serious again. "I think our business here is not yet finished. I believe we should still summon the spirit of your friend, Cameron. Not for what he might say to you, but for what you might wish to say to him."

He slowly nodded.

She reached out and took his hands in hers and the séance began.

The headlines of the Extra editions of all the Chicago newspapers issued after the dismissal of charges screamed with one voice:

INGERSOLL FREED!
True Murderer Revealed!
Reporter Faraday Breaks the Case!

Victoria did not see the papers because she had boarded the first train out of Union Station that morning. She did not need to read them because she knew what they would say. She and Nick Faraday had planned it carefully. She wished to have as little public involvement with the case as possible and the eager Faraday got his well-earned moment in the spotlight.

Her train was bound for Terre Haute, Indiana. She would be reunited there with not only her husband and her sister, but Blood had brought with him from New York her thirteen-year-old daughter, Zula Maud. He knew this would cheer her after the trying week she had endured.

The wire she had received from him the night before indicated that her brush with death had shaken him deeply. This touched her but not quite so much as to remove the information she had received in a letter from her mother. It had been dictated, of course, since her mother had never learned to read or write. Her mother claimed that Blood's first wife had shown up in New York in dire financial straights and he was now supporting her and who knows what else he was doing?

Victoria had to face the fact that she was jealous. There was no way around it. She experienced full force the painful complexities of a triangular relationship and felt their sting as sharply as Alec Ingersoll.

She knew that her mother despised her husband and loved to foment trouble between them, but the very possibility that she— Victoria—was destroying her health on this rigorous-beyond-measure lecture tour to now be supporting her husband's first wife? That, she could not abide.

As the train lurched southward and the shores of Lake Michigan rolled past, her thoughts turned to Medora Lamb Ingersoll, how she had used Victoria's own lectures to her advantage in order to justify her desire to have two husbands rather than one.

Victoria shook her head in disgust. If Medora had simply wished to leave a loveless mistake of a marriage and find happiness with another, that was fine, that should be the right of every woman. But Medora wanted more. She desired to retain the wealthy, virile husband who adored her and add to the bargain her pretty-faced, penniless lover.

Had Victoria's Free Love principles really created a self-serving creature such as Medora Lamb who wrecked the lives of the men who loved her?

Victoria did not at that moment have an answer. She had too many other concerns. There was the looming court appearance in Brooklyn next month. Would Theodore and Beecher be there in court? She sickened at the thought. She had no wish to lay eyes on either of them again.

Of all the emotions she could have summoned for this moment, she now felt only one: exhaustion.

She was tired of it all: the constant adversity, the relentless turmoil, the unjust vilification, the money woes, the unceasing need to clarify the misinterpretations of her philosophy. At some point, she—and Blood and the rest of the *Weekly* staff—would have to surrender to the possibility that America was not yet ready for their Free Love doctrine.

Trying to beat the concept into heads that did not yet want it had proved too costly a fight. At this point, she was so weary that even if she won the war, she was not certain the battle had been worth the victory.

Only four short years ago, the most prominent leaders of the Woman's Suffrage Movement counted themselves as her friends and sought to benefit from her remarkable oratory gifts that allowed her to hold an audience in the palm of her hand.

But all those leaders deserted her over a single issue: her adherence to the doctrine of Free Love. She knew they were being naive. Women needed much more than the vote. They needed the whole structure of society to change. But that was not going to happen this year, or this decade, or maybe even this century.

She tried to divert her thoughts to some more pleasant territory, but one theme kept resurfacing: She was tired of her present circumstance, tired of her husband, and tired of *America*.

They needed her a lot more than she needed them.

CHAPTER THIRTY-SIX

On their somber drive home from Carbondale, Flynn and Matt had both been strangely quiet. Each was lost in thought about the story that they had pieced together about the Free Love Murder trial, its antecedents and its aftermath.

At Matt's request, they made one special stop before Flynn took him to the airport. He wanted to visit the apartment where she had bought the photograph. They talked to Mrs. Belton, the chain-smoking landlady and got all the information she had on her former tenant, which proved to be a lot—Social Security number, birth date, and most tantalizing of all, her maiden name: Loretta Marie *Ingersoll*.

Flynn grabbed Matt's hand and squeezed it as they walked back out to her car. He promised her that his genealogy-loving aunt could dig up all kinds of things on this connection.

They kissed goodbye at the airport and he flew home.

"Did he call?" said Dan Keirnan as he entered his shop with a box of books he had just purchased for inventory. He and Flynn had swapped jobs on Thursdays. Now he hit the estate sale circuit while she slept late and opened the store at ten.

"No," she said from behind the counter. He had asked the same question every day that week and she was getting tired of it.

She heard him mumble under his breath, "That passive-aggressive jerk."

"Oh, Dad, calm down. It's not the end of the world." She shook her head. He was taking the situation much worse than she was, or at least worse than she was letting on.

"How can you be so casual about this?"

She shrugged, then turned back to the magazine she was reading. "I think he was just infatuated with the fact that I had known David Holloway, not infatuated with *me.*"

Her father frowned with concern. "You didn't tell him about Brody, did you?"

She jerked her head up in irritation. "Good God, no. Do you think I'm stupid?"

"No, sorry, of course not. But you could honestly use some better judgment where men are concerned."

"Don't start."

He raised his hands in surrender, then grabbed his box of books and hauled them upstairs to his office.

As one day of silence followed another, Flynn had slowly concluded she would have to content herself with seeing the week with Matt for just what it was: a nice little diversion.

They might occasionally keep in touch, a phone call or an email now and then—Hi, what's new? What have you been up to?—but in a couple of years, it would just be a Christmas card with a note, then just a card without a note. Such was twenty-first century romance, for better or worse, mostly for worse.

The first thing Flynn did when she returned to Weston was to find a beautiful Victorian-era frame at Mr. Heilbocher's antique store. The ghostly faces of Alec and Medora and Cameron now had a richly filigreed brass accent to call home. She hung it in the bookstore on the wall behind the cash wrap. It was a great conversation-starter with customers.

Flynn opened the store that Saturday as she always did. Her first chore after booting up the computer was to make a pass with the feather duster.

That damned spider was back at it again in the door to the children's section. Before she whisked the fragile web away she thought wistfully how she felt that, on some level, everyone spent their lives weaving some delicate web and hanging on to it, clinging however foolishly to a hope that some bigger force was not out there ready to knock them into oblivion.

The ringing of the antique-reproduction phone on the wall jerked her back into the present moment so fast she thought she might have whiplash. Its lovely, irritating jangle recalled the era when phones actually "rang" rather than beeped or whinnied or played the opening bars of the latest pop song, or reproduced some famous bit of dialog from a movie or TV show.

"Weston Books, Flynn speaking."

"Hello, 'Flynn Speaking,' " said a familiar voice. "When are you coming to Chicago?"

"Well, hello to you, too," she said, not knowing whether to be delighted he finally called or pissed off that it had taken him a week.

"Seriously, when can you come here? Ellen has invited us to dinner. I need to give her a date."

"Ellen?"

"The lady who owns the Prairie Avenue murder house. I think she'll try and sweet talk you out of that photograph, but then again maybe not. She's made a pretty amazing discovery of her own.

"When I told her about the mural that Alec and Medora had painted on the wall of their would-be nursery, she started in on her bedroom walls with a razor blade and sure enough, under two coats of paint, one coat of plaster, and two layers of moldy wallpaper, she found the mural. Just like Victoria Woodhull described it in her notes. Ellen's having it professionally restored now."

"Oh, I've got to see it," Flynn said before she remembered that she was angry at having been neglected. "So . . . uh . . . I was surprised you didn't call before now."

"I called Tuesday night and left a message with your kid."

"Oh, no. Really? He's not very reliable with messages. I'm sorry."

"And he wouldn't give me your cell phone number. He said you'd kill him." Matt sounded like he thought this was funny. "When you didn't call me back, I worried that you were mad about something. Then I started wondering if you got the message."

"Well, I'm glad you called again."

"It's been a hectic week," he said. "I was caught under an avalanche of work when I got back to the office. And my assistant quit—it was a nightmare. I spent the whole week putting out fires. Didn't even get out for a run until this morning. Can you believe it?"

She had to admit that sounded serious. Even after knowing him that short time she understood that running was a bellwether to the state of his life. Asking him to willingly give up a run was like asking a Buddhist monk to stop meditating.

"I guess you haven't had time to start on your book," she said. It was more of a question than a statement.

She heard a sigh at the other end of the line. "About that . . . you're going to help me on it, aren't you? I was taught how to write contracts and briefs. And I'm pretty good at that but . . . you're the one with the master's degree in English. You're the one who was a research assistant to the late, great David-fucking-Holloway, for chrissake. You *are* going to help me, aren't you? I'll never manage it on my own."

"Well, if you're going to whine about it . . ." she teased.

"Actually, I was just waiting to be asked."

"Consider yourself officially asked. Do we need to put it in writing? 'Cause I'm great at writing contracts. Did I mention that?"

Flynn laughed out loud. "I think I'll trust you."

She had already been writing the damn book in her head all week. She knew just how she would organize it: she would turn Victoria's notes into a third-person narrative and intersperse it with excerpts from Cameron Langley's notebook and the trial transcripts . . . she couldn't wait to get started.

She glanced around the shop. There were two women customers who probably wondered why she had such a loopy grin on her face. She turned her back to them and smiled at her spirit photograph instead.

"I've got even more news," Matt continued. "I think you'll like this. My aunt took that information we got on Mrs. Pilcher and we now have an answer to why she had the photograph."

"Oh, the *provenance*—at last. That's great." Flynn wasn't actually sure if she wanted this information. If they discovered a real heir, she might feel obliged to give up the photo to them. She was nowhere near ready to part with it.

"Well, there's a very obvious reason why her maiden name was Ingersoll. Our boy Alec remarried. You'll never guess to who."

"Garnet Langley?"

"Hey, you're psychic." He laughed. "It must be a girl thing. Anyway, Alec and Garnet had two daughters and a son. The daughters never married but the son did and Loretta was one of his kids, born in 1911. Alec died in 1916 at the ripe old age of 70."

"Oh, my God," Flynn murmured. The life of Alec Ingersoll was playing out in a whole new direction. She would have to readjust all her fantasies now.

"I guess Victoria Woodhull must have started writing his story that year—1916 or after—since she starts it out 'Alec Ingersoll is dead.' But she was really old by then. Maybe bad health or just plain old age prevented her from finishing it."

"Yeah, she must have been nearly eighty."

"My aunt has even more information but if you want it you've got to come to Chicago and get it, Keirnan."

"You drive a hard bargain, Holtser."

So F. Scott Fitzgerald was wrong. Flynn now had undeniable proof: Alec Ingersoll's life most definitely went on to have a Second Act. Come to think of it, Victoria Woodhull's did, too.

When she called home, Brody answered.

"Brode, would you mind if I went to Chicago for a couple of days next week?"

"Do I have an alternative?"

"Hey, kid, you always have veto power. That's our deal."

"I suppose you're gonna see that lawyer guy. He called last week. I forgot to tell ya."

"Thanks a lot, Brode. Write it down next time. Okay? But yeah, I'm going to see him. I'll also get to see the house that the people in my photograph lived in. It should be cool."

"Can I come? Wednesday's my last day of school, ya know."

"Well . . . I guess so. Sure, why not?" She had no idea how Matt would react to a family visit—a fourteen-year-old chaperone—as it were, but she had to find out what he and Brody thought about each other sometime. And better to find out sooner than later.

"I don't really want to come," he said, on reflection.

"Well, okay, suit yourself." She realized he was just testing the water, as always. "Let me talk to Grandpa."

"He's in the shower right now. You want me to give him a message?"

"Yeah," said Flynn. "Tell him . . . tell him I think my 'Second Act' is about to begin."

ABOUT THE AUTHOR

Michelle Black is the author of six historical novels. She is also an attorney and a former bookstore owner. She lives in Colorado. She loves to hear from readers and can be reached through her website: www.michelleblack.com. She also blogs on various Victorian and writing-related topics at: www.The VictorianWest.com.